BRENT EVANS'

LAND & SEA

FLOTSAM OF WAR

A LAND & SEA ANTHOLOGY

BLAINE LEE
PARDOE

BOOK
04

I dedicate this to my loving wife, Cyndi. Throughout this whole cancellation-thing, she held strong. To my daughter, Victoria—author, nurse, single mom, and tough as shit. To my son, Alex, extraordinary hair stylist to the stars and successful entrepreneur.

ACKNOWLEDGEMENTS

In the Land&Sea series, the entire world is dealing with the consequences of an alien invasion. This book is an anthology of the lesser known stories, battles, units, and people that are drawn into this conflict. As a reader, you will get the view of ASHUR and Trident pilots, technicians, nurses, and the militia. Some of these characters and units are destined to resurface again in future works . . . well, the ones that survive.

As always, my thanks to the Creative Juggernaut team—Brent, Eric, and Kevin. My sincere thanks to Walt, Nick, Lauren, and Jason at WarGate Publishing for helping us make this series a reality.

WARNING SIGNS

The challenge with intelligence systems is that the enemy rarely explains their intent or the nature of their threat. Enemies simply exist, and it is left to the professionals to sort through what is a risk and what is mere background chatter.

The warning signs were all there that something was happening in the oceans, but there was no easy way to connect those dots. The following snippets were some of those indicators that something strange and dangerous was unfolding in the oceans of the world. Most of these vignettes occurred before the alien threat had been identified and understood. Of course, understanding the extent of the alien invasion does little to abate the fear that the Fish generate. Wade into the water with caution . . .

Royal Malaysian Navy Ship KD *Jebat*, off the coast of Port Dickson, Malaysia

Kepten Ahmad Haqq Osman looked out from the bridge of the KD *Jebet* over the relatively calm sea and slumped back in his raised chair. Duty in the Royal Malaysian Navy was best described as days of boredom punctuated with minutes of rushed activity. Malaysia was a dominant regional military power but both she and her neighbors had no grand aspirations for growth. Most of what Kepten Osman and his crew did was patrol and render assistance to vessels that might need it. With the unstable weather in the region, complete with torrential monsoon seasons, their job was complicated enough. *I will be happy if I never have to clear my guns for action.* In fact, short of piracy, it was hard to picture a situation where he would employ his vessel's weapons in anger. *Pirates perhaps, but even then, most pirates prove to be cowards in the face of a warship.*

This was a standard patrol—one of eight patrol patterns the *Jebet* ran. There wasn't much to do other than for the navigator to update radar plots of commercial and private vessels in the Malacca Strait. Communications monitored for any emergencies. *It is what my father used to call a "Milk Run." In a day, we'll return to port for five days' leave.* He didn't have any plans for his downtime.

From the sonar station, Leftenan Komander Gestin spoke up. "Kepten, I am picking up a signal—dead ahead."

Osman sat up, then moved to the sonar screen where Gestin pointed. "It is massive, sir. It is reading like a reef."

He looked at it and was stunned. *This must be a mistake. We travel here all of the time; there are no reefs near this patrol route.* "Your settings must be incorrect."

Gestin shook his head. "Sir, I thought that too. I did a system refresh. These readings are correct."

"Then the unit is malfunctioning."

His sonarman shook his head. "I don't think so, sir. If it was, it would either work or not work. I am able to ping the two nearest tsunami buoys with no problem, so the indications are that the system is operating. This large reading is coming in loud and clear as a signal." He held up his headphone for Osman to hear. Clearly there was a signal being hit.

"That makes no sense," Osman muttered, more to himself than to his sonarman.

"We are closing on it fast, sir."

Kepten Osman looked out at the water and the brilliant blue sky in front of his ship. *Reefs just don't appear after two weeks. We were just in these waters, on this exact course and heading two weeks ago and there was no indication at all of a new reef formation. It must be a system failure. Still . . . if it is something, I will be putting my crew in danger.* "How deep is that reading?"

"Two to three meters, sir."

Osman narrowed his gaze. *At that depth, you would think I'd see the breaks in the water.* "Helm—reduce speed. Take us to one-eighth." The helmsman acknowledged the order, and he could feel himself lean forward as the ship reduced its revolutions and speed.

The bridge crew began to strain from their workstations, looking out over the bow of the ship as he was, hoping to spot the source of the mysterious readings. "Kepten, I am still reading the subsurface obstruction—dead ahead—220 meters. Sonar now shows that it extends perpendicular to our current course for over a mile," Gestin said.

For a few long moments, he said nothing, lost in his thoughts. *If there is something there, perhaps cargo dumped from a ship or wreckage of some sort—and I hit it at speed, I will be the laughingstock of the Royal Navy. If it is nothing, then I only must cope with some minor embarrassment—and Gestin will pay the price for that.* "Helm," Osman said smoothly. "Kill the engines. Duty Officer, post some men on the bow for observation. I want eyes on what this is, if it even exists." Komander Sherif, his first officer, saluted and left the bridge. Out on the bow of the ship, three men hustled into position.

"Range to this reading?" he asked with a hint of disbelief.

"We are now 78 meters, sir. With our drift and currents, we will be on it in just a few minutes," Gestin reported.

"Helm, turn us to port, 35 degrees," he replied. If there was something there, this would make his angle towards it little more than a glancing blow. *If it is there . . .*

"Signal from the bow, sir," Komander Sherif called out. Suddenly there was a lurch, not strong, but one that made the ship vibrate for a moment. A metallic sound, something grinding against metal, resonated throughout the *Jebet*. "Damn . . ." Osman said under his breath. "Helm, back us off, one-eighth. Take us back 100 meters, then all-stop and drop anchor. Komander, I want a damage report," he said as he turned to Sherif. "And I want to see this for myself." He left his post and made his way to the door off the bridge, then down to the deck. The air was warm, the sun made him feel energized. Osman made his way to the bow where the observers stood. One pointed down into the water.

There it was . . . a long line of coral just under the pristine waters of the Malacca Strait. From what he could see, it extended westward and eastward for considerable distance. His crewmen were in awe of it, as he was. *We were just here. How is this possible? Coral could not have grown that quickly.*

After a few moments, he felt the throb of the engines stop and heard the rumble and rattle of the anchor chain as the ship came to a stop. There was no protocol for this happening. His mind started going over his responsibilities. *Other ships could hit this and be sunk. We need to map it, place warning buoys, alert Royal Naval Command. Warnings would have to go out for small craft and commercial traffic. I wonder what the impact is on ocean currents?* His routine patrol had just become the most complicated mission that the Royal Navy had become involved with in the last decade.

I need to speak with Admiral Koniff. . .

Naples Pier, Naples, Florida

Jack Farmer adjusted his folding lawn chair, mostly because his butt was already sore from sitting in it. "Sally," he said to his girlfriend seated next to him, "How much longer do we have to stay out here? It's ten-thirty already."

Sally Jesmond was fifty-eight and five years his younger. She had dragged him out to the Naples Pier because she claimed she saw something in the water. It wasn't that Jack had anything else to do, but it was getting late, and so far, all he had seen was a sailboat moving silently off-shore.

"Oh, Jack," Sally said with a flash of that smile that had caught his attention a year ago at the dance in his retirement community—that and her buxom figure. "You just have to be patient."

"We've been here for an hour—I haven't seen anything. I've got to take my pills pretty soon or I'll be up all night," he complained.

"It's worth the wait. Besides, you are ex-Navy—maybe you can explain them." She had been going on about the mysterious underwater lights that she had seen in the warm Gulf waters passing near the pier for a week. He had finally consented to go with her, hoping that it would be more of a romantic night than sitting in an uncomfortable chair until all hours of the night.

"We've been here a while," he offered. "Like I told you at dinner, maybe what you're seeing is reflections off the water of a jet flying over. Sometimes those lights bounce off the water and fool people." Jack checked his watch again. *This has all of the fun of cutting my toenails.*

Suddenly Sally pointed out to the west into the Gulf. "There, Jack! Look over there. You can see them!" She popped up from her seat and for a moment he was worried she might go off the pier into the water.

At first, Jack didn't see them. He squinted for a moment and saw them, moving from the south to the north at what he estimated was about a half-mile off shore. There was one large yellowish light—from his estimate, something the size of a car. It was surrounded by two, maybe three, red lights which were intense. *What the hell. That's definitely manmade . . .*

The lights continued to move, and he saw, deep under the water, a string of blue lights. These led away from the yellow light and ran deeper—and farther back. His Navy experience kicked in. *Those are not a sub's running lights—not ours anyway. How big is that sucker?* Mentally Jack made an estimate. It had to be at least 250 feet long—maybe more. *And that's just the span of lights—God only knows how big the vessel is.*

It moved to the north and turned, sharply, toward the west and continued out to deeper waters. Sally jumped up and clapped her hands. "Isn't it beautiful, Jack? What was it? Was it a submarine?"

"I—I don't think so, doll," he said, still dumbfounded. "A sub could never make a turn like that. She pivoted at ninety degrees, spun on a dime. And no navy I know of lights up their subs that way."

Overjoyed at having him see what she had been watching for several nights, she said, "Isn't it exciting to see something like that? I told you it wasn't an airplane."

No. It wasn't. But what the hell was it? The part of him that was ex-Navy said he should report it. But the last thing he wanted was to have the vid-reporters trying to interview him and having him labeled as some sort of nut. Looking over at Sally, her flightiness would not play well on the net. *We'd be labeled kooks—that's what they'd say about us. Old people seeing things in the water—they'd probably diagnose us with dementia.*

"Yeah—it was exciting, all right." Jack got up and folded up his lawn chair. "We'd better get going."

Crab Fishing Trawler *Vespa*, the Bering Sea

It was a cloudy day but with relatively smooth waters, a rarity that Victor Torres embraced. Oh sure, the breeze that was on the Bering Sea was stinging, but it was not a penetrating cold that made your bones ache. The Bering Sea could be unforgiving but today seemed different. Even under the slate gray skies, it felt like a good day. *Now if that would only demonstrate it with a load of king crab.*

It was still early in the season, so even the best hunting spots had been sparse. Crabbing was a hard business, hard on the men and equipment, complicated by the fact that the crabs were unpredictable in terms of where you could find them. The cap was pissed, and took it out on the crew, which made matters worse. Victor understood his captain's frustration, but that didn't make matters any easier. Captain Hash was the one laying out the cash for fuel and he owed money on the ship—he made sure the crew knew that every chance he got.

As they winched up the baskets, Victor found himself hoping that it would be full of crabs, if only to take some of the cap's hostility away. The basket broke the water and was full. Victor allowed himself to smile. As he looked at the cage, he wasn't sure what it was full of. They looked like crabs, but were different—bigger—uglier.

As the basket swung overhead, they threw the catch and dumped the contents onto the sorting table on the deck. Over a dozen of the creatures piled on the wet deck. They had crab-like plating, but looked more like octopus, with bulbous heads flowing out behind armored torsos. As Victor stared down at the creatures, he decided the crab-like portion looked more like a lobster. They had forward claws, big ones, much more vicious-looking than those on a king crab. Their antennae were not a crab-feature either. They were large too—at over three feet long.

"What the hell are those things?" asked Samuel Koff, one of the more seasoned fishermen on the *Vespa*.

The "things" didn't move much at first, almost as if they were stunned, but seemed to be surprisingly agile after a minute. Most flipped over, landing upright, their bulbous heads bobbing behind them as their legs lifted them up. Their stance was like that of a scorpion, with the tail replaced with the softer head/body in the back. There was little that Victor could do but stare at them. King crabs were alive when they came up, but not incredibly mobile. These things were moving, bounding off the table, spreading out on the deck. Victor grabbed ahold of the staffs used to manipulate the cage and held it tight, almost in a defensive stance, unsure of these strange creatures. They moved almost in unison, forming a circle on the deck, claws facing forward. *These are no crabs . . . that's for sure.*

The grizzled and bearded deckhand Carl Koff grabbed one of the staffs and closed in on them. "I've never seen anything like these ugly bastards," he muttered, getting within two yards of them. With the staff, Koff prodded at them, as if to gauge their reaction.

The one he poked at seemed to tense—its rear bulbous head seemed to raise slightly. *It looks as if it's getting ready to fight.* Victor watched as the creature reached with its right claw and clamped onto the slender wooden prod being used on it and squeezed. The wood snapped like a twig, the metallic tip spinning on the deck. *How is that possible?*

The creature jerked forward towards Koff, then it sprayed a black substance, like oil or ink, right at Koff, hitting him in the torso and face. The burley Koff howled in pain, his hands reaching to his face. Koff spun and through the wet black substance, it looked like his flesh were melting off. *My god, it's some sort of acid . . .*

The creature grabbed at Koff's ankle and clamped it, tearing off his foot with an audible snap. Koff wailed, screaming in agony, as the creature tore into him on the deck. The man clawed at the deck as the creature shot up his back, its pincers flailing at his flesh. Another deckhand, Dane, swung his hooked staff and hit the creature. Suddenly, the other crab-like creatures sprang at him, one of them spraying the air with its black corrosive. The other crewman jumped in with their hook-staffs, stabbing and slashing away at the creatures. There was a noise, like the noise a lobster makes when it is cooked alive, a screech that filled the deck. The sound of agony and pain. *At least one of them is hurt or dead.*

Victor didn't wait—he bolted for the upper deck. As he cleared the top step, he turned around and saw a scene of horror on the deck below. The crab-like creatures were engaged in a battle with the survivors, tearing into them. Victor saw a severed arm fly across the deck, leaving a streak of blood. The inky substance was not just maiming the crew, but seemed to be burning holes in the deck.

It hit him then—these creatures could have gotten out of their cage at any time. *They deliberately came here . . . to do this to us.* The cries of the men fighting below spurred him to run for the bridge and the cap. He had been fishing for king crabs for fifteen years . . . he had to know what to do. He was always saying he had seen and done just about everything in the Bering Sea. As he burst onto the bridge, he saw Captain Hash looking down at the deck below, fumbling with ammunition that he was attempting to put into a pistol. Bullets spilled on the deck as his hands shook with fear. As he looked down on the deck below, it was awash with blood, the bodies of men, contorted in agony, lay about. The living crab-creatures shuffled among the dead and dying humans and their own dead. Holes from the caustic they sprayed ate through the deck plating, sending up wisps of gray mist into the air. Only one deckhand, Caster, a grizzled old veteran of the Bering Seas, had made his way aft, limping badly and covered in blood. He was followed by one of the crab-things, two of its legs dragging as it moved. *Move it, man!* Caster got through one of the bulkhead doors, slamming it shut as the creature sprayed the door with more of its deadly ooze.

Four men killed by those things!

It was in that moment that Victor knew just how deadly serious matters had become . . .

Exclusive! North Koreans Claim US Is Using Mutated Fish to Spy On Them! *(Global Enquirer Press Service Story)*

(Pyongyang, North Korea, UPG) In a stunning announcement out of Pyongyang this week, Quang Soon, Deputy Minister of Information in the North Korean government, claimed this week that the United States is using mutated sea creatures as a means of spying on his government. As proof, he has offered a vid of the creature that the Korean People's Navy captured last week off of Inchon.

The creature is 1.8 meters long but does not resemble any known aquatic species. With powerful forearm-flippers, the Koreans claim that it achieved speeds of nearly 17 knots before being subdued. Its lack of recognizable features indicate, according to Soon, that it is a creature genetically manipulated for the purpose of surveillance on the People's Navy. "This creature was sighted on three occasions moving in and around our vessels, clearly gathering data on our ships. Only the United States has the capabilities to produce such creatures."

According to Deputy Minister Soon, the specimen that was captured had been badly damaged in the fight. "The United States had bred this creature for combat—that much is evidenced by the struggle it put up against our valiant Marines."

Defense Department officials have refused to comment on the incident other than to state, "The Department of Defense does not have a genetics program and has never produced creatures of any kind. This is clearly propaganda that borders on science fiction."

Despite these rebuttals, the government of North Korea staunchly supports the accusation and has promised to provide evidence to the rest of the world once their own scientific analysis has been complete. Marine biologists at UCLA who have seen the vid have stated that the fish showed by the Koreans may be some sort of prehistoric creature that surfaced for some unknown reason. This has happened before such as the Coelacanth in 1938 and a prehistoric sturgeon which washed up on shore in Connecticut in 2014. "Such creatures which we believed were extinct do appear from time to time as a reminder of just how much of the ocean has yet to be truly explored," said Dr. Harold Cleen of UCLA.

"The thought that this is a creature genetically manufactured by the Department of Defense is laughable," added Dr. Cleen.

76 Porter's Landing Road, Freeport, Maine

Harriet Bates fumbled with her iPhone but finally got the code in. "Cumberland County 9-1-1 Dispatch. What is the nature of your emergency?" the voice seemed too very loud in her confined space.

"There is someone in my house," she whispered from the floor of her closet. "Send the police."

"I'm showing your location at 76 Porter's Landing Road—is that correct?"

"Yes," she said, curling up into a ball on the floor of her closet. "Hurry, there's a few of them here. I saw them outside through my kitchen window."

"I'm dispatching the sheriff's department right now. Where are you in the house?" The dispatcher's voice was oddly calm.

"I'm in the closet in my bedroom." The tang of mothballs stung at her nostrils.

"Okay—for now, stay right where you are. Help is on the way."

"I hear them breaking things in the dining room." She winced. The sound of shattering china made her wonder if her Hummel collection was being destroyed. The thought of that made her ball up her tiny left fist in fear and anger.

"Ma'am, I'm going to stay on the line with you. The sheriff is on the way. Do you know who is in your house?"

"They came through the door," Harriett whispered.

"Through the door?"

"Yes—in my living room. I heard a high-pitched noise and some grinding, then there was a boom and my front door came down, right in the living room. I only saw them for a moment—but they didn't look human."

There was a pause for a moment on the line. "When you say they didn't look human . . ."

There was a crashing sound from the kitchen. The thud of something hitting the floor was so hard, it shook the closet that she was in. A coat fell off the hanger and draped across her legs.

"Harriett," the operator said intently. "What was that noise?"

"They're doing something in the kitchen. Maybe you should call the FBI or whoever handles aliens in the government."

"Alright . . . now, is there anyone else from your family in the house?"

"No," she replied softly. "I'm alone." Ever since Harold died. The boys had moved out years before. This wasn't them—she knew that. There was her cat, Missy, screeching in the background. "Oh, Missy . . ." she whispered.

"There's someone in the house named Missy?"

"No, no, it's my cat. I heard her. They must have hurt her. She scares so easy." There was a rustling noise—and the sounds of things falling on the floor, large things. "Oh, please hurry!"

"They will be there in a matter of minutes. Harriett, I need you to stay in the closet until the officers open the door. Can you do that for me?"

"Yes," she whispered back in a lower tone. In the background, she could hear the wailing of police sirens. They got louder each moment. There was the sound of someone moving in the house, a flurry of activity in the kitchen. She heard a scraping sound, then a strange quiet.

"I think the police are here," she said.

"I show them as on-scene. Just remain calm and stay in the closet," the operator instructed.

It was another minute before she heard her front door creaking open. *I need to get that squeak fixed.* She heard whispered voices—human voices, which made her feel somewhat more secure. "Check upstairs," one said. Harriett winced. The upstairs . . . she didn't use those rooms except Chuck's old bedroom which Harold had converted to an arts and crafts room. *Oh my, that room is such a mess . . .* She worried what the officers might think of her. *I'm not one of those hoarder people. I just like to do quilting, and that requires a lot of scraps of material.*

Several minutes later, there was a rapping at her door. "Mrs. Bates—this is Deputy Hirsh."

She smiled. "They're here . . . thank you," she said into the phone and disconnected. It took a moment to stand up, but she opened the door and saw the tall blonde deputy standing there. "Are you alright, ma'am?"

"Yes, yes . . . did you catch them?" She tried to peer around the deputy to see if she could see the state of her Hummel collection, ignoring the front door that lay on the floor and the officers in the kitchen.

"Um—well, did *you* get a look at them?" The deputy was clearly at a loss for words.

"I only got a glimpse of them when they came through the doorway. They were big, taller than you by about a foot. Their heads reminded me of a cobra—big, tall. Their bodies were tentacles, a lot of them. There were two of them that I saw. I'm not sure what they were—but they were hideous." She held out her hands to try to give the officer the size of the creatures, as if she were showing how large of a fish she had caught. Mrs. Bates managed to step forward enough to see that the wall rack that held her Hummel collection lay on the floor. Harriet moved past the officer to the pile of her collection, walking past the doorway into the kitchen. "Oh my—Umbrella Boy is broken," she said, bending over and picking up the figure. "It took me forever to find him." Tears welled as she cradled the broken figurine.

Rising again, she turned to Deputy Hirsh. "Tell me you caught these—these criminals, or whatever they are." She was angrier than she had been in a long time. Her fingers trembled, she was so mad. *They broke my precious Hummels. What kind of vandal would do that?*

"Ma'am—can you please come with me to the kitchen?" He held out his hand and guided her through the doorway that she had just walked past.

The kitchen was a shambles. Food had been dumped out of the cupboards onto the floor. Her tiny dining chair was tossed into the corner. Then it hit her—the big blackness where the wall to the backyard had been. It looked like the wall had been cut out, an opening all the way to the ceiling and at least ten feet wide, taking out the kitchen sink with it. In the yard, she saw the wall lying flat, her countertop spilled out on the wet grass. The cut looked precise, almost smooth, with no straight edges but a flowing almost random way about them. *Someone has cut out an entire section of my kitchen wall and dragged it out into the yard. How did they do that?* The image stunned her for a few long moments. *Why did they do it?* Water gurgled from the severed pipes. *Oh my—it's flooding my basement.*

Turning, she saw that her refrigerator that Debra and the kids had purchased for her last Christmas was gone. The power cord had been cut rather than unplugged, and it hung limp in the hole in the wall where the fridge had been. There were scuff marks on the hardwood floor leading to the opening. *They cut out my wall and stole my refrigerator.*

"Mrs. Bates, we need to sort through what happened here," the deputy managed.

Her mouth hung open as the scope of the damage hit her. "My refrigerator—my wall . . . what did they do?" Her hand relaxed and she dropped the remnants of the Umbrella Boy figure onto the floor and it shattered.

Nuagarh, India

Vasur prepared his tiny one-man, 14-foot skiff for a day of fishing. The little skiff had been built by hand by his cousin Benj in the village, a gift to Vasur on his eighteenth birthday from his family. The little wooden fishing boat was his prized possession. It marked him as a man, someone that could provide for himself . . . a mark of independence.

His fishing the day before had been less than fruitful. The turtles were mating again, and he was catching them in his nets much more than the fish. They weighed a great deal and while they were edible, there was little money to be made with them. They simply were not worth the effort to catch them. On top of that, environmentalists complained that the fishermen were disrupting the turtle's native habitat. *What do they want me to do, let my family starve, so that the turtles can live?* Even at his age, he understood the folly of such efforts and ignored their protesters on the beach every morning.

With the turtles coming ashore, he had to fish farther out in the delta of the Devi River where the currents were stronger. Using his pole, he pushed off and angled to the open waters where another pair of skiffs were already poised. The morning sun felt warm but not yet oppressive . . . that would be later in the day. He stood for a moment to look around the river delta, drawing a long breath of air that stung with a hint of salt and a tinge of burning garbage from someone on the shore. Vasur didn't dream of going to the city or working in an office building. His dreams were more practical—he wanted to be where he was. *At least here I am my own boss.* A few minutes of pushing, angling his tiny skiff by shifting his center of gravity, Vasur reached the spot in the waters where he wanted to try his luck.

With a sweep of his long skinny arms, he tossed the fish net into the murky waters just as his father had taught him. Using his pole, he pushed up against the current enough to move up-river slightly.

After several minutes, he pulled the draw line to start to pull the net back. There was always a bit of anticipation that came with the first cast of the day. *Have I hit a good spot or do I need to move and try another location?* As he pulled the line, his muscles flexed—there was weight there. Vasur got a little excited, but that drag on the net could come from turtles, debris in the river, any number of sources. He craned in the net, one heavy meter at a time. With a final lunge, he dumped it onto the deck of his skiff.

There were some fish—about a half-dozen scad. There were two turtles who were still entangled in the net. Then there was something else. It was a crab—a large one, nearly a foot across. Its shell was a glossy gray color. It moved surprisingly fast but was still caught under the net. *Great—first the turtles and now crabs. My net didn't go that deep; I wonder how he got in it? I only make money catching things I can sell.*

The more that Vasur looked at it, the more it didn't look like a crab to him. The number of legs was wrong; this crab had ten. Its two front claws were oddly shaped, curved like sickles, larger than what he expected. The body was oddly shaped too, with a large bulging exoskeleton to the rear with a stalk-like projection the size of a straw that was caught in the netting. *I have only seen a few crabs before. Maybe this is some breed I have never heard of.*

It was jerking in the net, and Vasur bent over in hopes of getting it free. He lifted one end of the net and from the stalk-projection on the creature, he saw a gray stream suddenly lash out. It sliced through the netting over the top of the crab and when its arc hit the side of the skiff, it left an eight-inch cut. *What was that—some sort of laser?* Vasur jumped back, releasing the net.

The crab-like creature was free. It crawled up the narrow side of the skiff and paused, its shimmering black eyes seeming to look at him, then fell overboard, plopping into the water.

Vasur moved to the net and looked where it had been cut. It was a precise straight line, as if a sharp knife had done it. When he looked at the gouge cut into the side of his skiff, it was the same. Pausing for a moment, he wondered what to do next. *Great, now I need my net repaired.* As he looked at the brown waters of the river, he nodded once to himself. *No matter what, I will not fish in this spot again.*

Cu'a Viet, Vietnam

Phuc Giang saw the massive item on the beach and was unsure at first just what it was. Occasionally garbage washed up on the narrow strip of beach where he did his scrounging. Parts of a shipping container, a barrel, the flotsam of human waste . . . mostly trash. The thing he saw that Saturday morning was different . . . he could tell at first sight.

He had been out scouring for four days, and so far had little to show for his efforts. Sometimes he found scrap or salvage that he was able to trade or sell. One time he found a Chinese naval officer's dress jacket—soaked and stained, but it had earned him a fist full of dong. How it had gotten there was a mystery, one he liked to fantasize about. His favorite mental story was that an officer on a sub had fallen overboard and had shed the jacket to swim back to his boat. Phuc imagined him being dressed down by the captain and it made him chuckle. It paid to comb the trash that washed up. It wasn't his full-time job, he worked as a fisherman, but his employer's boat was in for repairs, and he had to help out the family.

Looking at the object on the beach, it struck him as strange, different from the usual beach rubbish he picked through. At first Phuc wondered if it was a small boat or raft. It was large, the size of a truck. The color seemed off for a boat or raft. It shimmered in the morning light, pearlescent, with a blurred hue of pink to it. It was a rippled round shape, with curved edges that rose upward, towering way over his head in height if it had been standing. As Phuc walked closer, he saw that it was indeed not a raft, but it looked like a shell of some sort . . . larger than any he had ever imagined.

Moving to the edge of the large object, Phuc reached out and touched it. Yes, it was indeed a shell. He squatted down underneath and saw a myriad of patterns on the outer portion of the mammoth shell. His hand felt the inside of the shell and it was smooth, almost glass-like to the touch. Phuc studied the edges of the large shell and found nicks and dings, as if it had hit something.

This is only half of the shell! It was large enough for him to crawl into and use as a boat if he wanted to. Phuc looked up and down the beach for the other half-shell but saw no signs of it. Glancing inland, he noticed that the trees and brush looked as if they had been cut down, either by a wave or by human activity. Several big trees were toppled over; their fronds looked as if they had been devoured, chewed by something. *Maybe a rogue wave washed this up and did that damage?*

He had spent the entire eighteen years of his life along the waters edge of the South China Sea and had never even heard of a shell of this size. *I wonder what it is worth?* Gripping it with both hands, he tugged to try to see if he could move it, but the weight combined with the wet sand made it feel as if it were anchored. His mind raced with thoughts of how he might recover it before someone else found it or the tide came back.

Grandfather . . . he will know what it is and what to do with it. Phuc reluctantly left it on the beach, running full speed back to his family's home.

The hike back the town would take most of the day, and he sped up at times to reduce the time. Such a shell was rare—and it was bound to be worth something to someone. There were a lot of tourists that visited the beaches of his hometown, Cu'a Viet. *Perhaps one of them would be willing to pay for such a beautiful rarity!* The thought of reaping rewards for his find propelled his legs even faster.

The first clue that something was wrong was that the beaches were empty. The tropical trees and plants that flanked the tourist area looked as if they had been battered in a storm. Beach chairs lay everywhere. Phuc's first thought was that it had to have been a tsunami—but he would have experienced it as well. *Perhaps a storm?* But the weather had been so clear.

He trotted closer and saw a few people milling about, almost walking as if they were the undead. Then, further away from the waterline he saw it, two of the shells like the one he had found. One was tipped over, but the other was upright, open like a massive clam. It shimmered in the early evening sun.

Seeing a man walking as if he were looking for someone lying on the beach, Phuc rushed over to him. "What happened here?"

The man raised his head slowly, a lost expression washing his face, his eyes almost glazed over. "These things came ashore. They opened up and millions of these devouring creatures emerged. People panicked, but that only seemed to entice them. They came as a swarm, ripping at their victims, eating them like a savage water funnel."

Phuc reeled with the man's words. He wanted to call him a liar, but there was evidence of something that had taken place on the beach. "We tried to run, but they followed us into the town. Nothing was spared. They killed dogs, children, everything."

The man gestured in the distance at a lump of clothing some ten meters away on the beach. Phuc took two steps closer to it and saw that it was not a pile of clothing, but the remains of a young woman. Flies covered the torn gashes of flesh. She looked as if she had been attacked by a pack of dogs. The faint smell of open viscera mingled with the salt air and his stomach locked up. Bending over, he violently threw up. Sweat drenched him as he staggered back from the woman.

"Where are these creatures now?" he asked the man he had encountered.

"Many are dead, the rest have gone inland."

"What do they look like?"

The man looked around the beach, walking several long strides. He emerged with something round in his hand, the size of an orange. It was grayish white, almost polished in appearance. As Phuc moved closer, he could make out that half of it was a mouth, ringed with jagged teeth. It had spindly white legs. While he saw no eyes, he had little doubt that it had some. It had a flea-like look to it, but much larger.

"They move in a pack. They spring and hop to move. When they attack, their bites have a poison to them. They are easy to destroy, but they are hard to hit. The police used their weapons on them, but they were so fast, it was impossible to hit only a few of them. The gunfire and movements only seemed to attract more of them."

"Why?" he managed to mutter.

"We don't know," the man said, tossing the dead creature to the ground. "Many people have fled. There are rumors that there have been other attacks, far more deadly. The Americans, the Chinese—everyone has suffered with these creatures. It is a sign . . . payback for all we have done to the oceans. Nature has struck back at us . . . that is what it must be."

Glancing farther inland, his mind shifted to something else, something far more important . . . *his family*. Had they been attacked? He rushed off, not even thanking the man he had spoken to. As he sprinted towards his house, he saw more bodies, some covered with towels or sheets, others simply left where they had fallen. Purple skin and torn flesh, and blood-splattered sand marked where they had been attacked and ultimately fallen.

When he reached the town itself, the scenes of death and destruction did not cease. Bloody smears in front of a café marked where people had died. Windows were shattered, and he saw a door that looked as if a ravenous dog had chewed it apart. There were dead little creatures lying about as well, some covered with dried maroon blood that was already cracking and flaking off of them.

Rounding the corner onto his street, he came to his house and found the door ajar. Phuc stopped there for a moment. Was it open when the creatures had come? Trepidation washed over him, a fear of what he might find inside. He rallied, slowly opening the door and stepping in.

Things seemed normal, no sign of carnage or chaos. Calling out, no one responded. There was an eerie quiet to the place he called home. Moving to the back of the small house, he saw a note scribbled and left on the table. *Phuc, we have gone to your uncle's in Dansavan. We pray you find this note and join us.* It was signed by his sister, which he expected; his mother had never learned to read and write well.

They're alive! His body shook with joy. It was the best news that he could have hoped for. Phuc knew he would have to pack his belongings and go find them. As he headed to his room, he wondered just how safe they would be in Dansavan. *Is anyplace going to be safe from these monsters?*

Canadian Freighter Collides with Submarine

(API) Halifax, Nova Scotia. Canadian officials today declared that a Canadian freighter, the *Trudeau's Oppression*, collided with a submarine approximately 180 miles east of its port in Halifax two days ago. The freighter was badly damaged by the collision, but officials claim that it was only in a marginal risk of sinking as a result of the collision. The damage to the ship and her cargo was extensive however, requiring a Coast Guard tug to return the vessel to port. Damage is estimated to be in the area of $4 million dollars CAN.

Initial photographs of the damage show a massive gouge on the bow of the *Trudeau's Oppression*. According to Admiral Jacques of the Royal Canadian Navy, "This damage is consistent with a submarine collision. The rupture of the freighter's hull shows impact damage which could have only been done by a submersed metallic target of considerable mass and speed."

The captain of the freighter indicated that he had no indication of a submarine, either visually or on sonar at the time of the impact. "Only a stealth-submarine could have gotten close enough for a collision—and only the Russians and Americans have such vessels in their fleets."

The United States Department of Defense issued a press release earlier today which said, in part, "No US vessels or submarines were operating in the vicinity of the *Trudeau* at the time of her accident and no US vessels had any part in the damage the ship suffered."

Russia's ambassador to Canada, Alexi Androvan, issued a short statement on the Royal Canadian, claiming, "This is clearly the result of a collision with a US submarine. Once more, the American Navy is lying to conceal their responsibilities to the sovereign people of Canada." The American ambassador could not be reached for comment.

The owner of the *Trudeau's Oppression*, Barrian Industries, has indicated they will be conducting their own investigation into this matter and that legal action may be pending as a result. "Based on the damage we have seen, the submarine would either be extensively damaged or sunk. Either way, we will be able to eventually determine which nation was responsible for this reckless action and will hold them accountable for the damages they have done to both us and our customers."

NORAD, Cheyenne Mountain

Captain Dennis Tunley stared at his screen in NORAD's Cheyenne Mountain complex, pausing for a few moments to rub his eyes. While he worked in a windowless environment in the heart of the mountain, that didn't mean he failed to notice the strains of working the "dark shift." The dark shift was a misnomer; the Command Center was almost always darkened. It made for better reading of the holographic displays that the tracking officers used. Captain Tunley had drawn the short straw, so to speak, in terms of working early mornings. He was only on the shift for twelve weeks before rotating off, but those weeks were hell.

Tunley's duties were mind-numbing at times. The true hot-jobs were manning the threat consoles—looking for signs of enemy missile and bomber launches. Captain Tunley's seat was orbital tracking. In a typical week, two to five objects would drop from Earth orbit to collide with the planet or burn up on their way in. The running joke was that his job was "to track space garbage." Unlike the threat consoles, no one scrambled fighters or went on alert when he spotted something. Now and then a crashing piece of space junk made the news vids, burning in like a meteor or actually hitting the Earth. Tunley's job was to identify the objects coming in and project their landing zones.

NORAD's tracking of space debris was far more sophisticated than the general public realized. Satellites tracked thousands of pieces of debris, their orbits meticulously plotted and tracked for deviations. There were projections for when objects would descend into the atmosphere and where. Now and then a piece of debris would crash to Earth that was not anticipated, usually older material from the last century that was not carefully tracked. Some pieces of trash broke into multiple signals as they neared the Earth. These types of signals were the ones that got his attention the most. *At least they break up the monotony.*

At 0244, his monitor flashed an unexpected warning. Tunley reached up and used his fingers to assign a tag to the signal: *Red 215.* Per his thick procedures manual, he toggled his headset for the duty officer. "This is low orbit watch, I have an unidentified signal at four-four-zero point two-one—tagged as Red two-one-fiver."

"Roger that," Colonel Thomas replied. "Project your object on the board."

Tunley responded quickly. His holographic display screen now appeared on the massive tracking board for everyone in the Command Center to see. Captain Tunley's fingers flew through the menu options, following SOP. *First confirm signal. Second, project target impact. Third, identify source. Fourth, alert if over populated area.*

The object, whatever it was, was heading out over the Pacific coming from the north. He tapped Eielson Air Force Base in Fairbanks, Alaska, and their long-range threat-radar system. Their system picked it up, if only for a few seconds. "Target is confirmed," he said, his voice now projecting throughout the entire Command Center—a result of his screen being tossed up. "I am projecting flight path and descent rate data now." The current position of Red 215 showed on the screen and a digital dotted line path leading to South Pacific Ocean some 200 miles north of French Polynesia.

Instinctively he accessed the long-range radar array in Hawaii and drew a bead on the object that was dropping. It was a standard procedure, simply to confirm its size and flight path. What he got back from NORAD's HiDish long-range radar was a strange set of signals. Tunley recalibrated and tapped into the National Weather Service's long-range Doppler array and got another set of data that seemed to confirm what he had already seen. *What the hell?*

"Duty Officer, I am getting a reading off an NWS radar on the target. It shows it measuring at over 250 yards across." Heads in the Command Center turned to him. Colonel Thomas came over to his station.

"Are you sure about that?"

"Yes, sir." He punched up the reading and pointed to it on the virtual display space in front of him. "See for yourself."

"Is it an asteroid or meteor?"

"Unknown, sir. NASA had none on plot."

There was a moment when the bald-headed colonel said nothing but stared at the image, then he shattered the silence. "Alright then. Comms, get me a discreet line open to the Pentagon."

Major Falkner, the deputy watch commander, spoke up. "Sir, do you want us to go to Alert One?" The Alert One status was reserved for potential threats to the US interests.

"Not yet, Major. Let's see what we're dealing with first." The mention of Alert One was enough to up Tunley's blood pressure. He had only been in the Command Center once when they had gone to that status. *The old man's got a cool head on his shoulders.*

Colonel Thomas turned back to Tunley. "If that's an asteroid, it's a big damn one. Punch up the NOAA Tsunami Tracking Site. Warn them we have an incoming bogey and tell them where projected impact is. If this thing is that big, it's going to kick up a big damn wave."

Captain Tunley's hands swung into action and opened a window with the NOAA. "This is NORAD. We are tracking an inbound object from orbit to the following coordinates." He dragged the projected impact location onto the call.

The voice that came back was one that sounded like someone that had been smoking weed rather than monitoring for tsunamis. "Really? Wow. Is this *really* NORAD or some sort of joke?"

Tunley rolled his eyes. "This is Captain Dennis Tunley, USAF with NORAD. We need you to monitor your wave buoys in that target area. This bogey is big. If it is an asteroid or meteor, it is going to generate a hell of a wave."

"Right," the voice said. "I'm on it."

New data flashed on his display. "Stand by, NOAA." He muted the channel and squinted at the data. *That's not possible . . .*

"What do you have, Captain?" Colonel Thomas asked from right behind him, his breath was so close that Tunley could smell the coffee he had consumed.

"The object, sir—HiDish is showing it as slowing."

"Is it breaking apart?"

Tunley double-checked the data and shook his head. "No sign of that, sir. She's moving fast, but looks to be slowing. We have impact in forty-five seconds." Tunley activated a timer in the upper corner of the virtual screen.

The communications officer spoke up on the Command Center's speakers. "Colonel, I have the line open to the Pentagon."

"Roger that," Colonel Thomas said. He leaned over Tunley's shoulder again. "Alright, Captain, paint me a picture."

"Object is slowing—it's down to Mach Two," Tunley said. "That's weird, though."

"What?"

"The bogey's trajectory hasn't changed. With debris, when it slows, the flight path is altered by the lack of speed. This one is still on its same flight path."

"So, is it debris?" the colonel pressed.

"Unknown, sir. In all of my training, I've never seen anything like this."

"Sir, bogey is at Mach One now. Still on the projected flight trajectory." Tunley looked up at his display. "Ten seconds, Colonel."

"Hey, NORAD," came the voice from the monitor at NOAA. "Still nothing here."

The radar plot registered the impact—right where he had projected it. "Impact, sir."

Colonel Thomas reached up to the holographic display. He waited for several minutes, sweating, wondering how bad the damage would be. *Did NASA screw up and not plot a meteor?* "This is Colonel Thomas at NORAD. NOAA, are your buoys registering any sort of impact?"

The silence was long and made Tunley's stomach clench. *What if this is a rogue asteroid? Something that big could wreak havoc all over the Pacific.*

"We got just a ripple here from one buoy—showing a four-foot wave."

"It should be much bigger . . ." Tunley said in a low tone just loud enough for the colonel to hear.

"NOAA," the colonel said firmly, "double-check your readings. All you got was a four-foot wave?"

"Right," the man at NOAA replied. "Sorry, Colonel. That's it."

The colonel shook his head. "Thank you for your cooperation, NOAA." He turned to the communications officer. "Kill the Pentagon feed."

"I don't understand," Captain Tunley said to the colonel, turning his chair to face the man that stood behind him. "I've never seen anything like that."

"I need you to log your data, Captain. It may have been an equipment glitch. We'll do an after-incident report. Maybe someone is running a diagnostic software or something that led to the anomalous readings. We'll look into it. File all of your readings into a 412 Report."

"Sir," Captain Tunley spoke up. "It was not behaving like space debris or a natural object. It didn't come from any of our known orbital plots."

The colonel put his hand on Tunley's shoulder. "We had something like this happen three months ago. Sometimes it's just a glitch in the system. Don't kick yourself in the pants over it, Captain. You did everything by the book."

Tunley turned back and looked at his virtual display. *If I did it right, then what was that thing?*

Island of Hokkaido, Sea of Okhotsk

Major Koji Nakao of the Japanese Self-Defense Force, 13th Brigade, took off his hat and tucked it under his arm. Four hours earlier, he had been on an intel audit on the home island when he had been diverted to the military hospital on Hokkaido. The reports he had been sent had been disturbing to say the least. "I am here to see Private Kamei." Nakao took out his digipad and transmitted his orders to the hospital attendant's workstation. She quickly read the authorization and nodded. "He's down the hall, on the left, room 5B."

Major Nakao bowed slightly. "Thank you." When she buzzed him through the door, he began his march down the white ceramic–tiled hallway. He came to Room 5B and swung the door open slowly.

On the bed before him lay Private Hikauru Kamei. Where his right arm had been, there was a short five-inch stump, wrapped in flesh-colored gauze. Private Kamei's jet-black hair jutted out from under the bandage that wrapped the top of his head and over his left ear. A plum-colored bruise the size of a baseball was on the private's swollen right check. The swelling distorted his mouth, raising a corner of his lip with an expression that made him somehow look mentally challenged. IV tubes and digital monitoring sensor feeds connected his body to the bed. The faint chemical smell of disinfectants hung in the air. Nakao was not surprised by the man's condition. Having read the preliminary report, he knew that Kamei was in bad shape after the events the night before. Still, knowing it and seeing it were two very different things.

"Private Kamei, I am Major Nakao of the Special Investigative Service. I have some questions for you."

The man nodded once. "I understand, sir." His speech slurred slightly.

"Are you being taken care of to your satisfaction?"

"Yes, sir," the private replied, his voice slightly muffled by the swelling on his cheek.

"Good," the major responded, moving in closer and activating his digipad to capture their discussion. "Tell me what led to the incident last night."

Private Kamei drew a long deep noisy breath before he began, as if he were bracing himself against the memories. "We were poised along the line of dispute. My squad was positioned on the east end of the island, along the beach."

"Tell me about your positions there."

Private Kamei shrugged slightly under his sheets, almost seeming to relax—which had been the major's intent with his question. "There is not much to tell. We have a series of trenches that run down to the beach. Set back in the wooded area are a series of bunkers. Each squad occupies two of these, each housing a machine gun. They have overlapping fields of fire, all connected in a network. The outer perimeter is manned by drones controlled by the company's drone command. Anyone attempting to penetrate the lines would hit our sensor net, then the drone net, then us."

The situation on Hokkaido with the disputed territory was a stalemate left over from WWII. The Russians occupied part of the island as did the Japanese—with both sides having claims. Since the era of Russian expansionism, there had been a few incidents between troops on the islands. "Accidental incursions" from the disputed islands and the Russian occupied part of the island—at least that was what the Russians called them. The Nemuro Subprefecture on the island remained a sore spot between the two nations, especially since the Russo-Bratva War with the United States, when the Russians used the crisis as an excuse to deploy troops to occupy Nemuro.

"I understand. Where were you?" Major Nakao asked.

"I was in the forward trench-line with three of my squad members on patrol there. It was around 0530 hours or so. Everything was normal. We were not detecting any penetrations by the Russians. Our sensor net and drones did not register anything from their lines other than normal patrols. We had been having some technical issues with the sonar buoys over the last few weeks, but that is typical."

The major pulled up his digipad and made a notation on the sonar buoys. *That was something that was not in the original report and might be of interest.* "I understand. Please continue."

"We heard a scream. It came from the bunker that was to our east—nearest to the beach. Oka and I took off down the trench line towards the bunker. Then there was a burst of gunfire from that direction. We went low, took cover. It was clear that something was attacking the bunker."

"This gunfire. Was it the sound of our Tora automatic rifles or was it different?" the major pressed.

"It was ours, sir. I have fired that weapon many times. I know the sound it makes. It was on fully automatic—most of a clip, from what we heard. From where we were, we couldn't see the gunfire flashes directly, but we saw the shadows. I knew it was coming from the bunker."

Private Kamei took a long ragged breath before he continued. "We readied our weapons and moved down the line. I heard another of our men yell out—I believe it was Corporal Shoda. We could see shadows moving in the bunker as we closed on it. I motioned to Norio to hold back. I went first."

"Norio?"

Private Kamei was quick to clarify. "Private Norio Oka."

"Ah. Very well. What did you see?" Major Nakao asked.

"It was dark—the interior lights were off. I was running with my visor and so the night vision made distinguishing colors very difficult. I saw bodies . . . my squad members . . . on the floor. I could make out their outlines. There were five of them there, in a heap on the floor."

"What else?" the major asked. He could sense the fear in the private; it dripped in every word he spoke. *He is the survivor, our only link to what occurred there.*

"There were figures there. Two kinds. I saw one that was short. Stumpy. Only a meter and a half tall. It was thick, though. Almost like a dwarf, though with no real neck. It had long arms—I remember that. Like a gorilla's, reaching all the way to the ground.

"The larger figures, there were two there. I couldn't make out any details of them. On nightvis, they were black, almost as if they were absorbing light—like the passive camouflage on our drones. They were like men, only taller. They were hunched over; the ceiling in the bunker was so short, given their height. Their hands were claws, claws like webbed fingers. One turned on me before I could get my weapon aimed. I felt a pain in my arm." Private Kamei looked down at the stump where his arm was.

"Did the weapon make any noise?"

"No," Kamei continued. "I remember a rush of air, like a breeze. My arm was gone in a second. I was spun around. Something hit me on the way down—a punch or a kick—I am not sure what. I remember Oka calling out my name. I—I must have blacked out."

"Did they speak at all?" Major Nakao queried.

"No. They were more like monsters than people. There was no room in that bunker for us to maneuver. If they spoke, I would have heard it."

"What do you remember next?"

Private Kamei closed his eyes, then opened them as he gathered his thoughts. "I remember hands on me—putting me on a stretcher. I remember the sound of a helicopter. I woke up here."

Major Nakao set down his digipad on the foot of the bed and crossed his arms. "I feel for your loss, Private. We are faced with a problem. Your descriptions of the attackers—they are not consistent with Russian power armor."

"Sir, with respect—I do not believe they were Russians. They did not trigger the sensor net, nor did our drones pick them up. They did not look like any Russians I have ever seen."

"Perhaps," the major suggested, "in the darkness, you mistook Russian scuba gear for these creatures you described."

Kamei slowly shook his head. "No, sir. I remember those images in my mind." He glanced down at the bandaged stump of his arm. "You can ask the others in the squad. Ask Oka. He was there with me. He will tell you what he saw as well."

The major paused. *He does not know.* Nakao was there to get answers; he had not planned on providing them himself. *I will need to watch his reaction, to see if he is lying.* "No one has told you then?"

Private Kamei shook his head.

"Your squad, including Oka, are all missing. When the alert team arrived at the bunker, you were the only one found there, in a pool of blood—yours, and that of the members of your squad, according to DNA tests at the scene. They did not expect you to survive, but someone had tied off your hemorrhaging. Perhaps you did so before you passed out. We discovered some strange impressions in the blood and dirt near the bunker, but they don't match any known animal."

He was stunned. The private said nothing for a few moments; his lower lip trembled. "I was the only one that was left? Why? Why was I spared? Where were the others taken?"

"To the shore. We assume they had some sort of craft there. Why would they take them, though? That is the question I struggle with. These were not officers vital to the defense of the border. These were simple Marines." *It is like assembling a puzzle when one does not know what the image is.*

"I do not know," Private Kamei replied.

"Let us talk about what you know about your squad mates," Major Nakao said, taking a seat at the foot of the bed next to his digipad. "Tell me about Private Norio Oka . . ."

OPEN AT YOUR OWN RISK

Tanks are fun and armored crews are a different breed of warrior. They are used to living in cramped quarters, with no privacy, with the knowledge that a hit on their large armored target could end their lives in an instant. It is a pressure that brings out the best and worst in people . . . where their training and discipline are all that stand between them and certain death.

Mission 0877—Operation Fast and Loud 16D
The Eastern Front, Lake Saltonstall Recreation Area, Branford, Connecticut

Staff Sergeant Daniel Thun maneuvered his Schwarzkopf fighting vehicle to a position where it barely crested the rocky and tree-covered ridgeline so they could get a view of the lake below. He crept the vehicle forward so that he could get a good unobstructed view down the lightly wooded hillside. "Battlespace Command—this is Whoop Ass. We are at our designated coordinates."

"Confirmed," came the gravelly voice of Captain Rolando. "Stay alert. Any enemy activity is to be engaged."

"Roger that," Thun replied, turning to his right and looking at his gunner, Staff Sergeant Heath Sparks. "Best order they could have given us."

"Yeah," Sparks replied. "As if we wouldn't just shoot first and take names later."

Thun shut off the Schwarzkopf to conserve fuel and surveyed the long lake. It was the headwaters of the snake-like Farm River that emptied a mile away into the Atlantic Ocean in Long Island Sound. When the aliens had come ashore, they had hit New Haven but had only secured a minor foothold in the city itself. Since then they had been making flanking maneuvers, using the waterways to try to find a way to get around the city. Lake Saltonstall was one of the bigger inland bodies of water to the east. A week before, they had tried to go west, coming up the Housatonic River. Thun and Sparks had been in that battle, one that had driven the Fish back. The big brains in their command presumed that the Fish would try again, this time to the east.

Both of the crew knew it was a guess at best; no one seemed to be able to get into the heads of the aliens since the invasion. They didn't seem to follow traditional tactics or strategy. Thun described their actions as more animal-like. Sparks firmly believed they were playing a different game altogether. "It's like we're playing Tic-Tac-Toe while they're playing Monopoly."

"I'd feel better if we had a fire team on board," Sparks commented. The Schwarzkopf had a rear passenger compartment that could carry a reinforced fire team into battle. The challenge was a remarkable lack of personnel on the part of the army. The American military had not been prepared to fight a two-coast war on the homeland. After the Russo-Bratva War, the politicians did what they always did, they cut spending for the military. When the patriotism faded, so did enlistments.

"No shit, Sherlock," Thun muttered. "It's not like we have to worry. So far BS command is batting about one-in-four, trying to outguess the Fish."

"We've at least got a full load of ordnance and the rest of the platoon is spread out along the coast." The war had put a strain on the military's logistics. Artillery rounds were still at a premium as was anything the Air Force wanted to drop. Their Schwarzkopf was a C model, outfitted with a rack of ten missiles on top of the turret, and an Mk 7 rail gun, as well as a light machine gun for close encounters. The missiles were configured with HEDP warheads, high-explosive dual-purpose. By and large, they were most effective against the Fish. The rail gun had been intended for anti-tank use. It was armed with a slender EFP round, an explosively formed penetrator. If it hit a crab or a boss, they were going down or losing whatever limb got hit.

"I've got your full load right here," Sparks said, cupping his crotch and flashing a wide smile.

"From what I've heard, that is small arms."

"Screw you."

"Your mom did." There was a pause and both men grinned. Sparks shoved open his top hatch to get some fresh air, and Thun followed suit. The small compartment of the tank possessed its own unique aroma of sweat, lubricants, and a hint of spent solid rocket fuel from previous engagements. The fresh air never stood a chance against the smell, but it was enough to make their tight space more comfortable.

Sparks changed the subject. "It's not like very much ever happens here. I mean, until we were assigned to this section, I'd never heard of Branford."

"I'm happy here now. When winter blows in, I think we should put in for reassignment to Texas or Florida."

"This is the army. If you want to go somewhere warm, you have to beg to be assigned somewhere that is freezing."

"Like Branford."

"Yeah—like Branford."

They spent the next four hours in mindless conversation. It helped them stay awake and focused. Perched on a hilltop, alone, looking down at the edge of a lake, was dull duty. The banter helped, even if it was insipid. They broke out lunch and ate in their seats, cold sandwiches purloined from the mess before they had left that morning. The biggest excitement they had was when they spotted movement near the water's edge. It turned out to be a doe and her two fawns. The sight of them wandering by stirred Thun. "You know, we could have venison steak for a week."

"What are you suggesting, shooting Bambi?"

"Not the rail gun," he said throwing out a proviso. "You could tag them with the machine gun. A few well-placed shots and we get steak. It's like hunting."

"Using the .50 cal on a deer is not at all like hunting."

"You can't kill them with harsh language."

"I ate venison once. It sucked. Tasted like eating a fat guy's sweaty underwear."

"It worries me that you know what that would taste like. I contend that you haven't had properly prepared venison."

"It tastes like ass," Sparks said. "Smothering it in seasoning can't camouflage the underlying horrible taste."

"I make a great venison steak," Thun announced.

"But you wouldn't be preparing it. We'd be handing it off to the cooks. Army cooks have the inherent ability to take mediocre cooking supplies and turn them into hot, steaming piles of shit."

Thun paused. "I see what you mean. Okay, don't shoot the deer."

"I wasn't going to," Sparks muttered.

Watching the deer move along the shoreline of the lake was the closest thing to entertainment for them. That show came to an end when all of them bolted away from the lake, running up the hill off to the left of their fighting vehicle. Sparks rose in his seat, looking downhill. Not satisfied with that, he used the optics on the vehicle to zoom in on the water. "You seeing this?"

"Seeing what? Is a beaver wandering through now?"

"Check the water where the deer were just at."

Thun zoomed in on his display. The water was stirring. Ripples were swirling some twenty feet offshore, and there were multiple potential sources. "Um, that doesn't look good."

"You want to signal the BS commander?"

"I am not getting my ass chewed if it turns out that some wayward wolverine or beaver is out there. You know the drill, no unconfirmed sightings. The last thing we need is the captain chewing our asses."

"I don't think that's a wolverine." There was a hint of nervousness in his voice that was hard to ignore.

"Until I—" Thun's words were cut off the water swirled hard and rising out of it was a number of different aliens. Eight of the hulking crab creatures rose out of the water first, a sickening almost greasy, glossy gray in color. They fanned out, forming the perimeter of sorts. Then came the frogmen—a browning green in color, they walked out of the lake, their bulbous yellow-ish eyes visible on their zoomed-in displays. The frogs were frightening; they came in large numbers—a dozen or two at first, then hundreds rose up out of the water, surging on shore. It was more than Thun had ever seen assembled. A pair of their recon troops, nicknamed Foxes, slid out of the water, their massive underslung jaws and distinct hunched backs making them stand out.

Then came the real threat to their fighting vehicle. The military called them the Soldiers, but the rank and file soldiers referred to them as the bosses, an homage to video games. As large as an ASHUR, they were roughly humanoid in shape, but the similarities ended with their form. They had massive webbed clawed hands that looked as if they could damage their fighting vehicle with a swing on their part. A strange pattern, almost lightning bolt-like was embedded in their muscular armored skin. The colors changed; no one knew for sure why. This one had a crimson, pulsating pattern.

Frogs were mass attack weapons. They had first appeared as big eggs that the Fish had floated ashore. They grew to almost human size quickly. They couldn't handle weapons; they didn't have to. They devoured anything organic—a biological weapon that had devastated entire swaths of Florida's Everglades. In many respects, they were an area of denial weapon. When they attacked, they came in large groups, swarming their foes, spitting a toxic paste, clawing. They seemed immune to pain, and were a lot like zombies when it came to killing them. Wounds only slowed them. Against an armored vehicle, they were not much of a threat, but if the crew was forced to bail out, the frogs could easily overwhelm them. *They are up to something with that many being put ashore.*

This boss looked different from the ones they had seen before. It had something else, a large ridge on its back on a bulge running down what might serve as a spine. The bulge had two tubes and arched across the shoulders, down the triceps, to the hands. Whatever it was, it was a weapon they didn't want to deal with.

"There goes the neighborhood," Sparks said.

Thun toggled the uplink for his feed to the battlespace command, then he hit the communications toggle. "Battlespace Command, this is Whoop Ass. We have multiple contacts emerging at," he checked the map coordinates, "H-five, three, zero. We are showing crabs, frogs, a boss, and some foxes. We have frogs numbering in the hundreds. Transmitting feed to you now." Sparks closed his top hatch and while Thun waited for a reply, he did the same.

He hit the release for the P-Drones. The fist-sized drones flew out of their compartments and fanned out around the Schwarzkopf, spreading out down the hill. They were expendable and unarmed— their purpose was to provide video and tactical data to both the crew and the battlespace commander.

Captain Rolando's voice was smooth and controlled. He could afford to be relaxed. Controllers operated in the rear areas, far from the action. "Confirmed enemy presence in your sector. Help is on the way. You are weapons free and hot. Good hunting."

"Good hunting?" Sparks said as Thun fired up the Schwarzkopf's beefy diesel engine. The sound alone seemed to make the enemy pause and look in their direction. His targeting screens came to life and the turret cycled right and left as part of the startup routine. "Spoken like an officer that has never spent a day at the front."

The alien crabs reacted in unison—they scurried toward their vehicle, maneuvering with sideways steps around trees and rocks as they came like over-aggressive spiders.

"You seeing this?" Thun asked.

"It's my job to see that shit."

"It's your job to kill shit like that."

Sparks said nothing as he used his joystick to adjust the turret. "One rocket—HEDP," he said, his gaze totally locked on the screen. The tone signal purred in the compartment. There was a hissing sound over their head as the rocket rack unleashed one of the large projectiles. Thun watched on his primary monitor as the warhead streaked down the hillside and slammed into the crab. The explosion was loud and so violent, it shook leaves off nearby trees, an emerald rain. The alien reeled around from the impact, and as the smoke cleared, two of the four primary legs of the creature were limp attachments. Holes pitted the long scorpion-like body, spraying an arterial-like blackish gray goo.

For a moment, the pair of tankers thought they had killed the creature because it was stationary. Then the ooze stopped, as if a spigot had been turned off. The crab curled up slightly, then continue up the hill.

"Please make that crab unalive," Thun said.

"Freaking rocket was made by the lowest bidder," Sparks growled. "Firing."

The second rocket streaked down the hillside, slamming into the alien. This time big chunks of the creature went flailing into the air, to the point where it almost looked fake. As the smoke from the blast rolled skyward into the trees, they could see the alien's opened body. One man-sized claw twitched.

The second explosion seemed to galvanize the alien force. They started up the hillside at a faster pace. "Come on, Thun, do that driver-shit you do," Sparks said as he tried to keep the targeting reticle on the closest of the crabs that was coming up at them.

The Schwarzkopf lurched to life as Thun backed it up a few yards, then turned riding along the crest of the ridgeline where they had parked. One of the crabs fired a cutter at them, hitting the side of the fighting vehicle. The ultra-high-pressure beam of water was designed to cut like a laser, but the fast movement didn't allow it to do more than to score an ugly groove along the sloped armor of the hull.

Sparks triggered a power round for the rail gun and a massive shell exploded in the generator chamber of the turret, converting the explosion into electrical energy. The capacitor of the big cannon hummed above them as he drifted it onto the lead-crab and fired.

The rail gun made a high-pitched *wee-ooh* noise as it unleashed the deadly projectile. A plume of superheated air roared from in front of the barrel as the projectile flashed downrange at hypersonic speed. It hit the raised torso of the alien. The EFP round was designed to penetrate armor, but that was how the carapace of the aliens' bodies performed. It was a shaped explosion that entered in a hole roughly an inch in diameter, and exited out the back at almost a foot—a plume of greenish gore, orange and crimson flames, and other unidentified body parts. The force of the hit was so hard it lifted the crab up and back, sending it flailing.

"That's gonna leave a mark," Sparks said with a chuckle.

The boss paused, holding his arms out in front of him, pointing at the fighting vehicle as Thun took up a new position, still keeping some distance from the aliens. The massive tree-like arms tugged, and two projectiles fired out from the tubes that fed to the bulge on his back. They were orange and streaked through the air right at the Whoop Ass.

One nicked a tree and the projectile erupted in a splatter of some yellow-orange goo. The other broke on the left side of the Schwarzkopf, apparently spraying the entire side of the vehicle. The shot that nicked the tree ate through its trunk, sending it toppling right in front of them. Sparks jerked his head at the moment of impact, knocking his tanker's helmet hard into the padding to his side. As the vehicle shifted again, both of the crew could hear a hissing sound along the side of the fighting vehicle. The intense corrosive managed to penetrate the rear area troop transport area behind them in just a few seconds. The stench made their lungs ache and their nostrils sting.

"Jesus," Thun said, his eyes watering. Not waiting for another round, he backed up, getting out of line of sight for a moment. "We need to send some pain their way."

"Agreed."

"I'm going to crest the ridge. You're gonna need to fire fast. Mess up that boss and his Little Mermaid buddies."

"Call it," Sparks replied.

They both knew that the moment they presented themselves to fire, that they would be a target as well.

"On three," Thun said, moving the fighting vehicle forward some twenty yards from their last position.

Down the hillside, it was clear that more aliens had emerged from the lake. At least four more crabs and a dozen frogs. They were all making the long climb up the steep hillside.

"Three, two, one—"

A bang went off above and behind them as the power shell fired for the rail gun. The capacitor throbbed with energy. "Eat this, you bastard," Sparks said as the rail gun released its round downrange with a slight tug of recoil.

The round missed the center of the boss, but hit it in the right arm right at the elbow, severing it completely off. The massive humanoid creature turned hard under the impact.

"Got him," Sparks said. "Switching targets."

Thun kept his monitor focused on the boss. Where the limb had been severed, it sprayed like a firehose, shooting out an incredible amount of oily black liquid. Word was that the bosses were encased in highly pressurized bodies—or so the G2 guys claimed. Instead of dropping, the boss rose back up. The flow of whatever liquid was in it ceased. Its strange marks flickered from red to a brilliant blue. "Sparky, I think all you did was piss him off."

Sparks's response was to unleash another rocket downrange. It hit the ground in front of a crab that was spider-climbing over a rock. Bits of granite shrapnel from the explosion riddled its body, but after a moment of recoil, it continued its climb.

"We gotta move," Sparks said.

Thun didn't have to be told twice. Swinging the vehicle around, he maneuvered behind the ridge again. He heard the cracking of several trees behind him, no doubt the victims of alien fire that had been directed at them. "Nice try, assholes," he muttered.

In his ears came the voice of Captain Rolando's smooth voice. "Whoop Ass, you are to leave that grid ASAP. We have an airstrike inbound. It is going to saturate your area."

Thun's stomach clenched. "We have company coming."

"Fish?"

"The Air Force."

"Wow. There's a first for everything, I guess." The Air Force had been spread thin on both coasts since the start of the war. Getting air-ground support was almost unheard of. Word was they had run out of munitions after the first few weeks of the alien invasion, but rumors were rarely right. It made sense for an air bombing given the number of frogs that had come ashore.

Thun finished his backing up and throttled for forward movement, turning hard to the right. "We need to haul ass, big time," he said, he said, gritting his teeth.

The Schwarzkopf turned in place and took off fast, pushing them both into their seats. It went about forty yards when suddenly, a crab cleared the ridge in front of them. It sprang at the fighting vehicle, landing right on top of it. "Fuck me," Thun said, slamming the brakes in hopes of shaking the creature off. It didn't work. The alien hung tight to the front hull. From what he could see through his viewport and monitors, it was using its big claws on the side of the vehicle. The thuds, even through the armor, were audible and frightening.

Sparks triggered the big .50 caliber in the turret, sending the bullets at point-blank range into the body of the creature. Some rounds ricocheted, others dug deep into the crab's body. Sparks fired a power round for the rail gun as the crab's big tail whipped down, slamming into the turret. He thought at first that the stinger would break off—irresistible force hitting an armored target. It didn't. Instead, it slammed into the rail gun, striking three times with such rapidity that it felt like the turret itself was going to be ripped off. The capacitor, which had been whining, exploded above and behind them. "Lost the rail gun!"

Sparks called out as the damage display showed it flicker to crimson. "Move it!" he called out to his teammate.

Thun accelerated, driving blind—the crab was blocking his field of vision. The Schwarzkopf slammed into a tree, or so he assumed by the cracking sound he heard as it toppled it. It did not deter the crab who continued to lash away at the vehicle.

He saw a whip-like tendril extend out from one of the claws on his monitor. It lashed at the fighting vehicle and brilliant blue sparks flew, both inside and outside. One of his monitors popped, the screen cracked. The computer shut down, as did all power. The fighting vehicle went dark.

"What the hell?" Sparks called.

"It's one of their shock whips," Thun said, hitting the three circuit breakers and then the start button. His damage display and forward monitor flickered on, showing that the computer was rebooting. "This is going to take a minute," he said, grumbling. "Can you please get that asshat off our tank? I'd like to not die today."

"Targeting is offline as is power to the turret," Sparks said, removing his straps. "I'm going to have to do it the old-fashioned way." He climbed back and went into the turret, somehow managing to squeeze in.

Thun stared at the monitor, sweat running down from his hairline as the indicator showed it was only 50 percent reloaded. "Come on, come on . . ."

Sparks reached the turret and took manual control of the .50 caliber. Using a small manual viewport, he angled the gun as much as he could to line up the crab and triggered the weapon manually. They had trained him to fire that way, in "emergency situations," which he felt that this qualified.

He fired a steady stream into the part of the crab where it raised up. The creature shifted and Sparks aimed at the tail. The machine gun tore into it so badly that he cut the tail in half, just as it was about the strike again. The bulbous end with the stinger fell on top of the turret with a crunching sound. The crab wailed an ungodly cry as it fell limp.

The system finished its reboot but the damage had been done. The communications subsystem was unresponsive, as was the forward viewscreen. Thun leaned forward, pushing his helmet into the padding in front of the manual viewport, and backed up, hoping to dislodge the remains of the crab. Backing up some twenty feet, he saw something that made his stomach sink. The left tread of the Schwarzkopf lay in front of him on the ground.

"Fuck—piss—damn!" he spat.

"What is it?" Sparks said sliding back into his seat.

"We lost a tread."

There was a moment of silence. "I guess we are in no position to call the recovery team."

"Comms is out."

"And there's an inbound air strike."

"Right."

"So what do you suggest?"

Thun pulled his sidearm from the rack next to him and put it in his shoulder holster. "It's not like we can use smoke signals to wave them off."

"The BS commander will see we're in the zone, right? I mean, he will abort if we're still here."

Thun didn't answer that quickly, which was an answer all on its own. When he did speak, it drove right to action. "I don't want to bet my life on that. They may assume we have been destroyed."

"The one time the Air Force shows up, and we are in their target zone!"

"We are going to have to make a run for it on foot."

Sparks grabbed his sidearm. "Well shit. Out the top or back?"

"Back," Thun said, twisting around the seat back and making his way to the cramped rear passenger compartment. The chemical stink from the corrosive attack still hung in the air and he saw a number of small holes where it had eaten through the armor, one section looking as if it had been hit by a shotgun blast, a spread of holes. The reports on that stuff were accurate . . . it can chew through armor. The corrosive was, in reality, a molecular re-arranger, breaking down material at the atomic level, transforming it to a worthless goo. All Thun could be assured of was that he didn't want any to hit him.

"How long do we have?" Sparks said, reaching the rear drop-hatch and holding the button. The rear of the Schwarzkopf slowly dropped open. The fresh air was refreshing, if only for a moment. It was more frightening as the two men realized that they were no longer protected by their armored cocoon.

"Unknown," Thun replied, stepping out and looking at the Whoop Ass. The crab had done a number on the treads and bogies. It had been a minor miracle that they had backed up as much as they had. The creature lay in front of the tank, but its gore covered the woodland camouflage. A sweet yet tuna-fishy aroma hung in the air.

The rail gun pointed skyward, bent and mauled by the attacks the alien had inflicted. The rear of the turret was still smoking where the capacitor had blown and the missile rack was caved in—forever inoperative. "Christ," Thun muttered, staring at it longingly. The tank had gotten them through several battles and had never failed. Now they were abandoning it.

In the distance, he heard the guttural grunting of the frogs. They did it in unison. According to the Army, it was a noise designed to intimidate their enemies. It seemed to echo all around them in trees. Both of them could testify that as a noise to induce terror, it worked.

"Isn't there an air strike on the way?" Sparks said, shaking him back to reality.

"Right—let's move," Thun said, breaking into a sprint away from the dead fighting vehicle.

They ran full out, heading away from the lake shore, down the sloping embankment. Sparks slid on some dead leaves, skidding to his knees at one point. Thun grabbed him by his tac vest shoulder strap and helped him up. Bobbing and weaving around trees and thickets, they didn't stop for some time. When they did, they dropped low, heaving air. Thun remembered his training and tried bringing it in through his nose and out through his mouth, but his nose was so clogged he gave up and simply panted quickly.

Behind them, they heard the faint distant roar of a jet . . . or possibly a drone. Both looked back but could not see their abandoned tank or, thankfully, any sign of pursuit. They tried to see the jet above but the gray skies made that impossible.

Above the lake shore where they had been operating came two dull explosions. The air was illuminated with bright white light and a shower of spark-like particles that slowly drifted downward on the trees. The particles were intense in their luminosity and heat; the trees burst into flames as they rained down. The particles were a shower that lit up a huge area, saturating the banks of Lake Saltonstall, setting it all ablaze. Orange flames lapped skyward for easily three-quarters of a mile of shoreline. It took a full minute for a ripple of heat to reach Thun and Sparks.

"What the hell was that?" Sparks asked.

"Phosphorus bombs—air burst, at least I think so."

"I didn't know we had those."

Thun knelt lower, watching the slowly falling bits of whiteness drift down, consuming the area where they had been. "After Vietnam that stuff got pulled from the inventory . . . it was supposedly inhumane."

"War is inhumane."

"Yeah, well, the people that don't fight it like to play games with the tools we use. I heard stories of these things being used in Afghanistan and Iraq, but for the most part that was it. The Air Force must have dug them out of mothballs for this fight."

Over the roar of the fires, there was a wailing noise—not at all like the crabs. It was deep, booming, agony filled. Both men assumed it had to be the boss creature, though they had been told that the mouth chambers of the aliens were incapable of producing sounds. There was some satisfaction that it was in pain. Neither spoke for a few moments but watched as the last floating bits of intensely burning chemicals drifted downward.

Sparks shattered the silence. "We probably would have been safe in the Whoop Ass."

Then came an explosion from where the vehicle had been abandoned. It might have been the remaining rockets cooking off, or the engine compartment and fuel finally getting ignited. The blast was human in origin, not the work of the aliens. Black smoke rolled over the white smoke from the burning trees and aliens. Sparks spoke up again. "Then again, it was probably a good thing we left."

Thun mustered a thin smile. "Ya think?" He stood up and held out his hand to help his gunner to his feet. "Come on, Sparky, we've got at least a five-mile hike back to the firebase."

Sparks rose and the two started off cross country. "I signed up to be in armor so that I wouldn't have to walk."

"You joined the army first," Thun replied. "You know how much the PBI love their marching."

"You think they will assign us another vehicle?"

Thun considered that. "This war is just getting started. Yeah, they'll put us behind the wheels of something. First we will have to fill out a mountain of paperwork explaining why we abandoned our tank, why didn't we hold our position—the usual battle damage assessment bull-shit on steroids because we lost our tank."

"Ugh," Sparks said. "I forgot about the paperwork. Yeah, the Army is going to want answers for the lost equipment. Knowing them, they will try to take the cost of the thing out of our paychecks."

That comment did elicit a chuckle from Thun. "Yeah, we will have to serve for sixty-eight years to pay it off."

"Fucking Army."

"Fucking Army."

They came up over a lightly wooded hill in silence when Sparks decided he could no longer tolerate the quiet. "The Whoop Ass was a damn good ride. Even you have to admit that. I mean we racked up a lot of dead Fish in her." There was a sense of pride in his words that was hard to deny.

"She was at that."

"What are we going to name the next one?"

"You amaze me, Sparky."

"How's that?"

"Here we are, having barely escaped certain death, almost bombed by our own military, and you are worried about what we are going to name our next tank?"

"Yeah—so what do you think about, 'Whoop Ass—The Sequel'?"

Thun simply shook his head and came to the conclusion it was going to be a long walk back.

VOICES IN THE NIGHT

There are few things more frightening than being trapped behind enemy lines, at night, and unable to shoot or move. While ASHURs are a dominant force on the battlefield, they are machines and sometimes hardware just dies when you need it the most.

Mission 2044Q—Operation Thumper Three Delta
The Western American Front, San Francisco, California

Corporal Shanice Raven swung her Bronco-class ASHUR rig around the corner of the destroyed school and glared off into John McLaren Park. In the darkness of the early evening, she had switched to night vision and the greens lit up inside her rig's interior, giving her a solid 270-degree view of the rolling hills of the park.

The city of San Francisco had been turned into a battlefield early in the war against the Fish. As she looked out towards where the sun had just set, she saw the smoke rising from several battle zones in the city. It was hard to remember back to how the city looked before the fighting. She couldn't see the ruins of the Golden Gate Bridge from this vantage spot but knew it was out there. *I never made it to San Francisco before the war . . . all I have are memories and images from old movies.*

No one knew why the aliens had come. The government had admitted that they had been landing in the Earth's oceans for some time, though no one had pieced together what the aliens objectives were. That didn't surprise her. One thing she had learned after joining the Army was that "military intelligence" generally was mislabeled. *I've had my ass put in harm's way too many times already thanks to bad intel. Give me a good battlespace commander any day over intelligence officers.*

The aliens hit the coasts of every continent. Their bioengineered fighters had wreaked havoc globally. Some cities were lost. Others, like San Francisco, became the front lines in a new kind of warfare—armored ASHUR rigs fighting alien creations. *It could be worse; I could've joined the navy.* Surface and submarine fleets were struggling to fight a race that was native to living underwater. The cost was staggering, not just in the dead, but in the destruction of many magnificent cities.

It hadn't all been bad news for mankind. The newer model ASHUR rigs had vastly improved power systems and weapons. They had been brought online remarkably fast. It turns out that corporate America understood that if they didn't roll up their sleeves, their factories were going to be laid waste. It took some time to organize counteroffensives, but they were raging everywhere. While mankind had no idea as to the motives of the alien invaders, they were putting up a good fight.

The Bronco was one of the new Gen III designs. It was a light rig but unlike a lot of light rigs, this one wasn't built for speed. The armor plating covered a layer of shear thickening fluid, a gel that was soft and gave the ASHUR flexibility, but when it was hit, hardened instantly into another layer of protection. With its medium weight L-2.5 laser and a M-2 rail gun, it packed a solid punch. She didn't just like it for the firepower and protection though. The Bronco had a look to it, stern lines like a rearing horse. The armored plates had a curve that, in profile, made it look like a well-muscled wild horse near the front. Even its legs used rounded edges that seemed to mimic muscles.

She had been on patrol with a squad of infantry when they had stumbled onto a pair of crabs, the large scorpion-centaur-like creatures. She had provided cover to the infantry, killing one of the genetically engineered aliens with a rail-gun slug to what she assumed was its head and a laser burn to its chest. The infantry brought their own kinds of death and destruction to the party engaging the other crabs in small arms fire and grenades. It had gotten ugly, though. The crab they had engaged had sprayed their position and her Bronco with a blast from its squirter—a corrosive spraying device. It had killed two of the infantry and splattered the legs of her Bronco before finally succumbing to the human's firepower. Her tiny damage display screen seemed to indicate marginal damage, but she knew that the corrosive had a knack for causing problems long after it was fired.

Corporal Raven set out after the remaining crab which had broken off, which is what had drawn her into John McLaren Park. "Angel Fire, in pursuit!" She knew it was injured; the occasional greasy greenish black ooze that she assumed was their blood stained the ground and grass, showing where it had been. Her night vision gear showed heat signatures from blotches of cold on the warm ground. As she maneuvered her Bronco around a pile of low boulders, she slowly became aware that she had gone out too far beyond her designated patrol path. With the darkness of nighttime starting to set in, she realized just how isolated she had allowed herself to become.

Turning the rig around, she prepared to head back. As she spun, the crab collided with her hard. The rig's hydraulics moaned and protested as she twisted, tossing the bulk of the massive creature to the side with her Bronco's arms. Her own arms were in control sleeves and she could feel the ASHUR rig protesting as she fought to regain her balance . . . all while the creature's claws stabbed down at her like organic battering rams, trying to rip her apart. The scraping of the claws feverously trying to rip her armor apart made a metallic fingernails-on-the-chalkboard sound around her. Gritting her teeth, she struggled to get her arms and their weapons free. It took a few agonizing moments, but she did it.

She triggered two power shells to augment the power to her laser and rail gun. The explosive shells went off inside a micro-generator chamber, converting the explosions into electricity. She leveled the laser with the crab's body and fired. Without night vision gear, the beam would have been invisible. In the darkness, it was a brilliant flash along the armored carapace of the crab. The superheated slashing hole that it left hissed vapor from it.

The crab twisted hard, enough to push her clear by a few yards. Raven staggered in her rig, falling back on every bit of her training to keep upright. As she struggled with a half-staggering step to the right, one of the crab's massive front claws opened and engulfed the right arm where her laser was mounted. It clamped on the arm; metal moaned and creaked as part of the exterior blast armor pinged and popped off or bent in. Her damage indicators showed a complete hydraulic failure in the arm even before she saw the stream of hot hydraulic fluid squirt into the night air. *That arm is toast!* Even if she managed to break away, it was not going to operate.

Raven twisted her waist in a snapping motion in an effort to get free, but only made the damage to the arm sound and feel worse. Firing another power shell, she saw the spike of energy available and channeled it instantly to her rail gun. The capacitor throbbed, humming in her ears as she spun around, putting the weapon into the base of the crab's long upraised neck. The armor there was thick, but there was no missing at this range. *Try this out!*

From her left-hand sleeve, she toggled the firing trigger.

The rail gun accelerated its slug to hypersonic speed instantly. When it fired, the superheated air from the sudden acceleration in the magnetic barrel always flashed a brilliant jet of searing hot plasma. Most of the time this was merely a visual effect, but with her barrel almost flush at the neck of the crab, it added to the damage. Her night vision gear blurred intensely emerald as the slug hit and the flash fried the crab's flesh. The round entered and exited in the flash, spraying hot alien gore into the air.

Its grip on her Bronco's right arm instantly released as the creature staggered back. She couldn't help but smile at the sight as the crab wobbled on its lower legs. The upper pair of spindly arms twitched. "Die, asshole!" she called out as it seemed to turn away from her.

It turned around and a deadly spray of corrosive shot out from a tubular projection under one of its big claw arms. Raven flinched away. The bio-acid, a nasty, corrosive, fluoroantimonic acid, splashed the lower part of her cockpit, her ASHUR's legs, and as she spun, spraying some on the side and rear of her Bronco. She reeled around and saw the crab trying to pull itself away. She fired another power round, hot-charging her rail gun, firing again. This time the plasma burst filled the space between them as the slug plowed into the side of the creature. The hit caused ripples on the armored carapace plates as the round tore through its armor and insides alike.

The crab went rigid, as if every muscle it had locked up at once. It rose on its spidery legs, then dropped hard and limp. Raven ignored the damaged indicators screaming for her attention, and kept her focus on her foe. Wisps from the acid eating at her rig were like a fog all around her, but she saw through them, into the night. The crab was motionless, then fell over with a dull thud.

Her own breath was ragged as she realized the fight was over. Sweat burned in her eyes as she tried to get control of her breathing. Glancing down at her damage display, she saw the horrors of the damage. Her damaged arm was now worthless scrap metal. Hydraulics for her legs were showing a catastrophic failure. Most importantly, her power system, a bio gel power source and battery on the back of the rig, was hit as well. The power signature was showing a slow and steady decline as the source of power for the Bronco bled out.

"Fuck me!" she wailed. She instantly regretted cursing—her mother would have been horribly upset at her use of profanity. That was another gift that the Army had given her. Ignoring the damage indicators, she tried to take a step, to head back towards friendly territory, but there was a whine and groan of protest from the hydraulics, and she was only able to adjust her stance a half-yard before the system locked up completely. Power for an ASHUR was life. Raven deactivated the rig's night vision gear, realizing the draw on the power the system had. The interior of her cockpit canopy returned to normal, and her nostrils picked up on a whiff of something metallic . . . a sign that somewhere below her, the acid had eaten into the cockpit. Coughing from the smell, Raven grabbed her tactical light and flashed it downward, worried that it might get on her legs that were surrounded with the armor of the Bronco and their mobility sleeves. Her legs were clear . . . *no, this smell is in the cockpit.* A lower transparent aluminum panel seam was the source of the stench. She activated the vent system and ran the fan awhile, enough to vent the fumes out. Her nostril hairs felt like they were burning, but eventually it cleared.

Training dictated in such situations to validate operations of the rig. She ran through the checklist mentally, double-checking each system, hoping and praying that the damage indicator was wrong. As she finished, she pulled her arms out of the sweaty control sleeves and pounded them on her seat rests. *Goddamn it! I'm dead in the water.*

She activated her emergency transponder and turned on the comms system while she still had power.

"Angel Fire to Stomper Squad, Six Seven," she called to her squad mates. A hiss of static was all she got back. *Shit . . . I hope nothing happened to them.*

Finally Sergeant Tilly's voice came back. "Where in the hell are you, Angel Fire? We got hit by some of their frogmen and have been forced back to the line."

The line . . . that meant they were across the front and in human controlled territory. "I chased down the crab; now I'm in a bit of trouble."

"We are no-joy getting to you," the sergeant responded. "Recommend you link with battlespace command."

"Roger that," she said, feeling the red embarrassment mixed with frustration on her face. *Damn it, now I have to admit to command that I went out a little too far. This is going to cost me some paperwork . . .* Switching to the tactical channel, she mentally prepared herself to make the call.

"Baker Two Seven, this is Angel Fire," she said into the throat microphone. "Baker Two Seven, this is Angel Fire. I am issuing a Class Two distress and request immediate extraction and evacc." If she had been personally wounded, it would have been a Class One distress signal. She had to admire the Bronco's design. It had taken down the crab and despite being a wreck, she had come through okay . . . so far.

She waited for the battlespace commander to respond. She double-checked her comms system and saw that it was operating. *Come on, you asshats, acknowledge!*

She cycled the cockpit fan again for a few moments to stir the air in the cockpit. Then she heard it, a crackle in her helmet's earbud followed by a voice. "Angel Fire, this is the Battlespace Commander. I am not picking you up on my board. What are your coordinates?"

She turned on her tactical display and it flickered blue for a moment as it came up. "I am at grid Hotel seven. Twenty-one by eight. Confirm."

"Grid Hotel seven. Two-one by eight."

"Roger that."

There was a pause. "I've got nothing on your transponder," the voice came back. "Toggle it off and back on please."

The perfect Army solution, shut it off and turn it back on. Following the instructions, she waited for a moment. "Back on Baker Two Seven."

"Still nothing here," the voice came back. *Damn, it may be damaged as well. Why not? The whole frigging rig is dying around me.* She banged the control with the bottom of her fist, but still nothing changed. She waited nervously, glancing out into the darkness of the night all around her. *Hopefully someone is close enough to come in and recover me.*

ASHUR rigs were a precious commodity, as were their pilots. The services all placed emphasis on recovering rigs and pilots as quick as possible to avoid their technology falling into enemy hands. She had always thought the policy as stupid . . . the alien's technology was bio-engineered—they didn't use war machines like ASHURs; they simply engineered combatants that were bigger and more deadly. Now that she was stranded alone in the night, she found herself an ardent supporter of the recovery doctrine.

"Angel Fire," came the male voice of the battlespace commander. "We show you are outside your patrol corridor."

"Forgive me for going after the enemy," she snapped, almost regretting it.

"Understood. The issue is our resources needed to get you out of there are already committed elsewhere. It will take some time to get to you."

She looked down at her still-declining power levels. "Roger that, Baker Two Seven. Be advised, I am bleeding power here with almost full system failures. How long are we talking?"

"Four to five hours," the male voice replied.

Shanice Raven wanted to scream. *This is bullshit!* She was behind enemy lines, in the dark, and crippled. There was always the option of popping the cockpit canopy and going back on foot, but that would be leaving her Bronco behind. Army doctrine said stay with your ride. Besides, out there, without armor, she would be more vulnerable. *They know where you are, girl. You just have to calm your shit down.*

Drawing a long deep breath, she gathered her resolve. She knew that the power levels in her rig were on a steady decline, so she shut off the interior cockpit lights, killed the mangled hydraulic systems power, and any other nonessential systems. Raven wanted to crack open the cockpit canopy but found that it wouldn't budge. *The acid must have melted the seal.* Pulling her leg in front of her she kicked it, but the egress hatch refused to budge. Reaching up, there was a small hatch that allowed viewing overhead. It was too small to crawl out of, but large enough for her to open and get some cool air in.

"You still with me, Angel Fire?" came the voice of the battlespace commander.

"Roger that. I was just opening the top hatch for some air. I have enough power for comms, but I have shut everything else down."

"I'm staying with you on this channel," he assured her. "Help will get to you. Just remain calm and do what you can to relax."

"Spoken like someone in a rear area," she said bitterly.

"I wasn't always in the rear," he said. "I have a half-dozen patrols under my belt. Then shit happened. You know the Army; never let a warm body go to waste."

Somehow that helped Raven . . . knowing that the man she was talking to was not some desk jockey. "I'm glad I have someone who knows what it's like to be out here."

"Oh yeah. I spilled my blood and sweat in this war already. I always knew that I was going to see some action in the Army; the politicians love sending us to do their dirty work. I just never thought it would be in my home country."

"I hear that. I was raised in St. Louis. I always figured I'd be killing folks in the Middle East or Africa or even the Russies. I never expected *we'd* be the ones that were invaded."

"I know how you feel, Angel Fire. I'm from outside Philly. My old neighborhood is now in the AIZ."

She leaned back into her seat, her knees in front of her, looking out into the darkness of night. Flickers of orange from distant flames in the city were visible in at least a dozen locations. Even in the muffled silence of her cockpit, there were occasional cracks of small arms fire in the distance. All around her the war was being fought. Yet she was stranded there, in her rig, unable to move or fight.

Reaching up, she checked her shoulder holster and made sure her M18 was there. It was oddly comforting, not that the pistol would be of much use if the Fish showed up in force. Holstering the weapon, she wrapped her arms around her legs, sitting in a ball inside the cockpit. Pulling out her canteen, she took a swig of the water and savored it. For long minutes, she looked out across the park into the darkness. *If you ignore the sounds of war in the distance, it's actually a pretty peaceful place.*

Raven's mind went to her parents. Her father had been a vet and had been proud that she had opted to join the Army. Her mom was even supportive, though she knew that she was worried, especially when the first reports of aliens coming ashore began. The aliens had sent aside big shells filled with goblins, small piranha-like aliens that indiscriminately attacked people. The images of mutilated civilians and the utter panic, combined with the attacks in Hawaii and Guam, propelled Raven into action.

She began to elevate her game—working hard to become ASHUR qualified. Only the best of the best could hope to become an ASHUR pilot, and they had to make it through a grueling and competitive training program. It burned out a lot of world-be pilots, but not her. It hadn't been easy, but Raven didn't show a bit of hesitation. *I earned the right to sit in this rig, to be one of the first Bronco pilots.* Her ASHUR tattoo on her right forearm was proof of her success.

"Angel Fire," came the voice of her battlespace commander. It jarred her for a moment, making her wonder how long she had been staring into the night, reminiscing.

"This is Angel Fire, go Baker Two Seven," she responded.

"I've got eyes on you now," he said. "A Wasp is overhead painting your position now," he said. The unmanned Wasp class drones were short-range surveillance devices. She turned on her cockpit's night vision and saw the laser beam stabbing down from the sky only a few yards away. She shut it off, knowing she had to conserve power.

"Roger that—I am being lassoed," she replied.

"Good. I've got a team moving on your position as we speak," he said. She glanced at her chronometer and saw that an hour had passed since her Bronco had been crippled in the fight. "They are still a ways out from you, though. Hang tight."

"It's not like I have an option."

"For now, you look like you're alone," his voice came back. "I'm not seeing any enemy activity in your grid or any of the adjacent ones. But that can change quickly."

Looking out the side of her cockpit, she saw the rail gun. *If I could get out there, I could manually fire it.* Like many of the heavy weapons mounted on ASHURs, they were detachable and designed to be used if the rig was as damaged as hers was. The rail gun was a beast, but she knew she could manage it.

It's all academic. I'm trapped in here. Besides, stepping outside of the rig would expose me. The aliens had a lot of ways to kill. Their "guns" were termed needlers; they fired organic needles at a speed slower than a rail gun, but more than enough to punch through blast plates and flesh. Worse, many were poison-tipped. They had gas projectors that used some sort of bio-agent gas-virus that could kill or cripple fast. Some of the bigger ones carried sonic weapons that could turn internal organs to a mush if you were hit at close range. She had seen dead troops before without a wound or sign of injury, whose insides were reduced to a pudding-like ooze. They had flashers, weapons that used a pulse of gamma radiation to destroy human vision and skin. Stepping out on the battlefield without protection was a risky business, only to be undertaken by the bravest of the brave. *For now, I will sit and wait.*

She relaxed her cramped legs, sliding them back into the legs of the rig, not to walk but simply to stretch. Pulling out an energy bar she had stuffed in her go-bag she opened it and ate something, helping quell the rumble of her stomach. Raven savored the quiet outside, the stillness. The lack of anything moving told her she was safe. It was a fleeting few minutes though. Even a slight breeze that made the branches of trees move was enough to ratchet her tension back up.

A familiar voice crackled in her earpiece. "Angel Fire, you still with me?"

"Where else would I be?" she responded.

"There's a little hang up on your extraction. It's going to take a little longer than planned."

She was disturbed by the news but appreciated that it was blunt. "Anything I should know about?"

"A Fish patrol has forced the XO team to hunker down, that's all."

"It's a bit lonely out here," she confided.

"I knew it would be. I'm off-shift, but they are letting me stay on to stay in comms with you."

Somehow she found herself liking the man behind the call sign. "Thanks," she said, taking another sip from her canteen. "Since you're off duty, you have a name?"

"Earl," he said. "Earl Brody, Lieutenant."

"You don't sound like an Earl."

"How are Earls supposed to sound?"

"A little more hillbilly. You know, redneckish."

He chuckled. "Sorry to disappoint you, Angel Fire. I'm not a big fan of country-western music or the lifestyle. I'm more of a Boston Pops kind of guy. I got named after a cousin of my dad's."

He's sophisticated . . . probably more than me. "I never listened to them before."

"When we get you out, I'll loan you some tunes. It will change your life."

"I doubt that," she replied. She liked old-school hip-hop music, not the shit that the kids played today. Stuff with real singers, not synth-voice work. *There's no school like the old school.* "I'm glad you're out there."

"I didn't want you sitting there waiting. How are you holding up?" Baker Two Seven asked.

"Physically I'm fine. My Bronco is toast—but I'm hoping my tech can fix it. The kid is good at his job." Hell, there were few things that her tech, Corporal Brantly, couldn't fix when it came to ASHUR rigs. He was young, but had a knack for troubleshooting problems and making them go away. As she glanced at the worthless hunk of metal that was her rig's her arm-mounted laser, even she had to concede he had his work cut out for him this time. *Good thing this thing is modular because no amount of banging is going to fix that laser.*

"You must be some pretty hot stuff to have qualified for ASHUR training," he said. "I've tried out before, it's grueling."

She was proud, but she also knew not to flaunt it. "I was lucky and I'm fast. Piloting these things requires serious muscle, especially the legs. I was a runner in high school and was an alternate on the last Olympic team for cross-country. My legs are what got me through the training."

"There's more to it than that, Angel Fire," he said.

"Call me Shanice. Since both of us are technically off the clock."

"Okay, Shanice," Earl replied with a hint of hesitancy. "As I was saying, it wasn't just your legs. There's a lot of schooling that goes into the testing, as you are more than aware. A lot of folks can pass the physical tests, but bomb on the intelligence side."

He was speaking the truth. "I had help, and worked my ass off. I'm lucky. Math always came easy to me in high school. I don't have a photographic memory, but I'm pretty close to it. Apparently that stuff stuck in my head." Memories of the ASHUR qualifications came back to her, along with a bit of the anxiety associated with it. The weeks of training, specializing in a specific rig, were exhausting and grueling. For Shanice, it had also been one of her proudest moments. *And now the damned Fish have gone and busted up my ride!*

"Well, we are going to get you out of there," he said with a ring of confidence that oddly was helpful.

"I'm glad someone is looking after me."

"How'd you get so far off the beaten path?"

"Our patrol got hit. We took down one crab, but I had it in my head to go after the survivor. He managed to get the drop on me." She paused. That had always been a problem with her, her impulsiveness. Her mother had constantly lectured her that it would get her into trouble—and now it had. "Once I get a head of steam up, it's hard to stop me. Besides, you can't win the war by letting the bad guys get away."

"I hear that," Earl replied.

For a minute or two, she didn't say anything. She embraced her thoughts. There were lessons to be learned, and a good ASHUR pilot knew that. *I should have known better. I should have made sure I had support. I should have made sure that the squad didn't need me. I should have remained in better contact with them.* Next time, she assured herself, things would be different.

Time became a blur for her. Her body wanted rest and sleep, but her mind was attuned to everything outside of her cockpit. She could see the city miles beyond the park and knew that out there, where the glow of fires and flashes from gunfire tore into the darkness, that the war was still raging.

It was as if Earl could sense her need for quiet, and he didn't speak for a long time—perhaps an hour. Her eyes kept sweeping the night every time the wind blew, but so far she only saw the darkness. His voice came back to her, as if pulling her from a dream. "You still with me, Shanice?"

"Roger that," she replied wearily.

"I spoke to your squad leader, Sergeant Tilly. He wanted me to let you know that the rest of the squad is doing fine. Minor bumps and burns."

She found herself nodding to his words. "Good." Then, "What's the word on that XO?"

"They are close to your position, about ten minutes out."

She sighed and allowed herself to smile. "Good. I was beginning to wonder how long I was going to be sitting out here."

"Well, don't thank me yet. I've switched out the drone that is monitoring you. The thing is, we have two Fish slowly closing on your position."

Her hand drifted down to her sidearm and her jaw set forward. "Type?"

"One Fox—one frogman. Now, there's a good chance that they don't even know where you are. It might just be one of their patrols and it'll just pass by near you."

"Only if my luck has changed," she growled, pulling her sidearm out, she chambered a round.

"We're hoping that our guys get to you first. If not, stay in your rig."

"Where else am I going to go, Earl?" she snapped. "A big part of my problem is I can't get out of this beast."

"Which is good, because that means the Fish can't get in."

Her eyes narrowed. "You always blowing sunshine up people's asses?"

His chuckle reached her ears. "All part of the pay grade. Besides, it's not like there's a playbook for this shit. Just keep your eyes peeled."

Time crawled for long minutes as Raven looked around her crippled ASHUR. Checking her power levels, she saw that she had enough for a few minutes of night vision, but after that, she wouldn't be able to use the communications system. It was possible to fire a power shell and shunt that power into the battery, but it wasn't recommended if the battery was damaged—which hers was. *I wish I'd crapped out during daylight . . . at least the armor's solar kit would have given me a few minutes more energy.* It was in that moment she realized that having the night vision would not help her situation. *I'm trapped here. Seeing the enemy isn't going to kill them.*

Her body tensed the moment she caught a flicker of movement off to her right. The Fox aliens were like the reconnaissance forces for the Fish. Their squat bodies were built for speed, not battle. According to

G2, they had more advanced optic and audio systems. This one poked its head slowly over the top of a boulder, the slight glimmer of moonlight hitting its eyes enough for her to see the glimmer.

For a long moment, their eyes locked. It turned its head slightly, almost mimicking a human looking puzzled. She felt her body tense as she pulled her sidearm slowly out and wrapped her hands around it, embracing it. The gun was useless unless it somehow pried open her cockpit, but that didn't matter. Standing there, facing an enemy only a dozen or so yards away, holding the gun gave her a sense of comfort.

The Fox slowly seemed to glide as it moved over to the fallen crab, the one that had crippled her. Its elongated webbed claw-like hands touched the dead crab in several spots, as if checking it. It was smart enough to keep the dead creature between her ASHUR and itself, giving her very little to see. *What are you up to, you little shit?*

"Angel Fire, what's your status?" came the voice of Earl. It seemed louder to her, but then she realized that was because of the tension she was feeling.

She spoke in a low whisper through gritted teeth. "I have Fox right in front of me."

"That's what I see too. Sit tight. The cavalry is on its way."

Like I have a choice about sitting tight! Her heartbeat banged in her head like a drum as she watched her foe slowly rise up, staring at her rig once more. *He's not alone, he is supposed to have another Fish with him.* Then she heard it, the sound of something scraping against the rear of her rig. *His buddy is behind me!*

The Fox stared at her as she extracted her legs from the rig, curling slowly into a crouched position. If it ripped open the cockpit, she had to be ready to spring out. After a few long moments of silent standoff, the Fox silently crawled over the dead crab, moving towards her. It lowered its stance and took on a jaguar's crouch, a cat stalking its prey.

Sweat rose on her skin. It came closer. It rose in front of the rig, only a few feet away. *All of these times of fighting—I have never stood face-to-face with the enemy.* Yes, she had collided with them, killed them at close range, but never had she seen one when they weren't trying to kill each other.

It had narrow slits near its mouth that fluttered open and closed as if they were gills or somehow tied to its breathing. Its mouth had an array of tiny shark-like teeth, like the ones she used to collect when her family went on vacations to the beach. Its eyes were dark pools, much larger than a human's, bulbous, lacking defined pupils. It had eyelids, multiple, that blinked independently.

As he approached the front of her cockpit, she felt a slight tug from behind. *You think you've got me trapped, but if you open that canopy, I will kill you!* Every muscle in her body seemed to tense as the Fox reached out and put its big clawed hand on the cockpit canopy between them. The elongated, razor-like nails hit the transparent aluminum and dragged slowly across it as it pulled the hand down. Shanice's breath became rapid, almost panting, and she held the M18 up, pointing it at her enemy, even though it would never be able to penetrate the canopy. *That's right, I have a gun here. Do you know what one of those things are? Do you know what I am going to do to you if I get out of here?*

"You still with me?" came Earl's voice.

"I've got this asshat right in front of me. He's got his paws on my canopy," she growled back.

"Alright . . . you've got this, Shanice. He can't get to you and we've got a recovery team almost on you. Just remain calm."

"That's easy for you to say," she said, her eyes never leaving the Fox. "He's right here, looking right at me."

"You are an ASHUR pilot . . . you are the best that the Army has. You are more prepared than anyone for this. Keep your cool."

"I want to kill him."

"I know."

She watched as the Fox leaned in, seeming to get inches from the canopy, exploring it now with both of its hands, spreading out in front of her. Its face leaned in closer and she could see that it had shark-like skin on it, with a complex pattern that shimmered in the moonlight. It was looking at her. *You don't know what to do, do you? You can see me, but you can't get to me.*

It balled its fist, and on the back of the hand she saw a tube-like vein ending at one knuckle. It aimed it at the glass, and with a high-pitched hiss, a high compression spray of water hit the upper corner of her cockpit canopy. *Shit!* She leaned away from that spot.

The Fish had these cutters. They fired at short ranges but were ul-tra-high compression water jets that could cut through steel. This one concentrated on the corner of her cockpit canopy and in a matter of a few seconds, a spray of hot water splattered her as it penetrated.

"He's trying to cut me out of here!"

The alien hand moved slowly as the water jet sliced through the top of the canopy. Looking around, there was nothing that she could do but avoid the water jet where it penetrated. The spray of water in the cockpit seemed to be everywhere but her attention remained on where it was cutting through. Shifting her body to the far side of her cockpit helped a little, but she was getting soaking wet.

"Stand by," came the voice in her ears.

Stand by? You have got to be kidding! Suddenly outside there was a blast of light from behind her. The beams of headlights cast a shadow in front of her. The Fox stopped cutting, jerking up to look at the light source over the top of her rig.

Then came the banging of gunfire. A few shots hit the rear of her Bronco, metallic pings against the armor. Her would-be assailant recoiled, looked at her, and opened its massive mouth. A deep, almost throbbing sound came out, a mix of a hiss and a bass guitar. Then it sprang away, fleeing into the night with four fast, jagged leaps. Muffled voices calling out behind her gave her hope. Voices meant humans.

A sergeant appeared in front of her canopy. "You okay, Corporal?" he called. She gave him a thumbs-up. "We're hooking you up for a tow out of here. We will get you out of your cockpit once we are out of the AIZ. Understood?"

She nodded, releasing a long sigh of relief. She felt the tug as the winches began to retract her rig, felt it jerk down in a steep list as it was dragged up onto the recovery vehicle.

Three hours later...

Corporal Raven had checked out her rig before she had hopped into a field shower to clean off. The damage to the bio-power unit was far worse than what her damage indicator had shown. Most of the energy-generating goo that powered it had seeped out from the nasty holes burned in it. Her arm-mounted laser was worse, twisted with components that were fused together. *If I had fired off a power round to charge it, the damn thing would have blown up.*

A team of techs was all over it like a pack of spider monkeys, prying off the damaged components, stripping it down to the inner frame in many spots. Hydraulic fluid was being captured in a half dozen pans where lines had been severed, melted, or cut off by the techs. It was going to take days to rebuild the Bronco, but they assured her they'd get it done. Her personal tech, Brantly, cursed and bitched about every piece that had to be pulled off and replaced, but she had long grown past listening to his griping. *We all have our jobs to do . . . his is harder when I bring back a rig in this condition.*

As she walked past it, she saw the two painted insignia on the remaining armor, distorted by the acid spray that had trapped her in the cockpit. One was the Bronco logo, a rearing black horse on a bright orange background. The right half of it was gone, reduced to fragments of blistered paint.

The other was her personal logo, Angel Fire. It was an angel holding an automatic weapon, rising on flaming wings of brilliant red, yellow, and orange. The lower half of it was gone, to the point that she could only read the stylized "Angel" from her call sign.

The shower had helped. She had been wet from the alien water jet and her own sweat. A fresh jumpsuit and underwear helped immensely make her feel more human. As she finished her surveillance of what was left of her ASHUR, she turned and saw a short man with blond hair looking at her. She gave him a quick salute when she saw his rank. "Sir," she said.

Then he spoke. "So, you're taller than me."

Instantly she knew the voice and a smile came over her face. "Lieutenant Brody," she said. "Damn good to meet you."

He nodded back. "I thought you might like some company. I haven't eaten all night."

As they started to walk to the mess tent, Shanice noticed that he had a fairly pronounced limp. He couldn't have gotten into the Army with it, so it had to be from an injury. Turning she faced him head on, stopping for a moment mid-stride. "I didn't get a chance to thank you for staying on the line with me."

He chuckled. "I know. And I'm pretty sure you know that you don't have to," he said, waving one hand as if to cut off her words. He then began to limp off in the direction of the tent.

"I thought you'd be taller," she said.

"So did my mom. We work with what we have."

Shanice smiled as she followed him under the flap into the tent where the aroma of coffee and eggs hit her nostrils in a full-blown assault. *Indeed we do.*

BY GUAM'S EARLY LIGHT

In the first Land&Sea novel, *Splashdown*, the bulk of the fighting takes place on Guam. A question often asked is, "Where are all of the officers?" We had an explanation for that question but fitting it into *Splashdown* felt awkward. Since it required introducing whole new characters' perspectives for a single chapter only, it was omitted from the novel—but this story does answer that question.

Sometimes in war, chance and timing conspire against you. Such was the fate of Guam and its wayward commanders.

Big Navy, Guam

Captain Michael "Shake-and-Bake" Ratliff entered the conference room as he had every Tuesday for the last nine months. Colonel Spearman liked his Tuesday leadership meetings, and if he liked them, then so did Ratliff. Sure, the chain of command worked for passing messages down—but sometimes those messages got diluted or downplayed. Having all of the officers of his command in one room made sure everyone knew exactly what was expected of them and the Marines under their command. Also the meetings were a great way for information to flow upward to him—with little or no filtering.

Today's meeting was larger than most. Many of the duty officers were invited. The biggest reason was that it was the colonel's birthday. The base XO, Major "Dusty" Phelps, had put together a golf outing. The rumor that Michael had heard was that the old man hated birthday parties, but loved his golf game. While most people thought of Guam as a military base or the site of a World War II battlefield, it was also known for its golfing. While Michael found the game boring, it was a chance for the senior officers to mingle and that made it important.

The Marine Corps CO, Colonel Arthur "Ajax" Spearman, was an icon of the Corps on the island and had a stellar reputation. During the

Russo-Bratva War, as a major, he had piloted one of the first-generation ASHUR suits in the Battle of Nome. His flanking maneuver, marching his Marines nearly twenty-five miles around the Russian lines, was now required study at the Naval Academy. They all called him "the old man," but never to his face or in his presence. The colonel went toe-to-toe with the Russian Bear and had kicked its ass, making him a legend. Spearman's victory had come at a high personal cost. He had taken a hit that had damaged his spine. While he had refused to be removed from the field until the fighting was done, the injury remained. They had done a lot of surgery just to get him to walk, and while Colonel Spearman showed no signs of injury, it had disqualified him for further pilot of ASHUR rigs.

Losing the right to pilot one of the ASHUR suits didn't sound like much to someone outside of the military—but within the armed forces, it was significant. The suits were the epitome of war machines—powered battle armor, armed with a staggering amount of firepower. Rig pilots were the best of the best in the Army and Marine Corps, and even then, the qualification to man one of the rigs was difficult to obtain. ASHUR pilots were not only trained to fight using the machines, but they qualified on the model of rig they drove. For Colonel Spearman to be medically disqualified was akin to having a world record taken away from you in a sporting event. He was promoted for his bravery and tenacity in battle, but he was not going to pilot a rig again. The old man wasn't bitter about it, but it was also not a subject that got brought up in conversation.

Captain Paul "Poker" Fredericks entered the conference room with almost a bit of swagger. Not really, but Michael still mentally pictured it. Ratliff hadn't liked the man from day-one. He considered himself part of a "new breed" of Marine officer—more educated, more sophisticated, more political. Fredericks savored his preferred pronouns. He was the product of parents that made sure he got a participation trophy throughout his life. *He's more weasel than man.* Fredericks was one of the men that talked a lot about war and tactics, but it was all book-learning. He'd never actually been in battle. Yes, he was a Marine, so Ratliff had that respect for him, but he wondered how such an officer might fare under real battle conditions. *I hope I'm not near him when I learn just how good or bad he ends up showing as his true self.*

Fredericks brought in a big sheet cake, prepared by the mess, decorated with the Marine Corps logo and the logo of the colonel's ASHUR, the god Ajax standing on a cloud, ready to hurtle a spear downward. It was a good decorating job on a generic military cake, like one of hundreds Ratliff had in his career.

Unlike Fredericks, Captain Ratliff understood warfare. His expertise was based on hands-on experience. During the Russo-Bratva war, he had seen some action as a green lieutenant fresh out of Parris Island. He had been in the Battle of Fairbanks—had gotten wounded there too. As his CO had said, "You've seen the elephant." Ratliff didn't know anything about elephants, but he had led his Marine rifle company against a pair of Russian battle armored suits in a particularly nasty encounter. He'd earned his call sign, "Shake and Bake," when he set fire to the structure that one of the suits was in, bringing the building down on top of the Russian. Ratliff himself had applied for ASHUR training twice after the war but had been declined. The competition was always fierce, even in peacetime. *All the ladies love an ASHUR pilot, and all of the men want to be one.* While he regretted not making the cut, he kept his focus on his command duties.

Second Lieutenant Anita "Emerald" Garret came into the conference room and sat rigid in her chair like a cadet at the Naval Academy. Mike respected her. While young and inexperienced, she didn't have that weasel-quality like Captain Fredericks. She was tough—even in the uniform he could see that she had the body of a Pumper—incredibly muscular. He had watched her working her company and she was strict and unyielding. She had made the cut for ASHUR qualification, but she had allegedly washed out near the end of the program. The scuttlebutt was that it had something to do with an accident that had killed or crippled another candidate. No one dared ask her about what had transpired. To have made it that far, she obviously had the right stuff.

Lieutenant Ayr Kempf casually shuffled into the conference room and took the same seat he always did. Kempf was quirky. He wore Corps-issued eyeglasses with big thick plastic rimmed BCGs—birth control glasses, which only added to his geeky persona. Kempf was supposedly a good officer but failed to stand out other than his looks. While he was thirty years old, he somehow managed to look seventeen.

Most Marine officers had a bearing—a physically imposing presence. His training had been drone operations, and allegedly he was damn good at it. By comparison to the other officers, he seemed mild mannered. *There must be more to this guy than I've seen so far.* His Marine rifle company was considered top-notch, the highest ratings on the base.

Other officers came in, filling the twenty-one seats in the room. Such all-hands officers meetings were monthly and while a rarity, it did give Ratliff a chance to see some faces he might not normally see.

The colonel walked in and everyone snapped to attention. He glanced over and saw the cake and shook his head. "Aw crap," he muttered. "As you were. I wish you hadn't done that. At my age, birthdays are not something to enjoy." A few other officers entered after the colonel and shuffled around the large oval conference table.

Lieutenant Fredericks led the singing of "Happy Birthday" and oversaw the cutting of the cake—a job that even Ratliff had to admit he was aptly qualified for. With their cake in hand, the colonel began their meeting—only to be cut off by Fredericks.

"Sir, we will need to keep this short. We have arranged for an 1100 hours tee time at The Country Club of the Pacific."

"Golf," the colonel said, letting a thin smile crack. "I didn't bring my clubs."

"I have them, sir," Lieutenant Garret said. "Your wife was kind enough to help us plan this."

That made the colonel happy. He still held his staff meeting as normal. There was a somewhat spirited discussion about training. The Navy had sent a formal request to cut back on the Marine's use of the Naval Magazine for exercises. The facility was inland from Apra Harbor and was a series of bunkers for storing munitions and expendables. For years the Marines had been using the jungle that surrounded the facilities for exercises and even calisthenics. Now the commander of the facility was requesting that the Marine Corps train somewhere else.

"What in the world do they think we're doing—going over there to practice our Goddamn chip shots? We use that facility to train our people, and not once have we ever had an issue with us violating any regs," Colonel Spearman cursed as his clerk read the message.

"Clearly this Captain Dresden at the magazine doesn't realize how much we count on access to this facility," Captain Fredericks chimed in. His propensity for stating the obvious was just one more thing that Major Ratliff didn't like about the man. "Maybe we should talk to Admiral Carter," Fredericks added.

Colonel Spearman shook his head. "No. I'm not going to see the admiral until we've tried to resolve this at the lower levels."

There were some logistics issues. Since China's brutal annexation of Taiwan, there had been a slowdown in shipping in the Pacific. No doubt it was a response to the sanctions that the US had leveled at China. As a result, the US military on the island had only twenty days of paper products remaining, including toilet paper. The colonel asked for other sources to be secured before it became a crisis. It was at this point that Ratliff wondered if this was what a peacetime officer's life was like. *I signed up to serve my country; now I'm in charge of finding toilet paper and napkins.*

At 1100 hours, not a minute before, the colonel adjourned the meeting. They had arranged for transportation, shuttle buses, to take them to the golf course. It was on the other side of the island from the base, called Big Navy by those that served there. While it was a six-mile drive, it was a different world entirely on the eastern side of the island. There were none of the trappings of the base, none of the pristine military rigidity.

They broke into groups of four and Ratliff was a little surprised that the colonel asked for him in his foursome. He was using a borrowed set of clubs; golf was not his sport. If nothing else, it was going to give him a chance to get some much needed face time with the base CO, which couldn't be a bad thing. *I just hope I don't embarrass myself with my swing.* He could feel the heat beating down on him in his short sleeved khaki uniform. They had talked about bringing civilian attire for the game, but that added a level of logistics that no one wanted to own. Besides, it was enough to be away from the base for the day and outdoors.

They teed off and he was pleasantly surprised that he had managed to stay on the fairway and even get some distance on the swing. As they climbed into the cart and started off, he heard a rumble off in the distance, a faint echo of what he thought was thunder. Storms could brew up out of nowhere in the Pacific, but when he had checked the forecast in the morning, there was no indication of it.

The colonel's phone chirped, as did his and then, like a wave rippling through the officers, everyone else's. The text was shocking. "NAVAL BASE GUAM UNDER ATTACK. THIS IS NO DRILL. NBGAF217."

"Is this some sort of joke?" the colonel asked. "Because if it is, it's not damn funny."

The answer came in another distant thunder-like echo from the other side of the island. "The battlespace just went active," Major Phelps said.

Ratliff checked his phone but had not gotten that signal. The colonel didn't miss a beat. "We need to get back to Big Navy—now!"

They raced the golf carts to the parking lot and the shuttle buses, abandoning them at random. "Who's the OD?" the colonel demanded.

"Lieutenant Fricks," Major Phelps said.

"Jesus," the colonel growled as they rushed into the bus. "He's never managed a hot BS before."

"Who's attacking us?" Lieutenant Garret asked.

"It's either the Russians or the Chinese," Captain Fredericks offered. "It's got to be them." While it was logical, it made little sense. The Russians were still stinging from the cost of the last war. China had taken Taiwan, and that had left them weakened in the process.

The bus jolted to a fast start as the colonel ordered the driver to punch it. "It's got to be the Chinese," Major Klark Hammontree said as the bus started into the jungle growth on the way to the Navy base, swerving hard around a tight curve in the road.

The colonel fidgeted with his phone. "I can't get through the BS command," he said.

Everyone immediately checked but Ratliff instinctively knew the answer. "If it's an attack, we are locked out on cell phones, sir. We have to be on the base-net." The measure was designed to keep enemy hackers from penetrating the battlespace command and disrupting operations. The irony was not lost on Michael. *We put something in place that is now preventing us from doing our job. Typical military op.*

As they reached the other side of the island, the scope of the attack was all too clear. Long drifting pillars of black oily smoke rolled skyward. In the distance, he could see the *USS Antietam* was in its port slip in Agra Harbor, but was in the process of sinking. Listing hard to starboard, it was colliding with the dock facilities with a sickening groan that they could hear over the erratic staccato of gunfire from the base. Along the hull of the ship was what looked like some sort of man-sized creatures, with massive flippers, scaling the sinking ship's hull. The way they moved was inhuman. *What in the name of hell are those?* They only looked slightly human to him; their legs were longer than he had expected. *Why would they be climbing the hull?*

"I need to get to the BS command," the colonel barked as the bus skidded to an abrupt halt. The road was blocked by a truck that was poised between the two buildings, blocking both lanes of the road. It had crashed into one of the welcome signs for the base. *What the hell is happening here?*

The colonel grimaced at the scene as well. "The rest of you, find your personnel and get them deployed for defense of the base. Phelps, contact Andersen and let them know that we are under attack by an unknown force."

Ratliff hit the hot pavement and broke into a run. Explosions echoed off the buildings. They got some thirty yards running, when suddenly something emerged from around the corner of one of the administrative offices. The sight of it stopped him dead in his tracks.

It wasn't a Russian or Chinese trooper. It was big, taller than a human, and looked like some macabre combination of a giant scorpion and a crab. It had eight spider-like legs, massive in size, holding up the armored carapace of the body. The front of it rose to a thick armored head. In front of it was two massive claws, each one almost the size of a man. The creature was greenish blue in color and made a clicking sound as it moved. When it saw the marine officers, it paused, raising both of its huge claws and jabbing them right at the officers. *What the hell is that?*

There was a long vein-like growth on the exterior of one of the claws that led back to the hulking body of the scorpion-crab-thing. It seemed to pulsate. A big bulge formed at the body and moved through the tube to the end of the claw. Spraying out of it was some sort of liquid, sprayed directly at one cluster of officers that were standing stunned and amazed at what they saw. The grayish oily substance squirted out at them like a firehose.

Then came the screams.

A mist instantly rose from the officers as they dropped in wails of agony. Lieutenant Garret writhed on the sidewalk, her uniform dissolving. Her dark skin opened to raw flesh as she twisted and screamed skyward. One of her fingers simply fell away as she flailed her arms trying to get free of her dissolving uniform. It hit him in that moment—it was some sort of acid.

His feet moved before his brain fully registered what was happening. Ratliff darted around the corner, out of the line of fire, followed by the colonel and four other officers. The others had run the other direction, instinctively moving on the crab-thing's other flank. "What is that thing? Where did it come from?" Major Hammontree asked as soon as he was out of sight of the creature.

"Where it came from doesn't matter," the colonel said moving along the outside wall of the structure. "They are here now and we have to deal with them. We need to get into position and do our jobs." Gunfire and the explosions of grenades in the distance told them that the fight was already well underway. *Fricks is likely overloaded running a battlespace like this, especially with this being a surprise attack.*

The colonel peered around the corner of the building and his head snapped back quickly. "There's a different one just eight yards down. Shorter, walking upright," he said in a tense whisper.

Ratliff felt naked without a firearm. Looking upwards, some twenty yards farther up, was another building. That twenty-yard gap to the next bit of cover might as well have been the Grand Canyon. Worse yet, they were still a good quarter of a mile from the BS command post. He girded himself for the sprint. "We can't win this battle hiding here," he said. Colonel Spearman looked at him and grinned, if only a little. "Spoken like a true Marine. You go first, check the enemy, signal when we are clear."

Ratliff did the mental count. *Three, two, one*—his body moved, without a bit of hesitation, sprinting the twenty yards in a blur. As he ran, he glimpsed the creature that the colonel had seen. It was turned away from him, hulking forward, with a thick almost oily-looking hide on it. Once on the other side, he controlled his breathing, in with the mouth, out through the nose. Moving along the building, he rounded the corner to make sure nothing was coming around the structure he was at. Thankfully it was clear.

He returned to look across the gap at the other three officers, then snaked his head around the corner to check the alien. It was moving away, towards where the crab still stood, the one that had sprayed down the others. Ratliff motioned with both hands for them to run across. They did, one right after the officer in front of them, led by Colonel Spearman.

They repeated the process for two more buildings, then they were surprised to find a cluster of civilians huddled down in the brush behind one of the offices. They were relieved to see the Marines. "They tore into our office—we managed to get out the back," one of them said, moving to hug the colonel who managed to hold him at bay.

"What are they?" a female clerk asked.

"Unknown," Major Hammontree replied.

"You have to get us out of here," another man said. His fear was something Ratliff could almost smell.

The major shook his head. "Not right now. We need to organize the defense of the base. You'll be safe here." It was a lie, but one that Ratliff understood. *We need to mount our defense of the base first, then concentrate on civvies.*

They were three buildings away from the battlespace command post. As they prepared to advance again, they saw a stunned young Marine rush towards them. His face was pale with fear and he didn't even seem to notice the officers as he tried to rush past them. The colonel grabbed hold of him. "Where the hell are you going?"

His coarse, crisp question seemed to slap the Marine back into reality. "My fire team—they're gone. One of those *things* wiped them out!" he managed as he realized that he was speaking to the base commander. "We've got to get out of here."

Ratliff knew the look on the young man. It is said that Marines never retreat, that they never run in battle. He had been at the Battle of Fairbanks and he seen a number of panicked Marines and army infantry run from the Russians. It happened, not in great numbers, but panic happened. No matter how much training you instilled in troops, some would want to run. What prevented that was good leadership, stern commands from officers and NCOs in the field. *Almost our entire command staff was off-site when they hit us here.*

"Get your act together, Marine," the colonel barked at the rifle-man. Reaching down, he took the Marine's M18 from his holster and held it as his own weapon. "No more of this running shit. You are with us now and you are going to help get us to the CP. You got that?"

The words washed away the panic from the young man. "Yes, sir," he said. His body went from rigid down to the stance of a man that was about to enter combat. In a heartbeat, the young man had been transformed from a coward to a Marine about to enter battle.

They inched along the edge of the structure to the next opening. Ratliff leaned out slowly, and saw in the road, at the other end of the building, another one of the crab-like creatures. Its head was pointed in the opposite direction they had come from and even at this distance, it looked menacing to him. The long body was bigger than his car and the tail, curled up like a scorpion's, complete with a hooked stinger, made him flinch slightly.

He slid back. "One of those crab things is out there," he said in a whisper loud enough for his fellow marines to hear. It looks to be heading down where we came into the base."

The colonel looked at him. "As before. Go across, give us the green light, and we will come in pairs."

Ratliff glanced out again. While the creature had not moved, it seemed to have its attention focused further down the road. He sprint-ed across, once more checking ahead and making sure that was clear before he came back. Confident that the crab monstrosity was not pay-ing attention, he gave the hand signal for the others to cross.

The Marine private and Major Hammontree came first. Hammontree checked and signaled for the colonel and Phelps sprint-ed.

He was stunned to see them both dive for the ground before they reached cover. Glass shattered from the windows of the building next to him, and the realization was that the crab must have fired something at them. The colonel rose slightly in the grass where he had dropped, holding up the M18, and fired five well-aimed rounds. Ratliff reached over to the private and grabbed his ACR. He tangled around the corner of the structure, using the building for partial cover.

The crab had turned and was looking right at the two prone Marine officers. Phelps started to crawl for where Ratliff was. Ratliff took aim at the creature's head, firing four rounds that would have made his range instructor proud. The shots hit, he could see that—but they didn't seem to penetrate the carapace shell. One seemed to crack it though; he took that as a good sign.

The colonel fired as well, then he too moved towards their position. For a moment it looked as if he was going to make it. Then the crab pointed its claw-like limb and a beam, grayish in color, stabbed out. It was like a primer-gray laser, stabbing down. It tore into the ground around Phelps, then raised up, catching the officer in the side. It sliced through his uniform and body like a hot knife sliding through butter. A spray of mist rose from the cut and Ratliff realized it was not a laser, but some sort of intense high-powered liquid, fired under incredible pressure. Dusty Phelps's mouth opened to scream, sheer agony crossed his face, and he collapsed.

The colonel got to his knees and dove for the cover of the building, as Ratliff fired several more rounds into the creature. It lashed the cutting stream at the colonel, catching him right as he rounded the corner. Part of the cutter hit the brick of the building and destroyed it as Ratliff reeled back.

He glanced down at the colonel who was withering in pain, pulling one leg up to his chest. There was no foot there. Ratliff glanced back at the opening and saw the severed foot lying out there in the grass, wet with a greasy watery substance. It had cut so cleanly, it had taken the cuff of the colonel's uniform pants and sock with it.

Ratliff rounded the corner to fire again, but the crab was moving off, apparently distracted by some other activity further down the road. Ratliff handed the ACR back to the private and knelt down to attend the colonel. Blood squirted everywhere from the severed foot. "Tourniquet!" Hammontree said. Ratliff pulled off his belt and wrapped it around the colonel's thigh, tightening it as the older officer moaned through gritted teeth. In the distance, he heard the purr of a chain gun firing, which meant that someone had deployed at least one of the base's ASHURs. *Maybe there is still hope.*

"We need a corpsman," Hammontree said.

"We will need to carry him to the CP," Ratliff countered.

Colonel Spearman's face shook as he fought the pain. "Leave me here," he said. "Protecting the base is more important than carrying my sorry-ass around."

"We don't leave Marines behind," Ratliff said. He looked up at the private. "Hand the major your weapon and help me carry him." The private said nothing but followed the orders perfectly. "Keep that tourniquet tight," Hammontree said.

"I am," the colonel growled back.

Ratliff grabbed and hooked one of the colonel's arms. "Alright— we need to forget this slow and careful shit. We are going to sprint to the CP. Major, you are our fire support. We move and move fast." The colonel reached up to the private's belt and loaded a fresh magazine into the M18. Even letting up on the tourniquet for a moment sprayed more blood on the grass. His hands were slick with sweat and his own gore as he regained his grip on the belt and hiked it tight. "You heard the captain," he said. "Let's haul ass."

Sucking in a deep long breath, they began their run. They rounded the corner and he never looked—his focus was on moving forward. Hammontree fired off a trio of rounds, as did the colonel, despite being dragged. They reached the next building and could see the command post. Smoke rolled through the air around it and there was a flurry of activity. Explosions thundered in the distance.

They didn't slow at all, but kept heading for the armored door where a lone sentry stood, weapon at the ready. "Colonel?" he asked as they approached.

"Clear the damned door," Hammontree ordered as they carried him in.

The outer corridor was filled with wounded troops and civilians, to the point where Ratliff accidentally stepped on one man's hand dragging the colonel in. "Corpsman!" he called, and one rushed up to him. "He's lost his foot."

"We are overloaded with wounded," the corpsman said. "Get him over here."

The colonel grabbed at Major Hammontree. "Take command, Klark," he said. Hammontree nodded, putting the ACR against the wall, and headed for the battlespace command. Ratliff helped the corpsman find a place to lay the colonel down on the floor. "Go to your troops," the colonel told him. For the first time, Michael hesitated. There, in the corridor, with all of the other wounded, he felt like it was going to be the last time he saw the old man.

Colonel Spearman seemed to sense it too. "Don't worry about me," he said, tightening his grip a little more on the tourniquet. "This is merciful. If I die here, I won't have my ass hauled up in front of Congress and have this debacle laid at my doorstep."

Ratliff understood. *We were out golfing with the entire senior staff when the base was attacked. It won't matter to the people in Washington that it was a surprise attack. Congress will want a scapegoat when the smoke clears. He's right—this is merciful. If he does die, at least he won't be blamed for what happened here.* "Yes, sir," he said softly as he rose to his feet. "Whatever these damned things are, we will drive them back to wherever they came from."

Spearman nodded quickly, slowly leaning his head on the concrete floor. Ratliff bent down and took the M18 off the colonel's lap. His next stop was BS command to find out where his people where, then to get out there and organize some sort of defense.

It's a hell of a way to start a war . . .

THE HERO OF ST IVES

Land&Sea takes place all across the globe. While readers enjoy the Mecha and battle scenes, it is important to remember that the alien incursion has struck at every level of society. War has a way of turning even the most common person into a hero.

St Ives, Cornwall, Great Britain, the United Kingdom

Callum Haines angled his bike down the narrow lane of St Ives on his way to the row of houses that were poised not far from the beach. It was early morning, the sun was just coming up, though he could only see it on the rooftops above him. A fog seemed to creep through the narrow streets of St Ives, wet with the chill from the night before. His bike jostled in a dip in the road, but he easily maintained control.

Callum had arranged to meet his friend Baskin Hart at the docks at the north end of town and do some fishing that morning. St Ives was a quaint community that had originally owed its existence and livelihood to fishing St Ives Bay. That had been many long decades past. Now the community was known more as a vacation spot far from the bustle of the larger cities. The locals appreciated the seasonal visitors, or as Callum's grandmum would say, "We tolerate them out of necessity."

The trip was one he made once a week to go fishing. Callum had retired early from his job at the bank and enjoyed going to St Ives, visiting his friend, and doing some fishing. The death of his wife Doris two years before had been the impetus for quitting his job. They had worked their whole lives and were looking forward to retirement and enjoying time with each other. With her gone, the realization hit him that he was both alone and facing the end of his life without having really lived. So he had retired. Callum traveled and went to the places he and his wife had planned to go to, although he made the journeys on his own. A part of him liked to think that his wife was with him; in fact, he was sure that she was, if only in spirit.

The Royal Navy's losses at Scapa Flow had hit England hard in her historical pride. While everyone talked about Scapa Flow, the real damage had been done on the Isle of Wight. The island had all but fallen in the aliens' onslaught by the time the RAF and the Marines landed. The fighting had lasted three weeks, leaving most of the settlements on the island in ruins. Losses to both civilians and the military had been staggering. People hesitated now in making trips to the shore. If Britain could suffer such attacks from the sea, was anywhere really safe?

The war with the aliens had changed many things, but not much at St Ives. St Ives was a beach community. There had been talk of evacuating, and some families had done just that; but most of the people remained. This was not just their home, but the homes of their families for generations. Tourism had diminished dramatically. No one wanted to venture into the water, but were willing to hang on the beach and enjoy the sun. There was a thought that they might be immune to the alien threat. After all, there was nothing of great value in St Ives for the aliens.

As he rode the street, he noticed something odd . . . the quiet. Usually on a typical morning there would be the occasional car purring along, echoing between the tightly packed buildings. Something was missing, the sound of gulls. Even if he was up early, they would be making noise. But the roadway was dead quiet. When he had started out a few minutes earlier, things had sounded normal, but as he made his way to the west end of town, a stillness and quiet engulfed the air. Callum reversed his wheels to stop the old bicycle, bringing it to a halt. Dropping his feet he stood astride the bike and stared out into the morning and listened. There were no sounds at all. St Ives had gone from quiet and quaint to oddly terrifying in a matter of moments for him. He looked around and saw no one. Not even Mrs. Ferguson who would be walking her pug Bentley in the summer mornings was to be seen. The streets were bizarrely abandoned. *Where is everyone?*

For a moment, Callum toyed with turning his bike around and heading back home. Was it the aliens? Surely if they had come to St Ives, there would have been an uproar. Perhaps it was a fluke—the deadening quiet. He summoned his courage and stabbed his feet onto the pedals, riding for Baskin's house.

It was three minutes later when Callum arrived at his friend's home. He propped up the bike on the small stone wall that surrounded the tiny plot of sod that Baskin called his yard. Still no sounds permeated the air. Callum dropped his stand and went to the door. When he got there, he noticed that the door was slightly ajar, barely noticeable from the street. There were scrape marks on the front stoop. They appeared fresh, as if something heavy and metallic had been dragged across the threshold recently. Callum wondered if it was something he had overlooked on previous visits, or if it was indeed new.

There was something else, a stain on the lower part of the door. Not colored, but almost a transparent film of some sort. He knocked but no sound came from inside. Squatting slightly, Callum touched the ooze on the door. It was cold and sticky, a semi-dried ooze of some sort. Lifting his finger, he smelled it and the odor was tangy—almost like an orange.

His mind raced. Callum knew he should go to find the constable, but he wasn't sure anything was really wrong. He could only imagine the trouble he would be in for calling the police when it proved to be nothing. No. The answers were inside.

Cautiously he pushed the door open. "'Ello!" he called out through the doorway. It sounded much louder because of the silence. No sound came back. The man opened the door the rest of the way and called inside again only to be greeted with silence. Baskin's dog, a terrier named Trevor, almost always came yipping when hearing a noise. Today there was no sign of Trevor, which only seemed to add to his nervousness.

Stepping up and in, he swept the dark entryway. Some things looked out of place. An umbrella stand that was usually poised by the door had been knocked over. Baskin's mother, Mrs. Hart, never would have allowed that. She always was a stickler for everything being in the right place and "just so." Callum bent over and picked up the stand, setting it where he had always seen it next to the door.

"Baskin!" he called into the house. There was no response. He took careful steps into the hallway towards the kitchen and breakfast nook. "Is anyone here?" His footfall on the hardwood floor caused it to creak, a noise he never noticed before the stunning silence.

Callum moved to the kitchen and peered in. What he saw overloaded his mind. The kitchen and small dining area were a shambles.

The contents of some of the cabinets were spilled out onto the floors. Oatmeal and sugar spread out as if randomly dumped by someone searching for something else. The microwave, usually on the counter, was gone. Its power cord was still stuck in the wall, but was severed. Who would do that to steal a microwave?

The refrigerator was open and pulled away from the wall slightly. The light from it spilled out eerily onto the mess all over the floor. Two of the four chairs around the tiny table had apparently been knocked over by whoever had been in the house. Callum stepped forward a half-step to get a better view of the room. Condiments dripped from the refrigerator onto the floor, making the floor a sticky ooze in some spots. The coffee machine which Baskin's father was so proud of was gone as well. A blender lay in shattered parts on the counter. At closer glance, it looked like more than that—as if it had been broken and some parts torn out from the motorized base. With each beat of his heart he realized this was not just a robbery, there was something more that had happened here. *Is every home here like this? Where are the people?*

Callum turned and saw Trevor in the hallway, Baskin's faithful terrier. The dog wagged its tail furiously but did not bark—it had something in its mouth.

Callum reached down to pet Trevor but recoiled at the sight. The dog didn't bark because in its mouth was a pale, almost gray, human hand. He recognized the hand, which made matters worse. It had a gold ring on it, an Oddfellows ring. It belonged to Baskin.

Panic dripping in wet fear swept through Cullum Haines as he made his way to the hall closet. *A weapon—I need a bloody damned weapon!* His grandfather had brought home a Luger from the World War, but the family had turned it in, over the old man's protests. At the time, it seemed like the right thing to do, but now Cullum wished to hell they had kept it and he had it with him now. *I need to protect myself!*

Opening the door to the closet, he didn't look inside, instead he fumbled around inside while he kept his gazed focused on the hallways, fearful that whatever had come to St Ives might still be there. In the groping, he got a grip on something hard, a wooden handle. Pulling it out, he saw an old cricket bat. He clutched it tight in both hands for a long moment. *Ey, this will have to do.*

Fumbling with the doorknob, he stepped outside, his wide eyes sweeping the stone-walled yard for any sign of people. Moving along the front of the house, he rounded the corner where Baskin kept a small garden. Lying there, on his back, was the pale dead body of his friend. Callum moved next to him, bending down and looking over the body. There as a deep cut, one that had slashed his friend's sweater, shirt, and undershirt, cutting his flesh deep. He was of course missing his hand. Another slash showed on Baskin's left leg. *Oh Baskin, you deserved a helluva lot better than this.* Reaching down with one hand, he closed his friend's eyes. For a long moment, Callum knelt next to his dead friend and wept.

As he rose, his gaze on his dead friend caught some details. He was not soaking wet, which meant that he had not been out during the rains that had blown up the coast yesterday. *This didn't happen too long ago, maybe just a few hours.* That thought sent a chill down his spine and he gripped the cricket bat tighter.

There was a temptation to call out, see if anyone responded. That was tempered by the fact that whatever had killed his friend might still be around. Holding the cricket bat as if it were some sort of holy avenger sword, he paused and listened instead of acting.

At first, there were no noises—but then he heard whimpering, then crying. It came from the direction of Porthmister Beach, swathed still in a low fog. Not from an adult, but from a child. The sound stiffened his spine and forced his body to shed years. No longer a sixty-year-old, Callum was young again, filled with rage and strength.

He moved to the direction of the crying, rounding a corner with the bat at the ready. Each few steps, he heard the cries getting louder. Callum had no idea what he was going to find or see, but the thought of a little girl in trouble was enough to propel him forward.

As he came around a small shop at the edge of the beach, he saw an incredible sight. There were hundreds of people lying in the sand in pristine rows, as if they were stretched out taking some sort of nap. The bodies were lined up to the edge of the water. There, he saw nearly a dozen large creatures—unlike the aliens he had seen on the television. These were hulking, with tentacles. Several were putting some sort of transparent film over the unconscious people; others were dragging them, three at a time, into the water.

All around the bodies were small soccer ball–sized crab-like creatures, with raised spines. They glistened in the low fog, gray to pale white. Their tiny legs made them skirt in the sand. These he had seen before on the telly. He knew that they could spray a powerful cutting jet of water. Like a laser in intensity, he knew it to be the source of what had killed his friend Baskin.

Callum took a gulp of air, not daring to move for a few seconds. His mind raced with fear, rage, and questions as to what was going on. *It looks as if the whole bloody town is here.* The people were not moving; they were laid out as if they were napping. Squinting, he could see they were still breathing—chests were rising and falling in shallow breaths. *They must have done something to them to make them sleep.* His hand fidgeted with the bat in his hand as he drank in the wild images before him.

Then came the cry. It wasn't loud, it barely came to his ears over the sound of the waves crashing on the beach. Turning slowly to his left, he saw two of the small crab creatures dragging a young girl by her shirt through the sand, dragging her by her dress. She was whimpering, struggling a little, but not nearly enough to stop them.

He thought to himself as if he were a different person. *If you rush out there, they might cut you down like they did to old Baskin. But if you do nothing, that girl will end up like the others.* Callum accepted that he could not save the rest of the population, but there was a chance at rescuing the young girl. She was farthest from the water's edge. All he had to do was deal with two of the small crustaceans. *They will all come at you once you start.* Reaching deep, he gathered his resolve. *You can save her, and by God you need to try.* His mind went for a moment to his deceased wife Doris. He could almost hear her say, *Get out there and help that girl!* They had never had children of their own. Saving that child suddenly had even more importance to him. *I have to try!*

He trotted out at the young girl, his eyes transfixed on the small but strong crabs dragging her through the sand. They stopped when he was just two meters away. Both creatures turned towards him as he began his swing with the bat.

The creature he targeted seemed as stunned as he was at his own actions. His swing was fast and true, hitting the creature hard enough for him to hear the cracking of its shell as he sent it flying towards water.

The other alien scurried to the right as he brought the bat around. It fired its water-cutter weapon at him, but Callum sidestepped so that he would not put the girl at risk with his swing. Its shot missed, but Callum's swing did not. He hit it hard with a *thunk-crack*, sending the creature flying, then rolling over several bodies that were laid out on the beach. *That one would be a short run!*

His hands were shaking as he bent down and grabbed the young blonde girl. She was only semi-conscious and didn't move. He dropped the bat and strained as he hoisted her over his shoulder and started to run. His shoulder throbbed under the additional weight and his hips protested, but Callum ignored the pain.

They would be coming after him, but he would not succumb to them. He ran as he had not done for years. The girl was weeping over his shoulder, jostled hard with each step. Despite the chill in the morning air, he was wet with perspiration as he moved as he had not done in a long time. In three minutes he was outside of St Ives proper, but he did not stop or even slow his pace. He ran down narrow Belyars Lane, lined on both sides with tall walls of ivy and growth. The road dropped off to one side down a steep hill and he almost stumbled at one point, giving him a wave of fear that they might fall down the slope.

He didn't stop for another ten minutes. His body was quaking as he lowered himself down to one knee, which screamed hot in protest, then carefully slid the girl off his shoulders. She was groggy, but alive. Tears ran down her cheeks. There was a glazed look in her eyes, one of confusion and possibly some drugs. When she finally locked her eyes on his face, she cried harder.

Callum wiped the tears from her cheeks. "It's alright, little one," he said between rapid, ragged breaths. Looking behind him, he saw no sign of pursuit. "You're going to be okay now." She reached up to him weakly, wrapping her arms around his neck. Callum hugged her back. "We need to get you someplace safe. We need to tell others what has happened here."

THE GOOD BOY

GRDs—ground robotic drones, are an integral part of the battlespace in Land&Sea. They are weapons platforms, additional eyes and ears, and transports for heavy gear, and lifesavers. Drone drivers are an important part of any unit, and often spell the difference between life and death when the shooting starts.

Mission 3434T—Golden Goose Charlie 445
The Southern Front, Firebase Herculoids, Galena Park, Houston, Texas

Private Toby Andrews stood in the kennel, a holding bay for the Ground Robotic Drones, GRDs, and considered his options. The kennel was a big warehouse, commandeered by the Army as a depot for repairing and maintenance of the drones. Long lines of drones by model were lined up, most having been repaired several times after missions. They were gray primer painted, their replacement parts standing out against their usual black, white, and dark gray urban camouflage paint patterns. As Toby surveyed his options, the smell of oil, grease, and hydraulic fluid wafted under his nose. *Somewhere in these rows are the last GRDs I took out.* They had been hit by one of the Fish's acid squirters, and he had barely managed to get them back to friendly lines. *They were good drones—despite the damage they'd taken.*

GRDs were generally named after dog breeds. No one knew why; no doubt some Mensa member at the Pentagon had cooked up the naming scheme and got promoted for it. Most were quad-legged creatures that only marginally looked like their namesakes. GRDs were utilitarian in nature, with attachment points for carrying everything from water, heavy weapons, to ammunition. Some were outfitted specifically for extracting wounded soldiers . . . depending on the model. A few mounted weapons for close fire support, if needed. All were semi-autonomous, requiring the driver to take control for fire missions or where specific movements were required. Their sensors and camera systems all fed the digital battlespace, mapping terrain and the enemy so that everyone on the field of battle had a better view of what they were up against.

Some GRD drivers simply took the first drone that was available. That wasn't Toby's way. He had tried that once before and got one with damaged circuitry. "Quirky," was the word he'd used, though "unreliable" also applied. When he had ordered it to a waypoint to wait for him, it had kept on going, forcing him to take manual control before it wandered into the enemy. When he got back, he saw that a lower panel on the GRD had been missing, exposing the circuit board, which likely led to the problem. After that, he took the time to do an inspection of each GRD that he took. Techs sometimes made mistakes or were in a hot-sloppy rush to get the job done, rather than focus on quality work. While he couldn't see internal damage, he took steps to ensure that his replacement GRDs were sound and fully functional.

The corporal who oversaw the holding bay for the drones watched him as he checked out several of the drones, checking their leg actuators and the hydraulic hoses. "What are you looking to take?" he asked with a deep Texas drawl in his voice.

Andrews who was on his knees, checking a Husky GRD carefully, not even looking up as he responded. "Our patrol is going into a refinery. Some sort of frog hunt," he said, moving onto the next Husky in the line. "We're carrying some support weapons, so I need a Husky. I want to take a Great Dane as backup." Huskies were designed to carry weapons, ammunition, and could be fitted to drag wounded soldiers out of the battlespace. They had a dog-like shape to them, if you squinted real hard or had thrown back a handful of beers. The squat drones were tough, with heavy leg actuators that could support the extra weight they were expected to carry.

"Great Dane, huh?" the corporal said. "Must be you are expecting contact with the enemy."

Toby raised his head, after looking over the third Husky. "This one will do just fine," he said, rising to his feet. "Yeah—you might say that. When you wander into Houston, you pretty much expect a few close encounters of the worst kind."

The corporal grinned. "Come on back here," he said. "I think this is one that will serve you well." Toby followed him down the line of Great Danes. They were stocky beasts, with a chain gun that was mounted on the hard point just behind their front shoulders. The four low slung ammo canisters were poised over their rear legs. The hard point allowed a driver to potentially swap out the chain gun with another weapon, but most left the Great Danes armed as they got them. If you mounted a laser, for example, you would have to fit on the power system and ammo feed for it as well. Like most good troopers, it was easier to use the GRDs the way they were outfitted, though some field modifications were inevitable.

The corporal stopped at one of the last Great Danes and pointed to it. "This one lost two of its legs on its first time out. A crab hit them with its claws. We hot-swapped the damaged legs, and it's running like a champ. If it weren't for the damaged legs, the thing would be brand new. I checked this one out myself. She is practically fresh off the showroom floor. She'll serve you well."

Toby squatted down next to it and checked it over, looking underneath the GRD to confirm its condition. The damage he saw was just as the corporal described. Tugging at the hydraulic connectors, Toby was satisfied that the leg was properly seated. "Thank you for the heads up. This one and that Husky will do just fine."

The corporal pulled out his pad and Toby did the same. A few short stabs on the controls and he gave Toby a nod. "They are under your control," he said.

Toby saw them sync up with his control pad. "I've got 'em," he said, hitting their activation controls. Both drones rose on their haunches as they powered up, the Great Dane next to him emitting a low hum as it cycled through its start-up diagnostics.

"Good luck fishing," the corporal replied.

Toby gave him a nod. "Thanks."

He plugged in the waypoints to his squad's rally point and the GRDs took off, moving smoothly, sensing any objects in their way and slowly skirting them. Once he was sure they were on their way, he powered down his pad and made his way through the massive tent city where the troops were quartered. At one time it had been a parking lot for a Walmart, but those days had passed when the Fish attacked the coast and the majority of the civilians had retreated. The commandeered Walmart itself had been used for quarters, showers, and a mess hall. The Army had left the signs still up, either out of laziness or as a message to the people that remained that someday things might just return to normal. As he approached, the automatic doors swung open, just as they had for shoppers thousands of times before.

It took a minute for him to get his tray of food and to find his squad mates who had started without him. The smell of hamburgers enticed his nostrils as he walked. Of course, these were Army burgers, a far cry from Whataburger back home. Still, the portions were good. During the first few weeks of the war, they had been forced to live off MREs . . . to the point where he couldn't stand the taste of the hot sauce he smothered most of the food with to camouflage its flavor. *At least they were finally feeding us something closer to real food.*

He sat down next to Private Jack Lubeski who gave him a nod and a grin. Lubeski hailed from Tennessee and had joined the 36th Infantry Division at the same time Toby had—in the first wave of replacement troops. The squad had suffered nearly 50 percent casualties during those first few engagements of the war, back when the Fish and their weapons systems were not understood. *Back then we were the green troops . . . now we are the seasoned vets. Then again so are the Fish.*

Looking down the table, he saw Sergeant Norris, the squad leader. Norris was of medium height, with dark black skin and muscles that seemed to have muscles all of their own. Light pinkish scars tore through his hard-to-see tattoos on his forearms. One went down from the corner of his left eye to his cheek—from when an enemy crab had hit him with one of its dagger-like claws. It was a glancing blow but a jagged bump on the claw had cut like a saw blade. *He doesn't have to tell people about his combat experience; he wears it on his face.*

There were two troopers sitting at the table he had just met yesterday. They were raw replacements, fresh out of boot. The female was Christine-something; he couldn't remember the other kid's name. The dude looked as if he still had baby fat on his cheeks. Both didn't talk much. If anything, they looked nervous. *Was I like that when I came to the squad? Probably.*

Two other members of the squad, Jon "Ripsaw" Baber and Traci "Topside" Cantrell came from the cooking area with Baber carrying a steaming tray of food. It was crab meat—not Terran crab, but a vanquished enemy. The aroma of buttered lobster drifted across the table. The veterans all broke into a smile, recognizing the plate of food for what it was, a rite of passage.

"Here you go," Private Baber said, sliding the big plate heaped with green shells between the two new recruits.

The kid leaned over it enough for Toby to see his name tag, Cee. *That's right, his name is Frank Cee—the kid from Tallahassee.* "Is this really one of the aliens?"

The sergeant, the only person not smiling, nodded. "Oh yes. We took it out yesterday on the afternoon patrol."

"And we have to eat it?" Private Christine Szaro asked.

"All of the fresh replacements do," Cantrell said. "Right, Toby?"

He nodded. "Oh yeah. It tastes like chicken mixed with lobster." That part wasn't a lie. He remembered the same treatment when he had arrived. Memories like that were hard to shake. *It's a rite of passage.*

"They told us in basic to not even touch the Fish," Private Cee said. "Let alone eat any of it."

"Think of it as a delicacy," Lubeski said. "You get to tell people you ate something that only a handful of people on the planet have." As he spoke, Toby noticed that the soldiers sitting at other tables were turning to watch, having seen the tray of crab meat pass them. This was not a squad ritual; this was one that everyone in the division had adopted.

Cantrell handed out two mallets for cracking the shell. "Bon appetite," she said, smiling.

The two recruits nervously picked up the mallets and began to hammer the cooked shell. Once the white meat was exposed, Cee winced, as if he expected some sort of surprise. When nothing happened, the pair picked up their forks.

"Go on," Baber said. "Take a bite of your enemy." His wicked grin was on the verge of spoiling the fun that was about to come.

Private Szaro was first, taking a small piece up, smelling it, then putting it in her mouth. Cee followed suit, chewing vigorously. He swallowed and turned to the rest of the squad. "It *does* taste like chicken."

"Have some more," Cantrell said.

Both of them ate five or six bites, each one more confident that the others. Szaro paused for a moment, and her body tensed slightly. Norris, who was sitting close to her, pulled his tray away, knowing what was coming.

Her explosive vomit came fast and furious, dumping the full contents of her stomach onto the tray. Within a heartbeat later, Cee did the same. Both gasped for air, then threw up again. Splatter hit the rest of the table as the squad backed away, chuckling at the plight of the replacements. Cheers and laugher rose from the surrounding tables as the spectators reveled in the ritual. A few soldiers handed money to each other, no doubt having bet who would throw up first.

Both replacements continued for a full minute. When they were done, rings of sweat showed on their collars, and their pristine fatigues were now splattered with bits of food and alien tissue. Cee wiped his mouth on his sleeve while Szaro's trembling hand wiped her face with a napkin.

"We all went through it," Lubeski said, patting Cee on the back. "That shit tastes fine, but there's something in it that . . . well . . . reacts with our stomachs."

"Oh my God," Cee managed. "I had no control."

"All the replacements feel that way," Toby said. "The only good news is that once you puke your guts out, it's over."

"Except for the explosive shits," Babar added.

Private Cee looked over at Toby with a look of terror on his face, but Toby shook his head. "He's pulling your chain."

The squad helped clean up the mess which Toby helped with. As he did it, he felt the beefy hand of Sergeant Norris on his shoulder. "A moment," he said, and Toby turned to him. "Did you get the replacement GRDs?"

"Yes, Sergeant," he said. "They are already at the staging area. I'm going over to make sure they are charging right now and run pre-op diags on them."

"Good. Talk to Baber about what he wants loaded on the Husky."

"We going in deep?" Toby asked.

"You could say that," the sergeant said. "Lieutenant Stoner is going with us. He says this is a 'strategic recon and strike mission.' Something about a new target class."

"What is that?"

The heavily muscled sergeant shrugged. "I don't exactly know. What I do know is that if he's tagging along, it means we are going to be poking at the Fish . . ."

"And nothing good ever comes from that," Toby said, finishing the sergeant's sentence for him.

"Right. Which means we need to be sharp and on our toes."

Toby nodded. *He only says that line when contact with the enemy in inevitable. Tomorrow is going to be riskier than normal; that's the real message.* With those words, he turned in his tray and made his way to the staging area. It was a tent, but one reinforced with sandbags. Inside, the heavy weapons were laid out, sans the ammunition which was not issued until they were about to go off, to avoid any deadly accidents. His drones had parked themselves in their charging ports, and he loaded up the advanced combat diagnostics on both of them, and let that routine run.

He had lost five drones since arriving at the front—the last one just a few days before. Fluffy 48 had been a Pit Bull attack drone. It had gotten by a dozen or so enemy grunts, nicknamed frogs—short for frogmen. Frogs were a nasty bunch. They weren't armored and could stand on hind legs, but had a frog-like look to them. They hopped too, able to jump huge distances. *One minute they were in front of you, the next they are on your flank or getting ready to butt-hump you.* They operated in swarming packs. Frogs didn't carry weapons. They didn't need them. They relied on their big webbed clawed hands and legs and jagged teeth to tear into their opponents. Additionally, they secreted a deadly neurotoxin from bags around their stubby necks; the infantry liked to keep creatures like that at a distance. They could spit out ugly toxic globs, which could incapacitate or kill. They had two big advantages in battle. The first was in their numbers—the Fish liked to breed them, and they were horrifically dangerous. The second was that they seemed to lack common sense, fear, or pain. If you shot a frog and didn't kill it, it would keep crawling at you.

While frogs looked only marginally like their upright Terran counterparts, they lived up to being grunts. They would individually make deep resounding grunting sounds. During a fight, their grunting would weirdly become coordinated, emitted in unison. It was a noise that made infantry seem to throb and vibrate when they did it.

Then there was the smell they emitted. It was from the neurotoxin that coated their thick hides, at least that was what G2 claimed. It was a mix of rotting fish and the spray of a skunk. If the breeze was right, the aroma was detected before anyone saw a frog.

Toby had kept Fluffy 48 moving fast on its spidery legs, using its anti-personnel rockets at nearly point-blank range. It mowed down half of the attackers quickly, but they leapt to his flanks, and one struck at it, mauling two of the Fluffy 48's legs. As he emptied his ACR's magazine, they sprung on top of Fluffy, tearing at it with their huge claws. He was able to throw off two of the attackers with some fancy spinning maneuvers, but there was no exit for the GRD, and soon it was torn to shreds.

Toby moved to the two new drones and grabbed a small can of red paint he kept with his tools. Squatting down, he reached over for a brush and pried open the can. Drone operators, often called "riders" or "joyboys," usually came up with nicknames for their GRDs. These were then fed into his controls and the battlespace commander, allowing for better coordination. Some of the names riders chose lacked flair. Sergeant Dinkins of Charlie Squad used five-digit numbers. Private Nearson of Delta used semi-obscene names–like Butt-Humper 27. *I'm sure he thinks that looks funny on the battlespace commander's display.*

Since GRDs were named after dogs, that was what Toby went with—dog names. The system assigned numbers if there were possible duplicates in the same theater of operations. He eyed the Husky first. *You're not a Fluffy or a Fido. You're a rescuer.* Everyone named their Huskies Balto, but that was a no-go for him simply because it was too common. Toby remembered his grandfather reading him a story once about a Sergeant Preston of the Mounties and his dog, Yukon King. That seemed fitting. He tapped it in and got the designation Yukon King 2 for that drone, and they synced in the new designation.

Turning to the Great Dane, he toyed with Rin Tin Tin—but remembered that was a German Shepard. Besides, everyone would use that name. *No, you need something else.* His mind raced through famous dogs he remembered. As a child, he had been to the Smithsonian and remembered seeing a stuffed dog on display from World War One on display. He remembered it wore a vest adorned with medals. A quick check gave him its name, Sergeant Stubby—the most decorated dog from that war. It was fitting, given that the Great Dane GRD did not have a large head but instead had an omni-camera array and forward sensors package. He checked, and got Stubby 15 tagged for the Great Dane. The GRD twitched once as it synced up . . . to Toby, it was a sign that it liked its name.

Leaning in, he began to paint their names on their sides, something of a tradition with him. People liked to joke that GRD drivers slept with their drones, that they were weirdly attached to them. Some of that was true, he thought as he painted their names on as best he could. It made sense to have an attachment to them. GRDs saved lives every day on the battlefield. They had personalities too, little quirks about them. Since they were semi-autonomous, he always felt like they had minds of their own, and sometimes showed it. Like a lot of drone operators, Toby saw them as more than machines. *They are like the pet dogs they are named after.*

Toby didn't care what people thought of him or his drones—as long as they all did their job, that was all that mattered.

***

At dawn the squad rolled out of their cots and made their way to the staging tent, this time wearing their full STG urban body armor. Everyone loaded up on ammunition, checked their weapons, and did a quick check of their active camouflage systems. Toby did the same, almost mindlessly, a matter of routine. His helmet was scored where it had been hit by a crab in a firefight that seemed like a lifetime ago, when in reality it had been a matter of weeks. Seeing the mark reminded him of how deadly the Fish could be.

His active camouflage system flickered slightly, so he banged the small round pack on his side, synced to his armor, and it stabilized. The cloaking system technology worked, but it was quirky at best. It didn't take much for it to fail, but until it did, it was useful for getting in close to the enemy. If you moved too fast or started shooting, it would overload and shut down. Toby shut it off to save power, then went and uncoupled Stubby 15 and Yukon King 2, smiling as he saw their names painted on their sides.

"Alright, people, listen up," Sergeant Norris said. "Welcome to Op 445—Golden Goose Charlie. We're going south into the badlands. According to a long-range recon GRD, the Fish are using the Shell refinery for a breeding area for frogs. These aren't your normal frogs; these are some Fish-engineered jacked-up frogs. Charlie and Tango squads are going to provide us with a diversion and our mission is to get in there, destroy their operation, and get out."

"What can you tell us about these frogs, Sergeant?" Baber asked.

"No one knows for sure," Norris replied. "Our target is some sort of water settling pond that we are targeting. Apparently, the Fish are using it as an incubator pond for these new frogs. Intel says that these are a different breed of frog. They are up-armored, and can use weapons—at least that's the initial intel on them."

"That's all we need, a new genetic variant of frog," chuckled Lubeski. "The old frogs are bad enough as it is."

"Button that shit up," the sergeant snapped. "Nobody was asking your opinion, Lubeski. Keep your focus. These frogs aren't like the ones we fought before. They are supposedly tougher, smarter, and can shake off damage a hell of a lot more." Those words brought about a low murmur from the troops.

"Chances are, this target pool will be defended. Complicating matters, while that refinery is shut down, there's a lot of oil and gas still in the system. G2 warns us that we need to be careful not to rupture any of the infrastructure or we might set off the entire complex."

That line brought about several moans, all of which Sergeant Norris ignored. Lieutenant Stoner spoke up, ending the complaining with a nasally, "Pay attention, people, because the sergeant is trying to save your lives. When we fell back, that facility was shut down, but it is dangerous to be tossing around your typical explosives. We are going to use thermobaric grenades on the target rather than fragmentation. We can't afford for shrapnel to be punching holes in that facility."

The thermobaric grenades were larger grenades that acted as small fuel air explosives. Their aerosol component was a highly compressed gel that released when they hit the ground. It mixed with the surrounding oxygen then detonated in a devastating fireball. They generated incredible amounts of heat when set off, but very little shrapnel. The problem was, they were heavier than a normal grenade, meaning you couldn't throw them far. Toby picked up two of them and put them in his belt pouch. Using deadly fireball grenades was the epitome of Army thinking. His sarcasm kicked in. *Much better than explosives—using intense fire around oil and gas. Only the Army would think that this is a good solution.*

He joined Baber over next to Yukon King 2 to load up their heavy weapons. Baber was taking a support rail gun. The magnetic pulse weapon was extremely effective, firing a metallic slug that didn't explode but punched through whatever it hit. He opened the left side hatch of the GRD and lifted the transport straps. They removed the shoulder stock of the rail gun and put both parts and a drum of ammunition inside Yukon King 2, snugging it in tightly. "This new one any good?" Baber asked as Toby closed the hatch.

"Should be," he said. "Don't worry, when you need your boomstick, I'll get it to you." Baber gave him a nod based on trust and experience.

They loaded into a truck for transport to the front. He used his pad to have the drones hop up first, landing with a *thunk* in the back of the vehicle. The truck lumbered and jostled them to the front line, which was little more than a barricade in front of what had been a Starbucks, now nothing more than the burned-out husk of a building manned by a dust-covered squad. Their squad, Bravo, jumped down and he had the GRDs join them.

Toby caught a glimpse of the replacements. Szaro had put on her war face, doing her best to hide any hint of fear. It was still there though. Not so much with Private Cee. The color was gone from his skin and his eyes darted around nervously. It was tempting to tease them, but Toby remembered his first patrol. *I doubt I was any different from Cee right now.*

"Get those puppies out there ahead of us," the sergeant said to him. Toby pulled them up, connected to the battlespace command frequency, then laid out a wide zigzag pattern of waypoints on his pad for the GRDs to move ahead of them. He programmed in that they were to be no more than 100 yards ahead of his position at any time on their circuit. The drones took off, kicking up dust as they bounded across the rubble that had been a bustling street at one point. In recon mode, they would stop if they detected movement that might be associated with the Fishes and feed that data to both him and the battlespace commander. Yukon King 2 bounced up a burned-out SUV, landing perfectly as he deployed where Stubby 15 kept low, maneuvering around the chunks of debris as if he were practicing parkour, jumping side-to-side and forward as if it could sense what was stable ground and what wasn't.

While he had a dozen pop-up windows of camera feeds, Toby concentrated on their prime cameras at the front. It was disorienting to watch them for any amount of time given the autonomous programming of the GRDs. Instead, Toby focused on his own movements, only giving the drones a few moments of attention, and then only fleeting glimpses.

Once they got out of the former city, the drones marked on both sides of the road, using the deep dry gullies on either side. The refinery loomed in the distance, a puzzle of pipes, storage containers, etc. It was a metal maze, with pipes filled with explosive fluids, with limited fields of fire. The smell of oil, no doubt from damaged tanks, hung in the air as they moved towards it. The heat of the rising sun hit them, making some parts of Toby's STG armor chafe against his flesh, especially around his neck. Pulling out a disinfectant wipe, he folded it and put it in place to reduce the friction on his skin.

Pausing as they reached the edge of the refinery fence, he could see that the chain-link material had been pulled down or crushed during the early stages of the war. At his feet were the dried skull-like husks of long dead goblins, the ground-based piranha-like creatures that the Fish utilized. They were nasty creatures that sprang into the air and tore at anything that was flesh that moved. For most people, their arrival on the shores around the globe had been the start of the war, the first shots fired.

He took a little joy crushing the dead ones under his boots. Goblins were a shock weapon, hard to kill. They were small, fast, and moved in a swarm. Guns were useless against them unless you had a shotgun loaded with birdshot. Toby counted his blessings that he had not been there when they had been alive. *Those damn things can shred anyone not buttoned up in an ASHUR rig.*

The sergeant held up his fist as they crossed what was left of the fence and took up a position behind a cinderblock building, and the squad came to a stop. Toby paused his GRDs, which were already ahead of them in the maze of pipes and pumping stations that filled the refinery.

The lieutenant spoke in a low whisper. "That settling pond we are moving on is about 150 yards south by southeast," he said. "Andrews," he said to Toby. "I'm looking for you to get those GRDs moving slow and low—get us eyes on the prize." He then looked over to the sergeant and gave him a nod.

Norris spoke next, "Cantrell, you and Baber are on overwatch. The rest of you, we will advance in two-by-two, slow and steady." Toby understood the game all too well—the lieutenant set the table, but it was the sergeant that was in charge of directing the serving of the dinner.

"I need my boom stick," Baber said.

Toby hit the recover button for Yukon King 2, bringing the GRD back. "On it."

Sergeant Norris turned to the pair of replacements. "You two will split up . . . I want you with people who have had boots on the ground." Both of them nodded to the sergeant.

Yukon King 2 arrived two minutes later, taking a position next to Toby. He and Baber bent down, opened the side panel and pulled out the rail gun and its ammo. When finished, Toby closed it back up, then set a waypoint out in front of the squad. Bending back down, he put his hand on the top of what served as a head on the Husky. "Go get 'em, boy," Toby said in a low whisper. He hit the execute button on his pad and Yukon King 2 took off.

"You *do* know they aren't real dogs, don'tcha?" Baber asked.

Toby grinned quickly. *Maybe not to you, Ripsaw.* "If you take care of them, they will take care of you," he said. It was a line from his training in operating GRDs, and it was something he took to heart. Toby had always had a pet dog until he joined the Army. A loyal hound was always a big part of who he was. As an only child, his pet dogs had been both playmates and best friends. Yes, the GRDs were drones, weapons of war, but every time he lost one in a fight, it hurt. *Maybe they are filling that gap in my life.* He pushed down such thoughts. This was a combat patrol. There would be plenty of time to reflect on his life when they got back to safety. His eyes watched the display as Yukon King 2 took his position out in front.

"You're the eyes and ears out there, Andrews," Sergeant Norris said. "Paint me a picture. Everyone, hit your ACS. It's time to go invisible."

The camouflage systems gave Toby a moment of disorientation. They didn't make you entirely invisible, but more of a blur that blended in with the background. The squad deployed, taking up their positions, weapons at the ready. Toby's eyes were focused between where he put his feet and the GRD control pad. The two drones moved slowly, angling around piping. Stubby 15 spotted a large puddle of oil that was leaking from a failed gasket or broken pipe, and Toby manually angled him to avoid it. They moved ahead of the squad, methodically. He had to adjust Yukon King 2 several times to avoid things on the ground that might make noise.

Stubby 15 spotted the target first. The settling pond was big, the size of four Olympic-sized swimming pools. The water was a sick green. He wondered if it was from algae or if it was something that the Fish had put in it. Toby brought Yukon King 2 around the flank to get a more complete picture of the target. *What the hell is that?*

"Sergeant, contact," he said in a low whisper that made Norris turn and move in front of him, a hulking shimmer of optically cloaked blur. "I've got eyes on target." Norris leaned into his ACS field and his face became visible as Toby turned the screen to him. Toby watched it as well, glancing at Norris's face. They were close enough that he could smell the coffee still on the sergeant's breath. The lieutenant also leaned in.

"Are those eggs?" the sergeant asked as the lieutenant squinted at the screen. The green brackish waters were covered with opaque soft white globes, each the size of a softball.

"I think so," the lieutenant replied. "That was why we were sent in. To be honest, I'm more worried about those." He pointed to the shapes in the piping infrastructure some twenty yards from the pond. "Zoom in on them."

Toby's figures adjusted the camera on Stubby 15.

"Those your amped up frogmen, sir?" the sergeant asked.

"Yeah, look at 'em. They have tails. Normal frogs shed theirs. These have tails—that makes them the beefed up variety."

"I make at least a dozen," Norris said.

"Check the images. These frogs look like there are armored?" Toby stated, looking at what appeared to be chitin plates grown on their chest.

The lieutenant nodded. "That also matches the intel we had on them. Tougher hides, some natural blast plating. Give me that image," he said pointing to the image that had caught Toby's attention first. He zoomed in on it with Yukon King 2. It was an enemy crab, but this one was yellowish, significantly smaller than ones they had seen before. It had strange bulbous growths, hose-like veins that ran down both of its big front claws. "Well, well, it looks like they are full of surprises today," Norris said as he squinted at the new foe.

They are like the uruk-hai orcs in the Lord of the Rings, nastier than the usual ones. "What are those things on its arms?" Toby asked.

"Could be slicers," the lieutenant said. Toby winced. They fired high pressure cutting beams of water that were somehow stabilized with ultrasonic waves. This allowed them to cut through steel at close ranges and slice off their enemies' limbs at long range. He had seen their handiwork before.

"Could be something new," the sergeant added. Rising up, he broke free of Toby's ACS field and returned to being a blur of light and imagery.

"Alright, people," Norris said in his best command tone, his voice ringing in the earbud in Toby's helmet. "We have at least a dozen of these uber-froggies in the infrastructure past the pond. We have a crab on the ground, one armed with what looks like slicers."

"Our objective is that pond and the things in it," the lieutenant said.

"You want to make the call, sir?" Norris asked.

The lieutenant waved his hand in front of him with a cutting motion. "You've got more experience than me fighting these things, Sergeant. I trust your gut on how we should crack this nut." Toby admired the lieutenant for trusting the sergeant. Far too many officers tried to outthink the NCOs under them who had the expertise. *Our odds may have just gotten better on this op.*

Norris didn't hesitate, but handed out orders. "Baber, you climb topside. Get lined up with that rail gun and target that crab. Cantrell, you get some high ground in the piping too, provide cover from above—hit targets of opportunity. I am going to take Szaro on the right; Lubeski, you take Cee on the left. We need to hit those frogs before they close the distance."

"What about the breeding pond?" Lieutenant Stoner asked.

"I'll get you some support," Norris said. "Andrews here," he said, jabbing his thumb at Toby, "will go with you, using his Great Dane for support."

"Stubby 2," Toby corrected him. That got him was an icy stare from the sergeant. "Fine, fucking Stubby 2. You guys toast those egg-things after we whittle down the defenders." Toby looked over at the lieutenant who gave him a nod.

He summoned Yukon King 15 and pulled out five thermobaric grenades, handing most of them to Lieutenant Stoner. Toby hated using them. He had seen someone not throw the heavy projectiles far enough, only to get burned in the fire plume they generated when they detonated. With Yukon King 15 empty, its purpose was to provide surveillance of the battlespace. He programmed it to deploy on the far right flank of the settling pond.

Stubby 2 was another matter . . . his was a combat mission. He set it to "Heel" mode, where it would follow behind him a half-yard, off to his right as he moved. As he finished, the sergeant checked the firing harness on Baber, making sure it was snugged up. Norris looked at the squad. "So we do this by the numbers. We engage the frogs first. Baber, you and Cantrell engage from on-high. Once you open up, Lieutenant, I suggest that you and Andrews make your move at that time." There were a series of silent nods that were barely visible with the ACS systems activated. *Everybody is a wise cracker until it comes time to go into battle.*

They moved out silently and slowly, weapons at the ready. Toby watched his step and the monitor, zooming in on Yukon King 15. The feed he was getting from the GRD was good, though there was a flicker every now and then, no doubt from all of the metal superstructure of the refinery around them. After a few minutes, he and Lieutenant Stoner took position behind a small concrete building as the rest of the squad fanned out.

"Talk to me, Toby," the sergeant's voice came over his earbuds in his helmet's comm system several minutes later.

"They are still there," he said as a low whisper as he adjusted Yukon King 15's head cameras slightly. "They are just standing there."

The disembodied voice of another officer came over Toby's earpiece. "This is the Battlespace Commander for Op 445—Golden Goose Charlie. We are detecting movement to your west, heading on a bearing straight towards your position. ETA, fifteen minutes. Recommend executing your mission ASAP."

Shit—they've somehow detected us! Sergeant Norris's voice rang out clear. "You heard the man, we have inbounds. Baber, are you and Cantrell in position?"

"Roger that, Sergeant," Baber replied.

"Then let's get this party started," Norris said. "Fish fry time!"

The banging of gunshots to the right and left of his position told him the squad had opened up. On his pad, he watched as the frogmen fanned out, not so much seeking cover, but spreading wide. Usually frogs simply rushed their foes—these were *reacting*, as if they could reason. Their grunting could be heard from the other side of the building where Toby and the lieutenant were taking cover . . . sporadic, then unified into one loud noise. The bang, hum, and whoosh of Baber's rail gun, above and in front of his position, sent a hypersonic projectile into the small crab, hitting its heavily armored side—sending it reeling around quickly . . . the image on the pad was not entirely focused, but he could make out that much. The crab turned to the attackers on its right and extended its claws. A long spray of greenish-gray gas shot out at the squad.

"Gas attack!" someone yelled. Everyone knew about the alien's gas weapons, and everyone dreaded them. They were corrosive as hell, apparently, on organic material—like human flesh. Intel said it was a bacterial agent, but everyone called it gas.

Lieutenant Stoner put his hand on Toby's shoulder and gave him a nod. The time for their attack had come. He saw the thermobaric grenade in the officer's other hand and nodded. With a few flicks of his fingers on the pad, he programmed Stubby 2 to move alongside him and engage with any targets he could lock onto. He put the pad in his chest pouch and pulled out a grenade as well. Drawing a deep breath, the two of them rounded the corner.

The battle was fully engaged as the frogs were spreading out, running, then jumping on their massive muscular legs. Two were already dead at the edge of the pool. The crab was moving to the right, aiming and unleashing another burst of its gas. Toby saw another hit from Baber's rail gun making it recoil back, its legs contracting either in pain or to make a smaller target.

As they got closer to the settling pond, a frog noticed them, racing right at them, its arms extended wide, its deadly webbed claw hands fanned out. Its guttural grunting made Toby's chest pound, and with his free hand, he pulled his sidearm out, taking aim.

Suddenly, near his feet, Stubby 2's mini–chain gun purred. A long black-green spray of blood hit the frog as it sprang at them in midair, tossing the creature back into the pool. It splashed in among the opaque white eggs. *Good shooting, boy!*

He knew he was in range of throwing a heavy grenade so he holstered his weapon and flipped open the firing switch cover, depressing the ground sensor and timer. Leaning back, he arched himself for the longest throw possible, catching a glimpse of Lieutenant Stoner doing the same, a blur with his ACS system activated still. With all of his strength, Toby made the throw. His grenade bounced at the edge of the pond, almost falling into the stagnant green waters of the pool. Stoner did the same, his throw being longer, landing on the far side of the pond, right near the water's edge.

There was a flash as the thermobaric grenade's initial charge went off, releasing the high pressured explosive gas. It gurgled in the middle of the pond, and for a millisecond he could see the ripples of it in the air over the eggs. Then came the deeper explosion that rose upward, igniting the gas.

Instinctively Toby sprang into the air, ducking and creeping fast when he came down, darting next to Stubby 2. The gas ignited in a fireball that engulfed the pond and surrounding area. The air rushed inward to the rising ball of flame, kicking up dust that stung Toby's eyes. His own ACS was overloaded with the dust, and flickered off—as did the lieutenant's.

Stoner readied another grenade, just to be sure. The alien crab, seeing the new threat, raced towards them, along the edge of the pond, its deadly big claws pointing at them. Toby's eyes widened as Stubby 2 locked onto the threat and unleashed a stream of fire. The tracers were so fast, it looked like a laser firing from a sci-fi film. The bullets tore into the head and raised torso of the crab but the majority of them slapped into the semi-armored hide and fell hot and worthless on the ground or were ebbed right into the shell material.

The lieutenant made his throw as the crab moved in. The grenade missed the pond, hitting the crab's armor-like hide, and bounced back. Toby's eyes were more open than they ever were before. *Cover—I need cover now!* There was none as the grenade's first charge went off. Then he saw his best option. He sprang at Stubby 2, curling up behind the GRD as the fireball went off. He made himself as small as he could, hoping that the GRD would give him some protection.

The flash of heat from the fireball washed over him in an instant. He heard two bangs above him, most likely ammo cooking off from the intense heat. His lungs ached as he tried to gasp for breath as a strong gust of air, sucked into the fireball, blasted him. Lieutenant Stoner wailed as the gust of air died down. Looking over at the officer, he saw his LT's armor on his torso was blackened and in some cases melted. His uniform sleeve of the officer's arm was burning and smoke trailed from gaps in the tactical gear as he patted the flames out. Toby's pad chirped, indicating that Stubby 2 was damaged . . . badly.

Toby sprang up, noticing that his own helmet was hot where it bumped his neck. His boots, which had been exposed under Stubby 2, were flash-charred, their paint peeling in some spots, in others it was blackened. Seeing them, he instantly felt the heat on his toes. *We were almost killed!*

The air had heated at least 20 degrees hotter, making his lungs feel seared. He helped pull some of the gear off the lieutenant and patted out the smoking areas out of fear they might flare up. He saw the LT's arm flesh was exposed, the skin underneath blackened by the explosion. Stoner lay on his back, hyperventilating from the pain he no doubt was enduring. His eyebrows were singed off from the explosion and he had a trio of blistered on his left cheek—testimony to the heat.

Toby reached down to his belt and pulled out an icer, a deep freeze patch that he hoped would ease his pain. A mix of chemical numbing agent and a frigid pack, it might leave a nasty scar but should help make the burn less agonizing. He folded the pack several times to activate it, crunching the chemicals inside, then he gently put it on the wound, using the small straps with Velcro to secure it.

Lieutenant Stoner got his breath as the staccato of gunfire continued. The relief from the icer was almost instant; he could see it in his face. "Can you move?" Toby asked. Stoner tried to sit up but winced in pain, then shook his head quickly. His right leg had a similar burn on his knee. Where the skin wasn't blackened, it was exposed flesh, festering and wet with pustules already starting to form. Crimson blisters surrounded the burn. *Damn!*

His pad chirped, and he saw the camera image of a proximity alert. One of the frogs had found Yukon King 15. It loomed over the GRD, swinging its massive left claw in a sweeping gesture, tearing into the drone with such a hard hit that it knocked it over. The GRD righted itself, its forward camera lens cracked down the middle. As the frog moved in to destroy the drone, Toby hit the recall routine. Yukon King 15 started to back away as the frog delivered a kick. The damage indicator on his pad showed that the right forward leg was inoperative.

Toby heard a wail over the roar of the battle. He had heard the hissing screech before, from crabs when they were hit or dying. It was like the noise an angry caged possum makes, only much louder. *Good! I hope it's dead.* Once he was sure that the lieutenant was stabilized, he moved over to Stubby 2 to check the status of the GRD firsthand.

The hydraulic lines on the left side that had been closest to the blast were burned through in several spots, leaking a pinkish fluid on the ground. The head-sensor array was blackened, and he doubted it would work. Two rounds feeding into the chain gun had blown apart, shattering the feed mechanism. Checking his pad, he saw that Stubby 2 was off-line. With only two working legs, on one side, it was a loss. Toby put his hand on the still-warm armor and patted it. *Sorry to lose you, boy . . .*

The voice of the battlespace commander came back on. "Attention Op 445—Golden Goose Charlie. You're drawing attention from everywhere. They will be on you in five. Recommend an immediate retreat."

"I concur," Lieutenant Stoner said. "Sergeant, get us out of here."

Sergeant Norris's voice came on immediately. "You heard the man, it's time to go." Toby glanced over at the lieutenant lying a few yards away.

"Sergeant, the lieutenant is wounded," he said.

"Can he move?" Norris asked as the gunfire started to drop off around him.

"Negative," Toby replied. Just then, Yukon King 15 moved in next to Stubby, dragging his damaged leg. It was clear that the blow had hyperextended the shoulder actuator, which was now a twisted piece of metal. The damaged leg was bent sideways as well at the knee.

"Can you carry him out?" Norris pressed as some of the gunfire got closer as the rest of the squad started drifting back.

"Not likely," he said.

Cantrell's voice came back. "Cee got hit with by one of those frogs; he's in a bad way too. These new frogs can spit in streams rather than a big glob and can fire a hell of a lot farther than the frogs we are used to. Baber got caught by the gas and it is eating his forearm up."

"Go on without me," Lieutenant Stoner said with a ragged voice. "I'll just slow you down."

No. We don't leave people behind. Toby drew a breath and looked at the two GRDs. Yukon King 15 was beat up, but operational. *Time to cobble!*

GRD legs had compatible attachment points, even if they were different. Moving to Stubby 2, he pulled off the functional leg that could replace the damaged one. Some hot hydraulic fluid hit his wrist and hand as he worked fast to make the swap out.

Removing Yukon King 15's damaged leg took every bit of leverage and strength that he could muster. He tossed it on the ground and seated the shoulder link of Stubby's leg. The socket purred for a moment and he pulled his pad and ran the replacement routine. He lost some hydraulic fluid in the transfer, but there was no time to worry about that. The taskbar popped up, but was moving painfully slow. *Come on—sync up, damn it!*

"Andrews," came the hurried voice of Sergeant Norris, close enough now that he heard him live and in his earbud. "It's now or never. Get on the move."

"Get over here, Sergeant!" he barked. Ordering a sergeant was a gutsy maneuver, but Toby didn't care. As the GRD ran its routine, he pulled out the carry straps from the interior of the drone. Securing them on the handholds on one side, he turned to Stoner as Sergeant Norris appeared.

"Pick him up and lay him on King's back," he said. Toby moved to the lieutenant's side at the same time the sergeant did. He could smell their intermingled sweat in the air as they lifted the officer up and laid him on his back on the GRD. He groaned, no doubt in pain, especially as his legs hung off the back of the drone and touched the ground. Yukon King 15's legs bent momentarily under the weight, then adjusted to the new load with a whining protest.

"You sure this is going to work?" Stoner asked.

"Trust me," he said, tightening the straps to hold him in place. "It's going to be a bumpy ride, but it's better than staying here."

Norris stood erect and swung his ACR in the direction he had come from and fired three rounds as Toby pulled up his pad. "We don't have time for geek-shit, Andrews," he said as he pulled the empty magazine and replaced it with a fresh one.

The pad showed that the syncing had worked, but with a yellow warning indicator. *It only has to hold up until we are away from this shit.* He jabbed his finger hard on the launch home routine. Yukon King 15 took a few awkward steps, then began to move faster.

Each bump and jarring step made Lieutenant Stoner moan, but the GRD took off on the pre-programmed return route. Toby slid his pad in his front torso pocket and drew his sidearm, moving alongside of Sergeant Norris. Together, they sprinted for cover to the rear, turned, and made sure they were not pursued.

* * *

Lieutenant Stoner was ghostly pale by the time Yukon King 15 stopped in the rear area. Medics moved to get him off the GRD and onto a stretcher. His pant leg was soaked with blood from his festering and blistered burn, and while he looked like hell, Toby took a matter of pride that his GRD had gotten him back. The lieutenant looked over at him and gave Toby a nod of thanks.

Dark purple storm clouds were rolling in. The air was wet with humidity—signs that the weather was about to change. *We were lucky. The next op may be doing their run in the rain.* While he felt somewhat lucky, he knew that Stoner, Cee, and Baber might feel differently. *Any op you come back from alive is a success, as far as I'm concerned.*

Cee had a blistering wound on his lower neck from some of the frog spit and was breathing hard. They had hit him with an Epipen, which seemed to help with his breathing. The pustules oozed a sickly yellow-white goo. Baber's arm had stopped corroding from the bacterial gas but looked hideous. Strangely his uniform and armor were not damaged at all, same with Baber who had similar patches on his arm. *I wish these bastards had showed up with guns rather than this bio-shit.* Cee's wounds got wrapped by one of the medics, making him wail in pain. Baber winced when his wounds were wrapped, but refused to let out a cry . . . though the tears running down his cheeks told the truth about how bad the pain was.

They boarded a truck, including the battered remnants of Yukon King 15. After he climbed up, Toby checked the GRD. It was in need of serious repairs, including the right leg replacement, but the drone had held up well. After he stored the mounting straps, he rested his hand on the GRD as if it were a real dog. *Atta boy! You saved his life.*

"What the hell happened to the LT?" Cantrell asked as a distant rumble of thunder slowly cracked in the distance.

"The lieutenant had a bad throw with the grenade. Those thermobarics are more dangerous to us than to the Fish. We got it knocked back at us," Toby said, pulling out his water pack tube and drawing a long drag of the warm fluid.

"Well, you two certainly lit up that pond," Sergeant Norris said, stripping off his STG vest. His fatigues were soaked with sweat, as Toby knew his were. "I doubt any of those eggs made it through the fires you guys set off." There was a bit of pride Toby felt from that. *It would have been a lot better if we hadn't almost gotten roasted ourselves.*

"Why were the Fish breeding inland?" Szaro asked, removing her helmet and revealing her sweat-soaked hair.

Norris shrugged. "Who knows what the Fish think or why they do what they do. I am hoping we are just as confusing to them."

Szaro looked off as the medics helped Cee to a cot. "Is he going to be okay?"

Norris nodded, though Toby knew that it was more positive thinking than reality. "The medics have him. Whatever that bacteria stuff is, it's nasty. You get it on your flesh and it eats you alive. He should be thankful he didn't suck any into his lungs. They've gotten good at patching folks up and getting them back on the line fast. You'll see."

Cantrell patted Szaro on the shoulder. "One thing is for sure, you're not greenhorns anymore." Her words made Szaro slowly unleash a broad grin.

Lubeski nodded over to Toby. "You lost one GRD . . . but the one that came through was the one that counted. What was his call sign again?"

"His name is Yukon King," Toby said, proudly reaching over to pat the GRD on its back. He saw the name he had painted on the side, chipped and stained with a thin layer of dust. *And he's a damn good boy . . .*

SAVANNAH NIGHTS

Militia play a critical role in the fight against the alien invaders in the Land&Sea universe. With every coastal city under siege, the armed forces struggle with defending the nation in a way they haven't had to in centuries. Not all militia units are created equal though. Some are ruthless killers; others are bands of good friends united by a common enemy. Some are wannabes. A few are looting criminals.

War has a way of sorting out which kind of unit is best. This is the story of a unit's origin . . . though unlike superhero stories, not all origin stories are based in tragedy. Some are simply good men and woman pushed too far.

Claxton, Georgia

Justin Birdsong watched the news in horror. At first he thought what he saw was some prank, a publicity stunt to promote a new show, but it was on every channel. The bizarre massive shells that slid ashore all along the coasts across the globe, some as big as buses, were proving to be Trojan horses. They were beautiful at first. The ones that got the local coverage in Savannah where he lived were pearlescent with a shimmer of blue in them. The ones down in Florida looked reddish and pinkish in color.

People gathered around them as police tried in vain to keep the crowd back. No one knew where they had come from or why, suddenly, they were appearing around the planet. The TV news did what they did best, speculate and guess. Experts came out and claimed everything, from that they were some mutation caused by man's pollution of the oceans to genetic manipulations by the Russians.

Then the massive shells opened up, disgorging hell.

They were golf ball–sized creatures that swarmed. They tore at the flesh of anything near them, like schools of piranha, hopping and jumping in the air. In horror, he saw a family turned into a spray of crimson as they tried to flee on a live news feed. The big shells disgorged hundreds of thousands of the creatures, sending waves of terror in the streets.

Justin did what a lot of people did—they got their guns out and made sure they were loaded. He was a hunter, from a long line of hunters. He was half Chippewa Indian on his father's side, and it was as if instincts kicked in. He made sure both shotguns were loaded with #9 shot, a good spray that would take out a lot of those bastards if they came. The fact that he lived some twenty miles from Savannah didn't seem to matter. *If they come for me, I will take a lot of them with me.*

The night of the first incursion, he stayed up all night, glued to the television, watching as the authorities urged everyone indoors and to lock up. Justin knew he should shut off the television, stop combing the net for information, but he couldn't. There was no point in trying to go to sleep that night; the entire world was awake and reeling from what seemed to be a senseless attack.

In Savannah, the mysterious white-ball-like-creatures fanned out from the riverfront area, swarming through the city. The footage was blurred and jumbled, mostly due to the cameramen's fear. One intrepid reporter had a dead creature, holding it up for the viewing audience with a rubber-gloved hand. It was round, with slender, almost fragile-looking, legs that were hard to see they were so small, but clearly powerful. While the little creature was dead, partially crushed by some blunt force trauma, its big maw-like mouth filled with tiny razor teeth was visible. What it had for an eye was battered, but was big, and seemed to lack a pupil. It looked alien and dead.

Normal gunfire was ineffective; they were small and fast. Shotguns proved more useful, but even then, the little creatures had numbers on their side. It was as if they had been created to negate the use of weapons against them.

Justin's first reaction when he saw the dead creature was that it was not from here . . . Earth. *I've fished a lot and have pulled up some strange stuff over the years, but nothing like that.* His suspicions were confirmed when word came that there had been other attacks, including on Guam. It wasn't the ball-creatures there; those were big. A Spanish news crew got footage of a massive scorpion-crab creature, as big as a SUV, tearing into a squad of soldiers. In the distance, he had seen another creature, more human in appearance, obsidian black in color with massive claw-hands, seeming to shake off a lot of firepower being dumped onto it. There were others that looked like giant frog-men hybrids that wielded weapons that were jets of water that cut people in half.

He was processing those images when his phone rang. He picked it up without even looking at the name. "Hello," he said, not lifting his tired eyes. He did rub them with his left hand, and bits of crust in the corners told him that he had been up far too late.

"You seeing this shit?" Donnie Wixom's voice said with a hint of a southern drawl. Justin liked Donnie. He was an intriguing mix of backwoods redneck and top-of-the-line website designer. Donnie didn't care much for his job, other than it enabled his hobbies like guns and hunting. During the war, Donnie had been a private on Justin's fire team. The guy had grit, a nastiness about him. He didn't shy away from a fight, which was both a strength and a weakness at times. It was an aspect of his friend that Justin deeply admired.

"I am—what the fuck," he said, leaning back in his chair. His joints ached slightly in protest, another reminder of how little rest he had gotten.

"Goddamn aliens," Donnie said. "It's got to be. It's just like that show on the History Channel. It's aliens, man! I've been saying it for years. We ain't alone!"

His hunting buddy and lifelong friend was probably right. Aliens. That was the only answer that made sense the day after they came ashore. "I take it you are locked and loaded, brother," Donnie replied.

"Damn straight. Nobody's going to work today—that's for sure."

"I am—I hit the Dollar General and grabbed every canned product I could get and toilet paper. I'm not getting caught short like during the last war. There was already a run going on—the store was packed."

It was a good idea, though he was a little concerned about going out—and how many others might have the same idea. "You talk to Frenchie?"

"I did. He's coming up, loaded for bear. He says if these bastards want a fight, they picked the wrong guys to fuck with."

That sounded like their friend, Frenchie. Originally from Louisiana, he had been the member of their little hunting club to introduce them to hunting alligators. Justin had seen Frenchie shoot a gator, wound it, then jump off the boat and wade hip-deep after it with a knife in the mud and filthy water. Nothing seemed to scare him either because he was always armed to the teeth or simply didn't understand his own fear. "What about Berri?"

"I talked to her," Donnie replied. "For now, she's hunkered down. She lives far enough from the coast that she isn't too worried. She said that we can come to her place if it comes to that."

Justin had not thought about fleeing. Savannah was his home. The thought of abandoning it to a bunch of alien Fish didn't seem right to him. But . . . it might be necessary. *What if this is only the beginning? What's next?*

Justin tried to process what was happening and how to respond to it. *I fought the Rooskies up north when they had invaded, but this isn't likely to be that kind of fight.* He had the skills still, though he had gotten a little soft since mustering out. *How are we supposed to respond if these are some kind of aliens?* From the sprinkles of footage that the media was getting, some of these aliens were strong enough to take on ASHUR rigs.

His military training kicked in. *We don't know what they want. We don't know their full capabilities. They are hitting us on every coast and we are not prepared for that kind of defense. Even if the Army mobilizes, it'll take weeks before it is ready to cope with a problem like this.* As he thought through the myriad of problems the United States was facing, it was Donnie's voice that brought him back to reality. "You still there, dude?"

"Yeah," he replied with a sigh. "Just contemplating the full extent of the suck."

"I hear that. I have no intention of sitting on the sidelines if it's goddamn aliens. I mean, this isn't like shooting at people."

"I'm not so sure about that. Let's face it, we have no idea what we are up against. All we know now is that they struck first. There's more than one species in play here, which means there's probably some baddies that we haven't even seen yet."

"I say we go on the hunt," Donnie pressed, his voice rising in tempo. "We get our little hunting group together and go out and mess these bastards up."

"Too early, Donnie, too many unknown variables. This isn't like going on patrol in Alaska, taking out Russian infil teams. You know me, I don't like going in blind."

"Dude, this is a hunt. We are a hunting club. This is the best damn hunt we could ever hope for." Donnie's excitement was practically crawling through the phone in his ear.

"No," Justin snapped back. "This is war. We've both been there before." Pausing for a long moment, he closed his eyes and remembered the last war. He had played war as a child with his friends in the woods, using BB guns to shoot at each other. Real war didn't sting when you got hit; you could die or worse, be maimed. Being in real war, all illusions of the myth of war dissolved the first time the Russians dropped an artillery barrage on their position. As a boy, he had always seen himself being a heroic character, but war had taught him that was far from the realities he experienced. "Don't kid yourself. This will be carnage and death."

Several weeks later ...
The Eastern Front, Claxton, Georgia

The carnage of the attack on Washington, DC, and other key coastal cities felt like a gut punch to Justin. Savannah had not been spared in the assault. The aliens had emerged from the Savannah River and along the coast at Wilmington Island. The Georgia National Guard had put up a fight, but the aliens, dubbed "the Fish" by the media, were fast-moving and ferocious. The Battle of Forsyth Park had been where the National Guard made its stand. It made sense, the open park had wide fields of fire, with an urban area to fall back on. Heavy armor and ASHURs were deployed and made the Fish bleed for every yard of ground they tried to take.

The result was that half of Savannah was now termed an AIZ, Alien Incursion Zone. There were skirmishes day and night, but it was clear that neither side had the momentum to drive the other out. *Would it matter? It's not like we can follow them into the sea.* The once thriving tourist trade was gone, probably forever. As much as he had complained about the tourists wading through the heat and humidity of the city, seeing empty streets cordoned off with barricades was far worse.

Horror had gripped Justin as he'd watched the invasion. This was his hometown. In his experience, people either loved or hated where they were raised. He loved Savannah. Its parks and green space, the old Southern charm mingled with the excitement of young people who made the city their own. Yes, the summers were sweltering and there were times he cursed the tourists, but seeing it being destroyed by alien invaders tore his heart. The huge art university, SCAD, had been forced to evacuate the city, and with them went the soul of culture. The magnificent old mansions framed by trees filled with Spanish moss were devastated under the onslaught of a biological enemy from another world.

The other part that ate at him was the unknown. No one knew what to call the aliens, so the term "Fish" was adopted. It wasn't accurate, but it weirdly worked. No one knew how to communicate with them or what they were after. All that anyone settled on was that they had come from another world and had waded onshore with a devastating array of biological weapons. They sprayed acid—fired deadly needle-like projections that could shatter body armor plates, and could shrug off most gunfire as if it were mosquitoes. It was the unknowns about the aliens that made them more menacing . . . that and people trying to guess what their motivations were.

Justin got word from his company that he was laid off—there wasn't a need for his services with their office now behind enemy lines. It wasn't that he loved his job. Computer tech support was a constant series of frustrations and people lying about what they had downloaded, but it had paid the bills since he had mustered out of the Army. He wasn't going to miss his job as much as he would the paycheck . . . not that it mattered anymore.

The economy was in a perpetual state of turmoil since the invasion had begun. Inflation had spiked overnight as everyone began to try to profit off the panic. The president froze prices, but enforcement of that edict proved next to impossible. Washington was funding the war with the sale of backed cryptocurrency—war coins—whatever the hell that was. Given the endless tension of the alien invasion, he had almost forgotten to file for unemployment. Like everyone else, he was glued to the net and to the media coverage. When he did finally apply, he was told that the backlog meant that he wouldn't be getting a check for at least three months. *I paid my taxes and never expected a penny back from the government. Now that I need the money, I'm told to be patient and wait.* It was a nagging reminder of how bloated the government had become.

Since the arrival of the goblins, the tiny piranha-like creatures which signaled the start of the alien invasion, grocery stores had struggled to keep food coming in. People were hoarding everything, probably with good reason. China and other countries were no longer able to safely ship goods across the oceans of the world. The supply chain, which had been fragile since the COVID outbreak in 2020, had been stretched far beyond its limits. A black market economy emerged overnight in America. Some staples could be secured, though the selection was often random. The last time he was in the grocery store, they got a shipment of refried beans, and he found himself grabbing six cans. Other goods, toiletries like toothpaste and deodorant, were now considered luxury items. Neighbors got together to pool their resources, help spread what little they had. *We haven't been in a true war economy since WWII, and it shows.*

Normally he would have embraced forced downtime, but with the invasion, it only filled his idle hours with thoughts of war again. He considered re-upping . . . *God knows the Army is going to need good people with combat experience.* While he was proud of his military service, it wasn't something he craved. Returning to that life, especially after being in the real world for years, was not something Justin desired. He had seen stories on TV of locals that had formed ad hoc militia groups and had joined the National Guard in the fight. If anything, that had the most appeal. It was like being in the military, without the burdens of a chain of command. It had a *Red Dawn* feel to it—partisans fighting the good fight. It seemed like a fantasy, one he toyed with between broadcasts.

His phone chirped for his attention and he saw it was Donnie. "What's up?" he asked as he connected the call.

"Did you hear the news?"

"What news?" The problem he had been struggling with was not a lack of news but too much of it.

"They are kicking off a formal militia program."

"What do you mean formal? I've been watching locals with guns on the TV for weeks."

"They are allowing the formation of units, giving them weapons and shit," Donnie said with glee tainting each word.

That was different from what he had seen on the videos. "So, how does it work?"

"There's an application process. They are going to pay the teams they accept. There's some training and the usual administrative bull-shit, but it is a chance to get into the fight without all of the 'joys' of being in the Army again."

Donnie's words made Justin smile. "What are you thinking?"

"We reach out to the rest of the club. Most of them are bound to want to be a part. You know Frenchie is going to be in as long as he gets to kill something."

There was a ring of truth to the last statement. As he chuckled, he found his mind actually starting to embrace the idea. *What do I have to do right now? I've lost my job, my hometown is under enemy occupation. I need to be doing something—something that makes a difference.* One of the things he loved about his time in the military was that he knew what he was doing was part of something bigger. That was something sorely missing in the so-called real world. *At work, I was just another face in the crowd. I was easily replaced at the whim of upper management. If we had our own militia, it would be ours . . . something no one could take away from us.* As hard as it was for him to admit out loud, he only really felt in control of his life when he was looking through the scope of a rifle.

"We can't do this over the phone," Justin finally said. "This is the kind of decision that has to be made face-to-face. Going back to war isn't for everyone."

"What do you suggest?"

"Let's meet up at the cabin. Get the word out. Tell them we have a proposition. Tell them to come out Sunday afternoon. We can talk it over and see if they are in favor of this idea."

"I'm on it, dude," Donnie said.

Newington, Georgia

The club's hunting cabin was best described as dingy. It wasn't used much during the summer by the members simply because it was not air conditioned and the small pond it was on became a breeding ground for mosquitos that were more like vampire bats in Justin's mind. In the fall, during hunting season, they would come there and go deer hunting. Late fall was duck season, which brought more activity. As he pulled up in his battered Jeep, he saw that a few of his friends had already arrived.

Donnie was there, greeting him with a manly hug and back slap as soon as he cleared the door. On the porch was Berri, half-sitting on the peeling porch rail. Berri owned a bar two counties over. She had served in the last war and since then she had put on some weight. Berri was tough as nails with one of the best records for taking down bucks in the forest.

Standing with his beefy crossed arms was Samuel Noonan. An inner city kid when the war had broken out, Samuel had come out of the housing projects of Atlanta and had become a Ranger. The massive muscles that his shirt was failing at hiding pointed to the shape he kept himself in still. He supposedly had washed out of ASHUR training in the Army, but he didn't talk about that at all, and given his size, no one pushed the matter with him. He gave Justin a nod as he approached the cabin.

Frenchie came out and gripped Justin's hand with both of his and shook them hard. Frenchie was wearing a T-shirt with the logo, *You can run, but you'll just die tired*, on it. He had been a sniper in the Army and had left the service with a bad case of PTSD that he addressed by purchasing weapons. One time he had gone deer hunting with a fully automatic antique Thompson submachine gun because he said it felt sporting. His big handlebar mustache and beard were grayer than the last time Justin had seen him. "You still driving that piece of shit?" he asked, nodding at the Jeep.

"Hey, it's paid for."

"So's my ex-wife," Frenchie said. "That doesn't mean she has any value."

Justin stood on the porch, surrounded by his friends. "I take it Donnie told you what he's proposing?"

Samuel spoke up first. "Hell, my gym is closed now thanks to the AIZ being declared. The government is not letting the bank foreclose on me, but we all know it's a matter of time. Nobody is hiring right now, so I might as well sell my services to the government as a mercenary."

"Militia," Justin corrected him.

"Same shit."

Justin was tempted to argue the finer points of difference, but opted to avoid the debate. He turned to Berri next. "What about you?"

"Ever try and run a bar when no one is able to delivery you booze?" she scoffed.

"I can't say that I have."

"People don't pay money to sit in a dark building and drink water. I shut down two weeks ago. If I can't earn an honest living, I might as well be killing some aliens. After all, those asshats started this." There was such a casual tone to her voice that it almost concealed the hardness in her heart.

"Donnie?" He turned to his anxious friend.

"Best goddamn prey we could ever hope for—a real test of skill."

"Not to mention doing something to protect the country," Samuel said.

"Hell, the world," Berri added, which got her a nod from Samuel in response.

Justin turned to Frenchie, who grinned broadly with his jagged-toothed smile, cracking the top of a can of cold beer. "The only good Fish is a dead Fish," he said. "I say we teach them a little Southern hospitality." He finished his statement with a deep swig of beer, leaving just a hint on his mustache.

"We need to pick a commander," Berri said, hiking up her camouflage hunting pants.

All eyes fell on Justin. Before he could speak, Frenchie did. "I volunteer!"

Berri rolled her eyes and Samuel bowed his head and shook it. "Seriously, Frenchie? All of your war stories begin the same way . . . 'I heard an explosion and rushed towards it.' No offense, but we need someone who is calm and rational."

"I was joking!" Frenchie replied, turning back to Justin. "Of course it should be Justin."

He hadn't considered being their leader. It wasn't something that he had desired. Yes, he was the president of their little hunting club, but that was something on a very different scale. Before he could argue against it, Donnie weighed in. "Justin here was my fire team leader in Alaska. While we all served, I fought with him, bled on the same tundra together. He's got the head for it. He knows when to fight, and when not to." Donnie's words conjured up memories of fighting the Russians in the last war.

"Look," he finally said. "I will do this if this is what you want. I didn't ask for it though."

"If you had, we wouldn't have picked you," Berri said.

"As long as you let me kill these aliens," Frenchie said, "I will follow you." It was conditional, but acceptance. Justin knew at that moment, he had no choice but to be the commander of the Knights.

Looking around at his friends, he spoke crisply to them. "I feel like I have to say this out loud. This isn't a hunting trip. You've all seen what these things can do. If we do this, we are putting our lives on the line. When you shoot at some buck in the woods, you don't worry about the doe spraying you down with some sort of acid or trying to crush your skull with a sonic weapon. This is no game . . . no hunt for wild elk or boar. Animals don't shoot back. We do this and there's a chance we will get killed."

"Great way to motivate," Samuel said with a smile. "You ought to get a gig running one of those big churches." His sarcasm was thick and Justin felt it.

"Look, Justin," Berri said, shifting her position on the rail. "The way I see it, we either fight them now or later. It's pretty clear they aren't going to leave in the near future and it feels like every day or so we are seeing new kinds of these bastards being thrown at us. We could play it safe and do nothing, but I think we all know that sooner or later we are going to have to fight them. We might as well do it on our terms."

"And get paid for it," Donnie added.

"Alright then," he said firmly. "Let's get the application in and see what happens."

Three weeks later . . .
Fort Stewart, Georgia

While Justin had never been to Fort Stewart during his time in the Army, he noted that every base had the same aroma in the air. The mix of fresh paint, body odor, and the semi-musty smell of the tents was something that was hard to forget. Fort Stewart had the addition of the smell of portable chemical toilets as well, brought in to handle the massive influx of new recruits and the teams applying to be sanctioned militia units.

Being sanctioned was important. Since the start of the alien incursion, there had been armed groups of civilians that had been engaging with them in battle. Being sanctioned meant there was support and a degree of coordination with the regular army. While no one had the exact details of what that coordination might look like, it sounded a hell of a lot safer than having armed groups of self-appointed protectors operating in the same vicinity as the enemy and the military.

They had chosen a name offered by Samuel, the Savannah Knights, not because it was a great name but because their first three choices had already been taken according to the application app. It seemed idealistic, calling themselves "knights," but even Justin had to admit he liked the sound of it. Berri said she knew an artist who could come up with a logo and maybe some patches—but Justin didn't care about that as much as getting through the vetting process with the Army. He had already seen a few teams leaving the base with dour looks on their faces, clearly at having been rejected. It seemed odd that the Army would turn down any help since the country was facing its first real invasion since the Russians had hit Alaska. The rejected teams he saw leave looked more like basement-dwelling gamers out thinking that this was *Call of Duty*, rather than real war. *The Army probably saved their lives by rejecting them.*

The physicals were every bit as thrilling and fun as he remembered. Berri was told she needed to lose weight; her response was a glare that would have killed the guy that had told her that. The standards seemed pretty relaxed for the militia. Unlike being in the army, there were no standardized uniforms.

Next came firearm qualifications. They were verified on the range using military weapons, rather than their personal weapons. Justin cringed at his first three shots, but was able to adjust enough to compensate. Frenchie and Samuel tied for the highest scores from the Knights, which was no surprise.

Next came an interview. It was in a tent set up in a parking lot at the fort, shaded but still sticky hot. These were not individual interviews but with the entire team. With so many veterans, Justin was a little worried that the talk might go off the rails. Frenchie and Donnie were likely to blurt out opinions about the military that might not play well with the officers doing the interviewing. Remarkably, they held their tongues and tried to respond with short answers, *yes*es and *no*s, just like good NCOs knew how to employ.

The officer, a second lieutenant named Sanchez, jabbed his fingers at his digipad a few times, clearly checking things off. Finally, he turned to Justin and leveled a question directly to him. "You meet all of our criteria but one; you are short at least one person for your unit."

Puzzled, Justin cocked his head and looked over at him. "What do you mean? I read every bit of the criteria, there was nothing about minimum unit size, sir." The "sir" was a courtesy on his part, hopefully enough to blunt his rebuttal slightly.

"I understand. The criteria just came down from the Pentagon yesterday. Apparently we were getting too many units that did not qualify as a militia fire team."

"We have five. A standard Army fire team is four."

"True, but you are not in the Army—you are militia," he said flatly. "The brass believe that militia units need larger numbers to be considered combat effective. If you don't have anyone in mind, there is an opportunity to have us assign someone to your unit who has volunteered but has no unit affiliation."

Justin surveyed the others. "Do we have anyone we can add to the roster?" What he got back were shakes of the head or blank expressions. Turning back to the lieutenant, he made the call on the fly. "We don't have much choice—we'll take a recruit."

"Excellent," the officer said. "Congratulations. The Savannah Knights are officially a recognized militia unit. Your official designation is the 66th Georgia Militia, at least that is how the Army will refer to you. Report to your briefing tent, yellow five. I will have your new unit member report there. You'll be briefed as to the basics and we will get you outfitted with your weapons and gear."

"Can't we use our own weapons?" Frenchie asked.

"The best way for us to keep you armed is to have you firing the same weapons we use. That doesn't prohibit you from bringing what we refer to as supplemental combat weapons, when you deploy."

That was good enough for Frenchie, who grinned and nodded in response. It was a long walk to their briefing tent. When they got inside, an older warrant officer greeted them and gestured to the folding chairs that were waiting. He checked his digipad, then turned to them.

"I'm Warrant Officer Peter Handcock. So, you are the Savannah Knights. Welcome to the militia program. I'm going to run down the highlights of how this will work, then turn you over to Corporal Kole who will be your embedded liaison." He gestured over to a blond young soldier who didn't look a day over 16. *Shit, I've got scars older than our liaison.*

Handcock continued. "Your operations will be coordinated through your liaison, as will all requisitions for equipment and ammunition. Your unit will be operating alongside regular Army forces in the field, and you are expected to communicate and coordinate with them. No solo missions. Understood?"

Justin nodded as the older man continued. "I know you all have some sort of military experience, but chances are you are a little rusty. Don't worry about that. At first you'll be pulling light duty, manning defensive positions, security, those kinds of missions. That allows us to get you back in the swing of things while freeing up regular forces for more dangerous ops against the enemy."

It was an amazingly logical approach to deploying them . . . *not at all like the Army I remember.* Frenchie spoke up. "What kind of gear are we getting?"

"Everyone will get an ACR-25 rifle and one hundred rounds of ammunition. You'll each get three standard-issue M27S stackable grenades. I'd give you more, but we are chewing through them pretty fast at the front. You'll get a standard-issue tactical knife as well as a canteen, med kit, some MREs—the usual stuff. Everything else right down to your skivvies is up to you."

Frenchie was disappointed and Justin knew why. He wanted a grenade launcher. When he had been asked on the firing range what his favorite weapon was, he had said, "Forty millimeter." When the range instructor asked, "You mean forty caliber?" Frenchie had replied with a grin, "Did I stutter?"

Handcock went over the protocols for dealing with the Fish. "The standing rule is simple: Touch nothing alien. Don't assume that because they are dead that they aren't deadly. We had a guy bayonet one of them and it ruptured some gland filled with their corrosive acid spray. We had to mop what was left of him to send to his parents. These bastards are full of surprises and the truth of the matter is that we are just starting to figure them out."

Their orientation went on for hours. He detailed the different classes of aliens they had encountered. The crabs were the best known, along with the hulking Bosses. There were others though. The frogs were relatively new, stout two-legged foot soldiers from the sound of it. There were others like the Foxes who seemed to be their force recon troops, and massive hulking ones that acted as armored personnel carriers. "In reality, we are seeing new breeds of the enemy every few weeks now. They seem to be adapting to us and the way we fight."

The Knights were expected to follow military orders and regulations which was something they had anticipated. Some protocols were not required, such as saluting and employing military discipline. None of that would have worked with the militia groups anyways, that much Justin was sure of. The military's flexibility was a bit surprising, but he knew it was a double-edged sword. *Things may be worse off than we have been led to believe for them to be willing to bend rules and regulations so much so fast.*

Handcock went on for hours talking about the routines and protocols they did need to follow. Essentially the militia were independent of the Army, but under Army control. Discipline was handled at the unit level, meaning that if they broke and ran from a fight, there wasn't a lot that the Army could do other than disavow them and take away their sanctioned status. There were plenty of rules about looting and profiteering, which Justin didn't think applied to them. *It does point to the fact that there are some bad players in the ranks of the militias though.*

After several long hours with the warrant officer, he finished and left them with Corporal Nate Kole. They went to dinner together and Justin listened to the verbal barbs from his troops at the young NCO. "Geez, Kole, did they issue you a diaper with that uniform?" Donnie asked.

"Alright," he said, blushing at the barrage of verbal barbs thrown at him. "Look, I'm here to do a job, just like you."

"You ever fire a shot at the enemy?" Berri asked.

He shook his head. "I've been at the front for a two-week stint north of Savannah. I didn't see any action." There was a hint of regret in his voice.

People always regret not getting in a fight—until they do.

"How'd you end up in this position?" Samuel asked.

"I volunteered."

Berri's eyes rolled back. "Aw hell, Kole, that's the dumbest thing you can do in the Army."

He blushed, which only served to make him look younger in Justin's mind.

"Why did you volunteer?" Justin asked.

"My family lived in Miami," Kole said slowly. "When the Fish came ashore, I lost my mother and sister. My dad's alive, but he's living in a resettlement camp right now. My family has a history of volunteering for the militia. I had a relative that fought in the Revolutionary War in the militia, and one in the Civil War too. I thought this might be my best chance to fight in the militia at the same time as the Army." The sincerity in his voice was compelling.

"He'll do," Samuel said with a firm nod that seemed to crack a smile on Kole's face. Justin appreciated the sentiment, but at the same time, Private Kole was untested. The same could be said of others in the Knights, other than Donnie. Justin and Donnie had fought together against the Russians. He had never seen Berri, Samuel, or Frenchie in actual combat conditions. Yes, he knew them as people, as hunters—but this was *not* a hunt.

"According to the Army, we are short one member for our merry little band," Justin quipped.

Kole nodded. "Tomorrow we will visit the recruitment tent. There's a lot of people that don't want to join the Army, but want to be in the fight. We should be able to find someone there to fill the slot."

While Justin hoped that would be the case, there was a bit of reluctance about the caliber of people that he might meet. Would they be good candidates, or the wretched refuse . . . people that wouldn't fit into any other militia unit?

***

Justin's worst fears were confirmed the next morning at the recruitment tent. There was no formal process for filling the empty slot in their ranks. There were three other militia units there as well, wading through the potential candidates. Some just picked a warm body based on looks alone, Justin could tell. That wasn't his style. *My life might depend on this person, which means I want to get the right person.*

One candidate elbowed his way to greet the Knights. He easily weighed three-hundred pounds and his Amazon.com-purchased camouflage was straining under his bulk. His name was Rusty and he insisted he had the skills that they were looking for, without bothering to ask what those might be.

"You ever fire a gun in anger?" Samuel asked of the portly would-be warrior.

"Oh, I've been in some tight scrapes before."

"That wasn't the question," Donnie pressed. "Have you ever been in a fight—a combat situation?"

"I got into a big fight in high school," he said with pride. "One guy had to be taken to the hospital."

Frenchie leaned in on Justin's ear. "Pork-rind here is going to die first if we pick him. You know that, right?"

Justin grinned at his friend's comment. "Look, we need someone that has experience."

"I go to the range every week. I have a huge collection of guns," Rusty insisted.

Berri planted her fists on her hips and leaned in on him. "Anyone with a paycheck can collect guns. We need people we can trust in a firefight."

"I'm your guy!"

Justin could see the conversation devolving quickly from there if he didn't cut it off. "Thanks, Dusty," he said.

"It's Rusty."

"I don't care," he said, turning to find another candidate.

Most of the men and women they interviewed were of the same, if not slightly better, caliber. Most were in a rush to get in on the war, without a good understanding of what war was. Movies and games had made them not fully understand the realities of what they would be facing in the field. Even the Knights, with their experience, had little idea of what it was going to be like facing aliens.

After two hours of such tedious and disappointing interviews, he spotted a young man who wasn't jockeying to get in front of anyone. The kid was skinny, with brown hair that looked as if he had cut it himself. He wore jeans—not designer jeans, but the kind you bought at Walmart because they fit. His T-shirt was plain white with dull yellowish sweat stains around the collar. Cowboy boots topped off his attire, as well as a look of not enjoying the process any more than Justin was.

Walking over to the young man, he looked down at him. "What's your story?"

Lifting his head to lock gaze with Justin, his look of almost boredom faded a little. "Same as the others here. I'm looking for a way to get into the fightin'." He spoke with a drawl, not quite southern, more Texan in nature.

"You got a name?"

"Josh Colson," he said, rising slowly to stand a few inches taller than Justin.

"What's your background?"

"I work as a ranch hand in Oklahoma."

"What brings you out here?" Berri asked as she moved up to the conversation circle.

"There's not a lot of chance to kill the Fish in Oklahoma. We are what ya'll might call beach-deprived."

"You ever see any combat?"

"I graduated the police academy back home in Austin after high school. Served on the Austin PD for three years."

"How'd you end up working a ranch?" Samuel asked.

"I got into a gun fight with some car thieves," he said with a half-sigh. "We rolled up on them and they got out guns blazing. I was hit in the shoulder, my partner got one in the shin. We got both of them, but it was too late."

"You lose your partner?" Justin asked.

"No," he replied flatly. "One of their rounds hit a kid a half a block behind us—killed her instantly. After that, I just didn't have the heart to be on the streets anymore. I needed to clear my head—so I took a job on a ranch."

In his mind, Justin was checking off boxes. Firearms, combat experience, a moral center . . . all very positive things. "Why not just join the army?"

"Working out on the range, you start to like not having to take orders from people. The army is all about telling you what to do and when to do it and how you need to do it. I like my independence a little too much for that lifestyle."

Justin surveyed the other Knights and mostly got subtle nods. "We are the Savannah Knights," he said. "You seem to have what we are looking for. Would you like to sign on with us?"

Colson slowly turned to make eye contact with each member. "What's your experience?" he asked back.

"We've got combat vets and semi-professional hunters," Justin said. "Savannah is our home and we don't take well to some alien assholes invading and destroying it."

He paused and stared intently at Justin, his gray eyes seeming to look through him. "Alright then. I don't want to go out with a bunch of weekend warriors or idiots looking for some glory."

He extended his hand and Justin could feel the gritty callouses as he shook it back. "Welcome to the Knights then."

Firebase Vampire, Savannah, Georgia

The first three weeks near the front were dull. The Knights provided escort duty for a week on convoys bringing supplies in. There had been no sign of the enemy, but it did get the team working together. For a few days, they were assigned as defense for a heavy mortar position not far from the front. Long hours of dullness punctuated by the occasional thump of outgoing rounds. There hadn't been a lot of firing since the armaments industry had not yet caught up with the demand, so the higher powers carefully rationed heavy firepower. For the Knights, it was a stark reminder of how desperate the situation really was. *We never prepared for this kind of war, with both of our coasts under assault.*

The sounds of battle were always in the distance. Most were random, shots here and there. Explosions were rare, but the occasional staccato of bangs and cracks of fire echoed through the streets of outer Savannah. At times, there was no noise at all, then suddenly the cacophony of combat. Civilians had been ordered to evacuate early on, but there were still some who defied the military and refused to leave. Justin had seen that in Alaska as well. Regardless of the risks, there were always some people that refused common sense and remained in the middle of fighting.

In their downtime, Justin had the unit doing light PE, training with their weapons, rekindling their former skills. It was starting to show. Berri was losing weight. Samuel seemed even more bulked up, if that were even possible. Frenchie was tired, and when he was tired, he talked less. Bit by bit, Corporal Kole and Josh Colson were starting to fit in, becoming familiar with the other Knights. They reminded Justin of replacement troops during the last war. At first, the seasoned vets didn't want to get to know them too well, because they often had a short life expectancy once the shooting started. Over time, the experienced soldiers would eventually take them under their wings and give them tips that might save their lives. Kole seemed to be a mental sponge, soaking up any advice anyone might offer. Colson, on the other hand, remained relatively quiet and aloof.

The other thing that filled their downtime was the rumors. They heard stories of a number of new alien species. One was said to be a cross between an octopus and a giant crab, with armored tentacles that whipped fast enough to cut a fighter in half. There were said to be hopping aliens, big nasty ones, that could bound over a three-story building and climb walls like Spiderman. Frenchie and Donnie liked gathering and sharing the stories from the other units, but Justin tended to ignore them. Rumors don't win wars. Most of the time they were simply lies, amplified by boredom, and spread by people starved for anything new and exciting. *If even a tenth of these are true, we are supremely fucked.*

Finally Corporal Kole came through with a new set of orders, posting to the front. Gathering their gear, they made their way towards the sporadic sounds of battle. They stopped on Louisville Road at an old brick warehouse that was flanked by sandbags and a makeshift barrier that blocked the road. Adding to the defenses was a metal cargo container that had been placed in one lane of traffic, serving as a roadblock and a place to keep the guards in the shade. Sentries, weapons at ready, eyed the incoming troops with squints and faint nods, motioning them to the side door of the old structure.

Once inside the building, they saw a squad of troops who eyed them with just a hint of disdain. Justin ignored their gazes and walked up to the staff sergeant who stepped forward. "Justin Birdsong of the Savannah Knights," he said flatly.

The sergeant had two days' growth of beard stubble on his face. The wrinkles he had were canyons, etched out by years of service . . . Justin had seen the same face a hundred times in his career. "Sergeant Fogle, Bravo Company, second platoon," he said, nodding over to a picnic table that was nearby. The two of them walked over and sat down as the rest of the Knights filed in and dropped their gear.

"I just got word you were coming in," Fogle said. "We got orders to head out and go fishing tonight."

"Where are you going?"

"There seems to be some enemy activity around the visitor center. Drone vids show the Fish doing something in that area. We are going up there on recon."

Justin knew the city well enough to know it was a four-block journey. For him, it was a stark reminder of how close the enemy really was. "What do you need us for?"

"You need to hold this position on the line," he said. "Should be a cakewalk for you guys. We've only had the Fish show up a few times and drove them back. Chances are you won't hear a peep from them. This is a few hours tonight, in and out for us. We need you to keep this base secure and not shoot us when we come back. Pretty simple shit."

"Experience has taught me that nothing is as easy as it sounds," Justin quipped.

"You've seen action before?"

He nodded. "Russians up in Alaska."

"Nome?"

"Fairbanks."

Just the mention of that battle was enough to take a little of the crease out of the wrinkles on Sergeant Fogle's brow. "I respect that. The Fish are different though. They don't think or act the way we do. We knew what was coming at us from the Russians. We don't get that luxury with the Fish."

"So I hear."

A thudding footstep at the far end of the warehouse made the concrete floor tremble. Justin snapped his head around and saw the ASHUR stepping out of its maintenance pod. He knew the model, a Croc. The shape of the cockpit canopy was like looking down on the head of a crocodile, which was where it got its name from. The right arm mounted a chain gun, not the light model M242. This was the newer M300—one that could chew through an armored vehicle if it got the right angle. The left arm mounted a grenade launcher. On each shoulder was a trio of missiles. The armored combat rig was painted in urban camouflage, grays, and digital black and white splotches. Justin wondered if the Fish were confused at all by the paint schemes.

"That's Corporal Herrington's rig," the sergeant said proudly. "Call sign Morningstar. Retrofitted with one of the new high-storage batteries too. She's saved our collective asses more than once."

ASHURs were the epitome of weapons systems. Armored fighting rigs, they carried a deadly punch and could get into places that normal fighting vehicles couldn't. The Croc was one of those. For all of its firepower, it only had to crouch down and twist sideways to get through a door—though it was likely to do some damage in the process. Still, for all of its bulk, it was the hottest commodity in the battlespace.

Only the best soldiers could hope to qualify to pilot an ASHUR rig. Even then, there was a highly competitive process they underwent to earn that right. Samuel had been chosen and had failed out at the very end of his testing process. He refused to talk about the process or where he had gone wrong. Justin glanced at him and saw Samuel staring at the Croc across the old warehouse with a longing on his face that was mixed with frustration.

Seeing the ASHUR, Justin felt that the sergeant's squad was going to be in good hands. He had seen them fighting in the last war. Despite their bulk, they moved with remarkable speed and, in the hands of a good pilot, could rip apart almost any opposition. Frenchie had sworn he was going to get a rig as salvage, but the odds of that were pretty low, given the Army's recovery rates on reclaiming their tech.

The army squad also had a GRD—a Ground Robotic Drone. These semi-autonomous drones fulfilled a number of different operational requirements, from carrying heavy weapons and ammunition to extracting the wounded. The one he saw was a Shepherd. On the back of the sleek drone was an anti-personnel laser and a drum of the explosives and generator used to power the weapon. It wasn't as big as the assault lasers that were issued to the troops, but it was enough to sear a hole through almost any normal target. Its operator was testing the GRD, making it bounce in place, checking the actuators to make sure they were clear. The gray-and-white streaked camouflage on the drone was so pitted and worn, clearly it had seen action more than a few times.

The two squads intermingled for a few hours, as much as could be expected. The regular army troops only seemed to warm up once they learned that the bulk of his personnel were combat veterans themselves. That was the glue that held armies together—mutual respect. Even Colson, who usually kept to himself, talked to the troops getting ready to go on patrol, gathering whatever tidbits he could about the area what they were likely going up against.

At 1900, Sergeant Fogle's unit set out heading towards the city, led by the Croc ASHUR and the GRD. Justin made sure his people were in place, double-checking fields of fire to make sure that the tiny outpost was secure from every possible direction. A few of his people wore their ACS systems and were little more than a blur as they walked. The adaptive camouflage systems were expensive—which was why the militia didn't have them—and were quirky. They got overloaded easily as soon as the shooting started, but up until then, they made it difficult to see and target soldiers wearing them.

Justin never said it out loud, but there was a feeling of pride. This is what he had signed up for, being at the front. Guarding convoys was dull; any contractor could do that. Being at the front, even in a defensive capacity, was akin to being back at war again.

The first two hours passed in relative calm. The random sounds of battle in the distance echoed from Savannah—gunfire bursts and the occasional explosion. None of it sounded like it was heading their direction, but it was a constant reminder of where they were poised. Justin moved near Corporal Kole, who was inside the warehouse, listening to the radio chatter. *All we have to do is wait here, hold this spot until the patrol comes back.* For a few minutes, he allowed himself to relax.

Then came a flurry of call signs and chatter over the comms system. Gunfire over the radio echoed back from the city outside. Whatever was going down was close. Kole leaned in with the headset on, rocking a little in his seat. Then came something that made Justin tense up.

"Morningstar is down. Broken arrow. Repeat, broken arrow."

Morningstar was call sign for the Croc ASHUR rig. The voice was that of Sergeant Fogle and the older man was clearly stressed. The call for broken arrow was the call for a unit whose position was overrun.

"Shit," Justin muttered.

"They have a drone moving in to support them," Kole said.

Justin didn't have much faith in the Air Force. They were low on munitions, so whatever support they might deliver, it was going to be limited. "Where are they?"

Kole checked the map. "They are at their objective."

The Savannah Visitor Center. It was an old railroad building that had been repurposed a few times in its life. *They might be able to hold it, but if they are calling broken arrow, they are in a world of hurt.* A large explosion went off in the distance and he instinctively knew it was the Air Force dropping a bomb—no doubt to try to take the pressure off the trapped army troops.

Justin tensed as he considered what to do. They could remain where they are; they had orders. Broken arrow required any available units to come to the relief of the besieged troops. *We have got to be their closest support. If we sit here, they could get wiped out.* The thought of their blood on his hands for their inaction was something he didn't want to think about.

"We're moving out," he said firmly, adjusting the optics of his night vision goggles as they started out. They were true color ones, much better than the green-light ones he had used back in Alaska.

Kole looked up at him. "We have orders to remain here."

"Screw the orders," Justin said. "The Fish have overrun those troops and we are close enough to help. The call was Broken Arrow, and we are probably the closest support those folks have."

Kole's mouth opened slightly, but no words came out. "Alright," he said in a low tone. "I'll round up the others."

It only took a few minutes for the Knights to assemble. No one questioned what they were going to do once Justin told them of the situation. *They have all been wanting a piece of the action, and now they'll get it.* The members of the unit loaded up with extra ammunition. Frenchie raided the Army's munitions with a sense of glee, fitting out his urban standard tactical gear with a copious number of stackable grenades and at least two claymores.

They moved out in a squad column formation up Louisville Road. Their pace was brisk, mostly out of necessity. It was not a long ways to travel to where the Army forces were calling for help, but within a block or so, he saw the billowing black smoke rolling upward from the general direction of the Visitor Center, difficult to make out with the nightvis gear, but visible against the moonlight. The sight of the smoke, and the popping of gunfire increasing in tempo, told him he was closing on their objective.

"Hold up," he said just loud enough for them to hear over the squad's comm channel. "We are almost on them which means enemy contact. Our goal is to get to them so they can fall back—which means we are going to secure a corridor. We are going to shift up to bounding overwatch formation," he said. "Donnie, you take the forward fire team," he said firmly. Donnie moved forward and gave him a nod.

They moved another eighty yards forward, and he saw Donnie and the forward team drop. "Contact," he heard in his helmet's headset as they unleashed short, controlled bursts of fire. Commotion stirred from up ahead as Justin took the second fire team on a wide flanking maneuver to the right while Donnie and his team held their attention.

Moving through a tangle of brush, they rose slowly over a large embankment and came up on their first visual contact. It was a crab, though that description didn't do it justice. The creature was massive, taller than two humans, with a scorpion-like tail that was curled up. It moved on eight spike-tipped claws, and then the front rose like a centaur. Bullets hitting the thick green-gray chitin-armored body plates simply ricocheted off or fell to the ground after impact—unable to penetrate the thick body. As the creature reeled to face the threat to its rear, he could see the huge crab-like claw in front of it.

The creature was at the rear of the visitor center and, from the looks of it, was trying to push its way through the brick exterior. Gunfire flashed from inside the structure as Justin moved his people along the flank and ordered his people to engage.

Given the massive size of the crab, he would have thought that it would be slower. It skittered across the road and was closing on Donnie's position as his team poured in fire, peppering its sides. Frenchie ran forward and threw a triple-stacked grenade, which exploded along the side of the crab with devastating effect. One of the legs of the creature flew off, spraying a greenish mist from the severed joint as it careened aside to face Justin's team.

"That got his attention," Berri said.

The crab finished its turn and lofted a huge appendage. A thick bulbous vein that ran down the claw swelled for an instant, then unleashed a long stream of silvery liquid. It splattered near Berri as she tried to dive for cover behind a tree. Her wail of agony filled his earpiece as the liquid devoured whatever it hit.

An acid sprayer. Bringing his weapon back up, he aimed carefully for the crab's head and neck and fired a three-round burst. One shot seemed to catch a gap between the armored plates, making the alien twitch and sidestep. Another pair of grenades rained down, from Samuel and Donnie. The explosions wracked the crab hard, making it recoil its right claw.

Justin's head was filled with the sound of his own thundering heart as his adrenaline surged. The crab sprang forward, a surprising move, landing right in front of Corporal Kole. Thrusting its right claw forward in a dangerous arc, it slammed into the crouching Kole, sending him flying through the air and landing him next to an abandoned tour bus.

Shit! "Pour it on," he ordered into his helmet's mic and the intensity of the fire escalated instantly. One shot from his people hit a place on the curled tail of the creature as it clattered to the right. The shot must have hit something vital as it sprayed a blackish gray ooze out like a geyser, wetting down the alien and the parking lot that it was maneuvering through.

Raising its left claw, the crab's vein once more start to pulsate. Justin concentrated his fire on the vein, and punched through. A gush of caustic acid burst out, washing down on the creature's legs and side. Wisps of smoke rose from it and the crab whipped about, illuminated by the full moon that was out that night. A sickening hissing screech rose from it, like a lobster being thrown into boiling water only a thousand times louder. It staggered several steps, then collapsed. Its huge tail uncurled and slammed into an abandoned car, crushing the hood as the creature fell.

"Someone, recover Kole. Grab Berri. We are moving in on the building. Move it, people!" Justin called out as a pair of explosions went off on the front of the building. He toggled his comm system to broadcast in the clear. "This is the Savannah Knights," he said as he started to run across the parking lot toward the visitor center. "We are coming in your back door. Do not fire at us, we are friendlies." The smell of dust and fired rounds stung at his nostrils. Memories of Alaska tried to surge forward, but his adrenaline rush thankfully pushed them aside.

The back of the building had a huge three-yard hold pushed through the brick structure leading to what looked like some sort of office. They scrambled inside over the bricks and were greeted by one of the infantry. Standing at the entrance, he watched as they dragged the unconscious form of Kole. Berri was pale and her arm was still smoking where the acid had seared through her armor and into her flesh. It made his eyes water as she passed, and he caught a whiff of a bacon-smell. Her gritted teeth were testimony to the agony she felt.

They were led to the front of the building where barricades had been put in place near the shattered windows. The Croc stood half in and half out of the structure, in a hole that it looked like it had made backing into the brick. It was hard to tell if it had made the hole, or had simply stepped into it. It wasn't firing, but the survivors of the Army patrol were, from every window and hole they could find. Outside of one window, he saw the crushed remains of the Shepherd GRD, nearly pinched in half—probably the result of one of the crab's forward claws.

Sergeant Fogle saw him and moved over, keeping low. A shot of something pierced one of the window openings and slammed into the wall just above Justin, making him duck. Bits of orange brick dust rained down on him. "I didn't expect to see your sorry asses here."

"We came in the back," Justin said. "We can get your people out."

"We've got a dozen or so frogs at the front, and a crab on the flank," Fogle said with a breathy voice of exhaustion.

"Scratch the crab."

"We can't leave our people or tech behind. Herrington caught one of their big spikes right through the cockpit canopy of the Croc. We have to blow her ASHUR or extract it. I have four people down, three more dead."

Justin looked at the ASHUR. "Is it operational?"

"Maybe," the sergeant replied. "Herrington's body is pinned inside."

"One of my guys has ASHUR training. If we can get the body out, he might be able to pilot it out."

"Make it happen," the sergeant said.

Before he could give the order, a loud throbbing sound filled the visitor center. The wallboard cracked on the interior walls and dust fell from everywhere. His head ached from the reverberation that shook every joint in his body. *Sonic weapon!* The Knights had been briefed on them, but experiencing them was an entirely different matter. The headache the followed surged to his brow and made him cringe. His ears rang, not like from gunfire, but something deeper in his skull. He felt something wet on his upper lip and wiped it with his uniform cuff, only to see a dark maroon smear of blood there. *Just how much damage does that damn weapon do?*

He quickly refocused on the mission. "Samuel, get to that rig. You and Frenchie, get the pilot out of it. See if you can pilot it," he ordered. Frenchie bolted for the ASHUR, but Samuel hesitated, making eye contact with Justin. He gave his hulking friend a deep nod . . . *You can do this.* With that, Samuel sprang forward. Donnie moved to a window next to one of the survivors of the patrol and fired away at the enemies outside.

"Getting the dead out of here will be tricky," the sergeant said, moving to a window and looking out. He used his sidearm and emptied the magazine.

"We can drag 'em," Justin said, moving beside him. For the first time, he saw a frog. They were human sized, maybe a little shorter. Their skin had an armored quality to them, a greenish color with gray splotches. They moved in a running hop, fast enough to make them difficult targets.

The one he saw paused, and the sergeant's bullets thwacked into its front chest, not seeming to penetrate. Raising its thick muscled arm, it fired what looked like a dull beam. It was a high pressured cutter spraying a stream of water that was somehow held in its form. The spray sliced along the front of the building, sending a few bricks flying down on the troops inside. Justin recoiled and ducked for cover. When he looked up again, the frog was gone.

I never thought I'd miss the Russians. At least in the last war, the weapons were all basically the same. He moved over to the ASHUR rig where Samuel and Frenchie were working to extract the pilot. The spike that had hit her had pierced the cockpit's armored transparent aluminum canopy—a freak unlucky shot. The spike was a foot long and looked like a conical bone of some kind, with razor barbs. It was planted in the center of her chest. *Poor girl never stood a chance.* It took some straining, but they managed to pry out her blood-soaked body. Frenchie and Justin pulled her away from the hole in the wall where the rig was poised as Samuel slid in and closed the shattered canopy.

Frenchie emptied the magazine of his ACR, then slung it behind him. He pulled out his personal .44 caliber auto mag and aimed it. Amid the din of battle, the booming of his hand cannon stood out as he emptied one magazine after another. *He's in his prime, fighting with weapons of his own choosing.* If the situation had not been so dire, Justin might have cracked a smile.

"Tell me you can pilot that thing, Samuel," he said over the Knight's channel.

"I was getting my rating on a Mustang," he said. "I can pilot it, but probably not very well." As he worked at the controls, a spray of smaller needle-like projectiles slapped and pinged off of the front armor of the ASHUR rig, shattering and spraying bits of shrapnel behind him, raining down on the others.

A half minute passed. One of the longest thirty seconds of his life. The Fish were not seeming to aim as much as trying to bring the building down on top of them. *Come on, Samuel, get that bitch moving!* Frenchie had somehow found a grenade launcher among the wounded and was emptying the drum, raining death and explosions from out his window.

The Croc emitted a low hum as it powered up and started to shift in place. Samuel raised the big arm with the chain gun and it roared, spraying bullets and tracers out into the darkness of the evening.

Justin didn't realize how bad the ringing in his ears from the sonic weapon was until the chain gun opened up. It was like putting his head next to a jet engine running with afterburners. The sounds made his eyes water and his headache go from a throbbing pain to a full blown roar.

The guns shut off, still whirling fast to cool for a moment. Then there was a scream of sorts, deep and grunting from outside—hopefully one of the frogs being cut in half by the chain gun. The Croc shifted in place, knocking over more bricks, as Samuel backed it into the room. Two more spike weapons slammed into it, hitting the shoulder and arm, furrowing the armor there and sending fragments of the shots splattering the walls and ceiling as shrapnel. Pain-generated sweat ran down Justin's face and soaked his shirt. *God, I hope he doesn't fire that gun indoors again.*

"Grab ropes," Sergeant Fogle called out. "Tie the dead to the handholds on the rig; he can drag them if he has to. Any wounded that can walk, do so. We are going to lay down suppression fire as soon as we clear the building and fall back by pairs, slow retrograde down the roadway."

At Justin's orders, Frenchie rigged the claymores aimed out two of the windows. Moving next to Berri, he looked down at her wound and swore that he could see the bones of her forearms with his night vision gear on. "Can you get yourself out?"

"Give me your sidearm and a fresh mag," she said. He handed it to her and she held it with her good hand. "I can walk—for now."

Kole stirred, moaning as the unit prepared to move out. Frenchie helped him to his feet and while he wobbled, he seemed to be recovering from the brutal hit he had taken. "You going to make it?" Justin asked.

"I think one of my ribs is broken," he said, half-moaning the words. "Don't worry, I'll be fine."

Samuel moved the ASHUR to the rear of the building to the office they had come through, knocking out the doorframe to get inside during the process. With one sweep of the armored arm, he knocked aside the desk that was there, breaking it into kindling wood as it smashed against the brick outer wall.

The rear opening wasn't big enough for the ASHUR, but that didn't stop the Croc from shoving its way through. Two bricks remained on the armored front as Samuel cleared the structure. The dead were being dragged on ropes through the hole, and Sergeant Fogle helped one of the wounded women in his unit who was walking with a terrible limp.

They moved out, backing away from the ruins of the visitor center. A frog jumped out from around the side of the structure, firing away with its high pressured cutting weapon. It hit one of the troopers, sending him flying back. Frenchie leveled the grenade launcher and fired at the threat. The blast tore the frog's body apart, one leg splattering up on the side of the brick building with an ugly smear.

Moving through the parking lot, they passed where the fallen crab still lay. There was a stirring noise from near the building and another one of the giant creatures emerged. *Aw shit!* Justin took aim and fired three controlled bursts. While he was sure he was hitting the raised upper torso of the alien, he had no way of knowing if any of his shots penetrated.

He wasn't alone. The rest of the survivors blazed away as well. The crab juked hard to the right as bullets thudded and thwacked into it. Suddenly the Croc opened up with its missiles. A trio from the right shoulder fired. The triangular missiles locked their fins as they cleared their tubes and their tips shimmered red in the darkness, crimson streaks that stabbed out at the crab.

The triangular-shaped LAW missiles had been designed with shaped charges designed to penetrate armor. Their explosions were more than a match for the crab. One of its big claws was severed near the back of the head where it was attached, flailing into the night. Another missed and went off under the belly of the creature, rocking it off its eight-clawed feet and throwing it a good two yards back. The third missile hit near the head, blowing off one of the large crustacean plates.

The crab screeched an ungodly sound, twisting around and running back, hopefully to die. The muffled blasts from both claymores signaled that the enemy had entered the remains of the visitor center, and hopefully were paying a price for their arrogance.

Frenchie moved over to the trooper that had been hit. His STG and body armor plates had been ripped off, the Kevlar was severed, but it seemed to have been enough to prevent a deep penetration. While he had a lot of blood drizzling down his body, he was able to stand, though he was wobbly.

"Alright, let's get out of here," Justin said.

Methodically, but with speed, the survivors began to fall back to the firebase. The grinding thuds of the Croc were oddly reassuring as Samuel swept their rear, looking for targets. It wasn't until they reached the warehouse that they were relatively sure that the Fish were not pursuing, and even then, Justin posted his people for defense should they be wrong.

Sergeant Fogle had called in the medics who were waiting for them when they got back. Berri and Kole were evacced in the field ambulance along with the other wounded. A separate team took the bodies of the dead with them.

Justin's hands were trembling as the adrenaline started to fade from his bloodstream. Sweat made every bit of dust and dirt cling to him like a new layer of skin. Checking his weapon, he made sure it was loaded with a fresh magazine and set the safety. The feeling of some relief was not new to him; he had felt it every time he came back from a firefight. The headache from the sonic weapon still throbbed, but was subsiding as well. He stopped and drew a long drink from his canteen.

Sergeant Fogle came up in front of him, taking a drink from his own canteen as well. "Thank you for coming after us. When the drone dropped the bomb on the Fish, we tried to break out, but they had us bottled up. If you hadn't come along, we might have Alamoed ourselves back there."

"It was our pleasure," he said.

"Other militia units would have stayed here, following orders."

"We are not like them," Justin said with a hint of pride creeping out.

"I can see that," the sergeant replied. "And I'm going to let my seniors know what you did for us."

Justin nodded and smiled. Walking over to the Croc, he saw Samuel crawling out of the battered cockpit. For the first time, he saw the damage that the Croc had sustained. Its leg armor was pitted with shrapnel, either from the Air Force's bomb or from grenades. Pockmarks from hits ruined the paint scheme. The arm damage was visible and disturbing, given the caved-in armor plates. The fractured cockpit canopy was a testimony to the precision force that had killed Herrington, the original pilot.

Samuel looked over at him. "I don't suppose the Army will let me claim this as salvage."

Justin shrugged. "They said whatever we recovered—but you and I both know you can't fully trust what the Army tells us."

"Possession is nine-tenths of the law."

"We're at war. The law has no meaning in war."

"Still," Samuel said, caressing the left arm of the rig. "It felt damn good to pilot one of these in battle finally."

"I bet it did."

"I always felt like I washed out, that I'd failed."

"You sure as hell weren't a failure today," Justin replied. "And that's all that really matters to us."

Frenchie came over. "I'm keeping this grenade launcher," he said defiantly. "Even if they won't let him keep the Croc, I got this grenade launcher fair and square."

Justin chuckled. "Frenchie—it's all yours."

TDDB

In a vicious war against an enemy that is not comprehended, people get wounded and die. It is the nature of all wars, but one against a biologically engineered alien race whose methods and means of fighting are entirely new—death is in every foxhole, in every firebase, lurking on every patrol.

There are those that defy death—the doctors and nurses who struggle to save lives. This is one of their stories.

The Western Front, Drain, Oregon

The mortar rounds that went off around Second Lieutenant Tabitha Thomas's foxhole made her entire head throb. Thick clods of dirt mixed with bits of pine trees and dead brown needles showered her with each explosion. She had to override the instinct to abandon the foxhole and run for the rear. Common sense said the foxhole was the safest place to be during a bombardment, especially with the enemy being danger-close to her position. Logic was being quickly eroded by fear. Drain had been a dismal place even before the war.

She was bent over, leaning over the limp form of her best friend, doing what she could to stop the bleeding with a freezer and a chemical suture. As much as she tried to shelter her open injuries from the dirt with her own body, she knew she was failing. The only solace was that she wasn't entirely alone. Corporal McGowan was next to her, and huddled in the far end of the hole was the Husky GRD that he still was able to command.

A screeching sound, definitely not human, wailed not far in the distance. If not for the cacophony of explosions and gunfire around her, the screech would have probably sent a chill down her spine. She hoped whatever kind of alien it was that it was in agony. She had seen what they did to their human targets, and the time for granting them any thoughts of mercy had long passed.

Another loud *whomp* from a nearby heavy mortar round going off made her lay flatter on the wounded soldier, if that was possible.

How the hell did I get myself into this? How am I going to get out?

Thirty-three days earlier ...
Field Hospital 222, Drain, Oregon

Second Lieutenant Tabitha Thomas stood before the CO of the hospital at attention, Colonel Coleman Salz. "You can relax, Lieutenant," he said, gesturing to the folding seat opposite of the Costco folding table that served as his desk. "We try not the stand on too much formality here."

"Yes, sir."

He glanced at his digipad, reviewing her records, then tossed the pad on the desk. "You volunteered to be posted to a forward position. Why? I hope you aren't one of those adrenaline junkies. The last one suffered a mental breakdown."

It was a question she had answered before, several times. "I'm a nurse. Anyone can serve in some hospital in the rear. This is a chance to push myself."

"It might just get you killed," he said. "We've had to fall back twice. The Oregon National Guard has not been able to contain the enemy very well. You go eight miles west and you are in the AIZ."

"So I was told."

The colonel leaned back in his chair. "Well, the Fish have pushed inland about twenty miles so far. The only good news is that we don't have a lot of people living in this part of Oregon. By the same token, there's not much to slow down the aliens when they want to advance."

"I'm not afraid, sir."

"I'm not sure that's a good thing, Lieutenant," he replied, crossing his arms. "I know you were a RN before the war. You went through the Army's program after you upped. Well, most of what you've learned is probably already obsolete. You got trained to treat bullet and shrapnel wounds. We don't get a lot of that. What the alien tech does to the human body is not like anything you can imagine."

Tabitha felt that his statement was an understatement, but held her tongue. The Army had given her some training on the kinds of wounds she might face. Their acid sprayers and caustic gases were known. She had seen videos of the kinds of wounds and been told the protocols for dealing with them. *I'm not in the dark as much as he thinks.* "I understand, sir. I look forward to learning more."

"This isn't a school, nor are we a typical hospital," Colonel Salz said. "Our job is to stop the dying process and get them shipped out for more permanent repairs. The kinds of surgery we do here is fast and furious. There isn't a lot of time to do much more than stop the bleeding. A lot of this alien tech can kill you as easily as it does the victims. That means you have to be smart. Don't assume anything. If you see something that you haven't seen before, say something—ask someone."

"I understand."

"Do you?" The older colonel shifted. "I've lost three nurses, including the one you are replacing, because the goddamned Fish unleashed shit that we hadn't seen before and she touched it. They were good and bright people, just like you. All they were doing was trying to save lives, but the alien tech flipped on them. They suffered and died as a result."

There was a grimness in his tone that she took note of. *He's not giving these warnings to scare me. He's trying to help.* "Sir, I will be over-cautious."

"I'm going to assign one of our other nurses to mentor you," he said. "Lieutenant Steiger will walk you through the paces. For the first week or so, you don't do anything unless he gives you the go-ahead. You follow him like a shadow. You watch, ask good questions, do what you are told, and you might make it through this war alive."

"Thank you, sir," she said. He dismissed her, telling her where to find Lieutenant Steiger.

Steiger wasn't in his tent, but was found in the mess tent, coddling a cup of coffee as if it were a battery that kept him alive. The lieutenant was of medium build, his hair a disheveled brown tangle. Dark bags hung under his gray eyes and his cheeks seemed to sag, as if he had lost a lot of weight lately. After their initial introductions, Thomas sat down across from him. "So, when do I start?"

"You're in a big damned hurry."

"I've been traveling for three days just to get here. The Army, in its infinite wisdom, sent me to the wrong field hospital. So yes, I'm in a bit of a damned hurry." Frustration leaked out between each word that she spoke.

"Our job," Steiger said, "is simple, at least on paper. We are here to stabilize the patients. We save them and get them ready for transport. You worked in an ER, so this is a lot different. Triage is king here in terms of our priority. We work to block death long enough to get patients to a rear area where they can do the delicate work."

She knew the role of field hospitals all too well from her training, but the fact that he was emphasizing this meant that there were nuances to it that she didn't understand yet. "I think I understand, but I will really get it by doing my job."

"That's true," Steiger replied. "A lot of people coming here out of civilian service struggle—despite their Army indoctrination. Your old skills are good, but you can't rely on them here. We do things *our* way. I'm not saying it's right or the best way, but it works. Some of our patients are lost causes long before they are brought in. You will be forced to make some difficult choices that involve life and death."

She only nodded slowly in response.

Lieutenant Steiger grinned, if only a little bit. "I'm sure you'll do okay. Alright, let's get you oriented—follow me."

They arrived at the recovery tent, and she was greeted by an almost stale cheese aroma mingling with sweat that hung in the air. "These over here are acid victims," he said, pointing to several patients on cots. "The stuff that the aliens spray at them eats just about everything," he said holding up a finger with a nasty blister on it. "We have to immerse them in water just to get it diluted enough for us to start surgery. Getting that stuff off is not easy, but there are some tricks we will show you."

Tabitha had been trained a little bit on the molecular acid spray weapon the aliens used. Seeing the damage, even bandaged, on the victims should have chilled her. One man was missing an arm; another had his face wrapped, and there was oozing yellow pus and blood splotches already soaking through the gauze wraps.

Steiger turned her attention to another aisle of patients. "These folks got hit with the cutters." The Fish used a special high pressure water spray that could cut through steel. What it did to flesh was horrific and brutal. "We've found out that the fluid they use contains a high concentration of iron and nickel. The current thinking is that they use some sort of natural magnet to keep the beam cohesive, allowing it to fire at extended ranges and be effective. The fluid has to be cleaned out of the wounds extensively or there is a big risk of post-op infection."

Steiger led her to a row of patients hooked up to ventilators. Some were missing limbs from recent amputations.

"What happened to them?" she asked.

"The Fish have this caustic fog they spray. At first, we all assumed it was an aerosol form of their acid. On closer inspection, we have found it to be organic in nature. It is a quasi-bacterial agent with an aerosol delivery component."

"What does that mean?"

"It's an engineered organism," Steiger said. "Think of an airborne flesh-eating virus, only on steroids. The individual organisms consume anything organic, including cotton and wool. They secret an acid as they do so, causing more damage. You suck some of that in your lungs, the most we can do is remove the affected areas. That was how we ended up losing one of the nurses you are replacing. She got some of that organism on her arm and in a matter of an hour, it had eaten up much of her arm before we were able to stop it."

That was a sobering thought. The weapons that the enemy used were just as dangerous after they were fired as when they were launched. "Is she going to be okay?"

Steiger nodded. "We were able to arrest it. It turns out that it can be neutralized with a little cocktail we cooked up using hydrogen peroxide and alcohol. It doesn't repair the damage. The acid that this virus secrets makes skin grafts and other replacement techniques ineffective, for the most part. She's going to be in a lot of therapy before she can use that arm again. That's a good lesson for you. We have safety procedures; never shortcut them, even if it means saving the life of the patient. The Army is counting on you being able to save a lot of lives. You take a shortcut, you end up being a casualty."

"I heard you were down three nurses."

"Yeah," Steiger said as they moved out of the ward area and into another tent that was staged for medications. "We go in with the field medics from time to time. That means going up to the front. We all try to dodge that kind of duty. The Army's view is that we are filling a need. They are short battlefield medics, probably more than nurses, so sometimes we get the dirty end of the stick and have to go up where the fighting is happening."

Tabitha kept her thoughts to herself. The desire to see combat was hard to suppress—it went beyond curiosity for her. "So they were injured at the front?"

"One, Wendy Baker, was killed up there. They were short on combat medic specialists and she raised her hand to go help. She was stabilizing a patient when their position was overrun. One of the crabs got into the foxhole she was taking cover in and damned near cut her in half. She was good people . . . a damn loss. The other nurse got wounded and is back home recovering. There's no room for heroes up at the front. A lot of Florence Nightingale–types think it's worth the risk, but trust me, it's not. If they ask for volunteers for that kind of assignment, you'd best keep your hand down." While it was sage advice, there was still a part of her that wanted to see the front for herself. *I didn't just join the Army to be a nurse—I joined to help fight the war.*

It was that kind of determination that had helped drive her decision to enlist. A lot of nurses were signing up because of the incentives the Army offered, such as assistance in getting them their doctorates. While it was a good enticement, given she could walk out of the Army a full doctor in three years' time, it wasn't what had driven Tabitha. Her father had been a Marine and had served with distinction in the Russo-Bratva War. Her brother was in the Air Force as a drone pilot. She had joined the Army, much to the chagrin of her father. "At least you didn't follow your brother into the Air Force," he joked, shaking his bowed head. She came from a long line of Thomas family members that had served in the military and felt it was her duty—especially now that America and the rest of the world was being invaded from the seas.

There was that fascination too. These were aliens. Not the kind of threat that Hollywood gloriously capitalized on. There was no magic kill shot on a mother ship that would end the invasion. *We can't even communicate with the Fish.* They were this great unknown and as such mysteries always enticed her. She wanted to see them, explore what made them tick, and if possible, be part of the solution that drove them off of Earth. Even Tabitha admitted it was a fantasy on her part, but becoming an Army nurse was a step towards making that dream closer to reality.

"I came here to help people," she said carefully. "That may take me to the front at some point."

Steiger studied her face for a moment, savoring a bit of her resolve. "I understand. It's my job to keep this hospital staffed as best I can and to save as many lives as possible. If you decide to go off and do something stupid, that's on you. I've warned you what happens when nurses decide to go up there and help out. It is a dangerous place. Here you will face exhaustion. Up there, things are trying to kill you—plain and simple."

The next few weeks of her life was a crash course in relearning her profession. She worked sixteen-hour shifts, during which she learned how to treat and assist the kinds of injuries that the aliens were inflicting. It was intense and emotionally agonizing. Death could come from a dozen different directions when employed by the aliens.

Field surgery was something she was familiar with, though the kinds of injuries were far different from traffic accidents or gun or knife wounds that she had seen before. The Army was still training for a more traditional war, with just a splash of what the aliens were inflicting. That was likely because of the highly fluid state of affairs at the front not reaching back to the rear areas. *What they trained us for is mostly obsolete when it comes to the kinds of things we are facing.*

The sonic weapons they used, the so-called boomers, damaged blood vessels and eardrums. She got the point where she could spot those victims by their crimson-blood-filled eyes or their bleeding ears. There wasn't a lot that could be done to treat them other than pain relievers. The spike weapons they fired were equally horrific. The tiny organic spikes were covered with nasty, almost microscopic barbs. Pulling one out almost did as much damage as when it went in. Worse yet, some of the spikes were treated with toxins. Some were extreme muscle relaxants, which would eventually stop breathing or heartbeat. Others were pain-inducers, lighting up the patient's pain receptors to the point where they were screaming uncontrollably from the agony. She accidentally got poked with a tiny barb through her rubber glove and her arm was numb from a muscle relaxant for two hours as a result.

It was a reminder as to the dangers on the battlefield. *If I had gotten a big enough dose, it could have shut down my heart and lungs.*

Several soldiers were brought in that had suffered electrical shock. Apparently the aliens had begun to employ whip-like weapons that delivered incredible electric shocks when the victims were hit. Word was they could cripple an ASHUR if they hit it, that's how strong the shocks were. They were organic. Sometimes they threw electrified barbs when the whip was cracked, sometimes the whip simply hit the target and juiced it. One patient had been hit in the chest and it had partially melted his dog tags and fried his embedded identification chip that the Army put in every soldier to track them. Even hours after they were hit, the tiny barbs still carried a charge and had to be removed with the use of specially grounded tools and heavy electrical gloves. It was unlike any sort of medical treatment that Tabitha had ever experienced working as a nurse in an ER.

She got to know some of the staff at the field hospital, though only on a limited basis. The problem was that everyone was so busy that you only got to know them professionally. A few were already emotionally strung out; she could see it in their eyes and the curt ways they responded to questions. Burnout was real and there was little relief. She had gotten to know a few of the nurses, but not well. The emotional distancing from the patients tended to spill over with her colleagues. *When you are surrounded by death every day, you don't want to get close to anyone out of fear they will be next.* Tabitha was so exhausted that she collapsed on her cot after every shift, regardless of how much coffee had been flushed into her system.

Adding to the gloom was that they were in coastal Oregon. The skies were gray most of the time and the air was damp, making everything feel slightly moist to the touch. There was a lot of rain and the few times the sun did poke through the clouds, they were usually working and unable to enjoy it. *When the war is over, this is a place I never want to live.*

She had explored all that Drain, Oregon, had to offer—or used to offer. There was a bar that got alcohol once a week via truck. It was usually open only three days before running out of stock. The grocery store and the Dollar General had food, but the prices were outrageous . . . the result of the supply chain being shattered. Many of the locals had fled, but she was surprised how many remained behind. They were sullen, most were thankful that the Army was in their town, but looked forward to them leaving. The townies, as they were called, didn't like to associate much with the military personnel. Rumor was there were a few prostitutes that had set up operations in an old motel, but she wanted nothing to do with them. *I bet the Romans had camp followers that plied that trade wherever the army went.*

Lieutenant Steiger had been a great mentor to her. He checked on her often, gave her useful advice, and had helped her avoid making deadly mistakes. *I must be learning because I don't see him as often as I did when I got here.* One night the off-shift nurses did host an informal party. Alcohol was broken out and a few drinks were shared, along with the contents of several care packages sent by family members. One nurse, Gail Underhill, shared peanut butter cookies that her mother had sent. Tabitha savored every bite, swearing they were the best cookies she had ever eaten. That was what weeks of living out of mess tents could do to a person, make them happy with even mediocre food, just as along as it wasn't prepared by Army cooks.

Gail was the one friend that Tabitha could claim. She had adopted a pit bull puppy that had wandered into camp, naming him Leon. In their off hours, the nurses played with the dog, feeding it, attempting to train it. That puppy meant everything to Gail, a bit of sanity in a place where mental stability was up for grabs.

She wrote emails home. Texting was spotty at best, even with satellite internet. The sheer number of people trying to connect their devices meant a rationing of online access and when you did connect, it was dog-slow. She assured her parents she was doing fine and the messages she got from them dealt with the mundane things happening back home. Her father wanted to know more about the aliens, but the orders from the Army were clear: share nothing about the Fish with the people back home. She knew that the Army was censoring her emails and messages, so there was no point in trying to sneak out any tidbits that her father seemed to want.

At her thirty-day mark, she was brought into Colonel Salz for a quick evaluation. To Tabitha, it was a bit of a joke, but she understood that the Army's administrative machine demanded it. He asked her how she was fitting in and read to her some comments from her peers, all of which were positive and incredibly generic. "She seems to be adapting well and is learning our procedures as expected." The colonel asked how she felt she was doing, and Tabitha was unable to articulate a true response. *How do I tell him that this is fascinating and frightening all at the same time? How do it tell him that I am exhausted from working almost every day and that this place is closing in around me? That my coworkers are mentally fried and that I've gotten used to shitty food or the smell of patients that are dying while they wait their trip to the rear area?* She settled on the word, "Fine," which seemed to be enough for the colonel.

When she was working the post-op ward, some of the patients wanted to talk to her. That was hard on her. They wanted to hear a friendly voice, to engage with some flirting or even just some bland conversation. It was seductive at first. She spent time doing it with some patients, and she found herself getting to know them, even if it was just superficially. Then they left, hauled out by ambulances. It was like ripping a Band-Aid off when they suddenly disappeared. She found herself wondering how they were doing, if they recovered . . . questions she would never learn the answers to. The solution she settled on was to not engage in too much conversation with the patients. It was better for her own state of mind.

Present day . . . six hours earlier
Drain, Oregon

Tabitha was jarred awake by the sound of gunfire in the distance. A Ma Deuce banging away, followed by a few mortar rounds going off, making her cot rattle. The war had been far away, but suddenly it seemed near. These were not faint echoes, they were close at hand. While she had heard the sounds of battle before, echoing like distant thunder over the dense forests that surrounded Drain. Now the fighting sounded nearby and it was a jarring reminder of the proximity of the war. As she made her way to the mess tent, she saw a platoon of armored vehicles rush by on the Umpqua Highway, heading west, towards the sounds of the fighting.

As she ate her reconstituted eggs and toast, fellow nurse Gail Underhill sat down next to her. "Something is going down," she said, dumping three packets of sugar into her coffee.

Tabitha nodded. "Sounds like the enemy is getting close."

"It was that way when we were in Elkton," she said, referencing the town some eight miles to the west. "We had to evacuate when the Fish pushed inland."

"You think they are doing it again?"

Gail sipped the steaming coffee then nodded. "Those sounds you are hearing are only three miles out."

Evacuating the field hospital was no small task. They had plastic shell cases for all of the medications and surgical gear, which was some of the first equipment shipped out. Ambulances came in and were overloaded with patients to be evacced. Enlisted personnel dismantled the tents and the hospital staff quickly packed their personal belongings in their duffels and tossed them into the back of trucks. The highway running east and west was clogged with vehicles heading towards the fighting, and the field hospital trying to head away. All the while, in the background, the sounds of battles grew closer and more ominous. What had begun as an orderly departure from Drain had become more panicked with each passing minute.

The highway's countless potholes made the trucks they rode in rock side-to-side violently. *You would think that after centuries of warfare, they might make a vehicle that was halfway comfortable.*

They arrived in the outskirts of Eugene in a burg called Goshen, two hours later, thanks to the traffic. The colonel and his staff directed the unloading and unpacking in an abandoned RV park. There was a flurry of activity as the tents went up and the search for trucks and transport containers began. Tabitha worked for four hours helping set up the field operating room. When she emerged, she was surprised to see that the camp was almost fully set up, just as it had been in Drain. As a drizzle of light misting rain began to fall, she went to her tent. Both she and Gail's duffels were there. She set up both of their cots and took her things out, folding them and putting them in a crate that served as a dresser.

At dinner, they ate MREs, the mess staff had not fully set up the kitchen yet. As she ate, Lieutenant Steiger sat down across from her. "Well, that was fun."

"We do this often?" she asked jokingly.

"Every now and then. We were lucky. According to the colonel, we beat the Fishes overrunning us by a matter of an hour."

"That close, eh?" she said, finishing off her beef stew from the MRE.

"From what I've been told, Drain is now the front line." Steiger paused, then looked around the tent. "Have you seen Gail?"

Tabitha looked around. "No, I haven't," she said as the realization hit her. "Not since we were loading up."

Steiger rose to his feet. "Go out and look for her on the south side of the camp. I'll take the north. I'll meet you at the CP." There was an urgency in his voice that told her that something might be wrong.

Sprinting through the camp, she asked three other nurses and one doctor—no one had seen her bunkmate and friend. *Shit, shit shit!* Her breath was ragged as she entered the hospital CP. Steiger came in right after her. "No luck?"

Tabitha shook her head and struggled for her breath. Her hair and uniform were wet from the falling rain outside. She ignored that. Gail was gone. *She never got on the trucks.*

Steiger turned and opened the flap into the Colonel's office. "Sir, we have a problem. One of our people is unaccounted for. I ran her ID chip and she's nowhere near the base." Every soldier not only wore dog tags but was chipped by the army. It allowed for better tracking by battlespace commanders and identification of remains should they die. The chips even tracked if the person was alive or not.

"How in the hell did that happen?" Colonel Salz asked.

Tabitha stepped in. *It had to be Leon, the puppy.* She wasn't about to say that the colonel. "It doesn't matter, sir, she isn't here."

"We are going to have a long discussion how we evacuated our position and left an officer behind, understood?"

Steiger nodded. The colonel still looked angry yet almost fatherly for a long moment. "Well, we need to get her back."

"Can you contact the front and see if they have her?" Steiger said.

"You've been to the front before. It's not like they have a lost and found up there. This is our problem . . . our people. We need to send a patrol out there and bring her back."

Tabitha heard the words and spoke before she could think it through. "I'd like to go, sir." Steiger's head snapped around and he glared at her, but held his tongue.

"Agreed, she may need medical aide. I'm sending a GRD driver and one of our security personnel for protection. You get up there, see if you can find her. If you can't, get your ass back here."

They exited the office and Steiger grabbed her arm. "You shouldn't be going."

"She's my friend."

"I told you not to volunteer, and you turned around and did just that."

"I'll be fine," she lied. There was no way to know what she had just agreed to. The thought of other people going after Gail was something that should could not tolerate.

"You watch your ass out there," he said sternly. "Don't try to play hero."

Nodding, she headed out to change her uniform to her green STGs. For the first time since coming to the front, she slid in her blast plates which pressed hard against her breasts. Her helmet felt heavy and awkward as always, but she tightened the chinstrap to make sure it was snug. Her last additions were several spare magazines.

Two hours later . . .

One thing that Tabitha had determined was that Sergeant Kant had only one setting—intense. During their ride back towards Drain in the Jolt scout vehicle, she had asked him about himself, but he only glared at her. He was an older infantryman, old school, and was armed with an ACR complete with laser sights, stackable grenades, and a sawed-off shotgun that was in an obvious custom holster. Sergeant Kant was clearly not happy at having been assigned to escort her back towards the sound of gunfire. While she found his attitude grating, she also fully understood it. *To him, I'm just a nurse that is dragging his ass to where he might get killed.*

The GRD driver that accompanied them, Corporal McGowan, was far chattier. He had brought along a single drone, named Scrappy-Doo 301. GRDs always had custom, if not goofy, names that their drivers picked. The drone was a Husky-class GRD, with a boxy body that had been rigged for a stretcher drag to get the wounded out of the battlespace. It had compartments big enough to carry ammo or even a Carl Gustaf, if necessary. McGowan was edgy, either wired up on caffeine or incredibly nervous—possibly a mix of the two.

Tabitha had taken an ACR and an M18 sidearm for protection. She had fired both weapons a lifetime ago, back in basic training. Her father had taught her to shoot at the age of six, so firearms were not something that intimidated her. While she had no intention of getting into a situation where she would need to use them. If she did, she was confident in her ability to use them effectively. In her mind, it was a matter of getting to the front, locating Gail, and getting out as fast as possible.

They had to stop outside of Drain because of both the traffic jam and the proximity of the fighting. McGowan got the Jolt off of the road and hidden in a thicket of pine trees. They quickly made their way back to where the field hospital had been established. It was a muddy mess with several Humvees using it as a parking lot. A mortar crew was relocating to the rear carrying their ammunition and tube to a spot further to the rear. The cracks of shots were ringing out everywhere. Several foxholes had been dug as well in the black wet soil and Tabitha could see soldiers continuing to dig and improve their positions.

An ASHUR rig, a King Cobra, marched nearby, moving into the woods on the opposite side of the road where their Jolt was parked. It ignored the low hanging limbs, bending and breaking them as it walked on through. It was oddly reassuring that the ASHUR was there; it provided a sense of security.

Following Sergeant Kant, they all bent low and moved fast with the GRD running just ahead of them. McGowen knelt down and worked his drone and communications controls as the rumble of artillery shook the trees all around them. "I'm getting a hit on Lieutenant Underhill's chip," he said. "According to my readings, she is sixty-two yards that direction." He pointed to the woods in front of them where the gunfire seemed to be emanating from.

Tabitha looked at the woods and gathered her will. "Let's move," she said as she started heading that direction. Sergeant Kant moved in front of her. Kant almost fell in a trench that was cut across their route. She remembered it from when she had explored the perimeter of the camp—it was a deep drainage ditch that had been dug to keep water away from the field hospital. Now it was part of the defensive front line. One of the infantry in the trench glared at him angrily but did not offer any assistance.

There was a hissing sound from ahead, and she glanced up, catching sight of what looked like a grayish beam. It stabbed at the trees above them, severing several with a cracking noise. The big pines collapsed downward, right at them, boughs ripping off on the way down, snapping loudly. Their small group jumped for cover as one tree fell right where they had been standing, plowing deep into the wet soil and dead pine needles with a thud.

Tabitha lay in the wet ground, a small limb draped across her legs. Getting one leg free, she used her boot to push against the limb to free her other leg. It ached from the hit, and she checked it with her hands, making sure that no bones were broken. *That had to be one of the alien cutter beams.* Worse, it had come from the direction they were heading in. She picked up her helmet and put it back on and found the rest of her small team. Only McGowen showed any signs of being shaken by the incident. "Damn, that was close."

"Keep low," Kant said as he moved forward. The Husky GRD bounded ahead of them, running in autonomous mode. They came down a small hillside and saw a machine-gun position some twenty yards in front of them. Spent brass littered the ground as the gun banged away. Lying next to their position was an alien crab. It was the size of a truck, oily green in color, ripped open by what she presumed was artillery or grenades. Its internal organs did not look like anything she could remotely identify; there were bulbous tubes similar to a distorted version of an intestine, all covered with a strange white webbing. A purple basketball-sized internal component was oozing a black blood-like substance. There was a smell in the air, semi-sweet mixed with the aroma of old fish.

The sound of incoming mortar rounds made them all dive for cover. The foxhole they had chosen was a shallow mucky mess, but it didn't matter as the explosions went off at dangerously close ranges. The purr of a distant chain gun mixed with the gunfire and the muffled explosions of grenades. Looking down, she saw a soldier laying against the side of the foxhole, his body limp. One of the alien needle projectiles had gone between two of his STG blast plates. Learning in, she used her tactical gloves to carefully extract it, checking him for a pulse. As she did, he groaned audibly. With his eyes still closed, he muttered, "Damn that hurts." *Great—he's alive.* "We need to get this guy back for medical attention," she said to Sergeant Kant who hugged the side of the foxhole for cover as another explosion went off nearby, mixing with machine-gun fire from where the camp had been. No doubt it was the Humvees they had passed. Their tracers lit the drizzle-filled air, streaking overhead.

"He's going to be fine. TDDB," Kant snapped, crawling up to the edge of the hole to see if he could spot the enemy.

"What in the world is TDDB?" she said.

"Later. We're here for Lieutenant Underhill," he growled.

"Her chip says that she's only ten yards or so in front of us," McGowan said.

"Send in your Husky," Kant said. "Let's get some eyes on her before we rush up towards the enemy."

McGowan used his digipad to activate Scrappy Doo. "Going manual on this one," he muttered more to himself than to his foxhole mates. The GRD rose up to the lip of the hastily dug hole, then darted off. McGowan's fingers slid all over the display as he guided it.

"Eyes on the prize," he said after a few minutes. Turning the pad around they could make out the form of Lieutenant Underhill, curled up in a ball. Right next to her was Leon, nuzzling her. "Her chip is showing her as alive," he said proudly.

Sergeant Kant looked over at Tabitha with a stern expression on his face. "We are going to do this by the book. I've got point. You and McGowan follow me. We move fast and low, understood?"

She nodded. One thing she had learned in the Army was to trust the sergeants, especially the old ones. Chances were pretty good that Kant had served in the last war. His face alone seemed to speak of experience. This was not the time to start throwing her rank around.

"Alright then," the sergeant said. "Stick to my ass like a hemorrhoid." He rose and set off after the GRD.

Tabitha followed, almost sliding on the wet mud. They darted around a trio of thick pines and ducked under some other low limbs to reach a spot where a tree had fallen, probably in the last winter. It had ripped a natural foxhole and the roots, filled with soil, made a natural shield.

She spotted Gail and checked her pulse. *Where are you hit?* Then she spotted it, a blood spot on her right thigh. Digging in her belt she pulled out a pair of scissors from her medical gear and cut the uniform cloth. Three large barbs were stuck in Gail's thigh. They were black and nasty looking with jagged little hooks that tore at her flesh.

I've seen this before—this is from one of their electrical whip weapons. The barbs were nasty on their own, but experience had taught her that if she touched them, it would set off an electrical charge. Based on their size, it might be enough to knock her out too. Tabitha looked at her tactical gloves, now soaked, and knew they would only assist in the conductivity of any shock.

"Let's strap her to the Husky and get out of here," Sergeant Kant said.

"We can't," she insisted. "Not until those barbs are out of her."

"Then pull them out," he snapped.

"They have an electrical charge. We move them and we will trigger it."

Kant seemed to understand. He fumbled with his own belt and pulled out a utility tool with thick rubber handles. "It's not much on insulation but it's the best I've got."

Tabitha took it from him and examined it. *It's not like I have a lot of choice up here.* She carefully opened the pliers and reached for the first barb. As she pulled it, she saw the bright blue spark as it discharge and Gail's body twitched as she jerked it free. *It's best to get these out fast then deal with the damage.* She pulled them all, feeling a tingling sensation in her fingertips as the last one came out.

Handing the tool back to the sergeant, she grabbed a freezer pack and chemical suture and attached them to the wound. The cold would slow down any bleeding for a while, long enough to get her out of there. As she finished, there was a high-pitched whining sound and then a series of explosions. *Mortar fire!* She leaned over Gail to shelter her from the rain of dirt and dead pine needles that fell in on them. It was close . . . too close for her tastes.

"Let's strap her to the Husky," she said and McGowan moved to help her. He rigged a dead-pull using a blanket and two expandable carbon rods he had taken out of Scrappy Doo's body. It was not going to be a comfortable ride, but it would be better than them carrying her out. Besides, they still had another soldier they left behind they had to get out. Tabitha checked her friend and was encouraged that her pulse was steady.

Leon whimpered as another mortar round went off nearby. *We have to get him out of here too.* The thought of leaving the dog to its fate on the battlefield was too disturbing to contemplate. "Can you fit him inside the Husky?" she asked McGowan as they carefully placed Lieutenant Underhill on the drag.

"Uh—sure," he said. It took both of them to get Leon into the compartment; his tail and legs tried to prevent it from closing several times.

Suddenly she felt a presence, something looming over her. Whipping around, she saw a figure standing atop the broken bits of root from the fallen tree. It looked massive. Its face was that of a frog or toad, its claw-like webbed hands were dangerous on their own—but it held some sort of organic staff or rod. Its bulging eyes shimmered a little bit from the tracer fire of the machine guns, appearing yellow and black.

The frogman grunted, deep and throbbing. The sac under its chin inflated slightly as it swung the rod it carried downward.

Sergeant Kant cleared his shotgun and opened up with three shots that sounded like one continuous burst, they came so fast. Tabitha pulled her M18 from its holster and emptied the magazine as well, her shops tearing into the bulbous sac and throat of the creature as the sergeant's blasts made the flabby body of the creature ripple under their hundreds of shotgun pellet impacts.

It stopped moving and for a second, everything went strangely quiet. Kant switched to his ACR, this time opening up with burst fire as Tabitha shifted to put herself between the alien and Gail. The sergeant's shots riddled the already chewed-up center torso of the frog, almost cutting it in half. The creature fell forward, limp and lifeless, one of its claws landing on Tabitha. She panicked, if only for a moment, and pulled it off. A tacky cold gray-green goo remained, what she assumed was blood. Her STG was smeared with it and the stickiness was greasy.

"Time to go," Kant said, putting in another magazine.

There were no arguments from her. McGowan stabbed away at his digipad. "I set the waypoint to the Jolt. Scrappy Doo will take her there."

The Husky moved, dragging Gail behind it. From inside the metal body, Leon barked wildly. The GRD took off before they cleared the edge of the makeshift cover. Tabitha darted, moving side to side as she had been trained to do in basic. The roar of the gunfire all around her made her ears ache, but she slogged on, heading back to their first foxhole. Over the explosions and the crack-rattle of gunfire, she heard more grunting, as she had heard with the frog. This was louder, as if there were a dozen or so making the noise in unison.

Jumping into the first foxhole, she was followed by McGowan, then by Kant. The GRD continued on, moving in wide sweeping arcs, heading back to their ride. "What are we doing here?" Sergeant Kant asked.

"We're taking him," she said, gesturing the injured man she had treated.

Kant glared at her and there was a moment when she wondered if he was just going to outright refuse her command. He certainly looked as if he wanted to. Instead he moved in next to the wounded man, shouldered his ACR and squatted down. The injured man was shifted to his shoulder and the sergeant rose up.

Tabitha rushed on. An inhuman shriek echoed off the trees around her and over the banging and booming of the fight. She wasn't sure what it was, and refused to turn and look behind her to see. Her only hope was that whatever had made the noise was dead.

It took a few minutes more to reach the Jolt. Gail and Scrappy Doo were already there, just as McGowan promised. Leon was barking inside the drone. *This is probably the only time one of these Hounds has actually barked.* She got down and with the corporal's help, managed to get Gail laid out in the back. She then assisted Kant in moving the other soldier in next to her. She reached down to check him, but he moaned loudly, wincing in pain. "He's fine," Kant assured him. "TDDB."

Another trio of men came over. "You taking wounded?" the one in the middle, limping on one leg asked as his comrades assisted him. He nodded at the white-backed red cross on the side of the transport.

"We're loaded," Sergeant Kant said.

She glared at the older man again, then turned to them. "Climb on board."

The Jolt had been designed as a light fast recon vehicle. It barely could hold four. Gail and Kant assisted the others in, laying them like logs onto and on top of the Gail and the other man there. There was no time to evaluate their injuries; Gail needed help and that was what mattered the most.

The Jolt's suspension sagged under the weight. McGowan and Tabitha shared the passenger seat while Kant took the wheel. He kept his GRD next to the vehicle in heel mode. Kant started the Jolt and it struggled at first to get moving, let alone build up speed.

Six hours later ...
Field Hospital 222, Goshen, Oregon

Tabitha shifted in her folding chair next to Gail's cot. Her friend's color had returned to her face and she seemed far more stable. Leon was back in their tent, McGowan had gotten him some food after checking back in. She had reported back to the colonel when they had returned. The older officer didn't say much; his focus was helping her get the wounded inside for triage and treatment.

Gail stirred slightly and Tabitha reached out to her hand that was being fed with an IV, and gave her a squeeze. Gail wearily looked up, cracking her eyes open slowly. "I must be dreaming," she said. "Last thing I remember was being hit and seeing stars."

"We got you home," Tabitha assured her. "You're going to be fine."

"Hurts like all hell," Gail said, trying to move.

"Just lie here and relax."

"Where's Leon?"

Tabitha smiled. "Safe and sound in our tent."

With those words, Gail slid back to sleep. Tabitha rose and saw Sergeant Kant standing at the foot of the bed. He had changed out of his STGs into a fresh set of fatigues. He actually looked relaxed for the first time since she had met him. "She'll be fine," he assured her. "TDDB."

"You've been saying that for some time. I don't have down all of the military acronyms still. Just when I think I have them mastered, people whip out new ones. What the green Army hell is TDDB."

Kant grinned. "The Dead Don't Bitch," he said with a single chuckle. Tabitha smiled. *Well, he's right about that.*

THE NATURE OF BAIT

The depths of the oceans have always been a dangerous place. It has never been the domain of humankind. There are vast stretches of the ocean floor that have never been explored. It is the homeland of the alien Fish in the Land&Sea universe. While the aliens have developed biological tech to come ashore, mankind has developed the means to take the war under the seas. Going deep, however, comes at risk. This is, after all, the aliens' home field . . .

Mission N101—Ryback 001
USCGC *Mesquite*, eight miles off the coast of
Vandenberg AFB, California

Lieutenant Rita "Bubbles" Kraus was aboard the USCGC *Mesquite*, pacing around her Moray, double-checking every joint and attachment on the undersea Trident . . . the deep water equivalents of the ground-based ASHURs. She had been one of the first Moray pilots, something she was proud of. It was one of the few times in her life that her short stature had actually qualified her for something, rather than ruling her out.

She had been chaffing for a chance to go out and fight the enemy, and that time had finally come. There was some tension that came from it. Not only would she be facing the Fish, she also had to contend with additional risk factors. The Moray was still classified as a prototype. The pilots that used them liked to think of themselves as test pilots. The biggest difference was that if a new model of jet somehow failed, a pilot could eject and land safely. If something went wrong on the ocean floor, there was no ejection. Death was cold, dark, and sometimes ago-nizingly slow. If you dared to try to leave the suit, no easy task, despite the drugs pumped into pilots, you still risked the bends. "Nature, the aliens, and the tech can and will conspire against you," or so one of her instructors had told her. So she took the time to check every aspect of the suit before it was pressed into action.

The *Mesquite* had begun its career as a buoy tender but had just been refitted into a Trident carrier. There were four rigs on board, and they could be lowered in a small rack/cage down and deployed. Like the Moray, every bit of that hardware was prototype as well. There were other risks as well. Ships were easy targets for the Fish and they had dozens of ways they could be attacked and destroyed from below. *There's about a million things that can go wrong for everything that can go right on a dive.*

As she moved around the Spindrift—the metal array that raised and lowered the Trident suits into the water; she saw that Lieutenant Anton "Deadlock" Gunther was doing the same with his Stonefish. The dull gray with streaked white and black highlights on the Stonefish were similar to those on her Moray. Both had a humanoid shape, but the Moray was sleeker, a little squatter. It had thrusters worn like a backpack and on the shins. The Stonefish was bulkier, thicker, more ominous-looking, with microtorpedo racks on both shoulders. It had a six-round spear gun launcher on top of the right forearm. It had maneuvering thrusters on the underside of both arms as well. The Stonefish had the range, but the Moray was devastating at closer ranges.

The other two Tridents were Tigersharks. They were smaller than her Moray, had an almost anime armored suit look to them in her mind. The Tigersharks were the first official Tridents and could be configured with a number of different underwater weapons. While they might have looked sleeker than her Moray, she'd developed a fondness for her rig.

She admired Gunther, and with good reason. It wasn't just his chiseled looks. The SEAL officer had been in the pilot program of testing the Tridents at DARPA. Glancing over at her, he gave a nod. "Everything look good on your ride?"

Kraus nodded as she spoke. "It's a virgin rig. So far, everything looks fine."

"They are all virgins," he countered, running his hand back through his short blond hair. "When we were testing these things at pressure, we learned that it wasn't the things you saw that could kill you. If there's a failure, chances are you will never see it coming."

She understood the risks all too well. Getting permission to even sign up for the Trident program was reserved for people in the peak physical condition and was on a volunteer basis. Your CO had to believe in you enough to put his name on your candidacy. The first pilots had been SEALs, but many, like Kraus, were failed SEAL candidates. It was a chance to serve on something that only the elite could. Her inability to meet the physical standards for the SEALs had been a big disappointment to her. There had been some shame she had endured. Getting approved for the Trident program was an act of redemption. She wore the Trident badge with pride. "I understand. I lost a knee seal during one of my tests." Memories of that incident were seared in her mind. *I thought I was going to drown in my rig. If I hadn't gotten that emergency patch on in time, I might have.*

"I hear you. I had a leak in my battery and lost power," Gunther said.

"It would be nice if we had some more time to train together as a team."

Gunther cracked a cockeyed smile. "Welcome to the Navy. Nothing like on-the-job learning."

Kraus checked her chronometer. "Time for the briefing," she muttered. Gunther finished his ad hoc inspection and followed her to the new CIC for undersea operations that had been built in the ship. It was dimly lit, cramped, with the centerpiece being a massive digital table with limited holographic capabilities. The monitors on the walls provided sonar and sensor data, as well as the status of the four Tridents that were on the deck. Rita was impressed with the fact that the Navy had refit the room so fast. *War has a way of getting the usual bureaucracy to act and move quickly.*

The other two other pilots were Chief Petty Officers Marc "Crackle" Lidell and Ric "Flashbang" Demars already stood over the digital table map display. Captain Jamie McKenna, an imposing ebony-skinned man made of muscles and scorn stood with crossed arms at the head of the map table. "Nice of you to take time out of your busy schedule to join us."

They weren't late, but Rita knew enough not to respond to the barb. As they shifted around the table, she saw the vicinity where the *Mesquite* was hovering, only from an ocean floor perspective.

"Welcome to Op, Ryback 001," McKenna began, his deep booming voice seemed to envelop the room. "As you know, we are eight miles off the California coast. The Fish have had a burr up their asses to take out Vandenberg Air Force Base since the start of the war. Say what you want about the Air Force boys, their security forces have put up a hell of a fight to keep that base. The Fish keep throwing troops at them, including one of their big-ass Cthugas. They have relocated the joyboys and their drones out of there, but the Air Force keeps holding the base. I guess old habits die hard; that, or the folks at the Pentagon think that holding a base right at the water's edge is a good idea strategically. That is for greater minds to ponder."

McKenna shifted on his feet. "The wonderful folks at Naval Intelligence noticed a bit of a pattern with their attacks. They seem to come in cycles of around four weeks. For those of you thinking of checking your calendars, I'll save you that time—it is any day now. As such, this mission calls for you to drop and determine if they are staging for another attack. If they are prepping for an attack, you are authorized to disrupt that to the best of your abilities, within what are considered reasonable risks."

"Sir," CPO Demars spoke up. "What defines 'reasonable risks'?"

"Common sense," the captain replied, making sure he made eye contact with everyone in the room. "Ryback 001 is not intended to be an all-out spoiler attack. To be blunt, we need everyone to get more time in their rigs and working in that environment. If they are planning an attack, you are going to give everyone topside some time to plan a defense."

"If there's a pattern, aren't they sure an attack is coming?" Gunther asked.

The captain nodded once. "Perhaps. Patterns with the Fish are difficult to interpret. There's a probability that the intel people got it wrong . . . that the Fish are moving onto greener pastures along this front. If they are not down there in force, troops could be reallocated to other fronts. San Diego and La are still a hot mess with expanding AIZs. So some eyes on targets would be of great benefit.

"Regardless of that, you will be going down there to take a look-see. If you see them readying to come, get the word to us and hightail it out of there. Questions?"

There were a few—mostly dealing with possible recovery logistics, operating depth, ocean current strength and direction, oxygen mix, mission duration and extraction details . . . not the kinds of things that ASHUR pilots had to address. They spent nearly an hour going over the map of the area where the *Mesquite* would be dropping them. They were given their first shots of Deep, a drug that had been developed to combat the bends. Another would be administered right before their drop. The Navy claimed it prevented the bends in 60 percent of the cases, which wasn't great in Rita's mind, but it would have to do.

When they finished, they went on the deck as the ship maneuvered out to its position. It was midafternoon with light clouds, making the sun warm. Before she began to suit up, Rita soaked in the rays and enjoyed the moment.

Lieutenant Gunther moved alongside her. "I'll never get used to the thought that we are already in enemy territory just being at sea."

"The world is turned upside down," she conceded, surveying the horizon. "Three quarters of the planet is ocean. We've fought down there in subs but never against an enemy that called that place home."

"I always felt comfortable working underwater," the SEAL officer said. "Our training makes us comfortable. Yes, we know the risks, but we prepare for facing those. Now when I go deep, I get a little paranoid."

"I was never prouder than when I got to try out for the SEALs. I embraced working underwater because it was required. Now I'm going back, just under different terms."

"You didn't make the cut?" There was enough surprise in his voice that she appreciated the question.

"In the end, I didn't have the endurance."

"Tridents require the same if not more of that."

It was true. Despite the enhanced hydraulics and power systems, just moving and adjusting pitch underwater was a challenge. It pushed the pilot to the limit. "I don't know how I made the cut, but I did. Damn glad I did too. Most of the Navy is shore bound right now, sidelined until we get better at fighting underwater. I'm glad to be one of the first."

"Watch yourself down there," Gunther said, turning away from the rail. "It's a dark and lonely place and even if help is close by, it is going to take time."

She turned and watched him walk away, then took one more glance at the ocean before joining him. *It's deep and cold down there, but I'm from Minnesota. I can handle it.*

Two hours later…

Rita shrugged her shoulders inside her Moray, just to make sure that it was still snug. Access to her Trident was through a rear hatch and on the surface, requiring two assistants. Most of the other assaults utilized the *Volturnus*, a large manned docking bay that assisted with decompression. The Spindrift was filling that task, without all of the bells and whistles. It was a heavy-duty cage with external power and emergency air feeds, if needed. It didn't have a downside crew but was little more than an exposed elevator down to the ocean floor. Checking her docking clamps on the arms of her rig, she saw they were still secure to the Spindrift.

"Commencing dive," came Captain McKenna's voice. The Spindrift sloshed into the water and she braced herself, more out of instinct than necessity.

The ride down was a drop into darkness. Rita kept monitoring her systems, checking her sensors for any sign of the enemy. Several times the Spindrift slowed to an almost stop, then it would continue the winch-driven ride down.

At one point, Demars spoke up. "I think the naming of our mission is good luck."

"How's that?" Rita asked.

"Ryback . . . you know, Casey Ryback . . . from *Under Siege?*"

"What is that?" Gunther asked.

"Only one of the best movies ever made!"

"Never heard of it," weighed in Lidell.

"Me either," Rita added.

"You guys are killing me," Demars moaned.

She was shaking her head, amazed at the thoughts that warriors have when under pressure. *When we get back, I'll have to check it out.*

Finally, after almost two hours, there was a gentle thud under them as the cage came to rest. Lieutenant Gunther had local command of the mission, with Captain McKenna acting as battlespace commander. A few minutes later, he shattered the silence of their dive with his crisp and clean command voice. "Alright, people—get your lights on. We will proceed west by northwest with Demars in the point. Kraus, you are in the number two slot, then me, and Lidell, you have the rear. Lidell, every 80 yards, deploy a comms drone. I want to make sure we can still communicate with topside. I've dumped the waypoints for this drop into your nav systems. Unless we are engaged, stick to these."

Communications underwater was a hot mess and while some innovations had been made, it could still get spotty. Like everything at that depth, everything was questionable. She toggled on her external lights and got her first view of where they had landed. There was no plant life at this depth, simply sand and stones and darkness beyond the limits of her Moray's LED lights. There was a stark, almost barren emptiness around her. *This is as close to being on another planet as I'm ever going to get.*

Rita disengaged from the Spindrift with a hiss and click and leaned forward, switching power to her thrusters. The Moray listed forward slightly and she adjusted her arms downward, the thrusters keeping her leaning forward as she slowly floated away. The suit's computer adjusted the ballast balancing controls as the Moray began to float over the surface of the ocean floor, stirring some of the fine particles from the ocean floor as she moved.

Adjusting her stance with a little leaning, she swung in behind Demars's Tigershark. They were in no hurry, and Demars was setting the pace. Her own passive sonar display showed that Gunther was in behind her, per the plan. The hum and whir of her thrusters slowly shifted into background noise to her. She listened for other sounds in her rig, something that might indicate trouble. *So far, so good.* For twenty-two minutes, they slowly made their way to the first two waypoints. Her eyes moved in a trained pattern, from the nav screen to the tactical display, to rig status screen, then to the small engineering panel to check power, then to weapons. She no longer even thought about the pattern, it was just how her head worked.

Suddenly Demars rose upright. "Contact—sonar. At 301 degrees. I'm picking up movement," he said coolly.

Rita checked her own sensors. There it was a faint flicker at the maximum range. "Confirmed. Movement, organic, now at 310." A part of her hoped it was a Terran fish, but the size was big, which meant the other kind of Fish—the alien kind.

"Weapons hot," Gunther said. She reached out and toggled the power shunt to her weapons, then slid her arm back inside its control sleeve.

"Motion is slowing," Demars said. "Moving right in front of me. I now have a second signal closing with the first."

"You getting this, Bubbles?" Gunther asked, using her call sign. She hated that call sign—she had gotten it when she had seen a stream of bubbles rising from a suit during training and overreacted, thinking she had a leak in her rig. It was actually a stream of bubbles from the training tank itself.

She eyed her sonar screen carefully. "I only have the first target and it is at my extreme range."

There was a pause, long enough for her to wonder if she had lost comms. Before she verified, Lieutenant Guther's voice came back. "This is Golden Eye Actual," came the voice of Captain McKenna from the *Mesquite*. "I am assuming these targets are hostile. Let's assume a pyramid formation." Hearing his deep voice was a reminder that he was monitoring what was unfolding far beneath his ship.

"Roger that, Golden Eye," Gunther said. "You heard the man. Pyramid. Bubbles, you are top point; Crackle, you go right; I'll take left. Flashbang, you hold your position." The shift to call signs was an indication that the situation was changing, as if she needed any validation of that.

Rita adjusted her arm and leg thrusters and increased their power slightly. The Moray rose upward, rising to a position above her teammates by twenty feet. She set that as her depth and the suit's computer moved to a hover mode, adjusting her ballast system accordingly. Her tactical display showed that her counterparts were deployed in an almost perfect pyramid formation.

"I'm getting motion," Lidell said. "It is shifting to the same area as Demars. That makes three contacts."

Another minute passed.

"They are just sitting here at the edge of our sonar range," Demars said. "What are they up to?"

Captain McKenna's voice came over the communications channel. "Can the chatter, Flashbang," he ordered. "Deadlock, what is your assessment?"

Gunther's voice was short and to the point. "There are three possibilities. They are either moving to a defensive posture, they are awaiting reinforcements before attacking, or they are trying to lure us in for an attack on their terms."

His words were sobering. The Fish were often portrayed as animals, creatures lacking in human qualities. Listening to Lieutenant Gunther's description of the situation implied thought, planning, even cunning. *Are they trying to lure us into a trap? Have we stumbled onto something they are forced to defend against? What the hell are they up to?*

"Advance on the enemy at your discretion," McKenna signaled back.

There wasn't a hint of hesitation in the SEAL's voice. "Alright, people, we are moving in slow. Keep your eyes peeled for motion on our flanks or from above."

Rita adjusted her stance and thrusters as they crept along towards the source of the signals. Usually in her thermal suit that she wore, the Moray was always cold. Now, however, she felt beads of sweat forming on her brow. Her eyes ran through her routine, concentrating on her tactical display, looking for any hint of enemy movement.

"They are just standing there, waiting," Demars said, less out of amazement than out of fear.

"Look sharp," Gunther said.

"In range, no visual yet," Demars said.

Would Gunther want to get confirmation of what they were facing first, or would he simply want them taken out? She got her answer quick. "Take them out, Flashbang," he ordered.

She saw the thin stream of tiny bubbles from the Tigershark's microtorpedoes as they launched. They moved fast, not bullet-fast, but quick. In a moment, they were in the darkness, outside of the sphere of their light. She saw the flash of explosions in the blackness in front of them.

Her sonar showed the trio of signals suddenly move, quickly, right at the Ryback 001 team. "Here they come," came Lidell's voice, followed with, "Firing."

Her Moray was designed for close-in combat, so the deep-sea firefight that erupted was something she only got to witness from afar. The Fish finally closed in enough to be illuminated. The DoD gave them a formal classification, but they knew them by the name that the Trident pilots gave them—Mermen. They had four crab-like legs that were flattened out to act like flippers, with larger fish-like fins in the mid-section. Like their legendary mermaid counterparts, they had arms that extended out with deadly claws that were also finned to assist in propulsion. Their heads were not human at all, but triangular and armored with shell-like covering. They were a greenish-white in color and moved fast, closing on Demars almost instantly, slashing at his Tigershark rig, knocking him off-balance.

Lidell fired a trio of his own microtorpedoes into the sides of one of the Mermen. Their warheads were explosive, flashing yellow as they tore into the flesh of the creature. A spray of what she considered blood swirled in the water. The one that was hit withered and broke off the attack for a moment—long enough for Gunther to hit it with a pair of speargun darts . . . adding to the green-black swirls of gore in the water. The wounded Merman broke off his attack, paddling weakly to get some distance from the Tridents.

Rita watched her sensors and what she was witnessing. She wanted to drop down and join the foray, but knew better. Battles, even those underwater, were not wild melees. Discipline was the key, no matter how much she hated it.

Demars's Tigershark fell down, kicking up a cloud of dirt, obscuring vision. Lidell unleashed his ultrasonic blaster. *He must think that Demars is clear of the shot.* The weapon in the arm of the Tigershark emitted massive ripples in the water and a deep, almost throbbing, noise. The ripples hit the two Mermen that were tearing into Demars, forcing them to break off their attack.

Gunther unleased a pair of his microtorpedoes at one of the aliens. One missed entirely, exploding behind the Merman. The other struck low on the torso. It was a small explosion and a brilliant white flash—

clearly a microwave warhead. The alien twisted and contorted in the water, swirling more dirt from the ocean floor.

Suddenly her eyes picked up motion at her level, coming in from the right. It was a large target, moving fast, right at her. "Contact—coming in at 15 fast. It's big." She cursed her last two words. *I know better—that isn't how to report a contact.* She pivoted her Moray to face the incoming threat.

It came at her, black as night, shaped like a man. "Aw shit—a Boss! Tagging him for tactical." The big ebony killers were the scorn of Trident and ASHUR pilots. It was swimming right at her like an incoming torpedo. The deep etched groves in its body shimmered orange, making him look like an orange streak in the water.

Rita swung her left arm in line with the Boss and triggered the microwave emitter. An explosive shell went off in the weapon's generator, giving her the spike of additional power she was going to need for the shot. The water rippled between the two of them as the beam hit the alien. Its head twisted to aside, but it didn't slow. Instead it came right at her Moray, hitting her as it charged past with one of its big claws. The sound of the claw scraping along the side of her Moray was jarring and she lost her balance for a few moments, fighting the suit and the crushing water around her as her rig attempting to regain balance.

The Boss had swum past her and put some distance between the two of them. She hoped that the microwave blast had taken some of the aggressiveness out of her attacker, but he twisted in place and started for another run. *Shit!*

Aiming as he came in, she opened up again with the microwave emitter. The power shell went off with a bang and she saw the green spike on the weapon display as she steadied her shot. This time she went for a prolonged burst, the wave of energy slamming into her adversary as he closed. *Come on, bastard—die.*

He rolled into a ball and then sprang at her, coming at a lower angle. The massive alien grappled with her for a moment, seeming to try to rip the left arm off the Trident. She could hear the actuators protest as the claws tore at her arm and the emitter there. She swung with her free arm, hitting it in the narrow crimson eye slit on its face.

It stabbed at her with its claws again as she toppled backwards. With the thrusters misaligned, her Moray dropped, back first, toward the ocean floor. Her back muscles flexed as she tried to break off from the Boss. Damage warnings went off on her right arm, showing that the microwave emitter was off-line. The sickening sound of protesting metal told her that much.

As she collided with the silt, Rita played a hunch and fired off a power round for the emitter. The bang filled the inside of her suit and no doubt the Boss heard it as well. It was enough to get him to break off the attack, unsure what she would unleash next.

It gave her a millisecond to assess her situation. No leaks, but the left arm of her rig was oozing a thin spray of pinkish hydraulic fluid above her. The enemy was still out there, probably getting ready for another run. All she had left was her right arm plasma cutter. *I've got to get upright, now!*

Her abs flexed to make the Moray bend slightly at the waist as she fired her thrusters. The muddy waters swirled around her as she rolled over, then rose to her feet. Damage displays for her right arm showed the leak of hydraulic fluid finally, flashing yellow on her status display. Her sonar picked up only her teammates, who were closing on her. *Maybe the Boss had enough . . . or he's waiting for the right moment for another run.*

"You okay, Bubbles?" Lieutenant Gunther asked. He moved beside her. Behind him she saw Lidell helping keep Demars rig upright.

"My right arm and weapon are toast."

"Can you maneuver without it?"

The thrusters in the arm were functional, but aiming it was going to be a laborious and ultimately would fail. Trident pilots trained for such situations in simulation, but this—this was the real world. "I've got this," Rita insisted, flexing her arm with all her might to adjust the pitch. "What are your orders?"

"Flashbang's rig is extra crispy," he said. "They attached something to it and it shorted out his computer. I didn't see any indication that his Trident is breached, so we have to assume he's alive." She glanced over as sweat trickled down to the corners of her eyes, stinging her. On the outside of the Tigershark rig was some sort of octopus or squid-like creature, roughly the size of softball with ten-inch tentacles that were stuck on the side of the suit. *Creative little bastards.* "We are heading back to Spindrift for extraction."

The loss of hydraulics in her right arm made for a struggle as she did what she could to try to keep trim. The rig attempted to compensate, which helped, but at the same time, made it hard to maintain balance. After they got halfway back, she killed the thrusters and settled into a standing position. "Deadlock, I need to walk the rest of the way."

"Watch your power," Gunther said. "Keep abreast of us."

Most of the time Trident suits relied on their thrusters. Walking was exhausting for the pilot and it used more power. Fortunately they were closing in on the Spindrift and a ride to the surface. Slogging through the muddy ocean floor stirred up a blur of sand as she moved. Complaining wasn't an option. If anything, Rita was happy that she was no longer having to force her arm. Her triceps and shoulder muscles were hot with pain, but she ignored them. There would be plenty of time to ice them down on the *Mesquite*.

They reached the Spindrift and she double-checked her power. *I can always pop off some power shells and reroute that energy to the batteries if I have to.* She thought that the engineering portion of her Trident training had been the most boring part of her qualifications. Now, however, it was proving useful.

She backed in and coupled up, though it took three attempts. Gunther and Lidell both maneuvered Demars's rig into his rack. There was no sign of life from inside, but somehow Gunther seemed to know that he was still alive in there. *Without his electrical heating unit, he's got to be freezing his ass off in there.*

"Golden Eye, this is Deadlock. We are ready to ascend," he transmitted in the clear.

The Spindrift jerked hard as it lifted off from the seabed. The raising would be done in stages, mostly to allow for decompression. It would be hardest on Demars. With this rig inoperative, he would likely have to be rushed into a hyperbaric chamber to avoid the bends once they were onboard.

As the Spindrift rose, she noticed a glow on her tactical display. "Contact," she said. "Single target. It is matching our ascent and circling us."

Deadlock's voice was calm and cool. "Alright then. There's not a lot we can do from the Spindrift and we are low enough on power that jumping off isn't a great option. Ready whatever you have left and look sharp."

All Rita had left was her plasma cutter. It was an intense hot combination blowtorch and sword for all intents and purposes. It chewed through power, but she was hooked up to Spindrift and could pull some from the ship, and she still had her power shells. *If I light this thing up now, it will draw attention. It is best to be ready to fire it up if I have to.*

Her lights spotted the fast-swimming image circling around the Spindrift first. It was the Boss. She assumed it was the same one she had been engaged with earlier, but there was no way to be sure. In the blackness, she could see the pulsating and glowing lightning-like etchings on its massive body. Where they had been orange before, now they shimmered florescent green. Like a shark stalking its prey, it swam around the rising Spindrift at remarkable speed, far faster than a Trident could go. *He's trying to figure out who to go for, who to kill first.* Her throat went dry and once more she felt sweat stinging slightly on her spine.

"What's he doing?" Lidell asked.

"He's planning something," Gunther said. "Stay crispy."

As he banked in front of her, he coiled up, turned towards Rita, and launched at her. In that moment, everything seemed to slow down. Her heart pounded in her ears as she moved her left arm across her body. She got it up, like a brace for the impact that was to come, and with her now free right hand, she put her finger lightly on the power button for her plasma cutter.

The Boss came right at her, its big claw hands pointing right at her heart as it zoomed straight for her. It got within a meter and she knew she had him, there was no stopping. Newton's Second Law of Momentum was in control of the Boss at that point.

She hit the power button to the plasma cutter.

The bolt superheated plasma flared between them, causing a scalding hot bubble to form around the flame. She backhanded the swing with her left arm as the creature's claws dug right into her cockpit canopy, scarring the armor in front of her as she swung the cutting blade. For a long moment suspended in time, she pictured the canopy shattering and the water rushing in. It would be an almost instant death at this depth.

She felt the blade hit the Boss. Black liquid obscured her view as the claws broke off their attempt to wrench her from her cockpit. Then it came, a bellowing noise, so deep that it made her entire rig and the Spindrift vibrate for a second.

Then it was gone. The goo which she presumed was blood stayed at the same level. Glimpsing down, she saw the Boss dropping deep, leaving a trail of the blood-like substance flowing behind him.

"Talk to me, Bubbles," Gunther said.

Suddenly her breathing seemed to kick in. *How long had I been holding my breath?* Time resumed at its normal pace. Her head throbbed and she held out the plasma cutter in front of her still. Her eyes surveyed the damage display and was surprised that the rig was still in one piece. She took a moment to gather her thoughts, then powered down the cutter. "I'm okay, Deadlock," she said. "I hit him with the plasma cutter. I think he's breaking off."

"Good job," Lidell said.

"Keep checking your sensors. You never know with these wagtards. He might try one more run at us."

She did fire off a power shell and dump the energy in the battery, not because she needed it, but to be sure she had power for the cutter if he did come back. It took a few minutes for her to get her breathing under control again. *I've never been this close to the enemy.* Part of it was exhilarating, another part of it was utter fear. The entire experience reminded Rita of going to her first horror film. The difference was that these horrors were real and quite deadly.

Five hours later . . .

The Spindrift rose out of the water on the crane and swung over the deck of the Mesquite. It came down hard—the seas had gotten choppy since they had descended. It was dark out, and only the deck lights made it possible to see the ship.

A team of doctors and corpsmen opened Demars's rig and rushed him out for the sick bay. She couldn't see much but could tell that he was unconscious and pale, even under the bright digital lights. Another team, wearing protective gear, seemed focused on the squid alien that was attached to Demars's Tigershark.

A few minutes later, a tech team and a corpsman came over and opened her rear hatch so that she could get out. An impromptu physical was done, just to make sure she was okay. Rita didn't mind, the air was warmer than it had been in the Moray. Her thermal gear was wet with her own sweat and she happily took a cold water bottle that the corpsman offered.

Lieutenant Gunther and CPO Lidell walked over to her. For the first time since she had come back aboard, she surveyed the damage to her Trident. The claw marks were not just scuffs on the paint, the Boss had actually furrowed the suit's metallic and carbon fiber protection. Seeing the gouges, she realized just how close she had come to death.

"What the hell . . ." Lidell said, bending over at the edge of the Spindrift. "Is that what I think it is?"

Rita looked down and saw the Boss's severed arm, caught between one of her footpads and the metallic rack of the Spindrift.

"I'll be damned," Gunther said. "It looks like you've got yourself a hell of a souvenir."

She eyed the severed ebony limb and its menacing claw with a mix of pride and disgust. "I doubt the Navy will let me keep it."

"No doubt," Gunther said. "Still, it does give you some pretty cool bragging rights."

"Any word on Demars?" she asked.

"Unknown. He was breathing, I could see that much. Even with his thermal gear, he's probably got hypothermia. At least he's alive."

"No joke," Lidell said, giving the severed alien arm a light kick. "You were right, Lieutenant, about them baiting us in. They wanted to suck us in and then that Boss was going to pounce on us. It was an ambush."

"They didn't count on us tearing them apart," Rita added. *He's right—we were walking into a trap, we just sprang it from the inside.*

"It cost them," Gunther said. "Then again, that's the nature of being the bait. You have to remember there's always a bigger fish out there. For now, let's go see Captain McKenna. I have a feeling we will be doing a full BDA on this for the next hour or so." Stepping toward the superstructure, he paused and looked back. A sinister grin rose to his face. "Bubbles, why don't you bring that arm along? Nothing like presenting evidence to the old man of our victory."

Rita grinned. "Okay. When we're done, I'm downloading *Under Siege*. Anybody wanting to watch it, swing by my quarters."

"You're on!" Gunther said.

That's one mission down. God only knows how many to go . . .

TECHNICAL DIFFICULTIES

There are realities about equipment maintenance in the military. Pushing a piece of hardware hard for an hour can require two-to-four hours of maintenance to keep it working at peak performance. Repairing battle damage can take even longer. While ASHURs are the pinnacle of military technology, they are not immune to the needs of technicians to perform their unique brand of magic.

Most pilots know that technicians are the key to winning battle, though few of them ever see action on the front lines. Most of them . . .

The Eastern Front, Firebase Hooligan, Wando, North Carolina

E4 Corporal Fletcher "Fletch" Tyson stood on the small gantry next to WO Correia's Grizzly, tugging hard on the hydraulic hose at the left elbow joint. He had bled the system already and the hose should just pop off, but it wouldn't budge. Jerking it hard, it came loose, squirting a tiny stream of the yellow fluid on his overalls. The new hydraulic stains were lost in a camouflage of oil, grease, sweat, and other stains that had preceded its arrival.

Looking at the small segment of metal-clad hose, he saw the problem. Two spots on it had holes melted through them. *It's that goddamn acid-shit the Fish use.* He eyed what was left of the hose to see if there was enough there to salvage, cut, and refit for use elsewhere. No—the holes rendered it all pretty useless. Turning, he tossed it to the scrap bin with a *thunk* that bounced around the repair bay, a sound lost to the other noises of pounding, cursing, banging, and sizzling all around him.

"She up and running yet?" came a voice from behind him as he pulled out the replacement segment of armored hose. Fletch didn't even have to look for the source; he knew it by tone and attitude. Warrant Officer Steve "Boomer" Correia. Correia was cocky, which was saying a lot for an ASHUR pilot. He wore that honor and his ego like medals on his chest. Fletch had offered to sit with him for dinner once and the pilot had scoffed and sat with another pilot instead. TGFT—Too good for the techs, that was the acronym they used for such personnel. Fletch didn't dislike him for it, but he did dislike the prodding. The Grizzly was Boomer's ride and his tendency to hover nearby while Fletch did his work was both legendary and annoying.

"It'll be done when I get it done," he said, straining to get the right angle to attach the lower end of the hose.

"We have a hop coming up in four hours," Correia replied. "The captain wants to know if I'm going to be able to attend the party."

"I still have to realign your targeting sensors for the toaster." He used slang for talking about the rig's M-D-01X Directed Energy Weapon. Cringer had said that the targeting system was off on the weapon after his last firefight.

"How long will that take?"

Fletch turned his head slowly to Correia. "It will take as long as it takes," he snarled, then turned back to the task at hand.

"Maybe you can get one of your other techs to help out."

"They are all busy," he said with a louder tone of voice as he stuck his head under the arm to see the connection. Using the wrench, he finished the lower connection.

"You haven't even asked."

"I don't have to. You pilots came go out and beat the shit out of these rigs. When you do that, it takes a while to get them functional. Every four hours you are out there is six back here in the bays."

"Is there something I can do to help?"

Fletch extracted his head slowly and looked over at Correia. "Yeah, you can. Go over to the mess tent and get me some coffee, black."

"I meant with the repairs."

"I know what you meant. Unless you are hiding fifteen weeks of training on how to fix ASHURs in your background, there's not much you can do . . ." *other than stop bothering me while I work.*

Correia took off, frustrated, from the expression on his face. Fletch didn't care. This was a conversation that happened far too often. Pilots always felt that techs were too slow, that they were deliberately dragging their feet to get the job done. There were a few that were like that, they slowed down when prodded by anxious pilots. Not Fletch. *I know my job and know it well. I need my pilot to give me the time I need to do the job right.*

With a straining twist, he felt the attachment was secure. Climbing down, he put the tool in the precise spot where it belonged on the cart, then connected the refill hose for the hydraulics. The refill would take five minutes as the system flushed and filled the react-hydraulic fluid. The system gurgled and chugged and he paused to make sure that there were no other leaks drizzling down on the concrete floor.

He laid a towel in the cockpit and climbed in. Powering up the rig, he felt it throb all around him as the displays came on to report status and readiness. Using the sleeve to operate the damaged arm, he raised it, twisted it several times, then checked the pressure again. It was exactly as it should be. Lowering the arm, he stood/sat in the rig and savored the power all around him. *They may pilot 'em, but we are the ones that keep 'em running.* Then he powered down and climbed out.

Fletch had worked at his father's heavy equipment repair shop since the age of five, fixing heavy mining equipment out in Colorado. Big CAT excavators, dump trucks, graders—all sorts of stuff. His lifetime had been spent turning wrenches and making broken things work again. *Dad would be shocked at the stuff we are working with if he were still alive.*

He had planned on retiring in a year when his term of service was up. At thirty-two years of age, Fletch was hoping to get a job working on heavy equipment repair and servicing. Some techs wanted to open their own businesses, but not him. Running a company would mean paperwork and less time turning wrenches and making things run. That was where his heart was . . . the sense of reward of taking something that was broken and making it work again.

Even the hydraulic fluid they used was different from what was in the big equipment. It was a nano-infused reactive fluid. Not only did it respond to pressure to move a joint, it also could be stimulated with a low-level electrical charge at the proper voltage that made the fluid collapse or expand, adding to the power of the system. The electronics of an ASHUR rig were incredibly durable. He prided himself at being able to repair many damaged boards, where many techs simply swapped out the plug and play parts. The power systems were sophisticated and simple at the same time, adding to the eloquence of the ASHURs.

Not everyone could be a tech privileged to work on ASHURs. The training program was rigorous and required a lot of different disciplines—"from welding to weapons" was the line often used to describe the program. You were usually trained on three or more rig types. You also got to pilot rigs as well, mostly so that you could do the work on them. That was a part he liked, the raw power of being in a cockpit and moving one of the war machines around the repair bay. Techs got to do things that other soldiers only dreamed of in that respect.

As much as the pilots could be a pain in the ass, they respected the techs. The reason was simple: their lives depended on having good techs in their corner. While there were no known instances of a tech sabotaging some twat-hat pilot's rig, that unspoken thought had to be in the backs of many pilots' minds. Even Cringer, whose arrogance and nagging were at the high end of the spectrum, made sure that Fletch had a donut waiting for him every morning at his station.

It took him a half hour to get access to the targeting system board. Inspecting it, he wiped the connections clean and reseated it in the slot—then ran the diagnostics. That fixed the weapons drift that Cringer had written up. *He probably got it banged up during the last fight just enough to make it not work.*

When he finished, he took the time to clean up his work area. Some of the techs were sloppy in that regard, which made the senior tech have to do her job and chew their asses. He knew that it wasn't enough to keep your pod and bay clean; it had to be organized so that you knew where every tool was when you needed it.

That also meant wiping down the rig when you were done. His instructors had drilled into him, "Take pride in your work." That meant keeping the equipment they were in charge of looking good. The hulking Grizzly took a good twenty minutes to clean up, but to him it was a matter of personal satisfaction.

The last thing he cleaned was the nose art for Cringer. It was a cartoon bear's face making a cringing expression. Its eyes were cocked and wide open with the mouth half-cocked open and an almost puzzled look. Fletch noticed a chip in the paint on the image. Walking to his tools, he came out with a brown Sharpee and carefully touched up the mark. It wasn't a perfect match for color, but only he would notice.

Satisfied that he was done, he took another moment to step back and look over the entire Grizzly. There was a brute force to the massive rig, a feeling of doom and despair it seemed to generate. Its camouflage paint scheme was a mix of digital greens and grays, hopefully useful in both the urban areas and the abandoned suburbs where it was deployed. Fletch saw that the paint on the replacement left leg was fresher from when he had put it on two weeks earlier, and that the right side armor plates were still painted their dull primer gray and lacked camouflage. *If we get enough downtime, I will make sure she gets a new paint job.* Satisfied, he pulled his personal communicator off his belt and sent a text message to WO Correia. "She's ready to rock and roll."

That was all he had to say. He wandered out of the repair bay to the rear. Firebase Hooligan had been set up in a small strip mall before the war. The furniture store in the plaza had been converted to barracks, albeit with nicer furniture than any barracks he had ever been in. The Subway and adjoining hair salon had been converted into a cramped mess hall. The firebase command post was in a Verizon store. One of the empty shops had been turned into a sandbag barricaded armory. At the far end of the parking lot, just outside of the defense perimeter, was a Popeye's Chicken. For a few weeks after their arrival, it was open, if only for a few hours a day. The price had soured for a sandwich, but most of the troops didn't care. Now it sat empty, only used for its deep fryers. The big surrounding parking lots, one leading to an abandoned grocery store, provided flat open fields of fire.

The technician repair bay was situated in what had been a Firestone dealership when the aliens had come ashore in nearby Charleston. Some of the stalls were dedicated to ASHURs, one each. Two were allotted to the base's Jolt vehicles—the Army's answer to electric scouting vehicles. The Army had commandeered the strip plaza and surrounding areas for a rear-area depot. The Fish had assaulted it once, however, forcing the Army to change its status to a firebase. All that meant was a sand-filled Hesco barriers and a concrete road barrier wall to be erected, and several checkpoints and two gun towers built, all topped with razor wire. *Like the wire ever deterred the Fish.* The techs liked to joke that the wire was there for their psychological well-being more than for defense. In the war against the Fish, there were no real delineations between the front and rear areas. Everything was a possible target.

At the rear, he stood in the salvage yard and surveyed the blasted armor plates stacked up neatly against the red brick, the various blown and devastated rig frames—retired from service. Two storage containers held weapons systems and electronics that had been rendered inoperative. It was a junkyard of cool tech.

Walking over to a shaded corner, he saw his pet project. At one point in its life, it had been a Battle Ram ASHUR rig. Combat damage had rendered it pure salvage, and the good stuff had been removed from it. The techs had talked about scrapping the frame, it had been bent and burned in battle, but Fletch had kept it. In the off-hours, he had repaired it, manufacturing his own replacement parts. All of the techs contributed to the side project. It was technical therapy and helped them cope with the tension and tedium.

The legs were cobbled together from seven different rigs battle refuse. While symmetrical, they didn't look like a Battle Ram's, but more like a King Snake's . . . though these were custom built. Its weapon systems were also built from salvage that didn't meet the Army's standards, but that he and a few of the other techs had pieced back together. The hulking shoulder-mounted rail gun had a custom frame and coil system that E3 Karter had built almost from scratch. Getting it to tie into the targeting system had been tricky, taking some reprogramming on the part of Corporal Martin—a genius at the coding. The heavy ACR had been built from the parts of three damaged guns. Its flamethrowers were built almost entirely from scratch except for the igniter assembly—the work of Private Coon's sweat-equity in the project. Parts of it were downright ingenious, such as the way he added an armor wrap around the flammable fuel tank slung under the arm where it was mounted.

The battery pack was a second-generation one. Batteries were always at a premium in the repair bay. It was bigger and bulkier than the gen-three rigs, but it was the best they could muster. They had to modify the frame to inset the battery so as to not throw off the center of gravity. Where engineers used complex calculations to determine this, the technicians did it more on instinct and feel. They had gotten it right; the hodgepodge ASHUR handled well in its test runs.

The parts on their little project were scrap. The hydraulic fluid was used, drained out of real ASHUR rigs that needed repair. The soft armor, the shear-thickening fluid—a precious commodity now that the war was on—had been salvaged from rigs that had been scrapped. Army regulations said to not use the material, but throwing it away made no sense to Fletch and the other techs.

The base commander had noticed their project, but said nothing about it. *The major knows we need an outlet. If we are out here working on this, we aren't causing trouble.* There was another thought about the fact they hadn't been stopped. *Maybe he sees no harm in it, or assumes the abuse the pilots are giving us about it is punishment enough.* When the technicians were off-shift, they came out and worked on it. Fletch had become the unofficial project leader on the Franken-rig, as some of the techs referred to it. When they made changes, they passed them by him for his approval. There was a sense of appreciation in what he had started those long weeks ago.

The work was a running joke with the ASHUR pilots. They quipped about it being a "junkyard monstrosity." Even Cringer had asked, "What are you guys going to do with that? No one is going to pilot it, not when they have *real* rigs." Fletch had simply looked at him and replied, "It's not about taking it into combat, it's about making something. We spend our days repairing the damage you guys generate out there. This isn't about fixing something that's broken; it's about making something new and different."

"It looks wonky," Cringer had replied.

"Looks aren't everything," Fletch had reassured him. "It has it where it counts."

Now as he stood looking at it, he saw that the armor plating on the left side of the cockpit was too tall—it would limit the pilot's ability to see out the side. Walking over to the cutting torch, he checked the gas levels and grabbed his mask. *It needs just a little minor adjustment . . .* he thought as he put on the helmet and grabbed the spark igniter.

Three weeks later . . .

Cringer was back from the paint bay, complete with an updated cam-ouflage pattern of grays, blacks, whites, browns, and dull green slashes and crosscuts. To the casual observer, Cringer looked like a brand-new ASHUR. Not so much to Fletch. He saw the imperfections, the flaws in his work. One of the shoulder armored plates was not a perfect fit—the result of the rig's frame being slightly bent when Cringer had fallen over and through a brick wall. The lower torso armor, the crotch-plate, was something he had been forced to make ad hoc from armored stock. To him, it needed more curvature, but it did fit the frame. In war, functionality took priority over looks.

WO Correia moved to his side, crossing his arms, surveying it. "Damn, it looks like it came off the showroom floor."

"I didn't hang a pine tree freshener in it," Fletch said.

"It looks great." It was a genuine compliment from Correia.

"I replaced your ACS," he said, referencing the adaptive camouflage system—a device that could mask the appearance of the ASHUR with its background. "They say the new ones are more reliable."

"I gotta have my cloaking device," Correia quipped.

"I tested it. On paper, it works just fine. That's the challenge. They always work great under nominal conditions."

"The minute you start darting around and firing weapons, the damn things get overloaded."

"It's imperfect tech, but you take what you can get."

"I have a hop this afternoon," the pilot said, shedding his thin veneer of humor. "Deep penetration run."

"Your rig won't let you down."

He patted Fletch on the shoulder hard with a single slap. "I don't worry about your work, I worry about the Fish."

There had been an uptick in the tempo of the fighting lately. The aliens were pushing farther out of Charleston, and in doing so, the army had been forced back in several sectors. The Fish seemed to have an endless supply of replacement fighters and weren't as prone as humans to break and run when the going got tough. So far, they had been pressing to the south of their position, some five miles away.

The rumors were constant, and the techs, despite their busyness, were not immune to them. There was talk of giant Fish—monsters that could crawl on land that were the size of several buses. There were tales of flying Fish that were harassing rear areas. One breed of alien was said to have laser-eyestalks. Fletch took the stories with a grain of salt. Most were so fantastic that they were borderline ridiculous, but in this war, he had learned that even the dumbest of rumors usually had some factual starting point.

Three hours later, Correia mounted his rig with Fletch watching on. As he powered up, the rig seemed to throb to life. He ran through the startup routine, checking all of the systems. The Grizzly stepped out of its repair pod, squatted for a moment, then stood. Cringer lifted his arms, testing them and the weapons. He stepped forward to check the gait, the heavy legs crunching hard on the concrete of the former Firestone shop.

Fletch stood in front of him and gave him the thumbs-up indication that he didn't see any issues. Correia did the same. Moving to the side, he watched as the pride of his work lumbered out of the bay and formed up with the rest of the platoon. Another ASHUR, Sergeant Lewis's "Roughcut," a Mamba, joined them along with both of the Jolt vehicles.

The patrol set out and Fletch immediately went to work prepping the repair pod for a hot battery swap. ASHURs could only hang in battle for a few hours before needing more power. If it was a prolonged fight, they would return to the hanger and hot-swap a new battery pack. It only took a minute to do, if you had it all set up. Fletch didn't want to be caught in a rush if it was needed. It took a few minutes to wheel in and hoist the new battery into place. *Better to be prepared than forced to do things on the fly.* It was a line he had picked up from his tech training and something he lived day-to-day.

Now came the quiet time. The troopers, with the exception of a handful left to guard Firebase Hooligan, were gone on patrol, as were the two ASHURs that were fully operational. One, a Swamp Rat, was in a state of disassembly under Corporal Bigger's hands. The Swamp Rat had been brand new and, on its first patrol, had gotten badly damaged by one of the Boss aliens. It had gotten badly mangled. Its pilot, Sergeant Maggie Gibbs, should have kept her distance from the big Boss, but opted to get up-close and personal. *Pilots sometimes do shit like that—they feel that the rig makes them invulnerable or immune to the aliens. That boss showed her.* The result was that the Swamp Rat had been crushed, its frame mangled, and Gibbs sent to the hospital with a broken arm and two shattered ribs. Now it lay in pieces, carefully laid out by Bigger, in hopes of fixing the multitude of damaged components.

The technicians knew the routine well. They would be out for anywhere from two to four hours. After that, the ASHURs were going to be running low on power and need to return to the firebase. For a few hours at least, there was going to be no one demanding to know when the repairs were going to be done or complaining about your workmanship. Despite the risks that the pilots face, this was the one time that the techs were guaranteed relative peace and quiet.

Fletch went into the salvage yard where his project rig stood. A number of the techs were there, smoking, relaxing. There wasn't a lot to do during deployments. The firebase mess had gotten in a pallet of Gatorade, now considered a luxury item given the supply chain issues.

Partlow, one of the more senior techs, handed him a red bottle of the prized drink, still cold.

"How'd you get the mess hall to part with any of this?" Fletch asked.

"Their freezer was on the fritz. I told him that if I could get a few of these little gems, I could fix it before the food went bad," Partlow bragged as Fletch opened his and savored the first drink.

"I'm surprised he didn't turn you in," technician Margaret Hix said. She wore a Jolt patch on her arm, but had proven herself a technician more than able to help out with ASHURs when pressed.

"He was happy to get rid of the stuff," Partlow said. "I think he was selling eight packs of the stuff to the officers. Some that couldn't afford it were threatening to complain to the CO. Besides, for him, his job gets better when he no longer has the shit. Then he doesn't have to figure out how to dole it out."

"You see anything good in the freezer when you working on it?" Bigger asked.

Partlow winced. "I didn't know they made Grade D meat."

"D?" Fletch asked.

"Yeah."

It was Fletch's turn to wince. "What is that? I mean what parts of an animal makes up Grade D meat?"

"It doesn't matter," Hix said. "They'll soak it in barbeque sauce and slop it on a bun and we'll all be happy that we have a barbeque sandwich." There was truth in what she said.

"It can't be any worse than that stuff he called meatloaf," Dexter Sherwood, the heavy vehicle mechanic, said. The mention of the meatloaf made all of the gathered techs flinch. It took a boatload of ketchup and hot sauce to mask the taste of the food. Rumors had abounded that it was gamy meat, a shot deer or a wild boar. The accuracy of the rumors didn't count for anything. What mattered was that spreading them and speculating on the source killed downtime.

Gibbs looked over at the Frankenrig. "You ever going to get that thing done?" she asked of Fletch.

"It is," he said with a hint of pride. "I took it for a stroll the other day for a trim-and-fit run to make sure we had the center of gravity set right. It actually pilots better than the Grizzly."

"The weapons and targeting system operational?" Hix asked.

Corporal Martin weighed in, putting out the stump of his cigarette as he started to speak. "I uploaded the latest patch for a Sidewinder in it. That's the closest counterpart for the size and armaments. And I did a cold test on all systems. The systems all work and track. The communications system is running independent of the main board right now; it was easier than trying to make it seat properly. Sure, it's wonky, but it operates."

"When are we going to hot test the weapons?" Bigger asked.

Fletch chuckled at the question. *If only it were that easy.* "I doubt we'll get that chance. The CO isn't likely to let me load it with live ordnance and fire it, not in the middle of a war."

"Seems like a shame," Hix said. "I mean, yeah, it's built from scrap—but it was built well."

Dempsey, the best welder in the lot and a man whose face was perpetually covered in the black grime of metal work, shifted on the drum he was sitting on and spoke. "I think we ought to get the CO to see if he can get one of those DARPA engineers out here to look at her."

"I mean, there are parts of this that are pretty ingenious," Hix said.

The techs had a strong sense of pride in their creation. Some of their modifications they had done actually improved on the existing components. The senior tech had even documented some of those modifications and sent them up the chain of command—no doubt sitting in an inbox on some second lieutenant's desktop, buried in obscurity.

"Now that you have her done, what's next?" Sherwood asked.

"We have enough parts here to start building another one," Fletch replied.

"The way these pilots abuse these rigs," Gibbs said in a deeply sarcastic tone, "we have a never-ending source of material to use."

Fletch wanted to pile onto that comment, but his thoughts were tempered by the reality of the fact that the reason that their ASHURs were so damaged was they were fighting the enemy—a relentless enemy at that. Between their acid projectors, their high-pressure water cutters, and brute force, the ASHURs took a hell of a beating in battle. The Grizzly was even equipped with a cutter on the right arm—essentially an alien-cutting chainsaw. The fact that the rigs were equipped with such weapons was a testimony as to the proximity of the enemy to their fighting.

Bigger took a wide-mouthed gulp of his Gatorade and said, "Well, I have to swap out the left arm on the Swamp Rat. It doesn't meet specs to keep in, but I think it's possible to use the frame as a starting point to build another arm."

"I heard the guys over at Firebase Hallelujah have a lot of spare cockpit parts," Hix contributed. "Not sure what they have, but a private I know over there said they got a number of extra parts that don't match the rigs."

Dempsey chuckled. "Leave it to the supply officers to screw up. I swear, ours could fuck up a one-car funeral." His comment elicited chuckles all around. It wasn't so much that their base supply officer was incompetent, but he was working with a system that was strained to the point of breaking. The entire US Army had not been deployed into action since WWII. Most wars that had been fought, including the Russian incursion into Alaska, didn't require the entire army. This was all-hands-on-deck for the entire military—which meant that stockpiles were being devoured at rates no one expected. Everything was high priority and a rush order. *You add up all that and screwups are inevitable.*

He savored the last of the Gatorade and started thinking about the rig they had cobbled together. *Maybe we can scrape up enough paint to make it look official?* So far, no one had complained about the scroung-ing they had done for their side project. He felt confident that no one would miss a gallon or two of olive drab and tan paint.

His thoughts were shattered with an alert siren. Instinctively he stood, as did all of the technicians. "Aw crap, here we go again—an-other drill," moaned Martin. He understood the sentiment. The base CO liked doing the drills, especially when the combat forces were on patrol. They made their way to the bays, grabbing and putting on their tactical vests, moving over to the personal weapons locker and grab-bing their ACRs. No one was moving slow, nor were they moving fast.

"Attention—all troops to their combat posts," came the voice of the CO over the speakers. "This is not a drill. We have incoming enemy forces. Repeat—this is not a drill!"

Fletch could feel the color drain from his face. Looking over at the other techs, he saw the shock and dismay in their faces as well. Suddenly the tempo of their actions picked up. In the rush, he almost dropped his helmet as he started out for his place on the perimeter wall.

"What the fuck is going on?" Bigger asked as he ran beside him.

"What do you think?" he said, shouldering his ACR and locking a magazine into it, chambering a round. "The Fish are coming this way."

"What are we going to do about it?" Bigger asked as he mirrored Fletch's movements. "We are a bunch of techs."

A new voice, that of Second Lieutenant Brooks, rang out behind them. "You are soldiers first and foremost," he said.

"Yes, sir," Bigger replied. "It's just that I haven't fired my weapon in two months."

"I assure you that it will fire," the lieutenant said. "Remain calm, remember your training. You'll do fine." With those words, he moved on down the line where the kitchen staff of the base were moving up against the Hesco barriers. One of them was wearing a kitchen smock under his tactical vest, but he was there—weapon ready.

"The LT is confident," Partlow said.

"He's paid to be confident," Hix replied, putting two magazines up on the barrier in front of her for quick access. "If he was really good, he'd be out on the patrol."

The alarm klaxon sounded again, adding to the tension. "The pa-trol must have run into problems," Bigger said.

"They always do," Fletch replied. "The difference is, this time, their problem became our problem." Looking out over his field of fire, he felt himself starting to sweat. His field of fire was a parking lot, long devoid of automobiles. Beyond it, set back another eighty yards or so, was a thin line of trees and a tangle of low dense brush. Just over a hundred yards of open space with which he could engage the enemy. *A hell of a lot can happen in a hundred yards.*

The waiting set in. Fletch tried to convince himself that they might not come. He had never fired his gun at the enemy. While he knew that was a possibility, in the back of his mind, he had hoped that moment might never come. While he liked his team members a great deal, he respected them as technicians. How they would react as warriors was yet to be seen.

The klaxon sounded, and again the CO warned them that the alert was not a drill. Wiping the sweat from his brow, he fixed his eyes on the tree line. A bird flew out and he clenched, almost taking aim and firing. Drawing a deep breath, he tried to calm himself. *Don't panic—just fire when you have a legitimate target. Slow is steady, steady is fast.*

Minutes ticked on by with nothing. Even the usual banter stopped. He was sure that his fellow techs were going through the same thoughts he was. Then came shots from behind him, on the east wall. He craned his head despite knowing he would not be able to see a thing. There as a moment of relief that he embraced. *At least they aren't hitting our side.*

That thought was squashed when the brush began to crunch and sway in front of him. *Shit!* Then they came. A half dozen of the frogmen warriors sprang from the trees, along with a massive crab-warrior. The frogmen sprang on their big rear legs, moving long yards in a single hop. Their green-gray hides shimmered as if they were wet, their bulging eyes were yellow and black. Under their chins, their skin filled like an inflated sack. They grunted, loudly, deeply.

He fired at the one on his extreme right. The first shot missed, but his second one hit it as it landed, striking the leg. There was no indication that the bullet had penetrated—that was one of the many problems with the Fish. They were highly resistant to full metal jacketed fun. He fired another and saw it hit the frog in the lower body, its skin pushed back, but again, no sign of punching through.

The crab followed the frogs, its shell shimmering green to brown in color. Its massive scorpion-tail darted from side-to-side as it moved in. Pausing, it pointed one of its massive fore-claws towards them and a stream of high pressured water stabbed at the Hesco barriers in front of Partlow. The barrier absorbed the hit, though it seemed to almost explode in the process, spraying sand everywhere.

The frogs opened their mouths in unison, spitting at the firing line. Fletch ducked down behind his barrier, narrowly missing the spray. The liquid splattered the higher row of barriers raised behind him. Frog-spit was a toxic goo; even a drop of it could cause a dangerous allergic re-action. He heard one near him and looked down to see that his ACR's extended handle had a small drop of the goo on it. The greenish goo was all over the weapon, dropping onto the pavement at his feet. *If that had hit me . . .* he paused for a second, using a thick work rag from his pocket to quickly and carefully wipe away the toxin, making sure none got on his skin, then tossing the rag on the ground.

Looking over at Bigger, he was shocked to see that his friend lay on the ground. *I never even heard him drop!* His face looked huge, swollen and bright crimson. His breath was ragged, struggling—and Fletch could see that his tongue was swollen. Bending down, careful to make sure none of the spittle got on him, he loosened the STG and his uniform's neck. His mind raced with what he could do to help his friend, but nothing came to mind. Bigger's entire body quaked with violent spasms and Fletch tried to help him by holding him down, but it wasn't achieving any success. Bigger's blue eyes were swollen, staring at him, wide and filled with terror. Then it all suddenly stopped—his body went from rigid to limp. Fletch wanted to give him CPR, but the frog's goo covered his friend's chest. He knew that such a gesture would be futile. Bigger was dead, and nothing could change that.

Rage overwhelmed Fletch. He had never lost a friend in battle be-fore. Now Bigger was gone. He rose and took aim at the frog he had fired at earlier. It was closer now, a mere thirty yards out. Aiming for its head, he fired three rounds in quick succession. Two hit, one piercing its yellow eye. It made a grunting noise as it whipped around. His other shot punched through the bag under its chin. He saw a greasy black liquid splatter from that—blood, he guessed. It staggered, then fell.

Then the tower up above him engaged with a string of rapid deafening bangs from the .50 caliber machine gun as it began firing away in a torrent of short bursts. Another two frogs dropped, shredded by the incoming fire, and the machine gun started raining shots down on the crab. The big bullets made the entire crab quake under their impacts, and at least a few of them managed to find gaps in the carapace of the massive creature, going deep.

Another frog dropped as the last two sprang again for barriers. A grenade launcher *thunked* and sent a grenade into one of the aggressive amphibians. The blast tore off its arm and sent bits of its flesh flailing. The other inflated its bag under its chin and fired again, spitting a glob of green goo at the barriers. Fletch aimed at its flank and fired another pair of shots at the new target, missing with both.

The .50 cal aimed down and dumped a spray of death of its own down on the frog. The shots chewed up the frog and it collapsed just a few yards from the barrier, dark gray-green gore spraying out behind it.

The crab unleashed its cutting beam of water again, this time aiming at the tower. The shot was not aimed at the gunner, but at the middle of the tower itself. It cut like a plasma cutter through sheet steel, severing the support legs in a quick swoop. The tower's metal legs moaned and protested as it slowly tilted and collapsed down hard on the Hesco barriers just behind Fletch and the other technicians.

The crab suddenly began to move backwards on its eight legs, angling side-to-side as it moved. The pop-crack of ACR gunfire followed it as it drifted back into brush and out of the field of fire. Fletch's ears rang, his heart thundered in his chest, but he was still alive. He deliberately didn't look at Bigger, averting his gaze as he saw Hix and Partlow. Hix was pale, for the first time ever he saw a look of terror in her eyes. Partlow was wet with sweat, his jaw set hard.

"We made it," Fletch said.

Lieutenant Brooks came in behind him, wincing at the sight of Bigger's lifeless remains. "Jesus! How are the rest of you?" he asked as several of the base staff tried to extricate the tower gunner from what was left of the fallen tower.

"We lost Bigger," Fletch said, stating the obvious because he couldn't muster any meaningful words. He was trembling. This was his first taste of combat. His mind began to wonder at how many things he had gotten wrong. Seeing Bigger lay there, he felt a crushing weight on his mind. *Was that my fault? Was there something I could have done differently?*

"So I see," the LT said. "We will get him out of here. You did good, but that was just the opening band. The headliner act is still coming. I need you on the line."

The words were sobering. For a moment, Fletch had felt victorious in fighting his first battle. Now he was hearing that it wasn't the big fight he thought it was—that a bigger threat was coming. Looking over at the collapsed tower, he realized they had fended off the enemy, but were weaker for it. *If they come in greater force, we are toast.*

His mind went to this Frankenrig. "Sir," he spoke up. "We have an ASHUR—the one we built."

Lieutenant Brooks leaned back at those words. "That erector set project you've been working on?"

"It's functional, sir," Hix said excitedly, maneuvering around Bigger to join the conversation.

The lieutenant seemed to drink in the words thoughtfully. "Who are we going to get to pilot it? All of our pilots are in the field."

Partlow spoke up. "Put Fletch in it. He has driven it the most—and it's his baby."

Fletch felt the eyes of the small group fall on him. Lieutenant Brooks moved in front of him. "We could use some firepower," he said. "You up to it?"

Fletch nodded almost unconsciously. "I can pilot it. We need to get it armed though."

"Get to it," the lieutenant ordered. "We only have a few minutes before the big thrust comes."

As the techs broke into a fast run for the scrap yard, Fletch thought, *Oh shit, what have I gotten myself into?*

When they reached the rig, he opened the front hatch and put his ACR inside the cockpit then turned to help Private Coon attached the fill line for the flamethrower under the left arm. Karter and Hix attached the ammo drum and rail gun rounds for the heavy weapon, having to hammer it a bit to get the shell canister to snap into place. "You've got ten rounds," Karter said.

"How's the bat?" Fletch asked as he started to climb in.

"You've got a hot charge," Partlow said as Fletch put on his helmet, one of the pilot's spares.

Dempsey wheeled in the big ACR on a cart and parked it under the right hand. "Good to go," he called, stepping back.

Fletch crawled in and toggled the startup sequence. The ASHUR hummed to life around him. There wasn't time to run a full fit-and-trim sequence. *I'll have to work through the kinks.* He checked the pressure readings on the flamethrower and the hydraulics and saw he was in the green. Bending at the knees, he put his right arm in the control sleeve and reached out for the massive ASHUR-sized ACR with the rig's hand. He grabbed at it, awkwardly at first, but then secured it. The connector between his fist and the gun snapped into place, giving him a feed as to the ammo level.

"You good?" Partlow called out.

Fletch nodded. *Am I? I never planned on taking this thing into battle.* Building it was one thing; piloting it in an actual firefight something else altogether. The techs drifted back as he stepped forward with the rig. Lieutenant Brooks rushed forward, coming up in front of the still-open cockpit. "We need you outside of the perimeter," he said. "The rest of you, get back on the line. We have company coming."

Fletch hit the button to close the cockpit canopy and it came down heavily, sealing in place. He walked it forward, slow and steady, towards the main gate of the firebase. Two of the base defenders opened the gate and he maneuvered outside. A voice came over earbuds in his helmet.

"Corporal Tyson, I need you to take position on the west wall where the tower was." It was Lieutenant Brooks.

"Yes, sir," he replied, moving along the outer protective barrier to the position where he had been ordered. From the main gate, he turned to the left and marched the ASHUR out in front of the position he had been on as acting infantry. He felt lonely and exposed standing out there, not quite sure what to do next. Shifting to the left, he checked the tactical display. Markers indicated where his friends and fellow techs lined up behind him. It was somewhat reassuring. A realization crept into his mind. *I'm the biggest target out here. When the Fish see me, they are going to come right at me.*

His fingers and arms were sweating in the control sleeve, and Fletch wished he had brought a bottle of water with him. The cockpit's temperature rose as the sun hit it. The tiny air cooler was struggling to keep up with it. *We will have to put in a bigger one.*

That assumed, of course, that he survived.

The brush at the far end of the parking lot stirred. He gulped down a breath. Suddenly the brush line exploded with three huge crabs bursting through. The muffled sounds of gunfire erupted all around him, and throughout the firebase. "We are being hit on all fronts," came the CO's voice over the open tactical channel. "Pour it on!"

Fletch brought the targeting reticle onto the crab in the center, raising the left arm of the ASHUR. The reticle drifted as he struggled with the arm sleeve to hold it steady. *Come on, you bitch—hold still.*

The crabs fired away, two with cutters, another spraying the firebase with a laser-like cutting beams of highly pressurized water. Several Hesco barriers were destroyed, spraying sand into the air as they burst. Several bits of the spray hit his right arm and leg, but he ignored them. Processing all of the images and the action was overwhelming. *How do real pilots do this?* His struggled just to keep the weapon aimed.

As soon as the targeting reticle drifted dead on target, the upraised armored torso of the crab, he hit the fire button in the sleeve. It felt as if the ASHUR was fighting him as much as the enemy. There was a big bang as the shell went off, half-startling him. The explosion fed a specially designed generator to add to the power from the rig. The rail gun tugged in a subtle jerk as the metal projectile was launched down a lightning-fast magnetic pulse. The round cleared the chamber and there was a plasma flash as the air in front of it was superheated by the rapid launch of the projectile.

Fletch couldn't see it in flight, but the round slammed into the crab hard. The raised upper body torso at the front of the creature was knocked almost flat on its back. The rail gun round had penetrated— big chunks of flesh flew in a line with the trajectory of the shot. A dark gray-black fluid sputtered out of the impact hole and from the torn pieces of the body. Ugly organs were visible, pulsating, strangely frightening. He had hoped that he had taken the giant crab out, but slowly, it raised itself upright. The alien wheeled about, getting what footing it could, staring at him and opening its maw, letting out a horrific wail, a sickening mix of screech and roar.

Raising his ASHUR's massive assault ACR, he fired. The ASHUR's larger weapon bucked hard as it fired. The shots slammed into the wailing creature, knocking it hard each time a round hit, rending even more alien flesh in the process. The crab flopped over on its side, its tail twitching.

There was no time for rejoicing—its two accomplices were closing fast. He struggled with the feeling of raw panic. *Am I too close? Where should I be positioned?* Angling the rail gun with more skill than the first time, he fired another round, priming the weapon. The bang of the energy shell made his head throb as it went off. This shot tore off the leg of one creature, sending it flying backwards toward the tree line. The kinetic impact alone shifted the alien back a good two yards. Its body was slick with whatever it had for blood from the ripping off of the leg.

Twisting slightly at the waist, he unleashed a stream of ACR shells at the other crab as the rest of the firing line blazed away with their lighter infantry versions of his weapon. The target crab advanced on the infantry, then paused, angling its left claw in his direction. The ASHUR jerked under an impact on the left leg, almost causing him to lose balance and topple over. He staggered the rig back, fighting the rig and gravity at the same time. *Probably one of them has needle weapons.*

As he fought to regain stability and continue the fight, the other crab unleashed a sonic weapon. The blast came in waves across the parking lot, the air shimmering in ripples, slamming into both him and the other defenders. The cockpit around him swirled with a throbbing and painful sensation that left him momentarily dazed. Jerking hard, his head ached and his ears rang, then painfully popped. His eyesight blurred and stomach roiled, but he managed to recover. Sweat rolled down his face as he fought back the urge to vomit.

Ignoring the searing pain between his ears, Fletch raised the rail gun again and aimed carefully as the two crabs closed on him. Shaking off the metal haze from the sonic weapon, he choose the one that was missing a leg, the one that had fired the sonic attack. The moment the targeting reticle fell on its head, he fired again. The bang of the power shell still jolted him, but less so. In a weird way, it was oddly assuring, acknowledgement that the ASHUR was still operational. The rail gun tugged as the round streaked out, its brilliant orange and red plasma plume flaring out the end of the barrel. The projectile slammed into the thick plate of its head on the right side. It snapped the head of the creature around, much farther than he would have thought possible. The crab fell over, flailing its legs as it struggled to rise.

Shots of smaller-grade needle weapons fired from the wood line, hitting his transparent aluminum cockpit canopy, shattering there, and marring the material. The metallic pings were muffled as his hearing slowly fought to come back. The shots were a reminder that just one could penetrate and kill him, something he tried to push to the back of his mind. He turned his focus on the charging crab. Someone from within the firebase unleashed a Carl Gustaf; the shot hit that alien's tail, almost severing it off. Instead of being raised like a scorpion, it fell lifeless on the ground, dragging on the blacktop of the pavement as the creature continued to charge forward, seemingly right at him.

Instincts overrode his tension as Fletch unleashed a burst of fire from his heavy ACR mostly hitting their target—at least one of the three shots made the alien rock back hard, almost killing its running gait towards him. Still, it closed, despite the damage it had taken. *What does it take to get these big bastards to stop?*

As the creature closed the distance with him, Fletch fired the power round for the rail gun and swung the arm and weapon to aim it. Before he could fire, the crab sprung at him, crashing right into his ASHUR. Metal moaned and the shear thickening fluid (STF) went solid under the kinetic impact. The rig fell back a half-step, right into the outer barrier of the firebase, thankfully stopping his fall. A screw dropped out of nowhere, hitting his lap. The capacitors for the rail gun hummed with energy awaiting release.

One of the crab's large claws locked onto his ACR, clamping down hard around the rig's arm and the weapon. There was a crunching sound and his damage display lit up crimson showing that it was compromised. Metallic moaning filled his muffled hearing. Whipping the arm with the rail gun around, he planted it under the head and chin of the creature and fired upward. The plume from the round was like a torch, searing the chitin-like armored plating of the crab as the round fired. It tore through the creature and exited skyward. Fluid, dark gray and greenish, sprayed down on the ASHUR as if from a firehose. Then the alien went limp, but in doing so, collapsed on Fletch's rig, pinning him against the outer barrier.

His damage indicator showed that the ACR was compromised—meaning it may or may not work. The armored plates on his arm were crumpled and cracked from the pressure of the claw which opened just enough to allow him to get it free. There was a small hydraulic leak in the elbow, something he hoped would hold out long enough for him to continue the fight.

Fighting the mass that was pinning him, Fletch had to twist and turn the rig hard to pry it from under the fallen crab, while all around him muffled gunfire banged and cracked. His arms and back ached as he finally got the ASHUR free. What he saw was the last crab lying dead only a dozen yards away with the infantry behind him laying down suppression fire at the tree line. Mortar rounds, fired from within the firebase, flashed and banged into the woods.

He wanted to rest for a moment, get his breath, but the CO's voice came over the tactical channel. "Corporal Tyson, we need you on the north side now." As if to accentuate his point, there was a new explosion that went off from the battle, the concussion making the rig quake.

"Yes, sir," he said with a ragged response, moving his already aching legs to a run, thundering the ASHUR to the north. As he rounded the corner of the perimeter defensive barriers, he saw three more live crabs and a group of frogmen starting to assail the outer barrier.

Time to see if the ACR will fire. The arm fought his efforts to raise it, no doubt due to the hydraulic leak. The weapon's online status flickered on his board, far from reassuring. *Come on, baby—help me out.* He aimed at the nearest frog who was pointing some sort of weapon extension that was part of his arm at the barriers, apparently slicing the Hesco barriers apart, throwing sand everywhere.

Fletch triggered the weapon with his index finger in the control glove. The ACR barked and kicked hard, the recoil seemed worse as the arm rocked back with each shot. The first two rounds slammed into the frog, knocking it to the ground in a splatter of gore. His other shots were misses—wide ones. *Controlling the recoil is harder than I ever imagined.*

One of its comrades, now seeing the threat, turned its cutter on him, slashing a diagonal cut across the front armor of the ASHUR. It was like a laser, only wetter, as the cutter tore into armor plating.

An ugly groove was chiseled out of the transparent aluminum canopy, right in front of him. A tiny squirt of water managed to penetrate, spraying Fletch in the chest with hot fluid. He glanced down, fearful that he had been cut, but only saw the fluid. His damage indicators flickered amber for several damaged armor plates and the rig stiffened a bit in movement as the STF went rigid.

There was no time to revel in his luck. The mix of energy, adrenaline, and white-hot fear seemed to come into a strange mental balance for him. He jerked the heavy ACR over towards the new threat and toggled full auto, spraying an erratic burst of shells at the frog that had slashed him, cutting the creature in half with several rounds missing and hitting the outer barrier wall. A new fear hit him—*I hope that didn't hit one of our guys!*

The ACR emptied its magazine with a *snap* and *thunk*. He hit the ejector control, but it refused to drop. With a downward thrust, he bounded the gun against the pavement, hoping to jar loose the magazine, but it refused to drop. The warning indicator of the gun went to full red. *Damn it—that claw damaged it, so I can't reload.* Shaking the weapon several times still did not eject the spent magazine.

Turning his focus away from the arm, he saw a frog wheel towards him. The alien looked different in a lot of respects, namely this frog, like one of the others, had a tail. The frog also had something on is back, something orange in color. It looked a lot like an enlarged or mutated starfish, with two of the legs wrapping up over the shoulders. A large vein-like growth snaked from the starfish-thing ending in something that the frog grasped. It looked at first like a small stick with a long piece of black rope at the end of it. As the frog leaped at him, he saw the rope-weapon whipping it around over his head. It seemed to be growing extending, with each rotation, each swipe getting closer.

Oh crap! Jerking the rig hard to the right, he started to move away from the perimeter wall, trying to put some distance between him and the bounding frogman. The alien landed and the whip slammed into the ASHUR rig. The end of the whip stuck on the cockpit canopy, and it looked like an open mouth with something in the middle of it, punching at the transparent armored protection. His eyes fixated on it.

There was a flash, bluish and bright—almost like a flashbulb going off. A crackling noise filled his ears as his eyes filled with dots.

Disoriented, he tried to sidestep the rig, but it was locked up, like a statue. *What in blue blazes was that!*

As his eyes returned to normal, he saw that his systems were off. Hanging limp in front of him was a half-meter of the whip-like creature, still sucking onto the rig, not just the mouth but the entire length of it as if it were a giant slug. Fletch wanted to ignore it, but it was hard since it was right in his field of view.

All the circuits have been tripped! He reset the breakers on the primary systems of the ASHUR, one at a time, praying that the monitors and rig would come back to life. The damage display flickered on, as did the targeting system and communications. He had a moment of minor joy when the weapons control display flickered back to life. The main motivator that provided movement for the rig, however, did not. He reset it again, then again . . . but it didn't come to life.

That thing hit me with some sort of an electrical shock—a big one. His nostrils caught a faint whiff of ozone, never a good sign. Looking out, he saw the frog who had hit him had turned its attention to the barrier, swinging the whip at the defenders as bullets rained down on it and around it, ricocheting off of the parking lot surface. *Great . . . a tough frog! That's all we need.*

Fletch attempted to move his legs in their control sleeves but got nothing in response. Checking his arms, the same non-response was what he had. His primary battery was showing an almost 25 percent loss of power, no doubt some of that from the electrical attack. *That whip will kill a human that it hits and has enough of jolt to fry an ASHUR.* His brain turned his attention to the problem at hand. He mentally checked off everything he needed to do to get moving. *What good are weapons if you can't raise your arm to fire them?* The technician in him settled on the most likely problem . . . *it's got to be the motivator controller board. That's just fuckerific!*

Pulling his arms out of the control sleeves, Fletch reached down and popped open the computer access panel. ASHURs had redundancy built in, so weapons had their own controller, as did energy control, damage control, and the motivator board—which controlled the hydraulics, balance, and mobility of the rig. He didn't have the gear for diagnosing the problem, so he went old-school, pulling out the board and reseating it.

Once more he tried to move but got nothing in response. *If I can't move, I can't fight. I'm just a big old target sitting out here.* Communications was working, so he switched to an open channel. "This is Fletch—my rig is down. I think the motivator board is fried. Can anyone get me a hot-swap?"

There was a long moment of silence then a voice, that of Partlow, said, "I'm on it, hang tight!"

Standing there, immobile, he felt like a sick spectator to the fighting that was raging on the north side of the firebase. Hitting the egress button, he popped the front hatch and pushed it open enough for him to climb out. Reaching back and down for his personal ACR, he maneuvered to keep the ASHUR between him and the aliens. While he felt exposed still, being on the outside of the perimeter, his gut instinct told him it was better than sitting in the biggest potential target in the battlespace.

Waiting for Paltrow was the longest three and a half minutes of Fletch's life. He'd been tempted to fire his weapon, but knew that would only draw dangerous unwanted attention. *It's better to wait and hit them when the rig is back up and running.* Glancing at the heavy ACR that the rig still held, he saw the problem. The lower part of the magazine was crushed, no doubt by the crab's claw. The bent metal was bound up, and without a crowbar, there would be no getting it free, let alone having a chance of reloading it. Finally he heard his fellow technician call him from the other side of the barriers. "Bro—I've got it!" He could barely see Partlow from behind the barricade. He held the board in its gray plastic packing case.

"Bring it out," Fletch called.

"Go long," Paltrow said, pulling his arm back and throwing the board as if it were Frisbee, whipping it into the air.

Damn! This is so damn stupid! He ignored the battle raging a scant fifty yards away and focused on catching the board. On his third step, he almost fell, but managed to right himself and catch the board before it rattled on the parking lot pavement. His hand clenched the plastic case tight.

Ducking low, Fletch sprinted to the ASHUR and climbed in. He fumbled with the latch on the case, his fingers shaking as he finally got it open and pulled the board out. Bending down, he carefully inserted the replacement board, seating it into the slot, then closed the access hatch. *Here goes nothing . . .* He hit the circuit reset and waited. A few milliseconds later, the rig started to hum and the hydraulics re-pressurized. In that moment, he realized he hadn't been breathing—and he gasped in a fresh rush of air. The ASHUR rose back up to a standing position and he closed the hatch, sealing it with the hopefully dead organic tendril still clinging to the canopy.

Game on! He dropped the heavy ACR that the ASHUR was holding—it was worthless now anyway. It thudded onto the parking lot with a hint of metallic grinding. Backing up, he aimed at the frog that was closest, the one with the whip. It wasn't facing him, but was lashing away at the front line defenders behind the barriers, bringing the whip down like Indiana Jones, only with sparks and flashes of electrical discharge shimmering in the air with the crack and hit.

The bang off to his left and above filled the capacitors of the rail gun with a surge of power that made them whine slightly. This time he was not startled by the bang. Fletch leveled the weapon at the frog that was assailing the line and the instant the reticle fell on it, he fired.

Crabs could shake off rail gun hits, but it was rare. Frogs . . . they exploded. The hypersonic slug hit its shoulder, passed through the alien's body, and out the other shoulder, liquefying the flesh, sending chunks flying and devouring the frog. A dark mist of blood splattered and both alien arms went flying. The whip fell free mid-swing, sliding in the air, moving a little bit on its own as fell. *Payback's a bitch.*

The ASHUR's movement and overkill shot caught the attention of one of the crabs who had torn apart the outer defensive line and was in the process of ripping down the last Hesco barriers to get inside the camp. The alien wheeled about on its eight legs, turning to face him, then broke into a rush that was stunningly fast. Fletch sidestepped the ASHUR and started to move out, away from the firebase, mostly to get some room to maneuver. As fast as he was moving, the crab was moving faster. He triggered another power round for the rail gun and brought the sight right on the rushing alien. The capacitor throbbed with energy, with a dull electric hum that seemed to mirror his anticipation.

There was a tug as the rail gun fired. The crab was so close that the plasma plume just reached it as the slug hit one of its massive claws, ripping the limb completely off. Before he could celebrate, the alien plowed into him, as if the loss of a limb meant nothing to it. The rig moaned and toppled over backwards onto the pavement, grinding as it slid with the crab right on top of him.

He had never thought about being this close to the aliens, not in the safety of his repair bay. Now it hovered right above him. There was no way to get the rail gun to aim. Rocking the rig side to side, it refused to budge, the thick legs of the crab holding him pinned in place. His left arm was up and he used his right as a club, beating onto the spot where he had just blown off one of the claws. If he was causing pain, the crab showed no signs of it. Its massive head dominated his canopy. Bits of drool-like spittle fell from its gaping maw. The tiny ball-like black eyes bore in on him.

Panic rose in him like a tidal surge, but he managed to keep it in check. *Wait—the flamethrower.* Karter had built it almost from scratch and it had never been fully tested. *It's all I have left.* He strained his arm in the control sleeve, flexing it far more than he ever had before, raising his left fist up. Fletch jabbed the nozzle along the side of the crab's head as its claw stabbed downward hard, bending in the canopy under the impact. The outer seals burst and he could feel the air, and the stench of the enemy on top of him. A sweet smell, with a hint of tuna fish fresh from the can.

From deep in the cockpit's control sleeve, Fletch toggled on the flamethrower and could hear the gurgle from the underarm tank. *Here goes nothing!* Depressing the firing stud, he heard the splash of the fluid as it hosed the side of the crab, running down onto his ASHUR's arm. Then there was a flash, orange and yellow and crimson. The roar of the flames was all around him, including some splashing on his canopy. The creature jerked, rocking the rig and tossing him hard in the cockpit, jarring his senses and his body alike. The temperature in the cockpit soared and the smell from the chemical burning made his eyes water.

The crab jumped off and he rolled to his side. The left arm of his rig was on fire and he was worried that it would set off his remaining fuel. As he pushed himself up, his body protesting every movement, Fletch jettisoned the small fuel tank. It ignited and fired off across the parking lot like a wayward rocket, leaving a burning trail all the way over to the abandoned grocery store where it finally sputtered out.

His alien foe whipped back and forth, its remaining claw attempting to beat the flames. Then it screamed, a sound out of a nightmare, primal and definitely not of Earth. The screech was both low and high and it had the effect of dragging fingers down a chalkboard with him, sending chills down his spine. Its agony was oddly rewarding. It finally flop over on its side, flames lapping skyward marking its death with a black and gray pillar of smoke. Two of its smaller legs twitched as the flames devoured the crab.

Pivoting, he looked down the line and saw the last of the crabs collapse under small arms fire from within the base. Dead frogs littered the pavement as well as the other crabs that had been taken down. Fletch surveyed the tactical screen but could not see any indication of other combatants.

"Hold your fire," came the voice of the CO on the battlespace channel and Fletch suddenly heard the din of gunfire that he had somehow mentally tuned out earlier. "The last of them is bugging out to the east. Apparently they've had enough for today."

Fletch didn't move. He just stared wildly at the damage to the firebase. Barriers were ripped apart and toppled. Sand was everywhere from the damaged ones. Only one of the towers that protected Firebase Hooligan still stood. From within the protective rings, black smoke billowed.

As much as he wanted to cheer, he was trembling. His breath was rapid and ragged, and his mouth was dry. Every joint and muscle seemed to hate him, sending pangs of protest to let him know. Fletch was unsure what he was supposed to do. His body was drenched in sweat and the sting of smoke in the ad hoc ASHUR cockpit still clung to his nose hairs. *I always pictured victory to look different from this—that I'd feel different if I ever did see battle.* A part of him wanted to cry as much as yell. When he saw a trio of fellow technicians scamper over the barriers and start to him, he held his emotions in check. *The last thing I need is the flak I'd get if they saw me all emotional.*

Punching the egress button, he raised what was left of the groaning canopy hatch and powered down the ASHUR. Waiting hands from his friends helped him down and he wobbled as he stood. Glancing at the rig, he saw the burn damage, the crushed armored plates, and the bit of the whip-tentacle that still somehow clung to the canopy. Their pet project was battered and beaten, but in his mind, he could see that it was repairable, given time.

Fletch forced a smile as the others peppered him with what they had seen and done. For a few moments, they were all heroes.

Ten days later . . .

"That's a hell of a creation," Lieutenant Calloway stated. He had been assigned from DARPA to look over their handiwork and had spent a full hour crawling over every bit of the ASHUR. He used a digital camera to take dozens of photos of it. It was easy to see that he was not just a lieutenant in a freshly pressed uniform, he was a tech. Up until now, he hadn't spoken a word, but had squeezed into every nook and cranny on the Frankenrig, checking everything from hose fittings to weapons mounts. Standing off to the side overseeing the inspection was the firebase's CO. Fletch was more impressed that the colonel was in the scrapyard for the first time than he was that the ASHUR engineering team sent someone to see what they had created.

The rig still bore the signs of battle. Emphasis on repairs had been to the weapons. Rebuilding the heavy ACR had taken Sherwood three days to get it operational again. The flamethrower had been Karter's pride and joy, and he got it working in good order in a week. Partlow and Hix had repaired the cockpit canopy with some castoffs in the scrapyard.

The lieutenant moved away from the rig and turned to Fletch. "How did you address the balance issues?"

"That was Corporal Martin," Fletch replied.

Martin stepped forward from the small line of technicians that were present. "Sir, I went through and eyeballed the center of gravity and reprogrammed it on the motivator board."

"You guys aren't supposed to be able to get into that code," the lieutenant said.

Martin shrugged. "This is war. What we are supposed to do and what we actually do are two different things."

The lieutenant nodded, then turned to Fletch. "And you had no training in piloting this thing?"

"We all went through the driver's class, but that's mostly maneuvering rigs into and out of the bay and running fit-and-trim tests."

The colonel spoke up. "As you saw in my message, Lieutenant, if it hadn't been for Corporal Tyson taking this thing into battle, we might have very well lost the base." For Fletch, that was the first time he had heard that sentence from the colonel—and he did what he could to hide his pride.

Lieutenant Calloway looked at Fletch, then at the colonel. "We have a lot of firebases along the front. From what I can see, your technicians used nothing but scrap to build this—they didn't put in anything that would have impaired operations. Some of these mods, like the igniter, may be improvements on what we are currently putting into service."

"My technicians are the best," the colonel said.

"Yes, sir, they are at that. I am going to recommend that we put together a formal program to have all of the techs undertake this kind of ingenuity. It's not necessarily a front-line rig, but ASHURs like this would be a welcome bonus for a National Guard unit or even the militia." Calloway turned to Fletch. "Do you and your colleagues think you can put together a training program on what you did and how you did it?"

Fletch glimpsed over at the colonel who gave him a nod, then turned back to the lieutenant. "Yes, sir." Fletch had never put together a training program before—but he found a degree of excitement at the prospect. *Who would have thought that what we cobbled together would be of interest to the Army?*

The lieutenant looked over at the rig, drinking in a final look. Turning back to Fletch. "Outstanding work, Corporal. There's some details I need to work through with your CO. All of you did a hell of a job. You should be proud."

As the colonel and lieutenant left, the other techs huddled around Fletch. "You know you're going to get a medal for that shit you pulled off," Hix said first.

"I'm just thankful they aren't pissed off," Fletch replied.

"Every tech out there will be clamoring to do what we did—especially after the results we got," Partlow said.

"If nothing else, you got the old man to come down to the scrapyard," Martin added. "Until today, I don't think he even knew this place existed."

The huddle of technicians started to move to the chow line in the old Subway. He was close to ordering when he felt a pat on his shoulder. Turning, he saw Boomer Correia standing beside him with a double lunch on his tray. "I've got you covered," he said.

"Oooh," Hix said as he was led off to a table where Sergeant Roughcut Lewis was sitting. Correia gestured to the seat and set the tray down. It felt like being invited to sit with the popular kids in high school, though he fully anticipated some abuse from his technician colleagues. "We haven't had much time to talk," Correia said. "I just thought you should know, that was an impressive bit of piloting you pulled off."

Sergeant Lewis spoke up before Fletch could respond. "Not everyone is cut out to pilot a rig. You did it—and did it under fire. Damn good work."

"I was lucky," Fletch managed as he unwrapped the sandwich that Boomer had brought him.

"Well, you're a pilot now," Correia said. "I hope they don't pull you off as my tech."

"I doubt that," he said, though he wondered if that was even an option.

"Well," the sergeant said. "You'll need a call sign."

"I'm a tech," Fletch replied as he chewed the first bite of the tuna fish sandwich. "Tech's don't have call signs."

Correia shook his head. "You're more than a tech now. If you don't pick one, we'll end up assigning you one."

It was hard for Fletch Tyson to deny that he was looking forward to his new moniker.

THE TOLL

This is a novella based on Claire Dalton—who appears in *Storm Surge* for a short cameo appearance. Her story gets dramatically expanded into this novella-length tale. This was fun to write because we get to see the Air Force Pararescue forces in action for the first time, along with their specialized XO gear. When you need to get out of town, sometimes you have to pay a toll . . .

Part I: Mission 612J—Operation Boll Weevil 3

The Eastern American Front, Free Boston, Massachusetts

Corporal Claire Dalton was not looking forward to her patrol but no sane infantryman ever did. Moving into "The Zone" was not something she enjoyed. The troops called it "The Zone" but the Army's designation was the AIZ—Alien Incursion Zone. Regardless of what it was called now, she hated the partially destroyed section of downtown Boston. It wasn't just that it tore at her heart to see the east side of Boston turned into a war zone, though that did gnaw at her. Gone were games at Fenway in the spring. Gone were strolls with a boyfriend along the Charles River. Hell, gone was the boyfriend, now a refugee somewhere in an Ohio camp. It was the fact that her life was at risk just getting near The Zone. There were a hundred different ways to die in the AIZ.

When I joined the National Guard five years ago, I never thought I'd be signing up to kill aliens in downtown Boston . . . Before the war, she had worked downtown on the eleventh floor of a skyscraper for a pharmaceutical company as an accounts payable representative. She had joined the National Guard because she liked the outdoors and the sense of belonging to something other than work. She had met genuine friends in the National Guard, closer than her coworkers ever were. There was the family history too—her father had served in the Russo-Bratva War after the cyberattack on Gray Monday.

The National Guard offered her something tangible that dealt with issues of real importance in life, unlike her day job. It was hard to bond with her coworkers—everyone fighting for a promotion, battling their own incompetence, or backstabbing to get ahead. Working all day, moving digital information from one electronic pile to another, was tediously boring. She hardly knew anyone in the office, and those she did know, she didn't care about. To her it was a vast sea of cubicles where she sat every day to make money in order to pay her bills. The invasion put that part of her life on hold. Her apartment was outside of The Zone, but she hadn't seen it since she'd been called up. Her employer was in The Zone, so she became instantly unemployed. Claire's memories of coworkers and her old daily routine were fading memories. She wasn't the same person anymore either. Claire had dropped nearly ten pounds and was stronger and faster than she had been since college. She had seen things, horrible things, people dying right in front of her, that made her old life feel as if it were a boring foreign movie with subtitles. That wasn't her in that life . . . this was who she was. *I wonder if I'll ever be able to return after this?* A part of her never wanted to go back. *Here I can make a difference.*

One-on-one, she was called Claire Dalton, but in the Zone, her call sign was Foxbat. It was a relatively new thing in the military—getting a semi-formal call sign. The informal rule was that to qualify for one, you had to be in battle at least twice. In the past, such tags had been for pilots, but in the last war, everyone adopted it. The 2020s had everyone wailing about equality and equity, and the military had acquiesced to doling them out to appease the whiners. Call signs were formally assigned by sergeants. Why he had chosen Foxbat-5 for her, she had no idea. She had learned there were four other Foxbats in the Army, though none were in her sector. Everyone dropped the numbers and went with the words.

This was to be a recon mission, an in-and-out for her squad. Try to probe the enemy lines and gather intel on their activities. When the invasion had started, drones had done most of the reconnaissance duty. The aliens, they had adapted and had started to take out the drones when they saw them. That meant doing things the old-fashioned way . . . sending in ground-pounders to do the job.

Fortunately this isn't my first rodeo. She had been on recon runs into The Zone before. Eleven of them in total, some more successful than others. Roughly half had led to engagements with the enemy. Her first one was pure terror . . . one of the guys, "Hotshot" Henderson, had actually wet himself in his first firefight. His new call sign became "Wetspot" until he bought the farm two weeks later. Replacement troops were that way—they came, went on a mission or two—the good ones lived, the rest ended up like "Wetspot." Claire considered herself lucky. Her sergeant, Ringo "Beatle" McRory, was a pilot of a second-generation ASHUR suit. These were the epitome of powered battle armor, a mix of a tank's firepower with an armored infantry suit. Just having him piloting the rig meant they had a better chance of coming through the mission alive. It gave the squad an edge, even if it was one of the older rigs.

The new ASHUR Gen III rigs were the new state of the art. The older Gen II suits like McRory's Mamba had been retired from active service and passed down to the National Guard. They were noisier, which bothered her because noise drew unwanted attention and attention could draw death. The older models had been retrofit with new fuel cells and weaponry, courtesy of the alien tech—but otherwise were still cumbersome compared to the new, sleeker Gen IIIs. The operator's movements were more limited and a bit slower. It could carry heavy weapons though and did provide fairly good protection. Having any battle armor leading the squad was welcomed and strangely reassuring. *Though it would be more reassuring if I were piloting it.*

Her appreciation of an ASHUR rig and a qualified pilot, even an older one, was well earned. The rigs were a cross between advanced personal body armor and a tank. Standing at over eight feet tall, an operator was strapped inside of a "rig" that was covered with STF (Sheer Thickening Fluid) and triple-infused ceramic armor plates, carbon-fiber molecular weave, and a stunning arsenal of weapons. ASHUR pilots were the best-of-the-best in the military, and even then the failure rate in the program was high. They fought in the armored suits as if it were a part of their body, with micro-actuators and integrated hydraulic systems that made the rigs eerily human in their movements. ASHUR pilots could go where tanks couldn't go, bringing with them enough firepower to devastate anything they came across . . . almost. The aliens had proven to be tough nuts to crack, even for ASHUR pilots. Still, they were the best line of defense against the new enemy. Sergeant McRory's Mamba-class rig had smooth contoured lines and an arched back/head that leaned forward slightly, almost like a snake rearing for a strike. He had his personal insignia painted on its right chest armor plate—a Pitbull wearing a Boston Red Sox jersey with the name "Fluffy Death" painted under it in bright pink. When pressed as to the origins of logo, he would only flash a smile. ASHUR pilots rarely revealed the origins of their "nose art" to non-pilots; it was part of the mystique of being the military's elite.

Her squad's trek to the AIZ was a barrage on the senses. The sights were depressing—blasted buildings, long abandoned cars. The stink of uncollected refuse mixed with the aroma of something dead and a hint of burned plastic. The emptiness, the lack of people, made it even more eerie for Claire. It didn't seem like the Boston she knew at all; it was like some alternate reality version of the city.

They reached the edge of The Zone. It was hard to miss. Bright green spray-painted warnings were on every building and standing wall. When the aliens had hit Boston, like they had in many cities, they advanced a short distance then stopped. Some of it was the human resistance, but that wasn't all. No one knew for sure why they had stopped. *They probably see us as more of an annoyance than a threat. That's how it was in the early days at least.* The aliens were operating according to their own agenda, and that made them more dangerous in Dalton's mind.

Boston had suffered two attacks, months apart. The initial alien attack on Boston had been insidious, aimed at stirring fear among the civilians. The aliens made themselves known when they had sent ashore eight massive bus-sized snail-like creatures that were filled with millions of alien sand-flea-like carnivores into Boston. Despite the physical similarities, the differences ended there. These were the size of golf balls. Their exoskeletons looked like deformed human skulls. Normally sand fleas would not have been an issue except these were large, ravenous, and when they swarmed, they moved in a wild frenzy of jumping and crawling. They fanned out into the city like a carnivorous plague, killing thousands and devouring them like a host of locusts born in the bowels of hell. The Army and the media called them "goblins" and the name stuck. Claire saw them more like piranhas. They were attracted to motion and noise. They went after those that tried to flee, clogging the streets as food for the creatures. The goblins gorged themselves on anything alive, spreading fear and panic as they swarmed. In a matter of a few days, the creatures simply died off, en masse. According to the scientists, it was all according to the alien genetic engineering of the creatures: a high metabolic rate that led to a short lifespan.

After that attack, many people understandably left downtown. There had been widespread looting during and following the goblins' rampage. For some reason she couldn't explain, people used such situations to steal and set fires. Entire neighborhoods were lost to the fires before the Fire Department could get them under control. While many people fled the goblin attack, a surprising number stayed behind. *Boston is a tough town, that's why.* The Army and National Guard moved in, prepositioning equipment, expendables, and gear. Larger scaled attacks had taken place in Iceland, Guam, Hawaii, and other islands, with other alien creatures and devastating weapons. It seemed that the aliens were testing mankind's capability to respond. Troops barracked in abandoned homes, set up defensive positions—preparing for an attack that no one hoped would come.

Hopes be dammed. The invasion came two-and-a-half months later. The aliens hit many of the coastal cities around the world, all at the same time. Even cities like Washington, DC, which were upriver, were struck with incredible precision and brutality. The scale of the attacks was staggering and devastating. Despite some preparations, coastal cities were overwhelmed.

In Boston, the aliens came in on three axes of attack—Dorchester, Logan Airport, and Fort Point. The Army and National Guard had expected them in Boston Harbor, so the strikes around their defended positions caught everyone off guard. The civilians that were left in the city tried to flee, but the aliens swung around as far inland as Cambridge, cutting them off. The Army dug in at East Boston and the North End. The fighting in the North End was the worst. They called it the Alamo. Two companies of Army infantry surrounded by the enemy, under steady alien assault. The aliens kept coming and their perimeter dwindled to a few blocks of rubble and ruin that were turned into a makeshift fort. If not for a daring breakout, the defenders would have been wiped out. With their departure, the Army dug in along a forty-nine-mile front, grinding the alien offense to a semi-stable standstill.

Without humans taking care of infrastructure, Boston's AIZ was left to decay. There were fires that broke out and were left to burn, sewage and water pipes that burst and were left un-patched. Power failed, as did the net, leaving those that remained in the city unconnected for the first time in a generation. The stench of garbage, sewage, and rotting flesh hung in the alleys and streets—enough to make Dalton's stomach pitch almost every time she entered the inner city. *It tears at my heart to see the city like this, rotting.*

The alien warriors were not simply a single race—there were multiple forms of them. The mainstay of the enemy were tagged by the military as Class I Alien Combatants—but they were known as crabs to the infantry. Massive creatures with six large legs and a dangerous tail-appendage, they were slightly taller than an infantryman, but deadly close-in fighters. Their exoskeletons were really a form of armor over their guts—the aliens didn't wear battle armor like Dalton and her squad, they were grown into it. They rose in their midsection like a mythical centaur, using smaller insect-like arms on their upper bodies to manipulate objects. Crabs struggled inside of buildings; they weren't built for human infrastructure. On the streets, however, they were vicious combatants.

There were other aliens to contend with too. Short stubby ones that seemed to be the alien scouts—called Foxes, mostly for their apparent cunning. They only seemed to fight when pressed. Then there were massive creatures, called Tanks by the infantry, though the Army preferred the referring to them as Turtles. On their own, they could plow into a building and knock it down with sheer strength. Some acted as transports, carrying other aliens when they sprang in the air, their preferred mode of travel. The size of a large truck, Tanks were all but immune to small arms fire. It took a lot to kill them, and if you didn't, they would maul a squad brutally, biting and stomping troops into the rubble.

There were smaller "Dillos" named for Armadillos which they resembled. These things moved like attack rats—hard to hit, small, and when they clamped onto your leg or arm, they secreted a toxin that could incapacitate or kill. Some were even armed with weapons. She had heard rumors of other alien species, everything from armored snake-like eels to octopus-like creatures that were allegedly the size of a building. *Rumors are free of charge in the Army.*

The worst of the enemies seen thus far were dubbed "Bosses." They had an oddly formed almost-human shape, two legs with flat clawed and webbed feet for support, massive in size—easily eight or nine feet tall. They were like ASHUR suits except they lacked the hydraulic hoses and actuators. They were biological armored suits as opposed to mechanical, with thick muscles and extreme mobility. Bosses had shell-like armor plates embedded into their armor-like skin on their torsos and thighs. Bosses' heads were flattened, with long black eye-slit visors. Their hands were more like three-appendage claws, powerful enough to cut off a human limb, yet oddly able to handle delicate activities. They were taller, bigger than many ASHUR suits, and heavily armed. They were heavy too—apparently their bodies carried a full ecosystem of cold water for them to operate in. When a Boss showed up, you called for fire support, checked your egress routes, and made every shot count.

The alien species were merely the start of the threat that Dalton faced. Their weaponry was almost as insidious as the aliens carrying them. It seemed like every day the DoD was issuing new specs and warnings. *Why couldn't these bastards just use guns like we do?* The aliens possessed a bizarre array of weapons: slicers—ultra-high-pressure water jets which were like lasers, melters—ranged weapons that fired an exploding burst of corrosive acid-goo, spikers—weapons that fired poisonous needles that could punch through many types of body armor, and a dozen other ways to kill. Their boomers were bazooka-like weapons that fired sonic blasts that could devastate personnel and city blocks, pulverizing buildings to dust. They had weapons that could disable electronics and others that sprayed nerve agents which left their victims contorting in agony. Claire had seen one of her squad, Jax Nichols, cut down by a crab using some sort of electrical whip once—it had cut the private's right leg clean off. The Fish (as the aliens were generally referred to by the troops) used a variety of mine-like devices too. Their artillery was a weird mix of death and destruction, combining the worst of their weapons. The thing that Dalton hated the most was that their weapons were not explosive—they tended to be quiet. You sometimes didn't know you were under fire until people started screaming in pain or dropped dead. *The Fish hate explosions as much, if not more, than we do.* Every foray into The Zone was like a series of deadly science experiments crossed with an obstacle course staffed by monsters.

Despite all of this, there were holdouts, humans that had barricaded themselves in their homes and apartments, who refused to flee. Corporal Dalton couldn't understand it. They voluntarily remained behind the front lines, their survival in question every moment. Sane people fled. No matter what, there were some people that stubbornly refused. Some fought, others scrounged for survival. *Damned fools . . . no apartment or townhome is worth dying for.*

At the sergeant's orders, the squad moved like a snake along the streets, slithering under the watchful firepower of the other members of the 26th Massachusetts Division, the Yankee Division. From windows, doors, and reinforced positions, their guns hovered over Claire and her squad, just waiting for the aliens to attempt to push out of The Zone. The problem was that the aliens advanced in jerks and stops—so far, unpredictable and sometimes in places that seemed to defy logic. It had been three weeks since they had last advanced. The Yankee Division had been called up and tossed into the battleground of downtown Boston to attempt to contain the Fish. The 26th was cobbled together from various National Guard regiments, including her own 102nd Division which had been absorbed into the 26th a month into the fighting. The majority of the division was dug in, huddled in buildings and makeshift fortifications, waiting for the next alien offensive. It was good to know they were out there for backup—but they were staying behind. Dalton's squad was going forward.

Sergeant McRory assembled the team at the brick wall, the florescent green painted warnings looming over him. The building had a big metal door that was closed and cross-hatched with green paint to add a further sense of warning. Even in his Mamba ASHUR rig, he was dwarfed by the wall. He spoke in a hushed but firm tone through the external speakers. "Alright, people—welcome to Mission 612J or as the brass likes to call it, Operation Boll Weevil Three. Word is that there is some sort of activity taking place in sector two, downtown. We sent in drones, but they took them down before we could get a good idea of what was happening on the ground. GRDs likewise went in but never even got close to the areas before they were intercepted. HQ has asked us to go in and check it out visually. This isn't a gunfight—it's a recon, plain and simple. We get some vid, gather intel, get out in one piece."

"Yes, Sergeant," they all replied in a low tone.

"I want the scout GRDs in first. Have the Greyhounds in map-mode, Roughrider. We need to get a good battlespace display of what is in this building first, Watson. Keep them in the building to start—no point in tipping off the Fish that we are coming." Ground Robotic Drones were used extensively by the military. Some, like the Greyhounds, were rigged with sensors and cameras. Greyhounds were excellent at helping map the BS, or battlespace, the digital battlefield that each infantryman could access. Others, like Huskies, were heavy weapons carriers, taking the strain off the soldiers. The drones were respected by the squad, and their handlers (controllers) were vital members of the unit. GRDs often stumbled onto the enemy first, and their loss often prevented the loss of human lives. The controller for her squad was Corporal Randy "Roughrider" Watson. He was an arrogant prick when it came to his GRDs, something everyone, including Claire, was willing to overlook because he was damn good at his job.

"Once we get into The Zone, I want sweeps with P-drones of the surrounding area before we move out." His nasal north-end accent came through the speakers loud and clear.

"Sergeant," Private Copeland queried. "Where exactly are we heading?"

"Charleston Navy Yard," he replied as his Mamba twisted at the waist to face Copeland. "Air Force drones picked up something seriously Fishy going on there, pun intended. Lots of alien activity in that area, more than in most neighborhoods. The Air Force is limited by what it can't see. That's where we come in. We're eyes and ears on the ground. Get in, see what they're doing, report back. Recon mission, plain and simple."

"Why doesn't the Air Force just bomb the shit out of them?" Private Adams asked as she did a quick check of her Remington ACR-25, adjusting the stock length.

"Didn't you study the ROEs, Adams? You don't just indiscriminately bomb the enemy. Everything you blow up is our property—our buildings. Besides, we know of a few Resistance groups working in the area. We don't want to risk killing our people in the process. That is why we have the damn ROEs." No one liked the Rules of Engagement, they hamstrung squads at times from doing what was necessary, but they *were* the rules.

The mention of the Resistance got a mix of nods and eye-rolls. Everyone seemed to have an opinion on them. Claire thought they were good. Most were highly motivated folks, armed to the hilt, fighting the same enemy as the Army. Others in her squad were frustrated by the Resistance . . . feeling that they were more in the way than helpful. The few she had crossed paths with were decent folks, even the former biker gang, the South-Siders, who had been wreaking random havoc for weeks with the Fish. Fighting in the Resistance was harder than being in the infantry. You had to scrounge for weapons and food. But there were no complicated ROEs telling you what you could and couldn't do. She envied them and their ability to wage war as they saw fit. Of course, once the shooting started, ROEs got tossed. Claire had seen that before.

She activated her Mark III ECH's (Enhanced Combat Helmet's) drop-down visor. In her left upper quadrant was a vague BS schematic of the building in front of her and about half of a block. There were plenty of fuzzy areas on the digital readout, which the Greyhounds would hopefully feed to her helmet and the rest of the squad. The digital map displayed the members of her squad as green, with no red enemy dots showing. *With any luck, that won't change.*

Sergeant McRory used his Mamba's armored hand to slide the door open with a loud grinding of metal on concrete. The shoulder-mounted articulated chain gun on the Mamba swept the room side-to-side as the sergeant leaned in slightly. McRory cracked it open about three feet, then pulled back. "Deploy the hounds," he said in a low tone. The two Greyhound GRDs jumped through the opening and he slid the door shut after them. The Greyhounds were two and a half feet long with chipped olive drab ceramic-plated torsos covering their sensitive gear. The "head" was a rounded oblong almost like a football, with a number of different sensors and cameras. They didn't as much run as they bounded on spindly foot-long legs. When they moved, they bounced forward and reminded Dalton of a toy. That motion and their small footprint made them relatively quiet, though no one knew for sure if the Fish could hear anything. Intel had said they hated loud noises, but no one knew just how the aliens sensed things beyond visual sighting. The drones, however, picked up everything: EM signatures, infrared, bio-sigs, structural mapping, temperature variance—the works. The data was relayed their field controllers like Roughrider, who fed HQ, which then fed the battlespace feeds in the squad's helmets—all almost real-time.

Roughrider had an armored digipad slung in front of him on his chest that he used to control the Greyhounds. "Deploying and mapping, Sergeant," he said as his fingers danced on the tablet screen. Claire could see the details of the building where they were standing in front of start to emerge. The four-story storefront had nasty tight spaces and many rooms. She hated that. Urban combat was the worst kind, and with lots of tight spaces, death was usually up close and personal. Corporal Watson left one Greyhound sweeping the street outside of the little store, while the other swept the rest of the building. It took eight long minutes, but he finally made the call. "We're good to go, Sergeant. No Fishies so far."

McRory transmitted a quick burst. "Battlespace Commander, Yankee Recon Two-Ten, entering AIZ at Bravo-Sierra Ten on Boll Weevil Three." The sergeant turned to the members of his squad, speaking with his Boston nasal accent. "Alright then. We're going in. I want a Victor six-by-six formation. Roland—you've got point and I'm in the middle. We move in and take positions along Bartlett Street. Maintain good fields of fire, know where your squad-mates are."

The interior of the small market had been looted, either during the panicked evacuation or by those still living in The Zone. There was a hint of rotting produce from some of the smashed cases at the front of the store which Dalton tried hard to ignore. To her, the whole Zone stunk of garbage and rot. With no trash pickup, those that lived there simply threw their garbage in ruins or empty lots. There was the stench of rotting flesh too. No one was there to bury the dead killed in the incursion . . . though she had heard of some Resistance groups, namely the Brothers of Samuel, taking on that solemn task. It was hard to say what was rumor and reality in Beantown. The whole world had turned upside down when the Fish invaded Boston.

They moved to the front of the little market, keeping cover behind the abandoned cooler near the shattered remains of the front window. There were the sounds of erratic popping in the distance, gunfire, somewhere out in The Zone. The sergeant's Mamba loomed behind a magazine rack, relying more on his armor for protection than the ballistic protection of the old magazines. He scanned the street. "Okay, sweep the Greyhounds down the street. Ajax and Falcone, deploy your pocket drones. Roughrider, I want those to hit the upper floors of those townhouses, make sure we're clear." Private Keegan "Ajax" Murray and Alphonse "Falcone" Ramirez broke out their collapsible and disposable pocket drones and snapped out their armatures for the rotors. They purred to live and whizzed off through the broken front window. Their range was limited to four blocks maximum, but their cameras gave Roland a camera view of the upper floor windows to make sure no surprises waited for the squad. The Greyhounds followed, half-jumping, half-bouncing out the opening as well. Roughrider's fingers moved like a conductor over his digipad as he deployed the drones. His visor wasn't down and Claire could see that he was smiling. *Only a joyboy would treat this like a video game.*

Five minutes passed where the squad relaxed a little. Claire leaned against one of the side walls but kept her ACR at the ready, just in case. Just because the drones didn't spot the enemy, that didn't mean that the enemy was not out there. The rule was that the Fish *were* out there; they were *everywhere.*

"Alright," Sergeant McRory said as he checked his wrist. "Paint me a picture, Roughrider."

Watson squinted as his digipad readouts. "So far, so good, Sergeant." Claire's battlespace refreshed and she could see more detail than before.

The sergeant turned to face them, his troops giving the bulky ASHUR suit some clearance as he pivoted. "We move up as far as the office building across from the Bunker Hill Memorial. Keep to the right side of the street. Standard H formation. We'll use the memorial as our waypoint." Off in the distance, there was a rumble, the sound of an explosion, probably miles away. Was it a gas leak that had ignited? *No, the explosion was sharp, crisp.* It was US artillery, Claire was certain of it. Full-out barrages were rarer in the AIZ. The Army simply did not have the stockpiles of ammunition that they needed for a prolonged domestic invasion. You didn't call in "Steel Rain" unless you had to, and most of the time, it still didn't come. The official stance was that production was stepping up, but so far the word was, "conserve ammo." There were a lot of rumors about shortages of munitions—but she tried to tune the gossip out.

They moved up the right side of street briskly—with the sergeant shifting to point. Two blocks down, they came to the office building and entered through a glass doorway, fanning out inside. Ajax and Falcone found their pocket drones nearby and recovered them. The Greyhounds were there already outside, like obedient dogs awaiting their master's next command. The squad moved into the office building and immediately sought cover. She looked around the offices on the first floor and found them dull and drab. Potted plants withered, lacking water. The office smelled musty—with the HVAC systems off, water had gotten in somewhere and was molding. *Even if they left today, it would take years to clean up the mess these Fish created.*

Across the street stood the obelisk of the Bunker Hill Monument, it was as stately as she remembered it. A smaller version of the Washington Monument in DC, she half-expected to see it blown apart. *I watched too many sci-fi movies as a kid.* Movies always destroyed monuments for impact on the audience. *In real life, the only thing that gets blown up is the infantry.* The park had been eerily abandoned. The monument was undamaged by the aliens, though the park, left unattended, had knee-high grass and overgrown bushes. There were paths through the tall grass where someone, or something, had strode through, knocking down the grass and leaving an erratic trail. Corporal Dalton didn't want to know who had made the paths. *I probably won't like the answer.*

The squad paused after nearly two hours, huddling down between the empty husks of cars. Most of them took their water pack hoses and drew a long drag. Even in the autumn, running in full gear, with a sense of danger in the air, you sweat. The one thing the National Guard trained you on was hydration. She pulled her water tube up and took a suck. It was warm, but it helped.

The sergeant's Mamba looked out longingly at the Bunker Hill Memorial. "Alright, people, the next hop we make takes us three more blocks under Route 1. We're going to stop there. I need you people roasty-toasty. We are deep inside the belly of the Fish. Engage your adaptive camo, do quick checks of your squad mates. You see something that is threatening, you warn, confirm, then fire. In that order—not like that last foul up." Private Warner on the last recon mission had gotten nervous and fired at a palm tree he saw through a window, swearing it was the enemy. Ten minutes later, the Fish flooded in and forced them to fight a withdrawal.

The Adaptive Camouflage System, or ACS, could render a soldier or a tank cloaked—nearly invisible. They were quirky; sometimes they flickered which made you stand out. The moment your armor got hit, they would reveal you too. They ate power, so you had to be selective as to when to use them. Claire had sat through the lecture about the technology and how it worked, but in her mind all she needed to know was how to turn it on and off and adjust it.

The Greyhounds and two more personal drones swept on ahead of the squad by several minutes. The next three blocks were expensive brownstones. All had a look of abandonment about them. As they moved along the right side of the street, Claire spotted one that appeared to being tended for. Unlike others where the doors were left half-flung open, this one was closed up. The upper windows had plywood covering the broken and pristine windows from the inside. Either there was a determined holdout here or it was a Resistance safe house.

The next waypoint ended at a wall. The road came to a T-intersection at Route 1. Back during the era of the commute, you would go right and you took the on-ramp to the highway. To the left, and you could cut over to the next street at an underpass. Cars didn't run in the city anymore; they drew immediate unwanted alien attention and response.

The squad held up at the wall, and Claire scanned right and left. At the intersection, in front of the wall, she felt horribly exposed and it made her edgy. It wasn't just her. She could see it in the eyes of the rest of her squad.

Sergeant McRory spoke in a whisper via his comm system which she could hear clearly in her earbud. "We're going down the ramp and around the corner. The shipyard will be in front of us. I will check to see if we're clear. If we are, you four," he pointed to Rodriguez, Trace, Copland, and Hendershot, "will cross the street. The rest of us will move on the right side. We go slow and careful."

The four troops moved briskly across the street, sweeping with their guns. They were quickly out of Claire's line of sight, so she checked the rear and flank—mostly out of instinct. Copland's voice chimed in. "Sergeant, the left here is a lot of debris. It looks like a firefight down here at some point. I see lots of brass on the ground. Whatever happened here happened a while back. I can't tell for sure, but it looks like these buildings have been demolished by the Fish. No burn marks from a firefight; they're just smashed. Moving on the left side of the street is a no-go."

Trace chimed in. "I have motion in the third house. I'm not getting IR on it. Possible Fish activity in the rubble," he said in a whisper. "They may be looking for something. We're still all fuzzy, so they couldn't have seen us."

At the corner, McRory peered his Mamba around the concrete wall. "Shit. New plan. We are all sticking to the right side of the street. Roughrider, send one Greyhound under the overpass and check the far side." The robotic drone skipped around the corner. "Lots of damage down there, Sergeant, but it looks like there's cover on the right."

McRory's hulking Mamba turned back to the rest of the squad, broadcasting to the earbuds they wore in their helmets. "Alright, listen up. The Fish are tearing down some of the buildings from what I saw down there. We've got a possible bogey halfway down the block. We are going to move out only on the right. After we come out from the overpass, right flank, grab whatever cover you can along the way. We are going to have to make this fast, people. Let's get past this bogey and not draw any unwanted attention. Remember, you have ACS engaged, so keep tabs on each other to avoid bumping into each other. Move in pairs. If we draw fire, hold positions and await my orders." Claire tightened the grip on her ACR-25 to the point where it was just like an extension of her arm. If the sergeant said there were Fish ahead, then there was trouble ahead.

McRory took the lead in his ASHUR, followed by Private Khianey. Despite the bulk and weight of the Mamba rig, McRory could make it sprint when he wanted to. His footfalls on the pavement were muffled slightly with padding on the large feet of the armored gear, but not by much. "Next," he signaled.

Claire and Ramirez took off. Claire ran hard and fast, crouching slightly to provide a lower target profile. Running in combat gear was hard, getting killed was much easier, so she pushed her legs to their limit. Every ten steps or so, she saw a shimmer of Ramirez's ACS for a millisecond as it readjusted. As she reached the end of the overpass, she rounded the corner and saw a massive pile of rubble that had been a business building at one time. Now debris was piled up to a full story in height with rubble of the collapsed upper floors. There was no sign of an explosion; she knew what battle damage looked like and this wasn't it. No, something had demolished this building. The first floor of the structure looked somewhat intact, but the upper two floors were collapsed into the shell of the bottom floor. It was a jumble of bricks, broken wood, wire, and bits and pieces of people's lives. A smashed microwave oven, parts of a crushed box spring for a bed, all were mixed in with the red bricks and bits of white mortar. *Probably someone's apartment over the store.* Very little of the debris was in the alleyway other than a few neat mounds of brick, most was concentrated in the structure—an indication that the demolition was deliberate. As she leaned into the pile of bricks to lower her profile, she looked across the street and saw the same sort of destruction. *It's as if they are demolishing the buildings—why?*

She heard sounds coming from nearby, further down the street, the sounds of demolition underway. *The Fish are up to something, that much is for sure.* That was what the sergeant was worried about. They moved up in pairs, McRory whispering, "next," until the entire squad had made its way to the alley with mounds of rubble near the demolished structures.

"Alright," he said in a low tone as he crouched. "I need a pair to crawl into this rubble and see if you can vid what these bastards are doing." His south-side of Boston nasal twang rang with his words into her earbuds.

Claire had learned one thing very well: you don't volunteer for anything in the Army. It was a lesson that the rest of the squad knew too, so no one raised their hands. "What a bunch of wusses. Rodriguez, you get your ass up there and handle the filming. Dalton, you go with her on overwatch. Both of you, move silently—go slow and careful." Claire nodded and shot a nasty glance over at Rodriguez and bit her tongue. Rodriguez was not the best soldier in the squad, not by far. She had a knack for not being around when the shooting started.

Dalton slung her ACR on her back and put on her thin-weave gloves. Some squad members wore them all of the time; they were durable and gave you the sensitivity needed for firing. A few like Copeland cut out the fingertips to allow you to feel the trigger. Claire didn't, she wanted full mobility and sense on her fingers. Climbing into the pile of debris was going to difficult enough and there was no point in getting injured by the debris itself.

The key to moving through the debris and keeping quiet was to go slow and test your footing and handholds first. The jumble of rubble made that difficult. Even moving carefully, things shifted and made noise and her ACS flickered momentarily. Rodriguez was a little clumsier, sending one broken brick tumbling down a pile, causing a minor avalanche and kicking up some dust in the process. She turned back to Claire for a moment and she gave her a scowl is if to say, "you idiot!" *One day her arrogance is going to get her in a world of hurt. I just hope I'm not around when it happens.*

They slowly snaked their way up a pile of bricks, broken lumber, and shattered housewares to where the exterior wall came to an end. The broken edges gave them adequate cover; their bodies sloped down the pile into the center of the ruined house. Both Rodriguez and Dalton took out their portable vids and put the tiny devices up on the exterior wall, aimed down at the old Charleston Navy Yard. "Transmitting," she muttered into her throat mike. "Roger that," came back Watson. What Claire saw feeding into her helmet visor pop-up was puzzling, and most likely why they had been sent on this recon mission in the first place.

The old Navy Yard was alive with activity, almost like a colony of ants. The crab-like warrior aliens were around the fringes, seemingly providing security. Gone were the structures of the historic site; they were piles of rubble just like the one Claire lay in, aged historic red brick in random piles. Several other buildings were being dismantled by large aliens that she had never seen before. They were easily two yards tall, if not larger, and looked like a mass of tentacles. Their bodies reminded her of man-sized snakes, like cobras, upright and ready to strike. *New Fish. Great. Just what we didn't need.*

Coming from the water of the old piers were massive tube-like growths—large enough for a man to walk through. These were not constructs, but not like anything a human manufactured. The way the material wobbled and the strange bulges and vein-like growths were on the tubes, they appeared to be organic. The opening for the tubes was a membrane, almost pinkish, with a slit down the center that the aliens moved in and out of. The tubes led into the water and through the "skin" of the walls she could make out the forms of creatures moving in the tubes. *They are like walkways for them . . . right back into the water.*

The scope of the operations that the aliens were engaged in surprised her. The Charleston Navy Yard was not the only area demolished—there were entire city blocks beyond the Yard that were now nothing more than shells of buildings like the one Claire lay in. Across the Charles River the once built up area in Jeffries Point was now more of mounds of rubble and debris than actual buildings. Oddly enough, some buildings were left relatively intact. *Why? What are these bastards up to?* She couldn't see the Boston Coast Guard base but had to assume that it was devastated as well.

What stirred her the most was that she could see the USS *Constitution* afloat near her pier. With all of the carnage, she expected to see the grand old ship that she had visited in her youth to be in ruins as well. But the aliens had simply moved the vessel to accommodate one of their bizarre transit tubes, and the antique ship looked just like it always had. Claire sighed slightly at the sight of the vessel. The fact that it was still afloat stirred her—it was not just a ship to Bostonians— it was a symbol of the city and the nation. She had been to the ship so many times in her youth, on field trips and with her father . . . seeing it meant there was a glimmer of hope. *It must not have been important to them, but it is important to me.*

The WWII era USS *Cassin Young* was not as fortunate as the *Constitution.* The destroyer had been on display for decades as a museum ship, but those days were gone. The aliens had begun to dismantle the ship, literally stripping her apart. Most of her superstructure was simply gone, apparently cut off. Two creatures, which looked more like giant walking squids than anything else, where on top of the remaining forward turret, apparently cutting into the turret with some sort of tools she didn't recognize. The *Cassin Young* had survived the battles and horrors of WWII only to be unceremoniously stripped in the safety of her pier. Claire adjusted her camera to zoom in on the squid-things. *Maybe the guys in intel can figure out what we're seeing.* After a few minutes, she un-zoomed the camera image for a broader view.

Large creatures, which were dubbed Tanks by the infantry, were dragging along material behind them. She aimed the camera there for a moment and noticed on the feed in her visor that they were hauling metal only. The metallic grating on the streets confirmed to her it was metal, and she could see girders and trusses, apparently ripped from buildings. Other aliens she had never seen before, huge creatures that seemed to be a cross between a squid and an armadillo, were using the aliens' high-pressure water cutters to break the metallic pieces down into smaller pieces. In the distance, she heard a rumble and another building went down beyond the Navy Yard, sending a plume of dust and dirt rising into the air marking its death. There was no explosion—it wasn't an Army action, there was no explosion from artillery or rocket fire. It was a controlled, deliberate collapse.

"Are you getting this, Roughrider?" she said in a whisper.

"Five-by-five, Foxbat," Watson replied. "I've been relaying the sigs to HQ. Checking out the new Fish in town," he added sarcastically.

"How long do we hang here, Sergeant?" whispered Rodriguez.

"Until we get the word from Battlespace Command," McRory replied.

Suddenly behind Claire, off in the direction of the rest of the squad, she heard noise. It was the sound of rubble shifting, then the sound of gunfire.

"Shit!" someone, possibly, Adams, spat on an open comms channel which rang in Claire's ears.

"I have multiple contacts! Holy flaming shitballs. BS is lit up—they're coming in force. Check your six! They got around behind us!" another voice, that of Ramirez, yelled. There was a *whomp*, a muffled blast of a grenade going off. A cloud of fine dust from the parts of the structure still standing in front of Claire drifted down around her and rose from farther down the alley. Gunfire came from below them, filling the alleyway. Even with the visor down, she could taste some of the gritty dust on the back of her tongue. Her battlespace display lit up with red Xs indicating enemy troops. She and Rodriguez grabbed their vid cameras and stuffed the units in their satchels. For a few seconds, gunfire picked up in intensity from the alley behind them. The purr of assault rifle fire rose from where they had climbed into the ruined structure.

We're screwed . . .

Part II: No Plan Survives Contact with the Enemy

Claire rose just enough to spot Sergeant McRory's Mamba moving down the alleyway, still cloaked but flickering with each thudding footfall. He ran nearly headlong into an enemy Boss. The onyx black aliens were unlike the crabs—they were human-shaped, hulking in size, dangerous. Their genetically engineered bodies were pressure suits, keeping them under remarkable water pressure and providing them incredible armor protection. The Boss lashed out with a slicer seemingly attached to his right forearm. The ultra-compressed water stream was like an assault laser. The thin gray stream hit the building Claire was in, then swept down onto McRory's Mamba, hitting him in the shoulder. One of his carbon-weave ceramic blast plates went flying as a part of the wall collapsed into the rubble pile they lay in.

McRory reeled under the impact but somehow kept his footing. He fired his heater—a newly issued microwave emitter. The weapon didn't just hum, it seemed to pulsate a deep throbbing sound.

The Boss spun with speed that she had not expected, thrusting its left arm out with a savage punch that hit the Mamba so hard, Claire could hear the metal rig inner frame moan from the stress. The sergeant's ACS failed completely, exposing the camouflage gray of his ASHUR rig for the world to see.

McRory toppled backwards with a heavy *thud* and rolled just as the Boss thrust its foot down onto the concrete, making the entire area quake. Dust flew in the air and Claire prepared to bring her own ACR into the mix. McRory beat her. He stabbed the massive barrel of his heavy assault gun into the face of the boss and fired a steady burst.

The Boss staggered back after a succession of direct hits, using its right webbed hand to protect its head. The sergeant rolled and pushed, rising again to his feet. His underarm-mounted grenade launcher went *thump* and a brilliant burst of light hit the Boss. *Flashbangs—they hate that intense light.* The Boss reeled back, stunned for a moment. A crab appeared behind him, stepping out with a weapon slung in its tiny forearms on the upright parts of its armored body. Two more creatures moved in between the squad, cutting them off from the sergeant.

There was a whooshing sound and she saw an oily black cloud billow into the alleyway, right where the sergeant had been. Another hiss added to the deadly fog that helped obscure their line of sight. "Shit—fall back!" he barked into her earbud. She huddled low at the sight of the cloud. It was a puffer—a deadly gas projector. The gas was a biological bacteria/virus of some sort, corrosive to anything organic—like human flesh. The sergeant's Mamba had been breached a few times from hits—so even he was at risk. Claire's mind remembered the training on the enemy gas. "If that stuff gets on your skin, you don't have skin—or bone, for that matter." For now, the deadly billows of the gas seemed confined in the alleyway.

"Oh God," gulped Copeland. On her battlespace display she saw his signal, concentric green circles, suddenly switch to a pulsating red dot. Copeland had tried to rush in to help Sergeant McRory, and the deadly mist had overwhelmed him. His ID chip was already showing his life signs had dropped off. The mist was a killer, and there was a dense cloud between them and the sergeant. McRory continued to pour out a blistering barrage of gunfire, but was slowly backing away, putting distance between his squad and the aliens rushing around him.

More firing burst out towards the Navy Yard. There was another scream; this time it was Private Adams. "I can't feel my legs!" Claire saw on her BS display that there were a dozen or so crabs, showing as red Xs, starting to deploy on the street, catching the squad in a crossfire from the alley.

"Fall back to the underpass," the sergeant commanded with a ragged breath. "Dalton—Rodriguez, we are—" then his voice cut off. Claire looked at the battlespace display and saw that he was still alive, still on the move—but his comms had cut off. His signal on the battlespace display was putting even more distance from where she was. The gap between them was growing, and signals indicating the enemy force seemed to be growing.

Rodriguez turned to her; Claire could see the shimmer of her ACS system. "What do we do?" she whispered. Another pair of explosions went off from where the squad had been. It was followed with a guttural howl with a screech of some sort near the end—not human, but alien. She saw one of the alien red dots disappear from her BS display. *Good!*

Do we move, do we try to help the squad? We're still cloaked, but the moment we open up, our element of surprise would be gone, and we would end up in the same crossfire. Her mind was on fire with thoughts, options, and probabilities. Her urge was for them to fall back the way they had come in, surprise the aliens hitting her squad, but if the sergeant was ordering them to fall back—then what good would two more infantrymen be in a falling-back action? Claire unconsciously gripped her ACR tight to her body. Each heartbeat put the squad farther away and more aliens moving in between where they lay and the squad. Her tactical assessment was clear. *Trying to follow them now will just get us killed.*

Looking back, she saw the mattress jutting up out of the debris. *Yes, it was big enough.* "Follow me. Keep quiet," she whispered as the ragged gunfire from below still raged. She moved daintily though the debris to the mattress. She carefully pulled it down over the two of them. With one end already anchored in the rubble, it arched over the two troopers, concealing them. She clung to the mattress material so tightly, her fingers ached. Claire heard her own ragged heavy breathing and that of Rodriguez and she tried to calm herself. No one knew if the Fish had infrared gear or just how they targeted the enemy. Huddled under the filthy mattress in a heap of rubble, she wasn't sure if she was safe or if death was about the come. So they waited.

"We should have gone," Rodriguez whispered.

"We would have been killed," Claire replied curtly. "Kill your ACS, we are going to have to conserve power."

"What if they lift up the mattress?"

"At that range, our cloaking won't help. Calm down and check your battlespace—zoom out. The squad is already falling back to the insertion point." She adjusted the image zoom with her wristcomp. It had taken them hours to sneak into the city—but they were already quickly falling back under fire, and were halfway there. From what she could see, the squad was battling their way out—a number of crabs were flickering off, Army kills. *Kill them all!*

Her tactical display in her helmet showed six members of the squad moving away, their green icons heading back at a full sprint to the overpass. The enemy, in red, was flickering. Their signals were no longer being fully tracked, but they were all over the alley where the squad had been. Without drone coverage in the area, the enemy positions were hopelessly out of date. Worse, four yellow pulsing signals were in the alleyway, signals of troopers that were wounded and the blinking red signals of the four dead from the squad. Sergeant McRory was not among them; he didn't show up on her screen at all. *He must be out of my range. At least he isn't down. He's probably trying to draw them away from us.* The names of the dead—Adams, Copeland, "Banger" Ballston, and "Ice" Ickowski were in the image—pulsating red dots surrounded by crimson Xs of the enemy, scattered between where Claire was and past the overpass. Copeland and Adams had been recent replacements to the Yankee Division; the others were seasoned vets. This was a disaster. The squad had suffered over 30 percent casualties. The Army would send in another squad to attempt to recover the dead, which was the Army way . . . leave no man behind. When they did, it might be a day, or two, or more though. The Fish were catching on and getting crafty at their own ambushes. *We sure as hell fell into this one. It's like the Fish knew we were coming.*

"Foxbat, this is Beatle," came the voice of the Sergeant McRory, faint in her earpiece. "Come in." Just hearing his voice made her sigh. *Good—he's alive.*

Claire spoke in the softest whisper of her life, not wanting to draw the attention of any aliens nearby. "This is Foxbat, go."

"Sitrep," he said as she adjusted his volume up slightly to hear him better.

"Rodriguez and I are under cover in the building where you left us." In the semi-darkness under the mattress, she saw Rodriguez give a short nod, she was listening too.

"They hit us on three sides, we had to fight our way clear. We lost four of the squad and couldn't take you with us. I have orders to fall back to the insertion point with the rest of the squad," the sergeant said. "Can you hold there?"

How the hell should I know? His mention of the insertion point made it feel as if it were a hundred miles away. "Unknown. Our position is soft. We need better cover if we are going to hunker down." Her thoughts went to the yellow signals on her display. "Should we move to recover the wounded?"

"Negative," he said. She could hear the remorse in his voice. "My feeds show them dying. If they got in that bio-gas shit, there's not much you can do for them in the field." As he spoke, one of the yellow signals on her display went crimson indicating a death. *Damn it!*

"We are going to be falling back out of range in five. Your mission remains the same—surveillance of the enemy, but given your isolation, that is at your discretion. Hold until nighttime if you can, then get yourself to a hard position. We will contact you at 2230 hours and figure how we are going to extract you. Remember your training, Dalton. We will get you out of there."

Rodriguez spoke up. "Sarge, you can't just leave us here!" her voice strained at just above a whisper.

"Rodriguez, we didn't have a choice. Orders came from on-high," McRory replied, obviously upset. Claire knew that he had never left a single trooper alive behind enemy lines. *They wouldn't have retreated if the situation wasn't bad.* "Foxbat is in command. Do what she says, and you will get out of this alive." His Bostonian accent was more pronounced as he spoke. "Wait until you have some darkness, then move."

"Roger that, Beatle," Claire cut in. "Talk to you tonight."

There was a hiss and static pop of the channel going dead. Claire shut off her tactical systems in her helmet with her wristcomp. There was no point in wasting energy at this stage. In daylight, the helmet's solar systems helped keep it charged, but she was in the dark under the mattress, and the Army had drilled it into her to manage her energy carefully.

Claire wanted to rescue the wounded, but even as she thought about it, another amber signal went red indicating another death. She gathered her resolve. *If the sergeant said don't go for them, I need to pay attention to that.*

"They left us here to die," Rodriguez moaned. "They ain't coming back for us."

"The Sarge said he'd come and get us, and he will. We just have to be patient and smart."

The night came slowly and when it did, so did Claire's urge to urinate. Out of fear of exposing herself, she squatted as best she could under the king-sized mattress. One thing about the Army, it crushed any sense of embarrassment or privacy from you. The stink of urine mixed with the dust and the smells from the old mattress to make their plight even more unpleasant. In her mind it was still better than the alternative, being dead.

She had contemplated moving positions, but thought it best to remain where they were. *The sergeant knows where are, and the Fish don't seem to see us. If we start moving around, both of those situations could change. Until I hear otherwise, we hunker here.*

There were periodic sounds of fighting in the AIZ, some far off, some seemingly close. The close ones made her grip her ACR tightly and hope that it was a rescue force. But then the gunfire sputtered out, or faded back, and with it the hopes of a relief force.

The last of the wounded passed away before 2000 hours, her regular checks on them told her. She had seriously considered sneaking out and trying to tend them, or at least put them out of their misery. Claire knew better. The bio-bacterial lingered on their bodies. Just touching them would risk getting the stuff on their flesh. Firing a shot to kill them, however merciful, would have potentially attracted the Fish. *Leaving them there is the right thing to do—and I'm going to have to live with the guilt for the rest of my life.*

Finally at 2230 hours, she activated the comm link in her helmet and got a signal. "Foxbat, this is Beatle; come in, over."

Just hearing his voice gave her a flush of relief. "Go ahead, Beatle, I read you in the clear, over."

"Battlespace Command paints you in the same position—confirm."

"Same position. All is quiet. Awaiting a lift home, Beatle. You on the way?"

There was a momentary pause. "Ah, about that, Foxbat, negative. We're having problems on this end. We tried to push out with a relief force but were engaged almost immediately and forced to fall back. Our insertion point has been compromised and sealed off."

She felt her body sag under the news. *God, I hope no one was killed trying to get to us.* The last thing she wanted was to be responsible for more deaths. "What about a chopper?"

"That's a no-go, Foxbat. We could land on Highway One, but it's too close to their operations on the waterfront. We've lost a lot of birds lately—the Fish seem to have adapted to our use of them. Every time we send up a VTOL or chopper, they send in ground forces. The Air Force and Army have ruled out chopper extract. Over."

"You're *not* going to just leave us here . . ." Rodriguez chimed in just above a whisper.

"No. But it's not a question of us getting to you, but more of a question of you getting to us, over."

"Go on," Claire pressed solemnly.

"I need you to make your way to incursion zone Baker. Recon says there is light enemy activity there. Once you get there, we will give you an extract exit point from the AIZ. It's the best bet to get the two of you out of there."

She activated her helmet's mapping system and zoomed out, then zoomed out again. "That's a good four miles, Beatle, over."

"Roger that, Foxbat. It's the best we could do. I'm going to download waypoints to your helmet. Based on our latest intel, this is the best path to get there, over." She activated her BS and on her visor's screen the path projected itself as a blue line, zigzagging on the long path to the extraction point. This was not a straight-line path. It was a jumble of streets, alleys, and buildings to get to where they could get out. For a moment, Claire doubted herself. *I'm here with Rodriguez, which is like being alone. I'm behind enemy lines and I have to sneak past the enemy to get out.* She wondered if it was even possible.

"Foxbat—you still there? Over?"

"Roger that, Beatle. Just looking at the map. Seems to be the long way home, over."

"Foxbat, you're smart. Keep your head clear. Don't kick the hornet's nest. This is all about stealth, noise management, and cover. Keep quiet, keep low, and you will make it. I *know* you can." Even through McRory's nasal Bostonian accent, she felt comfort in his words. It was just enough to turn the edge on her self-doubt. "We will contact you again in eight hours, over."

"Roger that," she said. Eight hours was an eternity behind enemy lines. It was dark, but sunrise would come far too early, making travel trickier. It seemed like a long time to reach where they were going, but she knew that moving quietly and keeping to the shadows was going to add considerable time to the trek. With a hiss and pop, the comm line went dead, and she could return to the sounds of her and Rodriguez breathing under the mattress.

"They have to be kidding," Rodriguez muttered. "They have left us out here to die."

"Can it," Claire snapped. "We have to go four miles tops—that's it." It was a little lie. Yes, it was four miles on a direct path. They would need to be doing a lot of maneuvering.

"The entire Fish army could be between us and them." Fear rang in every word Rodriguez spoke.

"Then we need to be fucking quiet," Claire said through gritted teeth. *I don't have time for her fear. We need to get moving.* "So, make sure you still have all of your gear, we are moving out."

Slowly, careful to not disturb any of the debris, they slid out from under the mattress and into the cool of the night. It hit her like a wall, the chill in the autumn air on her sweaty skin. The shell of the building they were in looked totally different at night. She tapped her wristcomp strap and activated the night vision, her passive lighting augmentation system in her visor. In the past, soldiers had worn bulky goggles to see in the darkness. The system in her helmet projected a good medium range view in the darkness. Moving delicately to minimize noise, they crawled to the alleyway where the squad had been attacked and checked—there was no sign of the enemy.

Her legs and knees ached as she lowered herself down to the street. Hours of lying still had made all of her joints throb as they moved. Claire toyed with having them activate their ACS, but at night, when the system recalibrated or flickered, it gave off light which could be dangerous. She helped down Rodriguez and the two flattened themselves against the building, weapons at the ready. Spent shell casings littered the alleyway where her squad had fought hours earlier. Also lying there were the dead of their squad. Claire tried not to look at them—her focus needed to be getting out of the AIZ. Still she couldn't resist. The images she saw tore at her already battered psyche. Two of the fallen were unidentifiable aside from tags on their STG—the bacterial gas had devoured so much of their faces that white bone was visible. A puddle of fleshy goo seeped out from one of the dead onto the pavement.

"We should have done something for them," Rodriguez muttered, but Claire shook her head. "There was nothing we could have done. You want to honor them? Then we have to move and survive." The horrifying images stiffened her in that alley—giving her focus. *We need to get out of here or we will end up like them.*

"Down this alley to the end, then through the underpass," she ordered. The underpass under Highway One was not a road. It was more like a dumping ground for gear that the DoT used. There were stacks of orange road construction barrels positioned there, along with dirty metal fencing, and other road construction gear covered in tarps. The space was cramped, forcing them to crouch. Moving under the now-silent highway was even darker and more forbidding. After passing under six lanes of elevated roadway, they methodically made their way to the edge of City Square Park. The grass was overgrown and garbage littered the park and sidewalks. Her night vision allowed her to sweep the park, but she didn't see any signs of the enemy. The tall buildings around the park made her nervous though. Hundreds of windows faced them, any of which could serve as an enemy observation point. She wanted to cut through the park but the decorative wrought iron railing that surrounded it could box them in if they were fired upon. *It's best to keep to the sidewalks, at least that gives us some flexibility of movement.*

They moved in short bursts, twenty yards at time, keeping low and taking cover behind the most insignificant obstructions—like a mailbox and an overflowing garbage container . . . anything to break up any line of sight that the enemy might get. It was slow going but necessary. Claire knew that rushing was going to cause problems. The eerie quiet stirred her. *I'll never get used to seeing the city this way, abandoned.*

They made their way to the old district court building at the far end of the park. The big wooden door under the stately concrete arch was wide open, left that way when the occupants had fled. She could make her way around the structure, but the building seemed to offer some protection.

The inside of the building was pitch-black, but her night vision didn't offer up any movement. The offices were almost as they had been left when the citizens had fled. On the floor were a handful of small ping-pong ball–sized tiny skulls that crunched when you stepped on them. *Goblins—probably from the first attack on the city.* The aliens had biologically programmed them to simply die off after a few days. These were remnants of the initial alien contact. Some soldiers kept them for souvenirs, which Claire couldn't understand. *Who wants reminders of those events?*

As she moved into the darkness with Rodriguez right behind her, she detected a rotting, moldy, musty smell. *Probably from a toilet bowl.* She had smelled the same aroma before on other missions. Structures like the district court were not meant to be left unattended. The lack of running water made most bathrooms little more than mold factories. Working her way down the hallway, careful to not make much noise on the scraps of paper that were discarded there, the pair sneaked their way to the rear door. It was locked and marked with an alarm warning. Power had been out in this part of Boston for a while—but some systems had battery backups. With the front door cracked open, she was counting on any backup alarm battery system being long dead. If she was wrong though, an alarm might go off and draw dangerous unwanted attention. Claire paused and licked her lips in thought for a moment. *Is it worth the risk? Was it better to backtrack and move outside?*

Dalton looked back at Rodriguez whose visored faced only gave her a nod . . . acknowledgement that she understood as well. Claire pushed the door but it didn't budge. Months of being closed made it stick. She leaned into it and pushed again, half-waiting for an alarm—but none came, only the light creak of the door opening against a tight weather seal. She let out a sigh of relief and opened the door the rest of the way into the alley behind the courthouse and activated her mapping system in her helmet. While it was not an actively mapped battlespace, it gave her the layout of the roads and a map as to their extraction point.

While Rodriguez swept the alley, Claire studied the map to chart a course through the city streets. She shut the BS display off with her wristcomp to conserve energy. When daylight came, the helmet could charge from the tiny solar power mesh, but at night, using night vision, the power got drained. Power management was second only to ammunition management in the battlespace of Boston.

They slinked their way to Harvard Street. Lined with old brownstone homes, these showed signs of being ransacked, either by surviving human looters or the Fish. Doors were left ajar, some windows were broken—with curtains half-in, half-out of the holes. The debris of human life littered the steps and doorways. There were thieves that crossed into the AIZ through Army lines to do looting professionally. Some were looking for valuables to steal. Others were holdouts who robbed their neighbors' dwellings for food and survival. Still others were well-equipped, sent in by corporations to recover alien technology. Both were dangerous since they were heavily armed and operating outside of the law in a war zone. Claire had heard of some of them tangling with the Army as fiercely as the Fish.

Moving in short bursts of speed, huddling for cover along the way, they went down a narrow alley to Old Rutherford Street. They then moved north for several blocks, coming to the Rutherford Union Playground where Claire paused and checked the time. Like the other abandoned parks the grass was deep and tall. There were a few spots where the grass seemed greener. She stared at one of them and saw an open jawed human skull looking back at her in the darkness. With her night vision, the image startled her, coming into focus like something out of a horror movie. As she swept the park, there were at least a dozen places where human bodies lay. There was still a hint of stench as the two of them avoided the park, sticking to the street and sidewalk, using a row of burned out cars for cover. Several of the surrounding buildings had been razed, including the nearby school which was little more than a tall pile of broken bricks. *Something went down here—a battle, or a slaughter.* She hugged her ACR close to her body armor and lowered her stance to make herself a smaller target. Taking in a deep breath, she centered her focus on where they had to go and how much time they had to do it.

Working north, the duo came to the Bunker Hills Mall Shopping Center. Half of the structure was collapsed, the rest showed signs of fire damage. *Probably artillery or air strikes.* Garbage littered the parking lot along with dozens of burned out cars. A few craters of blasted blacktop stood as testament to the battle that had taken place there. The flat open parking lot made Claire nervous. Even with all of the cars for cover, it seemed horribly exposed to cross into it. She activated her battlespace display in her visor for a few moments to try to find another path to the extraction point.

"We'll cut over up Green Street and work our way around the mall area," she whispered as the two soldiers huddled in the entranceway to a small clothing store.

"We should cut across the parking lot up to that old Whole Foods—it will save us time," Rodriguez muttered.

"Too open. We stick to side streets and move around."

"It will take us half the night the way you are taking us, and uphill too."

Claire stiffened at her words. "We have our orders. We do this my way, period."

"Look, all I'm saying is that we can cut across there and save an hour of this duck and hide bullshit."

"You heard the sarge, Rodriguez. I'm in command. I've been on a dozen missions on the other side of the wall, compared to what? The two that you have been on? We do this the way I say. Otherwise you will find your ass getting court-martialed." Even she was surprised by the crisp harness of her voice. There was a period of silence as the two visored soldiers looked at each other.

"Alright," the dejected Rodriguez replied.

The duo moved up the steady hill on Green Street Claire noticed additional telltale signs of battle. Two of the cars she passed showed damage, but not from conventional weapons. Both showed signs of corroded metal, nasty gnawed, distorted holes in them, where the paint chipped around the edges. The Fish used squirters and melters to fire a caustic goo that ate through almost everything. As the moved alongside the vehicles, she looked them over. In daylight she might be able to make out rust, to tell how old the damage was. With night vision it was hard to tell, the system merely amplified the light that was available.

The aliens had definitely been there though, that was clear. She saw a sprinkling of brass shells on the ground, some melted, some merely scattered around on the pockmarked pavement. *The battle here didn't go well for us.*

Claire slowed her approach. She motioned for Rodriguez to lower their stances. Rather than moving in a run, they went slowly, deliberately, carefully. Claire and Rodriguez moved forward one car at a time, careful of their cover. Then, in the darkness, she heard a whistling noise—a human whistle to get their attention.

Dalton swung her weapon across the street from where she heard the sound. The Fish didn't whistle—not that she knew of. But the sound was out of place in a war zone. A figure stood in a cracked open doorway of an older brownstone home across the street, barely visible in the pitch darkness. He then motioned for them to come across the street with one hand.

Part III: Of Rabbits, Dogs, and Fish

F'ers—Freedom Fighters, bands of people who formed an active resistance —were known to operate in the city. F'ers were not part of the Army's militia program. They were rogue and tended to play by their own rules. Some were good, others less so. Was this one of them, or a looter seeking to ambush them? She paused for a moment, tempering her reaction. *If he had wanted to kill us, he could have already.* Tapping Rodriguez on the shoulder to get her attention, the two of them crossed the street and went up the stairs into the home.

Inside were two men, both armed, and a pit bull which seemed more friendly than threatening. She paused as they closed the door, wondering if her assessment of the situation had been the right one. The one with the faithful dog lit a candle and she deactivated her night-vis and raised her visor, giving her eyes a few seconds to adjust. They silently led her and Rodriguez down a hallway into a family room, one where the curtains were drawn and taped shut. She heard the front door click shut behind them. Despite the unknowns of the strangers and where she was, she felt oddly more safe than on the streets.

"Hello," she said with a hint of apprehension.

"You can relax, Corporal," the lanky man that had waved her in said. She could see him clearer now. He was in his late 30s, with a scraggly blond beard that failed to hide his sunken cheeks. His face was weatherworn and wrinkled. His body was covered with a patchwork of STG and blast plates. He was much younger than he appeared, she could sense it. "You're with friends. I'm Frank Haskill." She saw an antique AR-15 assault rifle slung over his shoulder. *This guy is old-school.* The ACR she carried tied into her helmet, allowing her more accurate sighting. She had digital feeds for ammo levels, everything else. Even hunters had started using commercial versions of this gear. The battered AR-15 didn't even have a scope—it was a pure iron-sights solution. It had advantages, namely it was all mechanical. In a pinch, she could use her ACR the same way if she had to.

"Claire—Claire Dalton," she said, extending her hand. He shook it and she could feel the toughened cracked skin of his palm.

He gestured to the other man, a younger African American youth decked out in a hodgepodge of armor. Some was STF liquid plates, other bits were from older BA/2 armor. "This here is Tony—but he goes by the name "Rabbit." Rabbit gave her a nod of acknowledgement which she returned. Rabbit was so skinny she wondered if he was malnourished. The armor he wore was a complete set, but was frayed and worn—almost looking as if it had been dragged along the city streets for a few days before he put it on. He had a shotgun in a front sling on his body, along with a .44 Magnum with a ten-inch barrel. The gun was rigged with a shoulder stock attached to the handle and had the extended clip. *This guy likes his fighting up close and personal.*

"Angel Rodriguez," her squad-mate introduced herself as. Claire was a little surprised. She had always just called her Rodriguez. She had no idea what her first name was. Replacement troops were like that—you didn't invest a lot of time getting to know them until you were sure they might survive. Rodriguez took off her helmet and tucked it under her arm, shaking hands with both men.

"What's the dog's name?"

Frank bent down for a moment and patted the dog on the head. "We call him Ish, short for Ishmael."

"That's a strange name for a dog."

"I used to teach college lit. It's from *Moby-Dick*—the whale hunter . . . Ish here is a security system for us. When the Fish get near, he gets all nervous and fidgety. He's helped save our butts more than a few times."

She had heard word of some squads getting a K-9 assigned to them, now she understood why. *I wonder why* we *don't have K-9 units with us? Typical Army. We could have used an early warning system.* Claire had tried to read *Moby-Dick* in high school for a class, but had opted for the Wikipedia version instead. *A college teacher—I would have guessed a biker or street thug instead. War does strange things to people.* "Thanks for getting us off the street," she replied.

Frank moved behind a big easy chair and leaned forward, resting his elbows on it. "You're lucky. The Fish have rigged the street up another block with webbies. You wander into that mess, you'd be easy pickings for them." Webbies were nasty little mines that the Fish had just started to deploy. They were small balls that stuck on almost any surface. The Fish mounted them at various heights and behind things. You entered their field and they went off. It was nothing lethal, just a goo that formed an adhesive web that was tougher than nylon and sprayed out in every direction, often setting off a chain reaction. It created a spider web that was designed to capture and hold its victims. The Army slang for them were spider-mines, for their web-like qualities. Most webbie sites somehow alerted the Fish when they had been triggered too. The crabs would show up after you were trapped and either killed or captured you. Webbies on their own were nonlethal, but they often led to death—or worse. Only a few POWs had been recovered during the war, and the Army was keeping information about them secret.

"Dodged that bullet," she replied.

"Where are you headin'?" Rabbit asked.

"We got cut off from our squad. We're on our way to an extraction point northwest from here, around Davis Square."

Rabbit let out a sigh and shook his head long and slow. "Dang, girl, you are going the long way to get out of Beantown."

Claire shrugged. "That's where battlespace command wants us to go. Our mission was to go down and run surveillance on the Navy Yard—and that operation went south."

The younger man laughed and looked over at his partner. "I told you that battle was down by the Yard." He then turned back to Claire. "You'll never make it out that way," Rabbit replied. "The Fish are busy in that area, in-force, if you know what I'm sayin'. We were up that way last night. They are takin' down buildings everywhere. Lots of their worker bees, and a few forced labor prisoners."

"What are they doing there?"

"Steel," Frank cut in. "They tear down the buildings and ignore everything but steel. The higher the grade of the steel, the more they dig for it."

"The Fish will destroy an entire city block just to strip it of steel," added Rabbit. "It must be like crack or Duke for them. You go across the Charles and they are gutting parts of the city. They take what they need and leave us with big piles of rubble."

"You've been across the river?" Claire asked.

Rabbit flashed a smile. "Oh yeah. I'm not sayin' it was easy, but we've been over there a few times. It is Fish-city over there. You have to be extra smart when you're there. They have made that their turf, you know what I'm sayin'?"

She didn't fully understand. Claire knew that aerial drones often were shot down on low-level passes over the city though. The aliens were apparently content with keeping some things secret. "Why were you there?"

"To *mess them up*," Rabbit replied slowly, accentuating each word. "Frank and three of us set a bunch of booby traps up, some claymores the Army generously donated to our little cause. We put them in some pretty discrete locations. They worked too. We were just about to get wet coming back across the Charles and we heard the explosions. Boom, boom, boom—one right after another, just like we rigged them. We cooked us some crab-meat that day." He fist-bumped his partner Haskill.

"So you're a resistance cell?" Dalton asked, a little relieved she was probably not with looters.

Frank Haskill nodded. "You make it sound so official. Yes, we're fighting the Fish here. This is where most of us lived before the war. Boston is our home. We've all lost someone close to us in the invasion.

All of us are here to make the Fish pay for what they've done. We're called East Side Retribution."

"ESR," corrected Rabbit with a sense of pride.

Frank shot him a scowl. "You're the only one that calls us that." It was clear that this had been the topic of discussion before.

"How many of you are there?" Rodriguez asked.

Frank shook his head and smiled. "We don't say because none of us know for sure. We aren't sure if the Fish would torture any of us they capture or not. Part of fighting in a cell, you only know the folks in your cell. No chance of being compromised." For the first time since he spoke, Claire heard a hint of his Bostonian accent.

"We had two others in our cell— but they got frosted by the Fish two weeks ago, when *your* Army started poking around in the city. It seems like every time the Army gets into the city, it stirs up the enemy, and we pay the price," Rabbit replied bitterly.

Claire opted to deflect his criticism. "I'm sure that isn't the intention."

"Well, that's how it goes down," he said, crossing his arms.

"So . . ." she said, struggling for the right words to avoid a painful subject, "can you help us to get to our extraction point?"

Rabbit shook his head but was silent. Frank responded with hesitancy that came from experience. "Look, I'm not saying it's impossible, but not through any direct route. I'm not willing to risk our butts to lead you there. The risk is just too high. The Fish started concentrating along the edge of the AIZ a few days ago in pockets—we think they are preparing for another push. You try to get to the Davis Square neighborhood, you have to move around three enemy battle groups."

"What do you suggest?" Claire asked.

"Your best bet is to hunker down with us until we link up with another Army raiding force, then we pass you off. The truth is, that could be weeks. I know of a few folks that have tried to use a small craft to float down the Charles and get to the coast. The problem with that is that the Fish are, well, fish. They take exception to any human vessel on the surface. The other option is to try to go out where the enemy isn't. There are some of holes in the front lines; they are dangerous to get to in some cases, in others less so. One of them could be your best bet if you don't want to hang around."

The thought of waiting weeks behind enemy lines made Claire Dalton something she hated—afraid. A lot could happen in three weeks. If the aliens were preparing an offensive, it might put her and Rodriguez even farther behind enemy lines. The river seemed to be a death trap from the way Frank spoke about it. *This isn't working out at all.* "You said that there are holes in the front lines. That sounds like our best option," she finally said.

"He also said they were dangerous," Rodriguez said. "Maybe we should just stay with them, wait for the Army to get us out. Why stick our asses out? Sooner or later the cavalry will be coming."

Claire disliked the fact that Rodriguez felt so comfortable questioning her authority. *She's afraid, but we don't have time for afraid.* "Look, we need to do this my way. You heard him, the Fish might be preparing for another offensive. The Army doesn't leave a man behind, but this is war, and if we are so far behind the lines that it costs more lives to get us out—they *will* leave us here. Or worse, they might send another squad in that ends up getting shot trying to retrieve us. I have no intention of spending winter behind the front, and I certainly don't want anyone else's blood on my hands. We have a duty to try to get back on our own, plain and simple. Not only that, there are standing orders that if we are separated from our units we are to work our way back to our side of the lines. We are going to try. Consider it an order, Private."

Rodriguez's face tensed and she looked ready to strike, but Claire knew she wouldn't. Army discipline—it was all that stood between a fistfight and acceptance of reality. Claire turned to Frank Haskill. "We'd appreciate it if you could get us back to our people."

Rabbit shook his head. "We ain't going anywhere until we talk about the toll."

"The toll?" Claire responded.

"Damned right, the toll. You want us to help you, you have to reciprocate."

Frank interceded. "Corporal, we can take you to a hole in the lines, but there's some things we need from you in return."

"What things?"

"Ammo, weapons, your BA, your helmets—your gear." His tone was matter-of-fact.

Claire winced. "I'm not following you. What do you mean?"

"Look, your gear and firepower are a hot commodity behind the lines. The Fish tend to pick up every gun or clip left from a battle. Your firepower can give us a fighting edge. We'll get you to where you can get out, but once we do, we want your hardware so we can continue the fight. Plain and simple—that's the price for an escort."

This was not something the Army had guidelines about. There was a general announcement that, when practical, to render aid to any free-fighting group. But this felt different. She hesitated slightly at the request. The thought of handing over her armor and weapon made her feel vulnerable and horribly exposed. At the same time, there wasn't much in the way of options. "I agree. I don't see that I have much of a choice."

"You don't," Rabbit added.

Frank offered a thin smile. "Okay then. Let's figure out the path of least resistance to get you back to the USA."

* * *

Frank and Rabbit had their own way of moving through Boston. Army doctrine was to use the buildings and just about everything else for cover, entering them to reduce exposure to enemy fire—but primarily using the streets. Not so with the irregular soldiers of the East Side Retribution. The buildings were not cover; they were the roadways for how they moved. They only crossed streets and alleys when they couldn't move through the buildings themselves. The freedom fighters would enter a structure, move through it, find a door or window leading to the next building, and then enter that structure. Sometimes the entry required breaking down a door, rather noisily. After the fifth such building, Claire asked them to stop.

"I have to ask, why are we moving this way? It takes longer. It makes more sense to stick to the streets," she said as they entered an abandoned brownstone's back kitchen door. The house smelled musty, even with the filters on her helmet.

Rabbit shook his head and smiled. "That's the US Army talkin'. We got this down from experience. The Fish, they aren't as attracted to noise as they are to movement. That's what we've noticed. You go running across wide open spaces, that draws them in. Also, they have got little booby traps across some streets. They hunt us like animals, so the way you beat them is to not act like the animal. The streets can be your enemy especially the big wide ones." Both men checked the cupboards while the small group paused. Frank tossed Ish a dog treat, which he consumed in a single chomp. Frank pocketed two cans of tuna after he checked the dates.

Rabbit continued. "Weird as it is, they don't seem comfortable in our buildings. Definitely not the upper floors. You want to shake them in an office building, head upstairs. We're not sure if it is the height or the air pressure or what, but they don't like tall structures. I've gone entire blocks jumping from rooftop to rooftop."

Claire leaned back on the counter and let her weapon hang on its sling. She pulled up her water tube and drew some warm water. "These places still have power and running water?"

"Some do," Frank replied. "It's hit or miss. You get water pressure at the bottom of hills, but you have to boil whatever you are able to get—it's been sitting in the pipes a long time. The sewer system has some serious issues too. Some of our guys affect repairs if they have the skills, just to give us some of the basic comforts."

"Like cold beer," Rabbit replied.

"Like a furnace," Frank added. "With winter barreling down on us soon, it's going to be brutal."

Frank Haskill looked around. "Okay, we ready to continue on?" Wearily everyone gave a nod and grasped weapons. The party continued to shuffle through the neighborhoods building by building. Sometimes it was impossible to gain entry—in one case the door was barricaded with wood. Someone had spray-painted an orange circle on the wood planks and Rabbit pointed to it. "We don't go there. There's a local holed up in there. You see that sign, you don't enter the building or you're likely to get cut in half with a shotgun," he said in a low tone.

"Aren't the locals friendly?" Rodriguez asked in a husky whisper. "I figured you'd be connected with most of the people that chose to stay behind."

"We are," Frank said, checking around the corner of the townhouse. "The majority of them are pretty cordial to us, we share food and information. The rest? Not so much. Survival mode kicks in with some. Others were whack-jobs even before all this shit went down. Some have their own agendas—like the looters that come into the city to rob the abandoned places or try to steal alien-tech. We heard a blast last week and snuck up on it to find eight guys had blown an abandoned armored truck. The Fish showed up too. Then it got messy. Some of the more sophisticated organizations, like the mob or some tech companies, have their people embedded in the city. They tend to keep to themselves 'cause their agendas are less honorable than ours."

There was a sarcastic note in the way he said "honorable" that Claire smiled at. *This town has gone to hell pretty damn quick. The buildings and streets all look the same, but nothing is like it was.* She wondered if every occupied city was devolving the same way that Boston was. "So you don't just have to deal with the Fish, you have to deal with nuts with guns and explosives too . . . doesn't sound promising."

Rabbit flashed a smile. "It makes life interesting."

Frank tapped her on the shoulder. "You have night vision. Can you check this street? It looks good to me, but you may see something I don't. Ish looks a little nervous." The dog seemed to be pacing back and forth. Clair didn't see the difference in his behavior, but Haskill appeared to notice it.

She activated her Mark III ECH's visor and surveyed the street. The cold abandoned cars offered no signs of trouble. "Looks clear." Frank patted Ish on the head and the dog obediently sat down. "They may have been through her in the last day or so, sometimes he can't tell the difference," Haskill said.

Rabbit took point again and jutted in between cars, keeping low, making his way across the street. He moved to a townhome and sprinted up the half-flight of stairs to the front door which was ajar, entering as if he were part of the night—a shadow in the darkness, almost invisible. Claire followed him, though she became conscious how loud she sounded compared to the resistance fighter.

The house they moved through had been ransacked. Every drawer had been pulled and dumped unceremoniously on the floor. She shook her head. *Why do people always resort to robbery in times of catastrophe? As if money means anything now, here.* She lifted her feet carefully to navigate the mess on the floor of the once quaint living room. Rabbit didn't pause, he moved to the bedroom area, looking for an egress. Rodriguez nearly fell coming into the room as she slid on some papers and just caught herself from falling. If not for Claire's fast grabbing of her uniform, she would have been sprawled on the floor.

They followed Rabbit who had backtracked and was checking another room. "No way over," he muttered. "Back door."

Claire once more provided a sweep out the back of the old townhome with her nightvis gear. It was a narrow alley but the dark shadows made it look more menacing. Her optics didn't pick up anything out of order. Rabbit pointed diagonally to the back of another row of houses, several down. "That's our next stop." Getting there was tricky. The place had a fence protecting its tiny backyard. Claire wondered if the gate could even be opened—it looked as if it hadn't been touched in years. A dumpster butted up to the fence, making access to the gate questionable. While the fence was relatively low, it would require some climbing, and the shrubs on the other side obscured what was in the backyard. There were several cars in the wide alley, which made getting a good view of the entire area nearly impossible.

"What I can see looks clear. The FOV is limited." She kept her gaze on the alleyway as she talked.

"FOV?" Frank asked.

"Sorry, Field of Vision," she replied. It made her wonder how long it had been since she had spoken for any amount of time with real civilians.

Her words about the field of vision made Frank hesitate. "Rabbit, we been on this street before?"

His partner shook his head. "Nope. I think a few blocks south we've crossed. This isn't our turf as much as the Boston Knights." Claire knew the reference—the Knights were a well-known resistance group in Boston. The Knights had a tough reputation. When the Army had reached out to them to ask about their effectiveness against the enemy, the rumor was that the Knights had sent a blue plastic barrel filled with the heads of dead Fish they had killed. The sergeant told her that the Knights didn't work or play well with others. Then again, that was the rumor. Dalton had learned there were more to street scuttlebutt than reality at times.

Then she saw something. It was a bulge the poked momentarily up above the fence then went down. She stared at the place where she saw it occur, but it only happened once. "Movement," she said in a firm whisper. Weapons swung outward. Ish whimpered once and Frank knelt next to the dog, petting it to calm him. "Something is in the air," he whispered.

"What's poppin'?" Rabbit asked in a hushed tone. He held his shotgun painfully close to her head. *If he fires, it'll take days to get my hearing back.* With her shoulder she bumped his weapon to the side, letting her BA 2 shoulder plate adjust his sighting.

"In the yard, at 11 o'clock, where we were heading. I saw something rise and drop. Whatever it is, it's either short or hunkering down behind the fence."

"No weapons fire . . ." Frank said mostly to himself. "A Fox?"

"Shit," Rodriguez spat from behind Claire. She understood her squad mate's reaction. Foxes were the eyes and ears of the aliens. They were stubby creatures, shorter than most humans, and all muscle and speed. Like recon troops, they fanned out gathering intel. No one knew how they passed their information back to the Bosses, but they did. They got the nickname "Fox" for being crafty and fast. Claire had seen them in action. With their powerful arms, they could propel themselves quickly, looking like a gorilla running more than a sea creature. Its twisting, flicking, serpent-like tail made it seem like an alien that was ready to pounce. Foxes looked top-heavy because of their stubby but powerful legs and feet and their heavily muscled upper torso. They darted and dodged when on the move, making them difficult to hit. If you did manage to corner one, they were savage fighters. Their massive extended lower jaws were lined with dagger-like teeth that could rip apart an unarmored soldier up. Even with STF armor on, a cornered Fox was a deadly foe. Its hide was like a crocodile's, hard to punch through unless you got a straight shot. Their real threat was not their combat skills, but in getting away—to inform the enemy of your position. They were the eyes of the Fish and that made them something to be avoided.

"You think he saw us?" Rabbit asked.

"Unknown," Claire replied.

"We have to take it out," Frank declared.

"We should just change direction," Rodriguez countered. "Get the hell out of here before he brings in the heavies."

Frank shook his head. "He'll shadow us if we don't kill him, feed our position to the crabs or a Boss. That's what they seem to do. We take him out and move on."

Claire drank in the alleyway—looking at it from a tactical perspective. "The cars along the backyard fence line will give us some cover. We go low—use them to cover our movement."

Frank put his hand on her shoulder. "We'll need to flank it as much as possible, cut off its chances of running. Foxes tend to bolt at the first sign of trouble."

Claire nodded. "Right. Rodriguez—you'll move about four cars to the south. Rabbit will go the same to the north. Frank and I will come in on the corners of the fence and shoot it before it can run. If we miss, Rabbit and Rodriguez, you make sure it doesn't get away. You two will move into position first—then we will come up the center—got it?" She craned her head around and got the nods she was looking for. Rodriguez made her the most nervous though, she was gripping her ACR so tight, Claire could see her muscles flex. Haskill knelt in front of Ishmael. "Stay, Ish. Stay, boy." The pit bull licked his hand.

Claire chopped her hand down as a motion to move and the ad hoc team fanned out as if they had rehearsed it a dozen times. Rabbit and Rodriguez crouched and jogged into position, signaling to her with a nod they were ready. "Go," she whispered to Haskill as the two of them moved directly across the alley. They came to a garbage can near the fence and moved behind it. She held up three fingers, paused, then two fingers, then one. In unison, the two of them rose and moved to the fence, weapons at the ready.

Her night vision gave her and Rodriguez an advantage, though she assumed that Frank's eyes had adjusted to the dark. She could hear her breath in her helmet's faceplate, ragged, not physically exhausted but nervous. She looked at Frank and gave a nod. The two of them rose alongside the fence and swept their weapons over.

There was a blur off to her left, a figure that bounded in a single leap into the next yard towards Rodriguez. Another figure emerged in the darkness almost a yard from her ACR's muzzle. *Two of them! Fuck* The shape standing almost four foot tall and looking every bit like a monster in the darkness. It was a Fox . . . the closest she had ever been to one. Its massive forearms were like that of a gorilla and it stared at her, its extended lower jaw lowering as if readying to bite—or perhaps stunned with surprise.

There was no hesitation in her reaction. She swung her ACR into play and her targeting reticle in her visor dropped to the creature. Claire triggered a quick two-bullet burst, ensuring her aim would be true. Inexperienced soldiers would opt for more, less accurate fire—but she knew better. The Fox recoiled under the impact on its hulking left shoulder, dropping and apparently rolling away from her. The flash suppressor kept the light low and her nightvis strained to compensate as she heard bursts of fire to her left from what she suspected was Rodriguez. Frank fired at the Fox as well, his AR-15 unleashing a bright burst of light that made her wince. The sound of the older weapon was louder and sounded more deadly than hers.

The targeted Fox reeled, then hopped on its tiny but strong back legs, right at the fence where Claire and Haskill stood. It struck with such force that the old fence buckled under the impact—hitting her hard, disrupting her aim and sending both humans stumbling back into the alleyway.

The Fox leapt onto the fence feet first and sprang into the air high over them. Her night vision adjusted as Claire rolled in the alleyway, coming up with her ACR at the ready. Her targeting reticle tied to her ACR just barely crossed the figure as it descended, but it was enough for another shot, sending its left leg flopping limp. There was a deep animalic growl and in a blur of aggression, Ish jumped at the Fox, tearing into one of its forearms with his teeth. The Fox swung its arm, sending the dog rolling with a yelp. The creature dropped to the ground off-balance with a thud as a burst of automatic fire from Rodriguez filled the air.

The Fox closest to Claire tossed something into the air and she kicked toward a car, hoping to get partway under it. *Time for more drastic measures.* Her hands drifted to one of the stackable grenades on her belt. "Grenade!" she yelled as the object made a loud popping sound. She pitched the explosive towards the Fox and ducked just as it went off. Her ears throbbed, despite the protection of her helmet. Dust and debris obscured her vision.

Claire felt something hit behind her right shin as she re-aimed her assault rifle. It felt at first like a bee sting. *Damn, I've been hit.* Her target, the wounded Fox, was not jumping but instead was pulling itself along with its massive forearms, dragging what was left of its legs, now a hamburger-like pulp. She aimed her ACR squarely at its back and fired three bullets. It stopped mid-stride and seemed to quake for a moment, then collapsed. Frank raced past her, firing his AR-15 in Rodriguez's direction. She heard another burst of automatic fire from her squad mate and cringed. Automatic fire was a waste of ammo. She heard Rabbit cursing, "Damn it, girl—you let him go!"

Claire pulled herself from the car and noticed that her left leg tingled, as if it were asleep. She had hoped that it had been shrapnel from her own grenade, but now she realized it wasn't. Looking down, she saw two needle-like projections from the creature's weapon stuck in her armor, and three bits of broken needles that hadn't gotten through. She pulled them out and could make out a stain of blood on one of them. "Porcupine," she cursed. The Fish used a range of toxic needle weapons. Porcupines were grenade-like delivery systems. They didn't explode but somehow puff-burst, unleashing hundreds of little needles—each impregnated with some sort of neurotoxin. They weren't fatal unless they hit you in the chest or head. It was a numbing agent. If it got your brain, lungs, or heart you were toast. Anywhere else and you lost the use of that limb for a few hours. She rose to her feet gingerly. Her leg held, wobbly, but was numb from the knee down. Her leg worked but she would have to watch it.

Glancing down the alleyway, she saw Rodriguez coming back. Her armor was torn in her right shoulder, and a STF and ceramic blast plate were gone—signs of impact. "One got away," she heaved with a gasp of breath.

"Damn," Claire replied. "Anybody else hit?"

Frank Haskill held his assault rifle in his opposite hand. "Got three needles in my right arm. I'm a lefty for a while." Ish came up at his side and Frank patted him with his good hand. "Good job, boy, you tore into that one good."

"That *maldito* Fox plowed right into me," Rodriguez spat back, her voice ragged, and she winced when she moved her right arm.

"What's your ammo situation?" Claire pressed, stomping her leg to try to shake the numbing from the alien barbs that had hit her.

Rodriguez fidgeted with her wrist comp. "One mag down—three to go."

"We gotta get out of here," Rabbit chimed in with a voice just above a whisper. "Foxes always bring the heat."

"Right," Claire replied. "Where do we go?"

Frank nodded north in the alleyway. "We move up. Get some distance from here. They will hone in on this area, move to trap us." Haskill didn't wait for a response; he started heading north. *There's a time to lead and a time to follow—this is a time to follow.*

Stealth gave way to speed. The small party jogged up the alleyway. Four blocks up, Frank waved for them to stop. He jutted down a narrow space between two houses. When they reached the street on the other side, he held up his hand again and they stopped once more.

The image she saw on her night vision across the street was not like the abandoned city blocks they had navigated through. The row of townhouses across the street were little more than rubble and ruin. The brick shells of the structures were like bowls filled to overcapacity with the upper floors spilling their debris into the street. This was not explosive damage; Claire had seen that before near the Navy Yard. These were demolished structures. The cars that were usually abandoned on the street were piled to the south, as if tossed there. Moving through an abandoned Boston was one thing—but this area was clearly being used for some nefarious purpose by the Fish, and that heightened the tension she felt. All of them crouched low in the narrow space between the row houses.

She used her eye motion to activate the map of the area. *We are close, less, than five blocks from the edge of the AIZ.* Despite the closeness, it seemed like miles to her. Looking to the north where that edge was, it seemed like a hundred miles. Buildings, some standing, others in ruin, lay between. Big buildings—old warehouses and office buildings, blocked her line of sight in the distance beyond the rubble. *If we have to try to traverse all of that debris and the shooting starts, we'll get tangled up in that rubble.* Claire used the tiny break to take a drag from her water pack tube.

"Somebody's sure as hell been busy," Frank muttered.

This was not a part of Boston that she knew well. She studied her battlespace display in her visor carefully, adjusting it with her wristcomp. The path they had taken through the city had twisted her around. When she got her bearings, she still didn't see a good way to reach the front lines. "We're still five blocks from the front—damn it."

Ish growled. In unison, the four humans dropped. Frank pulled the dog close to calm him. "We have company," Haskill said as he stroked the dog behind the ears.

Movement off to her left caught her attention, forcing her to crouch lower. She saw them through her nightvis, the hulking distinctive shapes of crabs outlined against the dark ruined structures. Six were fanned out in an oblong circle formation, moving through the streets slowly two blocks south of their position. Their massive clawlegs poked at the debris, clicking on the road's surface. *They are searching . . . that much is clear. Probably for us.* Claire moved backwards as did the others in their party, into the narrow space between the houses. Her foot was still numb in her boot, making her be careful with each step.

"Six crabs to the south," she muttered for Rabbit and Rodriguez. "Check behind us." Rabbit moved like a shadow back down the alley, then quickly returned. "I've got two more about two blocks down."

"We are so screwed . . ." Rodriguez moaned.

"Shut up and focus," Claire replied. *If the sergeant hadn't made her my responsibility, I'd loved to have ditched her.* As much as she felt that emotion swell in her, she knew she never would do such a thing. *We've lost enough people already on this op.*

Frank didn't waste time. "I've got an open window here," he said, pointing to a narrow basement window. It was going to be a tight fit, but it was less exposed than in the narrow alley. "We've got shit for fields of fire here. Do it," Claire said. One by one, they dropped in the basement, Haskill carrying Ish. Claire went last, grappled and pulled in by several hands in the dark.

The wet musty smell managed to permeate her helmet's filters. It was like the odor of wet newspapers. The basement was filled with crude wooden shelving units stacked with plastic containers. A Christmas tree, draped in a white plastic garbage bag, stood in the corner like a ghost, making her do a quick double take as she got her bearings.

Claire checked her wristcomp and saw the time. In an hour or so, the sergeant would be expecting her to be at the extract point or damned near to it. That plan had been scrubbed, thanks to a dose of reality. The sooner the sergeant knew, the better. Dalton activated her transmitter in her Mark III ECH, making sure she was on her platoon's channel. "Beatle, this is Foxbat. Beatle, this is Foxbat. Come in, Beatle," she said as they moved through the basement and up the stairs. Rabbit was fast—he found a window to the next building and was already opening it.

"Foxbat, this is Beatle—you are a tad early, over," came McRory's nasal accent.

He's not going to like the change in plans—he never did. "Things are fluid here," she said with a strain as she made her way out through the window. "We've had some Fish issues. They are on our tails, over."

"We've just pinged your position—you are not where we had hoped you'd be, Foxbat, over."

"Roger that, Beatle. Change of plan. We have enemy troops pursuing us and options are limited. There's a warehouse just north of our position. I'm sending the coordinates. It is two blocks from the front but not near an insertion point. I think we can make it there. It has a flat roof. Can you send a chopper in for an extract of four?" She glanced over at Ish and corrected herself, "Make that five, over." Claire tapped her wristcomp control, pointed in the battlespace display on her internal visor, and clicked on the structure—transmitting the coordinates.

There was nothing back from Sergeant McRory as she followed Rabbit and the rest of the team into the next house. The interior of the house was eerily as it had been the day of the alien invasion. There was no sign of someone rapidly grabbing goods, nor a hint of looting. A film of fine dust covered everything, freezing it in a moment of time. For a moment, Claire looked around and wondered if someone was still living there, simply hiding as an armed band entered their abode. They made their way to a side door near the rear of the house when Sergeant McRory's voice cackled into her helmet's earpiece. "Foxbat, this is Beatle. No-go on a chopper. Too close to the front and worries about whether the roof could hold the weight. Air control will only allow two minutes of hover in your zone—not enough to get you out of there."

Her numb leg cost Claire her balance for a moment and she accidently bumped the doorsill and felt her STF armor plate stiffen under the impact. Despite that, the impact gave her an ache on her shoulder. *Shit! I don't care if they drop ropes for us to hang onto.* "Beatle, we are running out of options. I've got a case of the crabs and can't itch them. You need to find a way to extract us from that building or you can drop in some body bags to save time . . . over." Dalton added the "over" almost as an afterthought.

"Stand by, Foxbat, I'm working the problem here with BS command. We have something in the works. Proceed to the coordinates given. I will get back to you in five. Over."

Claire trusted McRory. Hopefully he was kicking the helicopter crews in the ass. *We're going to feel awfully stupid up on that roof with no way off.* Crouching low, they moved through another house's backyard, crawling through a hole in the fence into the next yard. Haskill fumbled with his hunting knife thanks to a numb arm, prying open the lock on the back door. They made their way in as quickly and quietly as possible. The kitchen had been sacked, cupboards were opened, and there was an all too familiar stink from rotting food in the unpowered refrigerator hanging in the stale air. "What's the word from your brass?" Frank asked as Rabbit rushed into the house looking for another point of egress.

"They're working on it," Claire said flatly.

"I hope the fuck they are," Frank replied, resting his gun for a moment on a counter and rubbing his injured arm and wincing slightly. Ish nuzzled his head up against his master's leg.

They made their way to the next house before Claire heard the chirp of a response from Sergeant McRory in her earpiece. "Foxbat, this is Beatle. Proceed to your destination. Air Force Pararescue will meet you there with the extraction gear. Signal when you are in position, and we will send in the cavalry. Over."

Extraction gear? "Roger that."

"What did they say? Are they sending a chopper?" Rodriguez asked. "Are they gonna fly us out of here?"

Claire was at a loss for words. "They said they are dropping extraction gear and an Air Force Pararescue."

"Gear? What the hell . . . are they giving us shovels to dig tunnels?" Rodriguez was clearly still shaken from the encounter with the Fox earlier.

"Enough with the whining, Rodriguez," Claire fired back with a tense tone. "You haven't been making this any easier. If you hadn't let that Fox past you, we might not be in this fucked up situation to begin with. Do what you're told and you might just make it out of here alive. If the sergeant wants us on the fucking roof and says they'll get us out, then we go on the fucking roof and get out. Is that simple enough for you?"

Rabbit moved in close to them. "We need to shit-can this conversation. We are still a block from the building we need to reach, and we have Fish hunting us."

Claire glared for a second at Rabbit then begrudgingly nodded. The small group moved from door to door, building to building, with a renewed sense of urgency and speed. After a block or so of movement, they came to the last brownstone of the block. The side door was cracked open. Haskill checked it through the faded drapes, then motioned for the others to go through.

Claire followed Rabbit to the door leading to the tiny side yard. There was a low wrought iron fence wrapped in vines. Dead leaves and litter covered the once quaint yard, now little more than a patch of tall grass. Claire activated her night vision and swept the wide four-line boulevard leading to the warehouse structure. To the east, a several random abandoned automobiles clogged up the street. They were smashed together—the remnants of wrecks long-abandoned. *Probably a pileup as everyone was trying to flee the city.* She remembered those first few days of the invasion—everyone trying to get out of the coastal cities, all at once. The smart ones went on foot. A lot of people never made it out because they refused to hoof it. By the time many did finally opt to walk, it was too late. They were already overrun by the Fish.

Across the street was the target building. Just the sight of it gave her a mix of tension and relief—a sensation that salvation might be near. The warehouse itself was an antique red brick structure—the kind of place that was often converted to loft apartments before the war. It had a look of permanence about it, a rugged utilitarian look. It had a few large metallic access doors for trucks, almost armor-strength from their look, locked into place. There were windows on the upper floors, a few of which were broken. Dark evergreen paint peeled from the window frames and the hefty metal entrance door. There was no sign to indicate who owned the structure.

As Claire looked down the boulevard to the west, she saw movement that made her pull back slightly. It was hard to make out at the range of nearly two blocks, but their distinct shapes told her more than she desired. *Fucking crabs.* They were moving slightly, as if they were patrolling the street—or looking for Claire and her little group. *I liked it better when we thought the Fish were stupid.* Ish growled slightly and Frank petted his head. "Damn it," she cursed in a whispered tone, pulling back slightly to stay out of sight.

"Based on Ish's response, I think I know what you see," Haskill replied.

"West, two blocks or so. At least two crabs." She decided to hold back her theory that they might be looking for them . . . things seemed bad enough. *No point in giving Rodriguez something else to whine about.*

"You have a plan?" Frank asked her. She felt everyone's eyes fall on her. *Do I?*

"We can't stay here—they are behind us. Our extraction point is the roof of that warehouse." Claire pointed to the structure. "The crabs are two blocks down. We move quick, get in, barricade the door. We just have to buy ourselves enough time to get out." She worked through the logic as she spoke.

Rodriguez countered. "We cross that street, they will see us and kill us."

"Claire is right," Frank replied.

"I ain't got a death wish," Rabbit added.

"Neither do I," Dalton snapped. "But if we don't move, we will get caught—they are coming at us from three directions and the fourth is questionable. We move across. Even if they spot us, it will take them time to get us targeted. We get inside, barricade the door, get to the roof."

"What if the Air Force doesn't come through?" Rodriguez countered.

Claire wanted to shake her squad mate—violently. *If we're lucky, there'll be time for that later.* "It doesn't matter—we go anyways. You have to have faith that the flyboys will come through." She had heard stories of pararescues, rumors really. The Army's informal communications circuit said they were "Two-parts balls, one-part crazy with a dash of maniacal behavior." She didn't care about the stories spread by her peers. All that mattered was they got her and the others off the roof.

Claire raised her visor to look into the eyes of the three members of her little combat team. "Alright. Rodriguez and I should still have some juice still for our adaptive camouflage gear. We go first and get the door open. If they see us, we will provide suppression fire for the three of you to come across. We go in and block the door. Rabbit—you've got a gift for finding your way through houses. I need you to find us a way to the roof. Preferably a staircase—there's got to be one. Got it?" There were nods. She dropped her visor and engaged her nightvis again.

Claire moved across the street, her eyes darting down where the crabs were. She nodded to Rodriguez and they both turned on their adaptive camouflage gear. Claire checked hers visually it and it seemed to be working. Rodriguez's was at about 45 percent; her torn torso armor where the Fox had hit her had been compromised and the cloaking system was dead there. Rather than light and images passing through the imagers, her side torso was there, visible, seeming to float in the air with a slight shimmer around the edges that was visible to the naked eye. It was better than nothing at all.

"I'm exposed," Rodriguez moaned.

"Barely. They may not even see you. Regardless, you're with me. We're so far out they may not even see you. We move in three, two, one . . ." She limped across the street, her injured leg still numb from the Fish toxin.

The two of them reached the metal door of the warehouse and tried the knob. *Of course it's locked.* The door itself had metal bands on the exterior, reinforcements. *Of course it's secure—it's a warehouse.* She tried to force the door with a short ram of her shoulder blade, but all that did was make far too much noise and made her adaptive camouflage system flicker. Nervous, she glanced down the street at the aliens.

They had heard her hit the door, she could tell because they paused, lifting some sort of weapons up with their tiny forearms. *Great, at least they don't see us yet.* She toyed with using the butt of her ACR-25 as a battering ram but given the strength of the door, it might never open that way and each hit would draw the enemy towards her. *Best to do this as quick as possible.* Claire cringed at the option she was pursuing though.

She took her ACR and aimed it where the lock was on the door and fired four rounds at point-blank range. Then she hit the door again with her shoulder and half-stumbled, half-ran into the opening. Both she and Rodriguez stumbled into the room. She pivoted and started laying down bursts of gunfire down the street at the crabs—providing cover for Frank, Rabbit and Ish to run across.

Gunfire erupted behind her as the rest of her small team rushed across the street, firing down at the crabs which had to be approaching at this point. In the darkness, she spotted an old metal filing cabinet and started to move it towards the door as the rest of the tiny band barreled through the door opening. "Help me use this to block the door." The frame and exterior of the building suddenly made a sound like a broom being dragged across bricks as the crabs fired their needle weapons. Rabbit slammed the door shut and the others helped her topple the filing cabinet in front of the door as a barricade. Frank found a heavy wooden crate and struggled to put it on top of the filing cabinet with one numb arm. It wasn't going to stop the crab, but it might slow it down for a few precious seconds. While Rodriguez helped drag another heavy box, Claire turned to Rabbit. "Stairs, Rabbit—find us a way up." Before she finished, Rabbit was on the move while Haskill dragged a chair in front of the blockaded door. There was a dull "thud" against the door, and Claire motioned for them to back away. *Those damn crabs move fast.* There was a scraping sound on the metal door, sounding like fingers on an antique chalkboard, which sent a chill down her back.

"This way!" Rabbit called from a maze of jumbled boxes. Claire didn't have to prompt the others—everyone sprinted.

When they hit the top of the first flight of steps, there was a bang and commotion from below. "Shit," she cursed as she reached the second floor of the warehouse. Boxes and crates were everywhere. The air was stale and musty. She glanced behind them several times but did not see any sign of the aliens yet. When they reached the fourth floor, there were pools of water—either from a leak or a long broken pipe. *After we get rid of the Fish, it's going to take forever to clean up the city.*

The final flight of stairs ended in a locked door. Haskill took his AR-15 and rammed the lock with the butt of the stock hard. On the third hit, he broke it off. Below them, at least two floors down, Claire heard commotion and movement.

They burst out on the roof, slamming the door closed behind them. "Give me one of your grenades," Rabbit demanded. Without hesitation, she tossed him one. He jabbed it in between the doorknob and the jam, then pulled the pin. Claire loved it and smiled at his ingenuity. If the crabs opened the door, they would have an explosive surprise.

The roof was flat, covered with tar and sheet metal with large weather battered vents. "Cover the door—I'm calling for our ride," she directed Rodriguez who made for cover crouching down behind one of the vents and aiming at the roof door. It was woefully soft cover, but did block line of sight. Rabbit and Frank fanned out as well, covering the door in a wicked crossfire that any Army sergeant would have been proud of.

"Foxbat, this is Beatle. We are in position." She heard the muffled rapid thump of a helicopter, but it sounded miles away, even farther with the crabs in the building underneath her. She rapidly repeated the message into her helmet mike.

"Roger that, Foxbat. We have pararescue dropping on your position in ten. Can you hold? Over."

She raised her ACR 25 and trained it on the door. "We have enemy forces in the building we are in. We are going to be hot and engaged soon. Tell those paras we are cutting it close. Over."

"Affirm. Watch the skies for your extract. Beatle out." She cut off her comms with her wristcomp. The sounds of the chopper were a long ways off.

Suddenly the door to the stairwell burst open and a crab emerged, firing a melter from its centaur-like waist. The spray hit Rodriguez as everyone opened up on the creature, and Claire could hear her squad mate's cries of pain. Then the grenade which had dropped at the feet of the creature went off. The blast overloaded Claire's nightvis for a moment and tossed the body of the alien up and back down the stairwell, leaving a massive crab-like appendage near the fragments of the door that still remained. Only then did she hear the *whomps* of the chopper blades in the distance.

Rodriguez's ACS had totally failed. She was completely visible. Claire darted over to her squad mate who was furiously tugging at her BA/2 urban armor, tossing off plates and padding as if a snake were under her uniform. Clair instantly saw why. The creature's melter had caught her with a good spray of corrosives. The acid blob had gone off near Rodriguez and the snot-like globs were eating through her armor and gear. Her helmet had a spot on top of it and was smoking, so Claire used her knife to cut the chin strap and toss it. "Get it off, get it off!" Rodriguez quaked as she struggled to strip off her armor as the disgusting wisps of smoke rose up from her comrade. Claire killed her own ACS so that she didn't hurt herself while aiding Angel.

"Watch your hands," Claire warned as she used her knife to free up the shoulder plate which was almost eaten through completely. It took a minute or two to remove the pieces that had been badly hit. Rodriguez's left forearm had a horrible splotch of blistered flesh where some of the acid had penetrated her armor. It oozed blood and she was clearly in pain. "You hit anywhere else?"

Rodriguez shook her head, wincing. "Damn it, that hurts," she cursed.

Claire reached into her utility belt pouch and found her medkit. She found the numb-kit, used for treating wounds. "I'm going to give you a shot. It should kill the pain." Rodriguez nodded furiously. Clair poked her near the wound. A few seconds later, the injured trooper started to breathe more steadily.

Gunfire burst near them and she saw Haskill firing at the doorway. "We have an infestation issue," he said between shots.

Claire pulled out one of her two remaining fragmentation grenades and chucked it at the already blasted roof access. It went into the darkness and down the stairs, erupting with an explosion that threw debris up and out onto the roof. She glanced in the air and saw something in the skies with her nightvis. It looked like a quad-blade aerial drone at first with something hanging down under it. Below the rotor assembly was a man and below him was a bundle of something dangling on a bungie, a bag of some sort. Whatever it was, it was heading for the roof and coming down slow but steady. *Where's his chute? Where's my damn helicopter?* The sound of the helicopter was in the distance, very far away. Her jaw clenched at the thought that somehow their extraction was not happening. *We're trapped up here—no place to go.*

The figure came down faster than she expected but with relatively no noise. It was a man, Air Force Pararescue, and hanging down under him was a bag which hit the roof first, skidding along. He had come in on something that looked like a modified drone. With four nearly silent rotors, it had made his landing lighter than any parachute landing Claire had seen. He lowered the unit down onto the roof, undoing his harness. Rabbit and Frank seemed to ignore him, firing a shot each into black hole leading to the floors below.

The pararescue moved up to Claire. "I'm Lieutenant Brockton." She glanced at his patch and saw his name and his call sign, "Husker," under it. "I'm here to get you out."

"Where's the chopper?" she asked.

"Can't get them in this low. The Fish go after them. We're going out on some new gear." He unstrapped the waist band that tied him to the bundle on the roof and dragged it over to Claire. Opening the specially padded jump bag was a similar set of backpack-worn rotor assemblies. "I'll need your help to get them assembled."

She grabbed the bag and moved behind one of the metallic vents. "Just do what I do—it only takes a few seconds to snap these together." The rotor blades were almost three feet long each and the unit had four sets. Claire was shocked at how light they were. Putting them together reminded her of Christmas when she would help put together her nephew's toys. The units consisted of four rotors and a lightweight power unit that came down to an eerily thin carbon-weave rigid strap that you sat on, and the straps to hook you up. She saw a pencil-thin camera on the assemblies too. She worked furiously with him to assemble them, following his instructions each step of the way. "We're going out on these?"

"That's the plan," he replied, snapping the last piece of his second unit together. "They are called EXs—Extraction Packs. They have limited range, two and a half miles on the power units we're using. Should be more than enough to get us out of the AIZ and to safety."

Should be? "This may shock you, but I don't know how to fly one of these," she sarcastically commented. "And I'm pretty sure these folks don't either."

Lieutenant Brockton only smiled back at her. There was nothing funny about her comment in her mind.

Off a dozen yards away, Rabbit fired three shots with his shotgun in rapid succession. "Whatever you are going to do, you had better do it quick. They are acting pretty pissed off."

Claire stopped her assembly for a moment to toss her last flashbang grenade into the stairwell. "Cover your eyes!" she called out as the brilliant burst of light went off on the floor below.

Lieutenant Brockton looked over at Rodriguez. "She wounded?"

"Yes."

"She's first then." He crouched-waddled over to Rodriguez and grabbed her shoulder straps and pulled her over to one of the units. "You need to sit up and I'll slide this under you and strap you in." The rotors towered over her like an umbrella. He took off her helmet and moved her ACR off to the side. "I need my rifle," she said.

"Sorry, it's a weight thing." He glanced over at Claire. "You'll need to remove your BA too. Ditch the helmet and your rifle, canteen pack, everything." Claire began to follow his orders, while watching what he was doing to rig up Rodriguez. "I don't know how to use this thing," she stammered nervously as he strapped the unit to her back.

"You don't need to," he said. "Just relax and enjoy the ride." Brockton activated the communicator on the upper shoulder. "Husker to Blue Jay. Ready on number two." He moved away from Rodriguez, taking with him the other units that were assembled. The rotors purred to life with a dull hum as dust and debris kicked up. Rodriguez seemed to go pale as the unit took off with surprising speed, whisking into the air with her hanging under it. It rose off the roof a good thirty feet, then veered sharply off for the safety of the Army's lines. Claire watched it for a second. "Wow," was all she could muster.

The lieutenant looked around. "I thought there were five of you."

Claire nodded. "Here, Ish," she called. The dog looked up at Frank who nodded, then he came over.

Brockton was dumbfounded. "We've never tested this with a dog."

"Strap it on him, sir. That dog is part of the team." Frank poured fire down towards the aliens as Claire pushed to get Ish out.

The pararescue fidgeted with the straps and finally got them tied tightly to the confused pit bull. Brockton laid flat on his stomach to keep the unit upright. "Husker to Blue Jay, ready on number five." The unit purred the life, kicking up dust on the roof. Ish slid a little in his straps, Claire almost feared he would fall out—but he only looked down, his tongue hanging out of the corner of his mouth.

"I ain't flying in one of those things," Rabbit said as he watched Rodriguez disappear into the night.

"You're kidding, right? The damn dog was willing to do it," Brockton replied.

"He didn't know any better," Rabbit said, firing another blast with his shotgun down the hole. Frank Haskill jogged over and sat down to get strapped in without a word.

"Well, you can't stay here," Brockton snapped to Rabbit. "I saw over a dozen of the Fish converging on this structure on my way down." He looked over to Claire. "You think you can strap that on?"

She nodded, shedding her gear faster than in any drill she had been in. He brought over a unit, and she slid onto the carbon-fiber "seat" which was little more than a rigid spoon-like holder under her butt cheeks. She pulled the straps and mirrored what Lieutenant Brockton was doing with Haskill. Rabbit still was covering the exit point, glancing from time-to-time over at the activities of his comrades.

The pararescue came over and cinched up Claire's straps. "That only leaves you," he called over to Rabbit.

"Who's going to cover the door?" he said, firing another shot down into the darkness.

"I've got this," Brockton said. He pulled out two grenades. One was one of the new phosphorous grenades and the other had orange stripes on it. She hadn't seen that kind before. He threw the phosphorous grenade down the stairs and a burst of brilliant light rose from the darkness and continued to burn bright white. Smoke rolled out of the hole as the building started to catch on fire. "Now move your ass."

Rabbit grumbled under his breath as he sat down while Brockton rigged him, still clutching his shotgun. "No weapon," the lieutenant said. Rabbit's eyes narrowed. "I love that gun." He looked over to Claire. "Fucking Army owes me a gun."

Lieutenant Brockton checked them visually and activated his communicator. "Husker to Blue Jay. Ready on one, three, and four." He strapped on the slightly larger pack that he'd worn in.

Dust and dirt began to fly, and Claire squinted her eyes. Without her helmet on and her ACR in her hands, Claire felt naked, exposed. The EX pack itself did not generate a lot of noise, but the rush of the four small helicopter blades made the wind hit her damp hair and whip in her ears. The pack rose and for a moment she thought she was going to fall. She grabbed the straps that were across her chest and held on for dear life. She rose into the air, followed by Frank and Rabbit. Looking down, she saw movement in the darkness around the outside of the building . . . the Fish were there in number. They were all around the outside of the warehouse. Dillos were scampering up the side of the warehouse. If they had stayed on the roof a few more minutes, they would have been overrun. *Holy shit, we cut that close.*

Lieutenant Brockton hovered over the structure when they drifted off, hopefully to safety. She barely saw him drop his orange striped grenade. It spun down into the night, landing hear the center of the mass of aliens. He rose and moved off, and twelve seconds later, it exploded in a brilliant ball of searing white-hot death, raining burning particles down on the aliens as an orange ball of superheated air rose up. Claire could feel the heat of the blast. Looking down, the building seemed to be sucked in on itself, consumed in the fireball. Claire presumed that the aliens were devoured in the blast a well. *I've got to get my hands on a few of those grenades.*

They moved quickly over the dark city as the sounds of chaos drifted behind them. She knew they had crossed to safety when she saw lights appear below. The aliens didn't care about electricity or lights, but humans did. The formation descended to Lincoln Park, or at least it had been Lincoln Park before the war. Now it was a landing zone and, from what she saw, a drone park for joyboys to control their drones. The array of antenna rose from countless portable domes. They came to a flat area where a small landing pad had been laid out, and dropped slowly to the ground. Field personnel moved in, attending Rodriquez, Ish, and Haskill, who were all in various stages of unstrapping as Rabbit, Claire, and then Brockton touched down. It felt good to feel her feet on the ground again. The EX pack shut off and she felt its dull weight on her back. An Air Force ground crew moved in and helped her unstrap from the gear. One looked at her pack carefully. "Wow, we only had another fifty seconds of power."

She spun to look at Lieutenant Brockton. "Fifty seconds?!"

Husker shrugged. "If I told you how close it was going to be, you might've flinched. Besides, you weren't in real danger. If it goes low, your joyboy would've put you safely on a rooftop." He flashed her a cocky grin.

"Thanks for saving our asses," she said, extending her hand.

"No sweat. It's my job."

"Where can I get one of those grenades?"

The pararescue chuckled. "You couldn't throw it far enough if you had one."

She turned and saw Rabbit as the crew worked to remove his EX pack. His eyes were closed and his fists clenched on the shoulder straps. "Rabbit, you're on the ground."

He cracked open one eye and looked around to make sure. Then he seemed to relax enough for the ground crew to do their job. "I ain't ever doing that shit again."

Medics moved in to help Haskill. "Let's hope we never have to." Ish appeared and rushed up to his master, jumping on his leg, tail wagging.

***

The battle damage assessment (BDA) and debriefs took a good three hours, especially for Frank and Rabbit. Rabbit was still mumbling that the Army owed him his gun, which got to the point where it was a bit of a running joke. Claire got it; she doubted that the G2 Officer, Lieutenant Waters, did. Rodriguez gave her testimony from a hospital bed. The burns on her arm were deep, eating into muscle. Claire had been tempted to pass on to Lieutenant Waters just what a pain Rodriguez had been, but when she heard how bad her injury was, Claire held off. *If she stays in the service, I'll give her some feedback in the Evaluation Reporting System (ERS) and let it go at that. No point in busting her balls if she might get booted for this injury. If nothing else, she'd earned a call sign. I'll tell the Sarge she needs to be Whiner from this point on.*

She finally got away for a shower, which was the longest one she had taken in months. Between the dust, dirt, and sweat, she felt like her whole body was covered in a film of grime. When she returned to the makeshift barracks, an old gymnasium, Sergeant McRory was waiting for her, sitting on her cot.

"So, how are ya feeling there?" he asked with his Boston accent. "Quite a little adventure you had."

"I'm fine—tired. No, exhausted."

"I'm sorry we couldn't get you out any other way. It was the hardest thing, leaving you there behind the lines like that. If we had tried to reach you, it would have cost us more men and women. I didn't have a choice."

"The wounded . . . they all died."

He nodded grimly. "I know. They were dead as soon as they got hit. We don't have field treatments for that airborne bacterial shit. There was nothing you could have done. It was *my* call to leave them there." While he accepted the blame, he didn't make her feel any better about their deaths. "I hate that I left you out there for so long."

She could see the worry in his face. It was the nicest he had ever been to her, apologizing like that. "I know, Sarge. It's okay. I have to admit, I was worried for a while that we were not going to make it back though. The Fish were everywhere and had us cut off."

"What was it like riding those Ex Packs like that?"

"I was too scared to enjoy it. I will say this—it got the job done."

"You're some of the first people they used those on. We kept losing choppers coming in low over the city—with these, the birds stay up high and the pararescues drop in and do their job lickety-split. I heard you even got them to use it on a dog; that's one for the history books."

"Given the choice of flying out that way or getting killed, I'll take the flying any day."

"Your, ah, new friends are going to be bugging out tomorrow. You might want to swing by the visitors barracks and see them."

"They saved our lives back there."

"So I heard. I also heard from them and Rodriguez. It seems their salvation was tied to you."

"Sarge, I promised them weapons and gear. I know it's out of the ordinary, but before they go back, we should outfit them. It's the right thing to do."

"It's already been arranged," he replied. McRory turned before she could say anything and moved to the door. He turned at the door and flashed her a smile. "Oh, and before I go, I wanted you to know I've put you in for a Silver Star for your actions. If it goes through, you'll get your ass promoted. No good deed goes unpunished in the Army. Good work out there, Dalton."

"Thank you, Sergeant."

"Don't thank me. Being a sergeant in this army and this war is far from a blessing."

***

Thirty minutes later, wearing a fresh uniform, Claire entered the visitors barracks, which was a commandeered school room. Rabbit and Frank Haskill where there—the latter with his shoulder in a thick bandage from his wound. Ish was asleep on his back, his legs in the air, ignoring Claire's arrival. Both of her F'er allies wore fresh OD T-shirts and pants, though Claire could tell from the way that Rabbit moved in them, he was far from pleased about the new wardrobe.

"Word is you two are heading back into the AIZ," she said coyly.

"It's our home," Haskill replied. "Though I have to admit, until you've come out of the city, you don't realize all of the little things you miss."

"Like a real meal," Rabbit added.

She almost felt embarrassed to thank them, her face flushed red as she spoke. "Well, I just wanted to say thank you. If it wasn't for you, we would've been killed or captured or worse."

Frank grinned. "I doubt that. You are a hell of a fighter, Claire."

"I was luckier than anything."

"Luck counts," Rabbit said. "But before we all get weepy eyed. There is the matter of the toll."

"The toll?"

"Your gear and weapons. You left them on that roof, but you still owe us. On top of that, I am still owed a replacement for my good luck gun." He was clearly only half-joking.

She smiled. "I've been told that's been arranged, Rabbit."

He eyed her. "Damn right, it's going be taken care of," he muttered. "I'd love one of those grenades that pararescuer had."

"*That* I can't promise."

Frank Haskill turned to her and extended his hand. "If you ever decide that this Army-shit isn't working out for you, we'll always have a place for you with East Side Retribution." She shook it and saw Rabbit wink at her.

"It's ESR, Frank," she corrected him. Haskill and Rabbit both chuckled at that.

"If you do come and visit us again, you need to bring some of those damn grenades . . ." Rabbit added.

"It's good to know I have options," she said, and she meant it. Things in her world had gone from infinite possibilities to the horrors of war. Options were a rarity.

ABOUT THE AUTHOR

Blaine Pardoe is a *New York Times* bestselling and award-winning author. He has been an author and designer in the gaming industry since 1985. He has written countless sourcebooks for games including the Star Trek RPG, Space 1889, the Robotech RPG, BattleTech/MechWarrior, Twilight 2000, Renegade Legion, and Leviathans. He has authored numerous science fiction novels in the BattleTech/MechWarrior universe. His political thriller, *Blue Dawn*, was an Amazon bestseller in its category. Outside of the gaming industry, he is an accomplished historian and bestselling author in the military history, business management, and true crime genres. He has twice won awards from the Military Writers Society of America and was awarded the Harriet Quimby Award from the Michigan Aviation Hall of Fame for his contributions to aviation history. He has been a guest speaker at the US National Archives, the Smithsonian, and at the US Naval Academy.

ABOUT THE CREATOR

Brent Evans is a long-time illustrator and an award-winning art director, as an artist and noted game line developer. Freelancing since 1987, Brent has worked in many genres including political cartoons, comics, and children's books. In 2005, he was hired by gaming visionary Jordan Weisman to work on several games, and immediately distinguished himself as one of the core illustrators for the *BattleTech* franchise. His creative design and project management style inspired his elevation to Senior Art Director in 2009 for many legendary gaming franchises including *BattleTech*, *Shadowrun*, D&D's *Dragonfire*, the *Valiant RPG*, among others. From 2017-2019, he took on the additional role as line developer leading the overhaul of the *BattleTech* product line, catapulting the brand into the industry-leading global success that it enjoys today. Of Brent, it is said that his "superpower" is the ability to recruit and develop creative talent.

Additionally, Brent is a graduate of and serves as a board member for the Game Design & Development program for the University of Washington.

www.ingramcontent.com/pod-product-compliance
Lightning Source LLC
Chambersburg PA
CBHW050926030726
47503CB00007BB/2487